Ken saw a ribbon of fluorescent light spilling from a doorway. Browne's office.

There was a continuous rapid-fire clicking coming from behind the door. It was a familiar sound, but Ken couldn't place it. He crept closer and peeked through the crack.

All he could see were bookshelves.

He placed his finger on the door and shoved. It swung inward, revealing more bookshelves, a window, a desk . . .

And a man slumped over the desk.

Ken froze. This couldn't be happening.

The man's face was lying on his computer keyboard, causing line after line of letters to scroll down the monitor screen. It was making the clicking sound.

What now? Maybe the man wasn't dead. Maybe he'd had a heart attack and was just unconscious. He should check.

Ken walked over—and saw a tiny bullet hole in the man's forehead, with only the tiniest trace of blood. Jesus.

Should he report the murder? No. He was already linked with two murders. How would this look?

First Carlos Valez, then Sabini, now this guy. Three people he had recently come in contact with. No way was it a coincidence?

What had he stumbled into?

If he didn't wind up in jail, he might just end up as corpse number four.

ROY JOHANSEN

THE ANSWER MAN

BANTAM BOOKS

New York   Toronto   London   Sydney   Auckland

This edition contains the complete text of the original hardcover edition.
NOT ONE WORD HAS BEEN OMITTED.

THE ANSWER MAN
A Bantam Book

PUBLISHING HISTORY
Bantam hardcover edition published April 1999
Bantam paperback edition / March 2001

Library of Congress Catalog Card Number: 98-41525

ISBN 0-553-58191-0

Published simultaneously in the United States and Canada

Bantam Books are published by Bantam Books, a division of Random House,
Inc. Its trademark, consisting of the words "Bantam Books" and the portrayal
of a rooster, is Registered in U.S. Patent and Trademark Office and in other
countries. Marca Registrada. Bantam Books, 1540 Broadway, New York,
New York 10036.

PRINTED IN THE UNITED STATES OF AMERICA

OPM   10   9   8   7   6   5   4   3   2   1

For Mom, who taught me
that anything is possible

THE ANSWER MAN

CHAPTER 1

God, he hated this job.

Ken Parker fastened two cords across the sweaty man's chest. He tested the cords' tension by pulling them taut.

"I'm a little nervous." The man was sweating even more.

"Roll up your left sleeve."

The man obliged. Quickly.

Poor bastard. What did the guy do to deserve this kind of treatment? Probably nothing. He was the last of five people Ken had seen that afternoon, and he seemed decent enough.

It didn't matter.

Ken placed a blood pressure gauge around the man's arm. Velcro fasteners held the wrap. He squeezed the bulb and pumped it up. The man's eyes bulged with each squeeze.

Ken looked at his polygraph. Lie detector. Truth teller. About the size of a small copying machine, it sat on a metal stand in the center of his shabby office. He'd always thought it was a scary-looking device. Which was probably the point. It was stark, angular, and boxy, with quivering, trembling needles that left jagged lines on the slowly rolling graph paper.

The nervous interviewee, one Carlos Valez, sat in an uncomfortable straight-backed chair. Can't have these people feeling at ease. No. Gotta keep 'em on edge. Nervous. Scared. Make 'em *believe*. Then maybe they'll fess up and bare their souls. If they believe this stuff works, maybe it really will.

Ken wrapped a perspiration sensor around Carlos's index finger. The man was dripping. His heart was pounding. Ken stepped back and took a good long look at his interviewee. Carlos was a wreck. Just the way he was supposed to be.

Ken reminded himself to find a new line of work.

"Why are you nervous? You're not going to lie to me, are you?"

"No, I'm just afraid—"

Ken plopped into his chair and rolled over to a cluttered desk. "You're afraid the lie detector is going to say you're lying when you're really not."

Ken didn't look up, but he imagined Carlos was nodding in response. That short, jerky, frightened nod he had seen too many times. He didn't need to see it again, so he continued to search his desk. Damn, there were a lot of bills there. He didn't think he was *that* far behind. And this phone number . . . Was this the woman who . . . ? No, probably not. He finally picked up a pack of playing cards.

"Don't worry. We're going to do a little test here." He rolled back to Carlos and fanned out the deck. "Take a card."

"What?"

"Take a card, any card."

Carlos reached over and his shaking hand hovered above the cards for a moment. His fingernails were dirty, and large, knobby calluses were peeling from his knuckles. He selected a card.

Ken put the rest of the deck away. "Okay, Carlos. I want you to lie to me."

"What?"

"Lie to me. Look at your card and say no to every question I ask. We're going to calibrate the machine to your responses. Ready?"

Carlos replied with a vague shrug. Ken flipped on the

polygraph and thumped it, shaking the sensitive needles slightly. The large roll of graph paper turned slowly, moving beneath the oscillating needles.

It recorded Carlos's every breath.

Every heartbeat.

Every drop of sweat.

Ken leaned over his machine with the authority of a scientist. *If they believe this stuff works, maybe it really will....*

"Okay. Is it a face card?"

"No."

"Is it a number card?"

"No."

Ken studied the graph paper. "All right. It's a face card, isn't it?"

The sensitive needles jumped sharply, indicating Carlos's startled reaction.

"Is it a king?"

"No."

"Is it a queen?"

"No."

"Is it a jack?"

"No."

"Is it an ace?"

"No."

Ken uncapped a felt-tipped pen and made a mark next to one of the indicator lines.

"Okay, let's talk about suit. Is it clubs?"

"No."

"Is it spades?"

"No."

"Is it hearts?"

"No."

"Is it diamonds?"

"No."

Ken looked up. "You have the queen of hearts."

Once again the needles jumped sharply. Carlos swallowed hard and revealed his card.

The queen of hearts.

Ken nodded. "Great. You're what we call an easy read. A lie detector's wet dream. You can stop worrying."

Carlos could not take his eyes off the smiling queen.

Ken put the card away. "Okay. Let's get started. Your employer wants me to ask you about some missing video equipment. . . ."

Springtime in Atlanta. Ken welcomed the arrival of warm weather, but the humidity sapped his energy. Less than an hour after giving the polygraph exam, he lingered around his favorite park, ostensibly stretching, but really deciding if he wanted to run the three miles today.

Never in his thirty-four years had he felt the need to exercise for the sake of exercise alone. He had always been active, and he enjoyed most of the sports he had tried. He kept a lean, athletic build long after most of his high school friends had porked out and gained an additional chin or two. But it always felt good to unwind here after a day of putting people on the hot seat. It was getting harder, not easier, to inflict his polygraph on the nervous souls who paraded through his office, and Ken often found himself finishing the day with his stomach in knots.

As he continued his stretches-cum-procrastination dance, he looked toward the cluster of skyscrapers that was downtown Atlanta. It seemed to be changing all the time. A real city. Not one infested with the redneck country music and lazy drawls the movies liked to portray, but a real honest-to-goodness international city. He had lived in and around Atlanta since he was twelve, yet he did not have an accent. Neither did most of his friends. The New South.

The late afternoon sun was disappearing behind the skyline, so he decided it was time to make his decision. Ah, hell. She'd be waiting for him. He started his run down the jogging path, as he ultimately did every Monday, Wednesday, and Friday of each week.

In less than half a mile he saw Margot Aronson.

"Don't slow down!" Margot shouted as Ken approached. She zipped her fanny pack and merged into the path with him.

He looked at her as they ran side by side. Margot was one of the few sane people he knew. She was thirty-three, pretty, and getting prettier with each passing year. Her female friends hated her for that.

She kicked off the conversation. "Tell me about Arlene." Ken's love life was now a big topic of conversation between the two of them.

"Not much to tell. I see her only once every week or two. We have fun. Not much more to it than that."

"Any future?"

He snorted as they rounded a bend in the path. Good old Margot. She still hoped he would find someone. Someone special. Someone like her, but not like her.

"There's not even that much of a *present*. You know, we've seen each other only a few times, here and there ... and she's *sure* she has me all figured out."

"You mean she hasn't?"

"After just a few dates?"

"What did she say?"

"She says I could never commit to her because I like her too much."

"Huh. Did she say you were a smartass?"

"No."

"Did she say you were stuck in a kind of extended adolescence, perhaps never to escape?"

"No."

Margot nodded. "You're right. She doesn't have you figured out."

Margot sprinted ahead.

They continued their run in silence, as was their custom. There would be plenty of time to catch up during the quarter-mile cooldown walk. Ken watched Margot running ahead of him. She was one of the few constants in a life that offered little in the way of stability. He hadn't known her during his high school glory days, when his grades were almost all A's and he led his football team to a state championship. Great days, Ken thought. What would Margot have thought of the person he was then?

He had his choice of half a dozen athletic scholarships, but instead took an academic scholarship to the University of Georgia, where he studied for two quarters until his father fell ill with a kidney disease.

The health insurance policy reached its cap in a matter of months, leaving the family in dire financial straits. In what was supposed to be a temporary move, Ken left school and took a job laying cable on the southern coast of Alaska.

He dutifully sent his paychecks home, but still the costs mounted. Fifteen months after entering the hospital, his father died, leaving behind over $140,000 in debts and medical expenses. Everyone had the same advice for his mother: Declare bankruptcy.

No way, Ken told her. His family always paid their debts. Though his mother pleaded with him to reconsider, he was determined to repay each and every cent.

When the Alaska job was completed, he worked on an oil rig, talking his mother out of the bankruptcy option with each phone call. It took him six and a half years, but he finally repaid the debts.

It was the right thing to do, he thought. Do the right thing and everything else will fall into place.

Wrong.

He returned home to find that his old friends had moved on with their lives, starting families and embarking on careers. But for him, with no scholarship and no money, returning to school was out of the question. After a few false starts, he finally found himself in the polygraph business, a field that required minimal training and low start-up costs.

But his finances had grown shaky since he started providing support for his younger brother, Bobby, who was laid up with a disease contracted in the Gulf War.

Same old story, Margot always said. So busy taking care of everyone else that you forget to take care of yourself.

Elwood's Pub was packed. As usual. A Hawks basketball game was on the big screen, and rows of electronic dartboards were in use. Of course, true dart aficionados would not have been caught dead playing this game—not with those plastic tips, and the board itself with thousands of tiny holes to accept the faux darts. Even the automatic scorekeeping rankled the traditionalists. They *needed* to breathe chalk dust. But the bar was too crowded for the old steel-tipped darts. Before the electronic boards arrived, more than one customer found himself on the receiving end of a poorly thrown projectile. On a far wall, along with a collection of road signs, antique car parts, and other knickknacks, was a formaldehyde-filled jar that contained the remains of an unfortunate victim's eye. The donor, who was still a regular at Elwood's, generously suggested the display after receiving a large settlement from the bar's insurance company.

Ken and Margot pushed their way through the overflowing deck and into the bar.

Ken held a hand up to the bartender. "Larry!" he shouted.

The bartender leaned down and picked up a small cloth bundle from behind the counter. Smiling, he raised it above his head and hurled it as he would a football. Ken completed the pass, letting the bundle unfold to reveal a long pair of sweat pants. He slid them over his running shorts.

Bill Aronson waved them over. Dressed in shirt-sleeves and loosened tie, Bill fit right in with the happy-hour crowd. He used to say he was not like everyone else there, who worked all day at fast-track corporate jobs they hated, then copped a buzz before heading home and passing out. The "weekend people," he called them, because weekends were the only part of their lives they could stand. Nowadays Bill often wondered aloud if he was becoming one of the dreaded weekend people.

Ken and Margot joined him at his table. Margot wrapped her arms around Bill and gave him a long, wet kiss. Rowdies at the next table looked away from the game and howled in appreciation.

Bill turned toward them and shrugged. "It's the tie. Drives women wild."

Ken took his seat. "How'd we do, Beave?"

Bill nodded. "Better, Wally. It used to take you four beers to do three miles. But now . . ." He pointed to his large mug. "This is only my third."

"Not good enough."

Margot spoke in mock determination. "I know we can finish under two beers."

The bar erupted in an explosive roar as the home team scored, and tables vibrated with the force of a mild temblor.

"So . . ." Bill leaned toward Ken. "How's the polygram business?"

Terrific, Ken thought. His favorite subject. "Graph," he replied. "Poly*graph*. Could be better."

"You mean there's a liar shortage?"

"No. Unh-unh. Never."

Margot cut in abruptly. "Don't get him started!" Ken smiled. His friends had heard enough on the subject. "Don't get him started."

Bill spoke above the cheering crowd. "If there wasn't a hiring freeze at the bank, I could've put a good word in for you there. Maybe someday—"

"Separating the American farmer from his land isn't my idea of a good day at the office."

"I'm just trying to help, Kenny."

"I know."

Bill looked down at the table, his eyes fixed on absolutely nothing. Ken noticed that the laugh lines on his friend's face seemed deeper, though Bill hardly laughed at all anymore. If Ken's financial problems had given him a sense of humor about life, Bill's success only made him miserable. Bill worked feverishly toward his goal of retiring early, even if doing it meant torching his thirties and forties. It didn't seem like much of a life to Ken, but who was *he* to talk, with creditors beating down his door?

He was about to offer some appreciation for Bill's offer, when someone caught his eye. Just a few feet away, sitting at a table by herself, was a stunningly beautiful woman.

And not just everyday, run-of-the-mill God-she's-a-babe stunning. He didn't want to take his eyes away, though he knew she would probably catch him gaping. He didn't care. He'd probably never see her again, and he wanted to remember what such a woman looked like.

She turned and caught him gaping. She sipped her drink and looked away, expressionless.

Ken didn't look away.

"Finish it," Margot said to Bill, pointing at his beer. "We gotta go."

"Where?"

"Graham's wine-tasting party. We said we'd be there."

"*You* said we'd be there. And I still got half a beer here."

Margot picked up his beer, chugalugged the rest of it down, and smiled as she wiped the foam from her upper lip. "No, you don't. Let's go."

She placed the empty mug hard on the tabletop, snapping Ken out of his trance. He turned to face them.

Bill stood and grabbed his coat from the seat back. "Ah, the ties that bind. And strangle. And suffocate. You still on for the game this weekend, Beany?"

"You betcha, Cecil."

Flag football with the guys. Three hours playing with a group that got winded after only twenty minutes, followed by a couple of hours tinkering with Bill's '55 Corvette. Ken wouldn't miss it.

Margot waved as she and Bill left through the ever-growing crowd. Ken glanced around, telling himself he didn't need to look where he really wanted. No, he could sit there and enjoy the atmosphere, listen to the music, and . . .

To hell with that. He turned to face . . .

No one. The table was empty.

"She's not there anymore."

The voice was so close, so unexpected, it made Ken jump. He could feel the moist, warm breath in his ear. He whirled around.

It was her. The woman. If anything, she was even more beautiful up close. Her face was a miraculous alignment of cheekbones, lips, and teeth that made Ken marvel at the wonders of human genetics. Her thick auburn hair shimmered as it spilled over her shoulders.

And those eyes. To say they sparkled would be an understatement. There was something there, a glint that let the world know she was on to it. Or so it seemed to Ken. Maybe it just meant she was on to *him*.

She sat in the seat across from him. "It's not polite to stare."

Busted. He shrugged. "You must be used to it."

"Doesn't mean I like it. Whether or not I like it depends on who's doing the staring."

He couldn't tell if she was pissed off or turned on. Maybe a little of both.

He threw a lazy arm over his chair back. It was supposed to be a casual move, but he wasn't sure if it was entirely successful.

"What's your name?" he asked.

"Myth Daniels."

"Miss . . ."

"No. Myth. M-y-t-h."

He almost laughed. "Myth Daniels. *Myth* . . . do you go by anything else? I don't want to thound like I have a lithp."

He smiled broadly and looked to Myth for a reaction. None. Zip.

He thought for a moment. "You've probably heard that one before."

"Only three or four thousand times. I don't go by anything else."

"I go by Ken Parker."

"I saw something interesting here, Ken Parker. The woman came in with you . . . and went out with the other guy."

"She didn't have any choice. He's her husband."

"And you're her . . ."

"Friend."

"That's all?"

"Not exactly."

"Uh-huh."

"I'm her ex-husband."

She raised an eyebrow. More out of interest than surprise, he decided. It didn't seem to him that she could be easily surprised. There was a directness about her, an intelligence he found mesmerizing. As if her looks weren't mesmerizing enough.

"Doesn't husband number two feel a wee bit threatened?"

Ken shook his head. "Bill and I have been friends since junior high. He trusts me."

"How did he and she—?"

"He stole her away from me."

"Most men would be bitter."

"I got over it. Had to. I could stand losing my wife, but . . . not my best friend."

She laughed. "You're a walking, talking, breathing country-western song. He's still your best friend."

He didn't join her in the laughter. It had been six years, and still this was not a funny subject to him. Maybe someday. Maybe not. "I'm talking about *her*. Margot. She was my wife *and* my best friend."

The smile faded from Myth's face. She looked around the busy pub.

"I need some fresh air." She had spoken quietly, forcing Ken to lean forward to hear her.

He mouthed his reply. "So do I."

"Fresh air" on a May night in Atlanta was hardly that, with the still, humid vapors threatening to smother anyone who dared challenge them. But at least the night offered solitude on a row of shops known as Little Five Points, where mom-and-pop stores attracted tourists and quality-unconscious locals. Ken and Myth walked along the deserted street, occasionally pausing to look in windows of the closed shops.

"What do you do when you're not intimidating men in the local saloons?" he asked.

"I intimidate men in the local courtrooms. I'm an attorney."

"Are there any lawyer jokes you haven't heard yet?"

"I doubt it."

"Then I won't even try. What kind of attorney are you?"

She ignored the question. "You're a polygraph examiner. Did I hear that right?"

He nodded.

"Those things really work?"

"Sure they do. It's *people* who are defective."

She gave him a sideways glance.

He nodded. "Nowadays people find ways to justify what they do. They rationalize. If someone steals from his company, hell, it's not really stealing. The company really owes it to him anyway, he figures, and he might as well take it. Whatever it is. That's not stealing. That's just getting your due."

"Do *you* think that way?"

"I don't know. All I know is it's getting harder to separate the truth from the bullshit. And the better we get at rationalizing away the things we do, the more useless my job gets. A polygraph can't catch a liar who doesn't think he's a liar."

"You're quite a cynic."

"Occupational hazard."

They passed a tall dogwood tree, the roots of which had burst through the sidewalk, loosening several chunks of concrete. As Ken guided Myth around the mess, he realized they were entering a neighborhood of recently restored homes. Houses that only a few years earlier were selling for peanuts but now were in vogue for the nouveau-riche baby boomers moving back into the city.

"Enough about me," Ken said. "Tell me about you."

"I'll tell you about me when we get there."

"Get where?"

"My house. It's not much farther."

Ken tried not to look as surprised as he was. Okay, so one of the most beautiful women he had ever seen was taking him home five minutes after their first meeting. Just another night in the city.

As they strolled through the neighborhood, Ken took note of all the little things that screamed money. The neatly trimmed lawns. The garden-club flower beds. The small security service signs pierced into the grass. The Porsches and Jags in the driveways.

Soon he found himself in front of one of the largest, most impressive homes on the street. Constructed in the style of a French château, it sat on a full acre of land in the middle of the block. A long driveway snaked around the side of the house, and a dramatic, curving set of stairs spiraled up to the house's main entrance, where a pair of double doors was flanked by towering stained glass panels.

"No way," he said.

She led him up the driveway. "Don't insult me by asking how I got it. I've never been married, no man bought it for me, and I've never inherited a dime. I earned it myself."

Even the grass smelled sweet. She probably spent more on her monthly gardening bill than he did on his car payment. When he could *afford* his car payment.

They walked up the front stairs. Myth fumbled with her keys, trying to insert one into the lock.

"Relax," Ken said softly.

Myth threw the lock. She turned around, smiled, and opened the door.

He followed her inside. The interior was even more impressive. He was no decorator, but he could instantly see that the furnishings, flooring, and accent pieces were expensive and impeccably chosen. Each room was a showplace, camera ready for a decorating magazine layout. Deep, dark, solid woods ran through the walls and furniture. The house's lighting scheme was low key, with sharply defined pools of illumination emanating from designer lamps in each room.

Myth led him into a cherry-wood-paneled study, where she turned on a floor lamp. Ken was startled by the sight that greeted him in the corner of the room.

A middle-aged man in a large leather chair.

The man had obviously been sleeping. He looked up at Ken and yawned.

Ken turned to face Myth. She was calmly hanging her jacket on a rack.

"Uh, Myth?"

"Hmm?"

"There's a man in here."

Myth moved to her desk and turned on another lamp. She put on a pair of spectacles and glanced through a file.

"Two men. Ken Parker, meet Burton Sabini."

The middle-aged man rose and stepped toward Ken. Sabini was thin and balding, probably in his late forties, though his bearing suggested a man much older.

"Hi, Ken. Nice to meet you." Sabini smiled warmly at him.

Ken looked back at Myth, who was still reading through the file.

"Kenneth Andrew Parker, born in Houston, Texas. You've been having a rough time of it, haven't you, Ken? Two quarters of college before you dropped out. A whole string of jobs, none of which held any long-term prospects. Except possibly this one. You've been at it almost two and a half years. You haven't been doing too badly, but your expenses are crushing you. It looks like you can last sixty days at the most before you'll lose your business."

Ken looked at Sabini, who was smiling and nodding.

The night was getting more surreal by the moment.

"What the hell is this?" Ken snatched the file from Myth's hands and scanned it. "Christ. My height, eye color, weight,

the grocery store where I shop . . . The weight's wrong, by
the way."

"It's what you put on your last driver's license application."

"You do this for every man you bring home?"

"Only men I do business with."

"Business?"

"Ken, do you recognize this man?"

Ken looked at him. "No. Should I?"

"Burton Sabini. He's being prosecuted in an embezzling
case, and I'm defending him."

Sabini was obviously surprised not to be recognized. "You
watch TV, read the papers? I worked for Vikkers Industries."

Ken studied the man a moment longer. "Sorry."

Myth took the file back. "The district attorney has
agreed to accept a polygraph examination as evidence."

"A stipulated test? That's what this is all about?"

"We need your help."

Ken looked from her to Sabini. Were they both nuts?
"There's nothing I can do. You get approval on the polygraph
examiner, but the D.A. makes the choice. Jesus."

"Just hear me out. They have a weak case against him."

"They must. The D.A. wouldn't agree to admit polygraph results otherwise."

"That's the way I see it. If Sabini takes the stip test and
passes, they might even drop the charges. We'd be home
free."

"Yeah, but if he fails, they could use that test against you
in court. You'd be an idiot to chance it."

"I don't intend to chance it." Myth took off her spectacles. "In the early sixties, there was a major study at the
University of Chicago. Researchers were trying to determine if it was possible to beat a polygraph."

"So?"

"I'm sure you know the outcome, even if you've never
heard of this study. It *is* possible to beat one."

"*You* said it, not me."

"My client is innocent, but we need to be sure his test

reflects that. We're not about to go blundering into a stip test unless we know he can pass it ten times out of ten."

"Then don't agree to it. There's too much room for error."

"I like that kind of talk," she said. "Most examiners will sing the polygraph's praises to the skies, but not you. You recognize that it's an imprecise instrument."

"I recognize the facts."

"And you're up front about it. If you can't clearly identify a deceptive interviewee, you'll go back to your client and say so."

"All examiners are supposed to do that."

"You and I both know that doesn't usually happen. The client wants results. In most cases, the examiner will point out a likely suspect even if the graphs don't completely bear him out. That's how polygraph firms stay in business. They produce results and cultivate those relationships. You, on the other hand, admit it when you can't spot the liar. Your business has suffered because of it."

"One of life's little ironies."

"Maybe it's time you made the polygraph's flaws work *for* you rather than against you."

"And how do you propose I do that?"

Myth smiled. "We would like you to teach Sabini how to beat the machine. Who better than a licensed polygraph examiner to show him the ropes?"

Ken stared at her. Did she know what she was suggesting? "That's interfering with the application of a stipulated test. I could lose my license, and you could be disbarred."

Sabini stepped forward. "*We* certainly won't tell anyone." He handed Ken a tightly wound roll of bills. "That's ten thousand dollars. If I take their lie detector test and pass, you'll get forty more."

They knew what they were suggesting.

Ken fingered the roll of bills. Fifty thousand dollars. Did he hear correctly? Fifty thousand?

"For that we're also buying your silence. No one can ever know about this," Myth said.

Fifty thousand dollars.

Ken wished he wasn't tempted by the offer. He wished he were angrier at Myth for luring him here.

"What makes you think I'd do it?" he asked. "Your pretty face?"

"Of course not. The money. I know you need it."

He did need it. *Fifty thousand dollars.*

Sabini spoke with a slight stammer. "I—I didn't steal from my company, I swear to God. The firm is pushing through a merger, and they're pinning this on me to show everyone they're still in control of their operation. I'm caught in the middle, Ken. It's torn my life apart. I know I can win this in court, but if this test will make the case go away more quickly, I have to try it."

Fifty thousand dollars.

"You have two weeks to train him to beat the polygraph," Myth said. "That's when we have to tell the D.A. if we agree to their stip test. If you work with Sabini and decide he's not up to it, the ten thousand is yours to keep."

"Please," Sabini said. "I need your help."

Fifty thousand dollars.

The peace of mind that money could buy.

He *needed* it.

But not that much.

Ken shoved the roll of bills back into Sabini's hand. "Sorry. I'm not your man."

"Why not?" Sabini said.

Myth frowned. "Not enough money?"

"More than enough money. If I was the kind of guy who would do something like this, I would've settled for half what you're offering. But you're asking me to help this man commit perjury."

"It's perjury only if he lies."

Ken looked at Sabini. He didn't look like someone who would have the nerve to rip off his employer. Tending to a butterfly collection or watching travel videos, maybe, but not embezzling.

Maybe his company *was* shafting him.

It didn't matter. What they wanted him to do was wrong.

"Listen," Myth said. "I know this is a lot to throw at you. Sleep on it. Sabini and I will be at Piedmont Park tomorrow night. There's a playground on the west end. We'll meet you there at seven, all right?"

"I won't be there."

"If you're not there, we'll take that as a no."

Ken nodded. They were both so matter-of-fact, as if they wanted to hire him to clean their rain gutters. He walked out. On the front stairway he stopped and turned around. Myth was standing at the door, her face lost in the shadows. "This evening didn't turn out quite like I expected," he said.

"Life is full of surprises."

"*You* certainly are."

"Do yourself a favor. Think about our offer. This kind of money could make a big difference in your life."

"I don't doubt it."

"Good night, Ken Parker." She slid back into her house and closed the door behind her.

Ken shook his head.

Fifty thousand dollars.

He thought about it all the way back to Elwood's, where his car was parked.

He hoped.

He was three months behind in the payments for his 1971 MG convertible, and the repo men were on the lookout. Ken had been successful in slipping them an occasional twenty to pretend they couldn't find it, but the men made it clear his bribes would no longer be accepted. Until things were squared away, he was parking his car in hiding places several blocks from home and work.

Fifty thousand dollars.

How could he turn away all that money?

Because it was the right thing to do. He knew he could

teach Sabini to beat the polygraph; a few tricks, some special exercises, and a lot of practice could do the job. But no matter how much cash they were offering, it wasn't worth it.

Things were bad, but they weren't *that* bad.

Right?

"Thank God you're here. I can't do anything with him."

Ken had driven from Elwood's to the two-bedroom tract home where his brother, Bobby, lived.

"What happened?" Ken asked.

Tina, Bobby's wife, nervously rubbed her hands together. She was a petite Asian woman who spoke with a distinct French accent. Bobby had met and married her while stationed overseas in the army. "He got some bad news," she said quietly.

"So what else is new?"

"The doctors at Walter Reed reversed their diagnosis. They told him the V.A. isn't going to pay."

"Can they do that?"

The sound of breaking glass came through a bedroom door, followed by a string of muffled curses.

"I can't talk to him," Tina said. "He won't listen. Anything he can reach, he throws against the wall."

Back to reality, Ken thought. Myth, Sabini, and their outrageous offer now seemed like part of an alternate universe. Ken knocked on the bedroom door. "Bobby?"

"Goddamn those bastards! Damn them all to hell!"

Ken slowly opened the door. The room was dark except for a tunnel of illumination shooting from a lamp lying sideways on the floor. Objects were scattered and broken all over the room. As Ken's eyes adjusted, he made out his brother sitting in bed. "I was in the neighborhood," Ken said.

"Bullshit."

"Okay, I wanted to see how you were doing." Ken strode inside and closed the door behind him. The room smelled of body odor and rubbing alcohol, like his father's room when he was dying. The memory made Ken queasy. "What did the doctors at Walter Reed say?"

"They said they've reevaluated my case. I can't keep food down, I got a fever, my heart races in the middle of the night. . . . Before, they said it was Gulf War syndrome. That my immune system was destroying my own body tissues."

"I know. What are they saying *now*?"

"Well, I guess I've been costing them too much money. Suddenly it's not that at all. Now it's somatoform disorder."

"What's that?"

"Hypochondria. Psychological shit. Goddamn bastards!" Bobby threw a plastic pitcher against the wall.

"Stop it." Ken righted the lamp and looked at his brother. Bobby had always been slight of build, but now he was bordering on emaciated. His hair was thinning, and his long face was half hidden by a scruffy beard.

"What the hell am I gonna do? It's tough even getting out of this bed. Tina's working two jobs just to pay the rent."

"Don't worry about it."

"How can I not worry?"

"I'll help out."

"You did your bit for Dad, Kenny. You don't need to keep doing it for me."

"Shut up and move your legs." Ken sat at the foot of the bed. "The V.A. should pay. Isn't there anything you can do?"

"There's a Gulf War veterans group. They're fighting this shit, but it'll take a long time. Jesus, Kenny—"

"Shhh. Don't get yourself worked up. You'll just make yourself sicker."

Bobby turned away as his chest rumbled with a deep cough. He wiped his mouth and turned back to Ken. "Have you seen Margot lately?"

"Yeah, I just saw her and Bill tonight."

"You never should have let her get away."

"I didn't have too much choice."

"Sure you did."

Ken quickly changed the subject. "The *Vivianne* misses you."

The *Vivianne* was a fourteen-foot boat that Bill had inherited from his parents. He and Margot never seemed to have time to enjoy it, so they entrusted Ken with the care and upkeep of the vessel. He and Bobby had spent many afternoons sailing the *Vivianne* on Lake Lanier.

"I'll have to get you back out there," Ken said.

Bobby let out a long breath. "God, I'm sorry."

"About what?"

"You shouldn't have to deal with this. You were there for Mom and Dad while I was off seeing the world. This is my thing."

Ken shook his head. "It's *our* thing."

Ken gave Tina sixty dollars on his way out, leaving himself with just enough money to cover meals for the next couple of days. He hoped his newest client paid his bills promptly.

Ken drove down the dark streets of Bobby's neighborhood. He cursed out loud. It wasn't fair. The Department of Defense still maintained there were no significant levels of nerve gas deployed in the Gulf War, despite a mountain of evidence to the contrary. Bobby was evidence enough, Ken thought. The guy had hardly been sick a day in his life, but shortly after returning home from the war, he was hit with the illness that had racked his body ever since.

Tina was the real hero. She never complained and was the one good thing in Bobby's life.

They deserved better.

Ken thought back to his meeting with Myth and Sabini. Fifty thousand dollars for two weeks' work? God knows he could use it. Bobby's condition had been a serious drain on his funds, and the situation didn't look like it was going to improve anytime soon.

But there had to be another way out.

•   •   •

Myth kicked off her shoes as she watched Burton Sabini through a window. He shuffled down the driveway, climbed into his car, and drove away. He had wanted only a "quick drink" after Ken left, but he nursed it for the better part of an hour. Myth supposed he wanted to talk. He was lonely.

She knew how that felt.

She walked back into her study, picked up the phone, and punched a number.

Her call was answered. "Yeah?"

"The polygraph examiner was here," Myth said. "I think he may do it."

"But does *he* think so?" the voice rasped.

"Not yet. But he'll come around."

"Perhaps he needs some persuading."

"Don't be stupid," Myth said. "I'm all the persuasion he'll need."

CHAPTER 2

Ken was late for work.

The traffic on Roswell Road was, as usual, stop and go. Less than a mile away from his office, north of the I-285 highway, he saw a motorist in need of assistance. She wore a tight white T-shirt, black shorts, and hiking boots, and she stood next to her convertible Mustang, peering uncertainly under the hood. As Ken approached, she looked pleadingly up at him.

What the hell.

He pulled over and quickly strode over to the young woman.

"What's the problem?"

She gestured toward her vehicle. "I don't know. It died on me, and I can't get it to start."

He looked under the hood, knowing he probably wouldn't be able to diagnose the problem with only a quick glance. He checked the battery connections. The young woman leaned over with him, offering a view of her ample cleavage.

She smiled. "Thanks for stopping. I didn't know *what* to do."

He smiled back. "I'm not sure *I* know what to do either. But if nothing else, there's a garage up the street. And if you need a lift somewhere—"

At that moment, a tow truck roared past and whipped around in a tight U-turn. It headed straight for them.

He turned to the woman. "Did you call him?"

She shook her head as the truck suddenly braked to a stop. The driver hopped out, and Ken instantly recognized him. It was Stu, one of the repo men from the bank. Stu ran to fasten his hookup to Ken's front axle.

Ken tried to stop him. "Come on, Stu! Don't do this!"

The repo man acted as if he had not heard. He worked quickly and expertly, with the proficiency of someone who had been doing his job for years.

Ken shouted, "Look, I'm gonna get paid up tomorrow! Tomorrow! Stu?"

Still, Stu did not respond. He walked back to his truck, stopping only to wave at the woman. "Thanks, Donna!"

Ken looked incredulously as the woman slammed down her hood, jumped into her Mustang, and started it up. The engine roared to life without hesitation. The woman blew Ken a kiss as she drove past.

It was a setup.

Stu climbed into his truck and laughed. He leaned out the window. "The one time Donna couldn't get me a car back, the guy turned out to be gay. You're only human, Ken."

He put the truck into gear and pulled away.

Ken ran alongside his car, collecting papers from the front seat. He managed to pull out the last of them before his MG, suspended from the tow rig, disappeared down the busy street.

Great. Just great.

Ken tucked the papers under his arm and walked toward his office. He'd been dreading this day for months, but at least now he wouldn't have to play hide-and-seek with the repo guys. That took almost as much energy as riding MARTA, the local mass transit system. MARTA was fine, but Atlanta was a hard city to negotiate without a car.

Ken broke into a sweat as he neared his office building,

which was located behind one of the city's more popular comedy clubs. The two-story structure was built in the late sixties, during a brief period in which adventurous "space age" architecture was the rage. The tide of fashion, however, was not kind to the L-shaped building; the pseudo-modernistic exterior stairways, rounded edges, and baby-blue molding contributed to a look more suited to Tomorrowland than to a place of business. Oval-shaped stairs led up to walkways overlooking the parking lot, and a thin layer of grime tainted the once-white building. Its only drawing card was the low rent.

Ken jerked open the building's glass door, climbed the stairs, and hurried toward the second-floor receptionist. What was her name again? He couldn't remember. Receptionists came and went so often. She was an attractive woman, about twenty-five, whose mouth was pulled into a perpetual smirk. She sat behind her desk, slightly swiveling her chair back and forth.

"Any messages?" he asked her.

"Yeah." She handed him a pink sheet torn from her pad. "Liz Benton from Packard Hills Mall called. She wants the results from your exams."

He nodded.

The receptionist sipped her diet Coke. "Did you catch a crook?"

"Maybe."

"Maybe? People pay you for maybe?"

"Not often enough."

She smirked. "The old man was looking for you."

The old man. Downey. The building manager was after the past couple of months' rent. So far Ken had been able to dodge him, leaving messages when he knew the old man would be out.

He shrugged, but the receptionist was still smirking. He smirked back and walked to his office.

●　　●　　●

Ken wanted to call the bank and find out how much it would take to get his car back, but first he had some unfinished business to tend to. He had administered five tests the day before. At sixty dollars a pop, they earned him grocery money, but he wouldn't get a dime until a report was sent to the mall management office.

Chicken feed compared to the money he could make from Myth Daniels and Burton Sabini. With that kind of cash, he could get his car back. And get caught up with his bills. And make sure Bobby was taken care of.

Don't think about it, he told himself. It wasn't an option.

His large electric typewriter hummed uncertainly as he flipped the power switch. He had bought it secondhand when a local high school switched over to computers for its typing classes. In fact, a metal plate still affixed to the typewriter read COBB COUNTY SCHOOL DISTRICT, accompanied by a lengthy serial number.

He reached for the graphs from the previous day's sessions. Of the five, he was immediately certain that three were innocent. They were pleasant, relaxed, and their readings were strong and stable. The other two were a different story. The readings were all over the place. They were clearly nervous, but that was only natural considering they were wired to a strange-looking machine and accused of a crime.

It was time to earn his pay.

Ken looked for baseline patterns on the questions he *knew* they were truthful about. Their names, places of employment, and dates of birth didn't leave a lot of room for fibbing.

The pattern for each of the interviewees was different. One answered each question only after inhaling. The other always exhaled first. One experienced a small rise in blood pressure before answering each question. The other's was relatively stable.

Both perspired throughout the exams, but so did the people he had already decided were innocent. Better juice up the A/C next time, Ken thought.

One of the men showed a spike in pulse rate each time one of the crucial questions was asked. He also stopped breathing for a moment after answering those same questions.

The other man's graph showed some erratic readings, but they were *consistently* erratic across both the control questions and the critical questions. Ken didn't believe he was lying.

Ken picked up the phone and dialed the mall manager. She answered it herself.

"Liz Benton."

"Ms. Benton, this is Ken Parker. I'm from Polygraph Associates. I did the exams on your employees yesterday."

"I expected to hear from you sooner."

"I'm sorry. I needed extra time to analyze the charts. In my opinion, Carlos Valez is the untruthful one."

There was a moment of silence on the other end of the phone.

"Ms. Benton?" he asked.

"Yes," she finally replied. "I've had my doubts about him. Thank you, Mr. Parker. Send a report and your invoice to my assistant, and she'll see that your payment is taken care of."

Half an hour later, Ken was almost finished with Liz Benton's written report, when he was startled by the sound of a dull pounding on his office door. It didn't sound like a knock exactly, but . . .

There it was again.

He went to the door and opened it.

Flash! An intense burst of light.

Standing there was Downey, the building manager, and he had just taken a picture with his Polaroid camera. The photo wasn't meant to be of Ken, but of an eviction notice pounded into the door.

Ken ripped the notice off. "Come on, Downey. Didn't you get my messages?"

The old man separated the photo from the chemical

paper backing and fanned it in the air. "I got your messages, but I didn't get your rent. You got thirty days, kid."

"Thirty days?"

"You'd be out of here tomorrow if I had my way. But that's the law. Thirty days."

"I'll get paid up. I will. I have some big accounts coming up."

But the old man wasn't listening. He turned and stepped down the hallway, still flapping that picture.

Ken stepped back into his office and slammed the door. Shit. What a day.

First his car, now his office. What did this mean? Was it a sign that he should take up Myth and Sabini on their offer?

Get real, he told himself. It wasn't a sign of anything except that he had screwed up his life.

He often tried to pinpoint where it had all gone wrong. When he left for Alaska? Possibly. But there were other guys out there laying pipe, and they probably hadn't made such a mess of things.

No, he decided. He couldn't blame it on that. He just didn't have the stomach to do his job the way it should be done. Myth was right. Polygraph firms stayed in business by delivering results, right or wrong.

Whenever he was unable to clearly identify a deceptive employee, the client often thanked him for his honesty but never hired him again. Successful examiners gave hard-and-fast answers, whether the readings supported them or not.

He couldn't play that game.

He picked up the phone and dialed quickly. The call was answered on the first ring.

"Margot Aronson."

Margot worked at a chemical lab, where she was developing an industrial petroleum cleanser. Her voice reflected what Ken called "the suit mood," a businesslike demeanor she effected whenever she was at work or even just talked about it.

"Hi, Margot, it's me."

"What's wrong?"

"Who said anything's wrong?"

"You did. It's in your voice."

He grimaced at the battery-acid taste in his mouth. He couldn't believe he was doing this.

"I'm in trouble, Margot."

"What is it?"

He sighed. "The bank repossessed my car, I'm about to lose my office, I have a small business loan that I'm four months behind on . . . and I don't even know how I'm going to pay next month's rent on my apartment."

She sounded startled. "I had no idea."

"I didn't want you to know. I didn't want anybody to know. I'm not exactly proud of it."

"I knew you weren't in the greatest financial shape, but—"

"The polygraph biz has been slow, and this stuff with Bobby has been pulling me under. He's getting worse. I'm funneling him all the money I can spare, and I guess some money I *couldn't* spare. I've been giving my creditors earnest money, but it's not enough anymore."

"Oh, Ken . . ." Her voice smacked of pity. He didn't want that. He wished he didn't want anything from her.

"Margot, I need to borrow some money. I'll pay it back right away, maybe in a couple of weeks. I hate to ask you, but I don't have any other choice."

She said nothing for a long while. Damn. He knew the call was a mistake.

"Ken, I can't."

"Okay," he quickly replied, trying to euthanize the conversation.

But she insisted on explaining. "We're just staying above water ourselves. We're up to our asses in debt. Between the house, the cars, student loans, there's not a lot left."

"I understand."

"Bill spends more than he should. He works so hard. He deserves to be rewarded, but he just gets carried away. I keep telling him I'm happy with what we have, but it's never enough for him."

It wasn't the answer Ken expected, but in a strange way it relieved him. He didn't want her money.

"I can give you fifty dollars walking-around cash," she offered. "If you want to swing by, there's an ATM downstairs."

"No, it's okay."

"Really, let me just—"

"No," he said firmly. "Come on, do you think I would've called if I had known your situation? Forget it."

"I'm sorry, Ken."

"Don't be. I'll talk to you later."

"Good morning, Ms. Daniels."

Myth did not have to turn to know Derek Rogers was greeting her. Rogers, one of the city's more talented district attorneys, always went out of his way to catch her attention. He was a lean, forceful type who had quite a reputation as a ladies' man. Myth, who had been dealing with his ilk since her teen years, knew the best way to keep Rogers off balance was to treat him with utter indifference. He was her opponent in the upcoming Burton Sabini embezzling trial.

"Good morning, Rogers." She didn't break stride as she paced through the municipal courthouse corridor.

He quickly joined her. "Slow down, will you?"

"Can't. Sorry. Some of us work for a living."

"Have you thought about my offer?"

"Which offer is that? The one where I walk on your back barefoot, or the one in which we go nude four-wheeling in the North Georgia mountains?"

"You remember!"

"Unfortunately I do. But I suppose you're talking about the stipulated polygraph test."

"Unfortunately I was."

"I've taken it under advisement."

"Meaning what?"

"Meaning, I'm thinking about it. The mere fact you offered a stip test proves what a flimsy case you have."

"Think what you want. But I need an answer within two weeks."

"You'll have it."

"Later, counselor." Rogers disappeared into a hearing room.

Myth continued down the hallway. She hoped to have an answer for Rogers a lot sooner than two weeks. Although she had made her name on high-profile cases, she would be happy to see this one go away quietly. Rogers, however, was making as much noise as he could, a tactic that could backfire if his case folded in on itself.

Rogers was ambitious. Cocky. Glib. Like so many men she knew. Like Tim.

Stop it, she told herself. Tim didn't matter anymore.

She caught sight of a padded envelope protruding from her briefcase. She had almost forgotten. It had been given to her on her way inside the courthouse.

She checked to see if there was anyone she knew in the immediate vicinity. All clear.

She stopped at a bench, pulled out the envelope, and tore it open. There were several black-and-white five-by-seven photographs, still damp from the lab. They all showed Ken Parker.

Arguing with a tow truck driver.

Walking to his office building.

Holding a paper with NOTICE OF EVICTION printed in large red letters.

An audiocassette tape was also enclosed, labeled K. PARKER PHONE CALLS 5/11–5/14.

A handwritten note said simply "So far, so good."

Myth stuffed the items back into her briefcase and walked down the corridor.

Ken spent the rest of the afternoon trying to come up with a way out of his mess, but each avenue dead-ended into a stone wall. His credit cards were maxed, his friends were tapped, and he had no equity to borrow against.

Of course, there was one thing he could still do.

It was an option he wouldn't even consider if it weren't for Bobby. Ken wasn't afraid of being broke; it wasn't pleasant, but he knew he could survive.

If only he could say the same about his brother.

Dammit.

At 7:02 P.M. he found himself walking down Piedmont Road, adjacent to the west end of the park. It wouldn't hurt to talk, he decided. His options were dwindling by the moment.

He scanned the park. It was dusk, and wicked shadows jabbed at the few kids left on the playground. A few parents and nannies stood on the sidelines. Over a hundred yards away, two figures sat on a bench—Myth and Sabini.

Myth called out as soon as he was within earshot. "Glad you could make it."

She rose to meet him, but Sabini remained seated, watching the playground intently. Then he glanced at Ken with tired eyes. "Thanks for coming."

Ken shook his hand. Sabini's attention immediately turned back toward the playground. He gestured to a small boy, about ten, playing on the monkey bars.

"That's my son," he said.

Ken looked at the boy. There was no resemblance between him and Sabini, but that was to the kid's advantage.

"He's here with his baby-sitter," Sabini said wearily. "I haven't been with him in over four months. My wife and I are separated. She doesn't want me seeing him until the trial is over. It's been rough on him."

Ken could see that it had been rough on Sabini too. The man's eyes were bloodshot and his face was ashen.

Sabini let out a long, tired sigh. "I don't like all this shady stuff any more than you probably do, Ken. But I want it all done with, and Ms. Daniels tells me passing the test might be the quickest way. Can you teach me to beat that machine?"

Sabini looked back at his son. Ken remembered his own father watching him play on the rocket-ship slide at Herman Park in Houston. Sabini looked at his kid with the same pride and wonder.

Ken realized that Sabini reminded him of his father. Dad never complained about anything, but as the years wore on, the stress of his job as foreman at a marble quarry took its toll. His posture slumped and he was always tired, but still he didn't complain.

Ken studied Sabini. He wanted to believe the guy was innocent, if for no other reason than he loved his kid.

Myth held up the roll of bills. "Do you want this?"

The moment of truth.

All that money.

What would Bobby tell him to do? Forget it, probably.

Not probably. Definitely. But after all those years of getting screwed for doing the right thing, this one act could make everything okay again. He could take care of Bobby and get his own life back on track.

He could feel his heart pounding faster. Was he really going to do it?

"How much time would I have?" Ken asked.

"Twelve days."

"It'll take some long hours and a lot of practice, but it can be done."

Myth handed him the cash and a manila envelope.

"What's this?" he asked.

"Everything you need to know about the case. Newspaper clippings, briefs, photos, miscellaneous documents."

The deal was done.

He was committed.

He felt sick.

Ken crammed the money into his pants pocket. His hands were sweating.

Sabini smiled. "Thank you, Ken. When do we start?"

"I'll need the weekend to get ready. How about Monday night?"

"Fine."

"Meet me at my office around nine. The building should be cleared out by then."

"I'll be there," Sabini said.

"Strictly confidential, right?" Myth said.

"I wouldn't have it any other way."

Ken turned down Myth's offer of a ride home, electing to ride the MARTA train. It probably wasn't the brightest move to walk around town with ten grand in his pocket, but he needed time alone to convince himself he hadn't just sold his soul to the devil.

It wasn't as though he was hurting anyone. If Sabini was innocent, he wouldn't know where the money was anyway. If he was guilty, chances were he would ride out a short jail term, then pick up where he left off with the fortune he'd stolen. The result would be the same. Vikkers Industries was out of luck.

Nice rationalization, Ken thought. He was almost as good at this game as his customers.

Vikkers Industries had outgrown its one-story complex several times in its twenty-six-year history, and rather than move to more spacious quarters, the company had merely built onto its existing structure, resulting in a sprawling, confusing labyrinth of corridors and offices. Employees who had worked there for weeks still got lost, and an extra receptionist was on the payroll just to guide visitors to their destinations.

Company president Herbert Decker felt it was his duty to walk through the corridors like a leader, his chest out and shoulders back. It was a habit he practiced even at night, when all the employees had gone home. His patchy beard didn't quite hide his weak chin, and he wore his hair in a comb-over that only accentuated his balding head.

He wished things would get back to normal. The Vikkers employees were already nervous and afraid for their jobs in the wake of the recent merger with Lyceum Metals, and Burton Sabini had only added to the chaos.

That ungrateful little prick. Decker had chosen him over younger, flashier candidates for the CFO job because Sabini seemed like the type who would stay put. The others would have bolted as soon as they were able to trade up to higher-paying positions at other firms. Who knew that the Milquetoast would perpetrate the biggest crime in the company's history?

That bastard.

Decker stepped into his office to see Ted Michaelson reclining on the sofa. Michaelson was a free-lance private investigator Vikkers often hired.

"Make yourself comfortable, Ted."

Michaelson laughed and sat up. "Don't mind if I do." The investigator was plump, fiftyish, and sported thick stubble on his chin.

"Thanks for meeting me so late." Decker sat at his desk. "Things are crazy here during the day."

Michaelson pointed to a collection of plaques on the wall, each commemorating a new metal formulation. "Busy putting more of those up there, huh?"

"Yeah." Decker patted his comb-over. "What do you have for me?"

"I'm covering all the bases. By the time I'm through, there's nothing about Burton Sabini we won't know."

Decker's eyes narrowed. "There's only one thing I want to know. Where's our goddamned money?"

"I'm working on it."

"So you keep telling me. What do you think of the D.A. offering him a stipulated polygraph test?"

"It shows they have even less of a case than we think they do. They're not even close to getting that money back, which is why you were smart to hire me. I'm sure Myth Daniels won't agree to the exam. She's smarter than that."

"Maybe."

"Is this what you wanted to talk to me about?"

"No, not really. Something else has come up."

"When it rains, it pours, huh?"

"A federal agent has approached one of our vice presidents about turning evidence against us."

"For what?"

"They've been rather vague. Some bogus charge, probably."

"Do they have proof?"

"I doubt it. They've been bugging the hell out of Matt Lansing in Finance. They want him to spy on us."

"Lansing told you this?"

"Yes."

"I should talk to him." Michaelson jotted down Lansing's name in his pocket notebook. "I'll put him under surveillance."

"Why?"

"To make sure he doesn't start talking to the feds any more than he admits to. He may be straight with you now, but once they start putting pressure on him, your boy could turn on you in a heartbeat. Do you know the agent's name?"

Decker handed Michaelson a small piece of paper. "It's here, along with his office number. Steven Lars. Heard of him?"

"No, but there's no reason I would have. I'll check him out." Michaelson flashed a toothy smile. "Are you sure there's nothing you want to tell me?"

"Positive. I want *you* to enlighten *me*. What are they looking for? How much do they know? Where are they headed with this?"

Michaelson nodded as he pocketed the slip of paper. "You may not like the answers to those questions."

"Don't worry." Decker leaned back in his chair. "I have some ideas about how to deal with that when the time comes."

CHAPTER 3

Ken wiped his brow as he stood over the engine of Bill's '55 Corvette. The perennial weekend project had consumed hundreds, perhaps thousands of man-hours since Bill had "rescued" it from the local scrap yard three years before. The car sat on concrete blocks in the garage of Bill and Margot's suburban home, and it was in no immediate danger of moving anywhere under its own power.

Ken and another of Bill's friends, Colby Lassen, spent many a Saturday helping him with the car. Each week another part of the engine was tackled, but every repair seemed to reveal yet another problem. Today they were installing new pistons.

"My ideal woman . . . She's gotta be small," Colby said. "Tiny. Not *dwarf* tiny, but petite. A lotta guys, they like the tall ones. Not me. I don't want a woman I can lose myself in."

Ken snorted. "I've seen you in the locker room, Colby. You could lose yourself in a tiny woman too."

"Blow me."

Bill looked at Ken. "What about *your* ideal woman?"

Ken paused with his pliers. "She burns bright."

Colby snickered. "Oooh, yeah."

"No, I mean . . . everything she does, she does full throttle.

All out. She never doubts herself. She always knows exactly what she wants and how to get it."

Ken leaned against the car. "She's beautiful, and maybe she even knows it. But deep down, she's scared."

"Scared of what?" Bill asked.

"Life. She's not neurotic or anything. But it's just enough to melt the 'ice queen' image she tries to put on. People like that need to feel they're in control. It's the only way they can keep their grip."

Bill and Colby stared at Ken, dumbfounded.

"Who are we talking about?" Colby asked.

"Yeah, who is she?" Bill was smiling.

"No one."

Bill stepped closer. "Come on. Who?"

"Nobody. Really. We're talking hypothetical here, right?"

Bill gave his friend a doubtful look. "I was gonna say my ideal woman is blond with big tits. I guess now I'll have to do better."

Ken stared into the engine compartment. He didn't know if he was describing Myth or merely an elaborate fantasy of who she might be. It wouldn't be the first time someone projected their soul mate behind a pretty face.

Don't get off track, man. Do her job, take the money, and run. That's what this is all about.

The money had already made a huge difference in his life. He had paid off his car, gotten the most persistent bill collectors off his back, and slipped five thousand dollars into his brother's mail slot. If only he didn't still feel guilty about the way he was accomplishing it.

He bent over and tried to look as if he was working. "This car of yours is gonna be on the blocks for *another* three years."

Bill laughed. He opened a mini-refrigerator and grabbed a cold Bud. "Hell, this car isn't for driving. It's for dreaming. It's for standing around, drinking beer,

and having conversations just like this. Haven't you figured that out by now?"

At the end of the afternoon Ken turned down Bill's offer to
stay for dinner. There was work to do.

He drove to the Emory University library, where he
hoped to find some background material on the various
methods of defeating polygraphs. There was a surprising
amount of literature on the subject, detailed in books, magazine articles, and scientific journals. Many studies in the
area were commissioned by the CIA and branches of the
armed services, but their methodology and results were
classified. Everyone knew the common-wisdom tricks:
biting your tongue, putting a tack in your shoe, and so on.
Examiners, however, were hip to these methods, render-
ing any such attempts worthless. It wasn't enough for
Sabini to pass the test; he had to do it with no evidence of
trickery.

Ken put down the last article. There wasn't a lot there
that he didn't already know, but he was sure he had enough
to get Sabini through the D.A.'s test.

And then, with an extra forty thousand dollars to his
name, he could stop worrying for a change.

A helicopter crash, a dead convenience-store clerk, and a
warehouse fire. A good night by any standards.

Hound Dog Barrett squeezed off four quick pictures of
the fire, finishing off her roll. Way to go. Things had been
quiet lately, but a night like this made it all worthwhile.
She flipped back her short brown hair as two other scanner
geeks drove up. Weirdos.

Like she was any better, Hound Dog thought ruefully.
She and the new arrivals spent their nights roaming the
streets, listening for broadcast crime and accident scene info
on a portable scanner. They would often get to the scene before the police, snapping away with their cameras. Though

scanner geeks occasionally made the leap to professional photojournalists, they generally preferred to keep their photos to themselves, showing them only to interested friends, relatives, and other scanner geeks.

At twenty-one, Hound Dog had seen more than most people would see in a lifetime. Decapitated corpses, mangled automobiles, and exploding buildings greeted her in her nightly adventures. She could only imagine what her parents would say if they knew she did this until at least dawn every morning.

She wound the exposed roll as she walked back to her motorcycle. Time to leave. She didn't like to be around other scanner geeks; seeing the socially awkward young men only reminded her that others saw her the same way.

She zipped her camera into its bag and kick-started her Harley-Davidson motorcycle. She adjusted the scanner headphones beneath her helmet and roared away, leaving the burning warehouse behind her.

One-ten A.M. If she went home now, it still would have been a good night. But she wasn't tired. And besides, she was on a major roll. Who knew what the rest of the night would hold for her?

Scanner geek.

Sometimes she felt like a geek, without a real life. In some ways, her hobby did isolate her from the rest of the world. Except for the time she spent with her live-in boyfriend, Mark, she had almost no social life. She spent most of her days at PhotoSmith Studios, one of the best-known photography houses in the city. There she made her living by retouching models' portfolio shots, and she had a standing offer to shoot as a studio photographer whenever she felt so inclined. But she just couldn't get enthused about telling snotty fifteen-year-olds how to pout.

She usually arrived home from work at four P.M., spent some quality time with Mark, then slept for a few hours. At around eleven she set out on her motorcycle, scanner on, searching for those photo opportunities. The time she spent alone, riding the city streets, was her favorite; these nights defined who she was.

She pulled into the parking lot of a Kroger supermarket, nicknamed by locals the "disco Kroger" for its proximity to a popular dance club. She went inside, bought a croissant and a pint of chocolate milk, and consumed them on the sidewalk outside. She flipped through a newspaper as she ate, reading up on the crime and accident scenes she had visited the evening before. As always, the reporters got many of the facts wrong. How could they be such screwups?

She was about to trash the paper, when a photo caught her eye. It was on page one of the business section, a beautiful woman with a middle-aged man. Hound Dog studied the woman's face. She had seen it before.

But where?

The caption told her that the woman was an attorney named Myth Daniels, and she was walking with Burton Sabini, her client in an embezzling case.

The woman's neck was arched and her face was tense, turned away from the camera in a three-quarter shot, accented with the tiniest hint of motion blur. Hound Dog had seen that pose many times before. It was the classic "avoidance reflex," the posture people adopt when trying not to have their picture taken. She saw it in her photos almost every night, so she considered herself an expert on the subject.

She wasn't used to seeing it from attorneys though. They *wanted* to see themselves plastered all over page one. But not this woman.

She looked familiar.

Hound Dog was sure she had never seen her in person. It had been a photo. Probably a black-and-white shot.

Not a newspaper picture, she didn't think. It was somewhere else.

Damn. She knew it would bug the hell out of her until she remembered where she had seen this woman.

She had to find out.

It was after one-thirty A.M. when Ken whipped into his parking space. He had been at Winston's bar, watching a Braves night game in Los Angeles. He was feeling good, both because his team had won and because it was nice to park in front of his home again.

He had just climbed out, when a blow sent him back against the door. He whirled around to see a familiar face.

The man was unshaven, and sweat dripped from his messy hair.

He leaned into Ken's face and screamed, "You son of a bitch! You screwed me. You fucked me over, man."

Before Ken could reply, the man landed a boulder punch to his stomach. The wind whistled as the fist flew into him.

Ken tried to double over, but a pair of arms locked under his armpits and pulled him up. He looked back at this second man. He hadn't seen him before. He would have remembered the brown tooth.

"Look at me. I said, *look* at me!"

Ken looked back at the first man. Then he remembered. One of the people he had tested . . .

Valez. Carlos Valez.

Whumppp!

This punch landed higher on his torso, near his rib cage.

Ken closed his eyes, momentarily losing himself in hallucinatory flashes of bright, white-hot light. His insides were exploding.

He opened his eyes. Carlos was still in his face.

"Remember me? Do you?"

Ken nodded.

"You said I was a thief. A goddamned thief!"

Ken grunted out, "I only—only said—"

"Shut up!" Carlos delivered what felt like a sledge-hammer to his lower jaw.

Ken's teeth gnashed. His face throbbed.

"You wrecked my life. My wife, my baby, and I were living with my dad. He threw me out after I got fired. Now I got no job, no home, no family. All because you said I lied. You're the liar. *You* are!"

Ken tried to form some words, but his mouth wouldn't cooperate. A thin string of drool escaped from his lower lip.

It was getting harder to breathe.

"Make a phone call. Tell the bitch you made a mistake."

His face still throbbing, Ken swung his legs and kicked outward. He aimed for Carlos's chest.

Contact.

Ken pushed himself back, slammed Brown Tooth against his car, and spun around with a punch to the man's stomach.

Brown Tooth tried to strike back. A miss.

Ken dodged a second punch. Another miss.

His whole body was killing him. How much longer could he keep this up?

Answer: Not long.

Because in the next instant Ken felt as if a truck had smashed into his back.

His legs buckled beneath him. His head struck the warm pavement.

He rolled to see Carlos standing over him.

The man had given him a kung-fu kick with his black-heeled cowboy boots.

Ken wondered if he was paralyzed. No. He wouldn't feel the spasms of pain shooting from every nerve ending.

He prepared for more, but at that moment two neighbors drove into the parking lot. College guys.

Carlos and his friend backed off. "Make the call," Carlos warned, "or you're dead."

Carlos and Brown Tooth ran from the parking lot.

Ken's neighbors climbed out of their car and looked at him lying on the pavement. The college guys whispered to each other for a moment, trying to decide what to do. Ken waved them on.

Hell, he *always* took naps here in the parking lot.

After a minute, he pulled himself to his feet, grimacing. He staggered to the stairs and slowly climbed toward his third-floor apartment. Each step was like another blow.

To his stomach.

To his chest.

To his back.

Carlos gave the gift that keeps on giving.

Ken's hands shook as he tried to put his key into the lock. Slowly, patiently . . . There. Finally.

He opened the door, stumbled inside, and made his way to the bedroom. His futon was on the floor. It hurt to bend at the waist, so he kneeled on the futon's edge and gently lowered himself down.

He stroked his jawline. He didn't think it was broken, but he could feel it swelling up. He wondered if he should see a doctor before going to sleep. But the thought of a four-hundred-dollar emergency room tab didn't appeal to him.

He also thought briefly of calling the police. Nah. Maybe he deserved it. Maybe he *was* wrong about Carlos's exam.

The uncertainty.

It was the worst part of his profession. Even when he followed the rules and tried to play fair, he could never be sure how accurate he was. How many careers had he ruined? How many families had he torn apart?

How many?

He had no idea.

Over the next few hours, he tried to sleep, waking whenever he turned or rolled over. He still hurt like hell.

He played a game with himself. Where would he be *if* . . .

If he hadn't done "the right thing."

If he hadn't screwed up his life.

He wouldn't be nursing bruises in this shitty apartment, he knew that. And he wouldn't be making a living from a gadget that might be about as accurate as a coin toss.

He had to get a real life.

Maybe, just maybe, Myth Daniels and Burton Sabini held his ticket to that life.

CHAPTER 4

Herbert Decker hated parties almost as much as he hated the watery Tom Collins he was sipping. He stood in the massive atrium of a rented mansion on Habersham Road, surrounded by a cast of characters who regularly appeared in the *Atlanta Journal-Constitution*'s society pages and trendy "Peach Buzz" column. The party was being given by a Belize diplomat with whom Decker was negotiating to supply raw materials for the country's public works projects. Before the deal was concluded, Decker was sure a bribe would have to be arranged. It was already factored into his company's internal budget, just as such payments were in the books of many firms dealing with foreign governments.

"Herbert, we've been talking about you behind your back," Governor Walter Holden said with the dazzling smile that got him elected. His popularity had never been lower, and with the next election only months away, he was almost certainly in his final year in office. Tonight the governor was sticking close to the party's host, Marco Vincent.

Decker handed his glass to a passing waiter. "It can't be worse than what you guys say to my face." He laughed, and the two men responded with polite chuckles. He hated cocktail chatter.

The governor stood close to Decker. "Mr. Vincent has expressed some concerns about your company."

" 'Concerns' is a tad harsh," Vincent said with only the slightest trace of an accent. He was a handsome man with dark skin. " 'Musings' is more like it."

Decker spoke through his frozen smile. "And what were you musing?"

"I was telling Governor Holden that as much as I wish to do business with your firm, I still must sell the idea to my country's public works ministry."

"Of course."

"That, I'm afraid, will be more difficult with the negative publicity your company is receiving."

Holden spoke quietly. "He's afraid the embezzlement case may scare off some of his country's decision makers."

Decker felt his face getting flushed. He knew it would appear that he was embarrassed, but he was enraged. He looked up at the ceiling. "I see."

"Please don't misunderstand me," Vincent said. "I have the utmost respect for you and your company. But as you know, perception is important. And to some people, the perception is that Vikkers Industries cannot control its own employees. My government needs assurances that you will be a reliable supplier of the materials we need."

"The actions of *one man*—?"

"I'm sure it will not be a problem, but it is something we must be aware of. Those who favor other alliances may try to use this as ammunition against you. That's all I'm saying." Vincent caught someone's eye on the other side of the room. "Excuse me." He walked away, leaving the governor with Decker.

"When does the trial begin?" Holden asked.

"In less than a month." Decker was still fuming.

"I know this Belize contract is relatively small, but there's no way to assess the total damage done. Perception is everything."

"You should know, Holden."

Holden ignored the comment. "I'd hate to see you suffer any more than you have already."

"What am I supposed to do?" Decker snapped.

"Get your house in order." He patted Decker on the arm and walked away.

"That's my plan," Decker said under his breath.

Four minutes past nine P.M.

Ken had never been alone in his office building before, and it wasn't a sensation he particularly enjoyed. There were sounds he never heard during the day. The creaks. The water rushing through rusty pipes. The air whistling through dusty vents. And finally, two sets of footsteps echoing in the hallway.

Ken's body ached as he rose and stepped toward the door. His face had stopped throbbing in the past few hours, but his stomach and ribs still hurt. He looked outside and saw Myth and Sabini.

"What happened?" Myth asked, her hand lightly caressing his bruised face.

"Just another satisfied customer."

"That looks bad," Sabini said. "You want to do this some other time?"

"No. We need to get started. Are you ready?"

Sabini nodded and stepped into the office. Myth started to follow, but Ken blocked the doorway with his arm. "Where are you going?" he said.

"I thought I'd watch."

"I can't allow that."

"Why not?"

"Every variable can affect the outcome. As his attorney, you might give him a feeling of security he wouldn't have otherwise. When the D.A.'s examiner tests him, nobody else will be in the room. I need to do it the same way. I'm sorry, but you'll have to leave."

She stared at him, then finally nodded. "Fine. Call me tonight after you finish."

She said it like an order, Ken thought. Making it clear she was still in charge. But she wasn't in charge anymore, at least not in his office, and it was driving her nuts.

Good.

He smiled. "Sure. Good night." He closed the door and turned back to Sabini.

"How are you this evening, Mr. Sabini?"

"Fine, thank you."

"Glad to hear it. Have a seat."

Ken went over the ten-question test with his interviewee, making sure he understood it all. Sabini was polite, but not too polite. He was agreeable, and the only questions he asked were to clarify some of the test's finer points.

So far, so good.

Ken hooked him up to the polygraph. He turned on the machine and thumped the top panel, unsticking the pulse needle. He elected to forgo the card trick. A D.A.-appointed examiner probably wouldn't do it, though Ken thought it helped reinforce the notion of the machine's accuracy.

If they believe this stuff works, maybe it really will . . .

Ken asked the first question. "Did you attend school at Rockport College?"

"Yes."

"Will you be completely truthful to me regarding the Vikkers Industries embezzlement case?"

"Yes."

Ken always wondered how he would react if he ever got a no in response to this question. He never had.

"Do you understand I will inquire only about issues we have discussed?"

"Yes."

"Have you ever stolen anything from an employer of yours?"

"No."

"In your capacity of chief financial officer of Vikkers Industries, did you misdirect company funds so as to derive personal financial gain?"

"No."

"Have you ever lied to keep from getting into trouble at work?"

"No."

"Between February and November of last year, did you arrange electronic fund transfers between your company and personal bank accounts in Zurich, Switzerland?"

"No."

"Is your full name Burton Charles Sabini?"

"Yes."

"Have you ever violated any laws in the preparation of business or personal tax documents?"

"No."

"Do you presently have access, either directly or indirectly, to the funds illegally transferred from your company's accounts?"

"No."

Ken looked at Sabini's readings as the paper spooled over the polygraph stand's edge. The responses were strong and distinct. Not much gray area here.

He unhooked Sabini from the polygraph, ignoring his client's questioning look.

"Well?" Sabini asked.

Ken tore off the graph and held it in front of Sabini's face. "You know what this is? It's Illustration 1-4 in the polygraph textbooks—the classic liar. Every reading points to that: breathing, skin perspiration, pulse rate. This is bad."

Sabini slumped. "Shit. I was afraid of that. Is there any hope?"

Ken studied the graph in his hands. This was going to be harder than he thought.

He stood and walked to his desk. "First of all, forget every bullshit story you've ever heard about what it takes to beat a polygraph. You're not going to be biting your tongue, pressing your foot against a tack, or anything like that."

"Okay, so I know what I'm *not* going to do."

Ken picked up a pack of cigarettes. "Do you smoke?"

"No."

"Start. It'll draw oxygen from your skin, make your perspiration levels less volatile. You had a tough time with that."

He slipped the cigarette pack into Sabini's shirt pocket.

"Great. I'll pass the test but die of lung cancer."

"That's the breaks."

"What else?"

"Can you . . . pucker?"

Sabini shifted uneasily. "Look, I'm not going to kiss you."

"I don't want you to pucker with your mouth."

"Then what with?"

"Your asshole."

Sabini stared at him, then abruptly stood up. "I don't know what you have in mind here—"

Ken pushed him back into the seat. "Sit down, you're not my type. Now, try it. Pull your asshole in. The old anal pucker."

Sabini was obviously still uneasy, but he concentrated, sucking it in. His eyes darted from side to side.

"Yeah . . . yeah!" he said excitedly.

"I knew you were a tight-ass. Good. That sends your blood pressure north. You'll be in good shape if you can do that on all the nonrelevant questions."

"What?"

Ken wired him to the polygraph. "There are a couple of basic kinds of questions: There's the nonrelevant control questions and the relevant questions."

He tried to think of a way to explain it simply. "Basically, nonrelevant questions are things they think they already know the answer to. Some will be harmless, Is this your name?—type questions. They figure you'll be straight with them on those. Other nonrelevant questions will be mildly threatening. On those, they're counting on you to lie."

"They *want* me to lie?"

"Yeah. They'll ask you things like, Have you ever stolen anything from your employer? They think that everybody has taken at least some pens or paper clips home with them. If they can see what your responses are when you lie about this, they think your readings will be even more extreme if you lie about something related to this specific case."

Sabini nodded. "The relevant questions."

"Right. What we have to do is level out your responses on everything. Then, depending on how well you do, we might try to give 'em some slightly higher readings for those mildly threatening questions. They would expect that."

"Just tell me when to pucker."

Ken smiled as he thumped the needles. He shook a can of WD-40 lubricant and sprayed the indicator mechanism. There. That took care of the sticky respiration needle.

He started the graph paper rolling again. "The first question is always a harmless irrelevant. Always."

"Okay."

"Did you graduate from Rockport College?"

"Yes."

"Are you puckering?"

Sabini nodded.

"Don't do it so much. Loosen up just a little . . . a little less . . ."

Ken watched the graph as the blood pressure readings dropped lower, lower, lower . . .

"There! Try and pucker just like that on the nonrelevant questions. Okay?"

"Got it."

"And don't hold your breath. You can pucker and breathe at the same time."

Sabini tried to take slow, normal breaths, but he clearly still felt awkward.

Ken went to the next question. "Will you be completely truthful with me regarding the Vikkers Industries embezzlement case?"

"Yes."

The blood pressure needle dropped.

Ken smiled. "Relevant question. You stopped puckering. Good. Okay, stay calm, breathe easy. . . . Now, do you understand that I will inquire only about issues we have discussed?"

"Yes."

The readings were stable.

Ken explained, "This is just to assure you there will be no questions out of left field. In the pre-interview, the examiner will go over the test to make sure you understand it. They don't want you worrying about any outside issues that might throw off the readings for the questions they *are* asking."

Sabini snorted. "Like anything could worry me more than being accused of stealing twelve million dollars."

"Still, you can count on it being there. Probably the third question. Okay. Have you ever lied to keep from getting into trouble at work?"

"No."

"Okay, this is one they *expect* you to lie on. Just relax, keep your breathing regular. . . ."

Ken nodded as the readings leveled off.

"Now . . . In your capacity as account financial manager, did you misdirect company funds so as to derive personal gain?"

"No."

The needles jumped sharply across the graph.

"You took a sharp breath, and your other responses went up too."

Sabini glared at the machine. "I just need some practice," he mumbled.

"You'll get it. But you have to stop being afraid of this thing. It will catch you only if you think it will."

Ken picked up his deck of playing cards. "There's a trick we do to convince people that polygraphs really work. If they believe in the machine, they're more likely to have strong nervous responses to the relevant questions."

He fanned out the deck. "Take a card."

Sabini selected a card, looked at it, and held it close to his chest.

Ken put the rest of the deck down. "Normally, I'd go through this whole bullshit routine about asking you to lie to me about the card. I'd ask you about the number, color, suit, and so on. And then, thanks to my wonderfully perceptive lie detector, I'd be able to tell you that you have the queen of hearts."

Sabini looked up in surprise. "That's right!" He turned his card around.

Ken picked up his deck and fanned it out faceup.

They were all the queen of hearts.

"The polygraph works only if you believe it does. Ready to try again?"

Sabini smiled as he threw his card down. "Yeah."

The next few days were a blur to Ken. He spent his mornings and afternoons exploring different methods of beating polygraphs, his nights training Sabini on the machine.

He taught Sabini breathing exercises calculated to smooth out the jagged respiration readings. As Ken had expected, this proved to be the easiest response to control. Sabini had almost mastered it by the end of the second day.

More problematic were the skin perspiration readings. Sabini would have to smoke for a week or so to deprive his skin of enough oxygen to make a difference. That alone, however, wouldn't be enough. Ken would have to think of something else.

For the pulse rate, he turned to the methods of biofeedback, the seventies-era relaxation technique in which subjects monitor their own heartbeats and even brain waves to bring them under control. He showed Sabini his indicators on the rolling graph paper and designed several exercises that allowed his student to consciously manipulate the readings.

Since the training sessions didn't begin until after ten every night, Ken and Sabini always worked until two, sometimes three, in the morning. It was a punishing schedule, made worse for Ken by the lingering soreness from his beating. And as hard as he tried, he could never get past how wrong it all was. It gnawed at him every minute of the day.

He couldn't wait to be finished.

It was a slow night on the streets.

Hound Dog revved her Harley, cruising up and down the city's major thoroughfares as her belt scanner crackled through the headphones. The scanner wasn't picking up anything interesting—some minor fender-benders, a robbery, a bar fight, all of which were decidedly unphotogenic after the fact.

For the past couple of days she had racked her brain trying to remember where she had seen the woman in that newspaper photo. Maybe it was in a shot taken by another scanner geek.

She checked her watch. One forty-five A.M. It was a bit early for "lunch," but since she was using more gasoline than film, it would probably be good to knock off for a while. At that hour, the best prospect was the Varsity, a cavernous fast-food restaurant located near the Georgia Tech campus. An Atlanta institution for over half a century, the establishment was geared toward high-volume traffic. The counter personnel always barked quickly, "What d'ya have, what d'ya have?!" and slammed the counter impatiently if the customers so much as hesitated to place their orders. This, of course, was nothing compared to the treatment in store if the patrons didn't have their money out and ready to give. This was true if the restaurant was packed with over a thousand or just a scattered half dozen. The Varsity's brand of customer relations reduced some to tears, but it added character to the place, and the food was delicious in its own greasy, artery-clogging way.

Hound Dog rolled up the ramp to the restaurant's parking structure, cut the engine, and dismounted. She could already smell those onion rings.

After getting her food, she held the red tray, glancing around for a place to sit. There were several large rooms, each of which had a TV blaring. She spotted a group of five scanner geeks sitting in the newer wing. Normally this would have prompted her to walk the other way. Tonight, however, was different. She headed toward them and took a seat at their table.

"You must really be bored if you're hanging out with us," said Vince, a thin, spike-haired young man with wire-rimmed glasses.

Hound Dog shrugged. "Just as long as I don't have to listen to you guys whine about how little sex you're getting."

Freddy, a portly man in his early forties, snickered. "What makes you think we're not getting our share?"

"If you guys were getting laid, you wouldn't be out doing this every night."

Freddy leered at her. "So I guess that means *you're* hard up."

She shook her head. "No, I get plenty, and I *still* do this. Which means I'm sicker than any of you."

She took a sip from her Frosted Orange as she pulled the newspaper photo of Myth from her camera bag. She tossed it onto the table in the center of the group.

"Any of you guys shoot her before?"

The men passed the picture around, making various "hubba-hubba" and panting noises, reminding Hound Dog why they were called scanner geeks rather than scanner enthusiasts.

"Where did you get this?" the smallest of the guys asked. His name was Laszlo, and his preppy appearance contrasted with the others' grunge look.

"Sunday paper. She looks familiar to me. I thought one of you guys may have shown me her picture in your book."

Freddy tossed a worn pocket-sized photo album on the table. "Speaking of which, I have something to show you guys."

"You have her picture?" Hound Dog asked.

"No," Freddy said. "But I have some awesome shots of that ambulance accident in Roswell the other night."

Vince leaned excitedly toward Freddy. "*That* was a pile-up!" He turned toward the others. "Some guy had a fender-bender, minor injuries, and the ambulance was taking him to the emergency room. But then it jumps the median on Holcomb Bridge Road, and *wham*!" He clapped his hands for emphasis. "It hits the pole of a Burger King sign. Everybody's okay except the patient—he gets a broken back!"

Laszlo shook his head. "By the time he's through with the ambulance company, he'll be a millionaire."

"What good is it if he can't move?" Freddy asked.

"Please," Hound Dog persisted, trying to get back to the original subject. "I know I've seen this woman somewhere before. None of you have shot her?"

"Even if it were fifty million dollars, it wouldn't be worth it to you?" Laszlo asked.

"To be paralyzed for the rest of my life?" Freddy grimaced.

"Guys . . ." Hound Dog implored.

"Okay. What if it were just the waist down?"

"That's the best part!"

It was no use. Hound Dog took the photo back, picked up her tray, and moved to another room.

"Idiots," she muttered.

Carlos Valez slumped against a brick wall facing the Inman Park apartment complex. He'd been there only a few days before, the night he kicked the shit out of that lie detector guy. Now he was back, sitting next to the Dumpster, smoking a joint he had found in his buddy Jesus's bathroom. He had been hiding out with Jesus since being thrown out of his father's house.

It had been a nasty scene between him and his father. When the lie detector test came back and he lost his job, his father yelled and slapped him around. Alicia and the baby can stay, the old man said, but you're outta here.

Carlos got him back. He beat the hell out of him.

Stupid old man reported him to the police.

Maybe Ms. Benton had reported him too. She was the manager who fired him from the custodial staff at the Packard Hills Shopping Center. Carlos exploded when she gave him the news. Didn't that bitch see what she was doing to him? He pushed her desk over, pulled the phone cord between his hands, and advanced on her. Scared her shitless. But after she cried and begged him to leave her alone, he ran out of the office. She wasn't worth the trouble.

Carlos glanced around the parking lot. He didn't think he would come back here. One visit had accomplished all he set out to do. He wanted to scare the lie detector guy, make him hurt, and keep him looking over his shoulder for a few days. But now Carlos wanted more. This guy had screwed him over, and he should pay. How? Carlos wrestled with that one for a while, but at about two in the morning he decided Ken Parker should die.

He played with his long razor, flipping it open and closed. He would take one clean swipe at Parker's throat, and if he was lucky, his victim wouldn't make a sound.

Carlos had never killed a man before, but there was a tightness in his chest, a burning, and it would go away only when this guy was dead. He had to make it stop.

Afterward, he would detour to his father's house, where he'd pick up his son. He knew it was risky, since his wife would report him. Maybe he would tie her up to buy himself some time. Or maybe he would waste her too. She deserved it for believing that lie detector over his word.

He sat still as a young couple stepped outside one of the buildings. The girl was going home, and they stood next to her car, kissing and tonguing each other for a while. Carlos didn't have a watch, but he figured it must be almost three A.M. Maybe Parker was staying with a girlfriend that night.

Carlos considered giving it up, until he heard the distinctive roar of an MG as it turned into the lot. It was him!

Carlos watched as the examiner pulled into his space and killed the engine. But the couple was still out there. He couldn't risk it. Not yet.

Parker bounded quickly up his stairs, climbing toward his apartment.

Apartment 332, Carlos remembered. It was in the phone book.

He waited another few minutes until the couple finally surrendered their lip lock. The girl drove away, and her boyfriend ambled to his apartment.

Carlos squinted into the darkness. He thought he saw someone several yards away, slinking in the shadows. He struggled to focus. It was no one.

He wished he hadn't smoked the whole joint.

He moved quietly toward the stairs and started the long climb. Only a couple of the landings actually had bulbs lit, so most of the journey was cloaked in darkness. He stopped.

There was a sound.

A footstep.

A rustling.

He couldn't tell if it was above or below him. He climbed a few more steps and listened. Nothing.

He continued up to the third floor, stepping on each stair on tiptoe. Once he reached the top, he glanced over the railing at the parking lot below. It was deserted. He walked toward Ken's apartment, swinging open the blade on his razor.

His face was hot and his mouth went dry.

He didn't want to do this anymore, but he knew he'd hate himself later if he wimped out.

He could break the door open by throwing his weight against it, but he'd have to work fast. Parker would probably be in his bedroom.

If only he had been able to nail him in the parking lot . . .

Carlos stood still, letting his body adjust to the sudden surge of adrenaline. His head was pounding in time with his heart.

He heard the rustling again.

It was behind him.

He turned just in time to see a glint of steel and the sight of his own blood spurting on his killer's face.

Carlos was dead before he hit the ground.

CHAPTER 5

Lieutenant Thomas Gant loved his sleep. He worshiped it. His wife, Diane, was a music teacher at the Sprayberry School for the Performing Arts, and she knew better than to wake him when she began her morning routine. Sometimes Gant stirred when she kissed him good-bye, but usually he didn't achieve consciousness until his clock radio blared at seven-thirty A.M., always in the middle of a commercial.

This morning it was an ad for tires. Gant punched the off button and rolled out of bed. He flipped on the TV and shuffled past the full-length mirror his wife had cruelly placed on the closet door.

Gant was a stocky man of forty-six, and though his dark red hair was giving way to traces of gray, his paunch was covered with fiery red fur.

He brushed his teeth as he gazed wistfully at Katie Couric. The phone rang. Gant continued to watch Katie as he answered it.

"Hello."

"Good morning, Gant." It was John Burke, the captain of his precinct. "I hear the TV. How does your heartthrob look today?"

"Al Roker's wearing a blue blazer and striped tie. He looks damn good."

Burke chuckled. "I need you to make a stop on your way

in. Some garbagemen found a body in a Dumpster. Looks fresh: 1067 Sycamore Creek Drive."

Gant jotted down the address. "I.D.?"

"Yeah. His name was Carlos Valez. His father had sworn out a warrant for him a couple of days ago. Assault and battery."

"Think maybe his old man whacked him?"

"Doubtful. He's still in the hospital."

Gant walked across the apartment complex's blacktop parking lot, approaching one of the many hundreds of crime scenes he had investigated in his twenty-five years on the force. He had been with the Atlanta P.D. since his days as a rookie beat cop. He liked his job and planned to stay through the rest of his professional life. More and more of his colleagues were deserting the force for positions with private investigation and security firms, but Gant had no interest in that. If he had been truly interested in money, he wouldn't have become a cop in the first place. As a homicide detective, he felt he was an advocate, a representative for a constituency that had few champions.

The dead.

Bereaved families all too often were quick to retreat into their grief, chalking up the death of their loved ones to unexplained random violence. And while such crimes were on the upswing, the vast majority were still committed by persons known to the victim. ORDER OUT OF CHAOS read a stenciled black-on-white sign tacked to a bulletin board near Gant's desk. That was as apt a description of his job as he had ever heard.

"Hi, Gant. How's it going?" Hound Dog raised her camera.

Gant smiled. Most cops despised scanner geeks, but he had a soft spot for Hound Dog. The year before, she rescued two children who had been kidnapped by a satanic cult. Her photo of a tire tread led her to their location even though a special police task force had turned up nothing.

This did not endear her to the force, however. Cops were furious that the high-profile case was cracked by a scanner geek, and they resented Hound Dog's presence at their crime scenes more than ever. She snapped a picture of Gant as he walked toward her.

"Don't you have enough pictures of me yet, Hound Dog?"

She shrugged. "I want to shoot up the end of the roll before I go in to work."

"I'm flattered."

What kind of job could she do after staying out all night? Gant wondered.

He approached the uniformed officers who were taking statements from two sanitation workers. The garbagemen were not happy.

The larger of the two men was practically shouting at the officers. "Goddammit, we got a route to finish! We've been here an hour. You got our addresses. Can't you talk to us later?"

"It won't be much longer," Gant assured him, knowing it probably would be. "How did you find him?"

The other man spoke. "We hooked the Dumpster, and the lift took it up. I was watching it. When Charles started to dump it, I saw the body tumble down. We fished him out of the truck ourselves."

Gant walked over to the body, which was covered by a painter's tarp. He lifted the covering and peeked underneath. The corpse was a mess. Besides the stains of dog shit, coffee grounds, and fruit rinds, the face was broken and bloodied, and a large puncture wound in the chest had dyed the white T-shirt with a crimson shield.

One of the uniformed officers stepped closer. "Messed up pretty bad. Stabbed, then maybe run over by a car?"

Gant shook his head. "Not run over. Looks more like a fall." He glanced at the four stairways situated around the parking lot. "Then he was dragged over here."

"Right." It was obvious from the officer's tone that he did not have the slightest idea how Gant arrived at his conclusion.

"Look at the shoes."

Gant lifted the tarp higher to show the victim's tennis shoes. The backs of the heels were scuffed and colored a dirty yellow. Pollen.

"And it's all over the back of his jeans, down near his calves. It's obvious he was dragged. Whoever dragged him probably wasn't very strong. Or very tall."

A clicking sound suddenly made Gant aware that Hound Dog was snapping pictures of the exposed body. Gant threw the tarp back over and shot a cold glance in the kid's direction.

He turned back to the officer. "Did you run the victim's record?"

"Yes, sir. He had an outstanding assault and battery warrant, and he had been convicted of one count of vandalism. He was a tagger, a graffiti artist. But that was over four years ago."

"Okay, I need a door-to-door. See if anyone in the complex heard anything, saw anything. I'll have a photo transmitted. See if anyone here knew the guy."

"Yes, sir."

Gant turned from the scene and looked at the small crowd of onlookers gathering in the parking lot. Vultures. Why were they here when they could be home watching Katie Couric?

Sabini wondered about the food in prison. Couldn't be worse than this crap, he decided as he finished his chili burger and fries. Sitting there in a grease pit two blocks away from the motel where he'd been staying since being kicked out by his wife, he imagined what day-to-day life in prison would be like.

Sit-ups before breakfast, an hour of letter writing, a shift in the prison library, dinner, then maybe some TV in the evening.

Oh, and gang-rape in the shower before bed.

He couldn't go there. The weekend he had spent in the

city jail was bad enough. The D.A. had secured his arrest warrant late on a Friday afternoon, meaning that the bail hearing had to wait until Monday. It was intentional, Myth Daniels told him. The bastards hoped that a couple of days in the slammer would persuade him to cut a deal.

He didn't say a word to anyone the entire weekend.

And now, with the trial only a few weeks away, the pressure was killing him. He *had* to pass the polygraph test. Maybe then this hell would be over.

He couldn't wait to see his kid. God, he missed Jeremy.

Sabini threw a few bucks on the table and left the restaurant. As he walked to his car, a black Porsche cut in front of him.

Herbert Decker climbed out. "How are you, Burton?"

It was the first time Sabini had seen his old boss since the arrest. The Vikkers president's thin lips were contorted in a smile.

Sabini stepped around Decker's car. "Excuse me."

"What's the rush?"

"My attorney wouldn't want me to speak to you."

"After all that's happened, I think I'm entitled."

"Your right to talk to me ended when you involved the police."

"We can help each other."

"I doubt that."

"We just want our money back. Give it to us and we'll square things away. We'll take another look at the books and say, 'What's this? *Here's* the twelve million!' Your reputation will be unsullied, and you'll be free to work for another company to rip off."

"Sounds like a good deal, if I had the money."

Redness spread from Decker's face to his ears. "What if I make you a better deal? What if you kept a few hundred thousand for yourself? As sort of a bonus."

"*Now* you want to give me a bonus."

"We always treated you fairly."

Sabini looked at Decker's Porsche. "Tell me, did you buy this car before or after the merger?"

"That's what all this is about, isn't it? The merger?"

"What makes you say that? The fact that twenty-eight-year-old sales managers became instant millionaires, and all I got was a handshake?"

"Stock options were part of their deal. Their guaranteed salary was lower than yours."

Sabini nodded. "That's what I keep telling myself. But for some reason, it doesn't make me feel better. I wish it did, Herb."

Decker was losing the battle with his temper. "You pathetic little prick."

Sabini managed a smile. "This trial will be over before it even begins. You don't have the proof. And you never will."

"Just wait and see," Decker said. "Wait and see."

The forty thousand was almost as good as his.

Ken sat in his office, studying the graphs from Sabini's most recent sessions. His client's progress was amazing. The breathing was flawless and the pulse rate was stabilizing. Even the perspiration levels were evening out. Much of this, Ken knew, was due to the demystification effect that had been noted in the studies. As soon as the interviewee becomes comfortable with the polygraph and aware of its limitations, the device's effectiveness diminishes.

Beyond that, Sabini was an apt and willing pupil. He remembered everything and applied his lessons immediately. On the rare occasions he made a mistake, he softly apologized, then proceeded to correct himself. Ken couldn't have hoped for a better student.

Sabini didn't even get rattled when Ken told him about the Reid seat, a chair that was designed to detect the pucker. Not many examiners used one, but if Sabini was asked to sit in such a chair, he was ready to utilize his most powerful weapon against the polygraph.

His mind.

"Psych yourself," Ken told him. "It's one sure way to beat every sensor they strap to you. When you sit down, you have to *know* you've done nothing wrong. Find a spot on the wall, look at it, and don't look away. Believe what you say. Sit there and tell me you're the pope, and the machine will believe it if you do. You've never done a thing wrong in your life. Anything you got, you earned. Believe it. *Know it.*"

Sabini believed. And bit by bit, so did the polygraph.

They usually took a short break around midnight, and Sabini always talked about his son. The kid's batting average. The songs he could play on his trumpet. The nonstop calls from his little girlfriends. It occurred to Ken that he should have been bored by the stories, but Sabini's enthusiasm touched him.

Ken's thoughts were interrupted by a sharp rap at his door. He threw down the graphs, stood, and opened it. The first thing he saw was a silver badge.

"Ken Parker?"

"Yes?"

"I'm Lieutenant Thomas Gant. Atlanta P.D. Can we talk?"

Ken felt his own sphincter tighten.

"Sure. Come in."

Gant stepped into the office.

What the hell could he want? Had he found out about Sabini's training sessions?

"How can I help you?" Ken said.

Gant handed him a photograph. "How do you know this guy?"

Ken looked at the photo. "I gave him a test last week. His name is Carlos Valez."

"When was the last time you saw him?"

"Saturday night. He didn't like how his test came out, so he and a buddy came by and worked me over pretty good."

"Is that where you got those bruises?"

Ken felt his cheek, which was still a pale shade of

magenta. "Yeah. Why are you asking me this? I'm really not interested in pressing charges."

"I'm glad to hear it, because he's dead."

Ken stared blankly at Gant. He tried to understand what he had just heard. Carlos Valez. Dead. "How?" he asked.

"Murdered at your apartment complex. Early this morning. I'm surprised you didn't see us there."

"I saw the police cars. But there's a couple in the complex who fight a lot. I figured the lady beat up her husband again."

Gant smiled. "We have four witnesses who saw your Saturday-night fight from their apartment windows. Two of them identified Carlos Valez from his picture. Apparently your parking lot is pretty well lit."

"People were *watching*? Nice of them to give me a hand."

"What happened?"

"I told you. He disagreed with his test results." Ken gave his full account of the exam, the outcome, and the confrontation that followed. The words tumbled out, occasionally sticking in his dry mouth. Was this really happening?

"So you saw him only two times," Gant said. "Once when you gave him the exam, once when he roughed you up."

"That's right."

"Why didn't you report him to the police?"

"I didn't think it was worth it. The guy lost his job because of me. He was upset. I just wanted to forget the whole thing."

Gant stared at him for what seemed like an hour. "Is there any reason why he would have been at your complex last night?"

"None that I know of."

"Look, we're pretty sure he was killed near the stairwell just down the hall from your apartment. We found traces of blood, his type, on the walkway. We figure he was stabbed, pushed over the railing to the parking lot two stories below, then dragged to the Dumpster."

Christ, Ken thought. The cop suspected him of murder.

"The guy had it in for you," Gant said. "Let's just say he came back to your building and attacked you again. You guys rumbled a little bit, maybe you picked up a few extra bruises, and in the end, he gets stabbed. He's dead. You didn't mean to do it, but you were scared. You panicked. You pushed him over the railing and stuffed him in the Dumpster."

"That didn't happen."

"If it did, it would be best if you told me now. It would be self-defense. Those witnesses saw Valez pound you into the sidewalk less than a week before. You could still come out of this all right."

"I didn't have anything to do with it. I didn't even know he was dead until you just told me."

Gant stared at him again.

Ken knew the game; these long pauses were supposed to rattle the interviewee and make him spill his guts. Even though he had used the tactic many times himself, he was surprised at how effective it was. The impulse to fill the gap in conversation was overwhelming.

The seconds ticked by, and still Gant did not speak. Ken relaxed and stared blankly at the detective. Finally Gant turned and circled around the polygraph.

"So you're an Answer Man."

"Excuse me?"

"That's what they used to call you polygraph examiners, isn't it? Answer Men?"

"I haven't heard that in a while." It was a regional expression, popular with the old-time examiners who still worked downtown. "It's pretty funny, because our business is really about asking questions."

"Yeah, but it's the answers you work with, sort out, and sift through."

Gant kneeled next to the machine and peered at the tiny needles. He picked up the blood pressure wrap. "I've never believed in these things. When I was a kid, maybe seventeen, I had to take a lie detector test when I was applying to work at a fast-food joint." He shook his head. "A fast-food joint. I didn't get the job. According to the machine, I was lying when I said I had never taken drugs on the job before. Funny thing was, I never took drugs in my life."

Ken shrugged. Whenever he told people of his profession, maybe one person in six had a story similar to Gant's.

Ken spit out his stock answer. "It's not an exact science."

"That it isn't." Gant put down the blood pressure wrap and handed Ken a business card. "If you think of anything else, please give me a call. I'm sure I'll need to talk to you again as our investigation moves along. Will you be around?"

The implication bothered him, but he nodded. "I'll be around."

Static filled the line as Ken spoke to Myth on a gas station pay phone. He kept his voice low so as not to be overheard by a teenage girl wailing on the adjacent phone about a fender-bender.

"They found his body in my complex. They think I had something to do with it."

"They obviously don't have any proof. Do they?"

"No."

"Naturally they would want to talk to you, but there's nothing more they can do. If you didn't do it."

"What do you mean?"

"If something happened, and if you did—"

"You mean if I killed him?"

"You could tell me, Ken. You *should* tell me."

"Jesus Christ, you sound like that cop. I didn't do it!"

"Okay. Don't get mad. I'm just trying to help. This is what I do for a living, remember?" She paused. "I'll need your final decision by tomorrow, Ken."

"I'm giving Sabini a final run-through tonight. A full mock exam. We'll pretend that we've never met, and I'll take him through the whole thing. By the book. I'll give you my answer tomorrow morning. Do you want to meet somewhere?"

"Yes. There's a pier on the lake, just off Gower Road. It's a little out of the way, but there's never anyone there. See you about ten tomorrow morning?"

"Fine."

"And, Ken," she said softly, "I'm sorry. I know you couldn't have done anything like that."

"Whatever."

Ted Michaelson walked through the narrow corridors of Vikkers Industries. Where was the conference room? He had gotten lost many times there, and it was happening again.

He looked at the workers in their offices and cubicles. He was sure they were laughing at him. People had been laughing at his obesity all his life, but now it was more than that. They thought they were better than him. If only they knew how many times he had saved their miserable jobs . . .

Snotty bastards.

Michaelson finally found his way to the conference room. Only one man was there, sitting at the long table.

Matt Lansing, Vikkers' VP of Finance, was trembling. Was he afraid of losing his job?

Lansing had been approached by Securities and Exchange Commission investigators on several occasions, but he still wasn't clear on what they were after. Michaelson had given Lansing a wireless microphone to wear, but for some reason it failed in his latest meeting with the SEC agents.

Michaelson pulled the wire out of his battered leather satchel. "I checked it out, and it's fine. Are you sure you didn't turn it off?"

"Uh, yeah. I did it just like you told me."

"Have you been wearing it every day?"

"Yes. I never know when they're going to come, so I've been keeping it on me."

Michaelson glared at him. "And on the day that they decided to show up, it stops working."

"I'm sorry," Lansing said. "I don't know what happened.

I didn't want to talk to them at all. I thought I should have an attorney present."

"Not yet. We need to find out what they're fishing for, where they're getting their information. We're hoping to derail this before it gets to the point where we need lawyers."

"Right." Lansing wiped his perspiring forehead with the sleeve of his shirt.

"So what did they say?"

"They had a lot of questions about the merger. They suggested that they might give me immunity if I talked to them about it."

"Why would you need immunity?"

"That's what I asked them. They said something about anticompetitive practices."

"Like what?"

"I don't know. I think they were waiting for me to fill them in."

"What else did they ask?"

"They wanted names of other people who might be willing to talk to them off the record."

"What did you tell them?"

"I said I'd think about it."

"Good. Did they ask for anyone in particular?"

"No."

Michaelson leaned back and clasped his hands behind his head. "So tell me, why do you think they picked you?"

"I don't know. I've been asking myself that. Maybe because I'm younger. I have a pretty high position, but not high enough to be part of the company's inner circle. They figure I know enough to help them, but I'm probably not powerful enough to be involved in a major way."

Michaelson played with the wireless mike for a moment. "If you were going to be completely truthful with them, what would you have said differently?"

"Nothing. I told them the truth as I know it."

Michaelson reached into his satchel and produced a legal

pad. He tossed it to Lansing. "Write down the entire conversation. Don't leave out a syllable. If you so much as burped, I wanna read about it here. Got it?"

Lansing nodded.

Michaelson pulled out another wireless mike and slid it across the table. "Here's another wire. If this one stops working, consider yourself officially unemployed."

"Good evening, Mr. Sabini. My name's Gary Marsh."

It was a name Ken plucked out of thin air. He was trying to simulate the entire polygraph experience for Sabini, and that included a new persona for the examiner. He had prepared Sabini for the doctor's-office–like atmosphere of many examiners' places of business; there was often an assortment of impressive-looking diplomas lining the walls, and it was not uncommon for the interviewee to be kept waiting. This was primarily to maximize the importance and authority of the examiner. In many offices, a one-way glass was utilized to spy on the subject during his waiting time. In polygraph school, Ken had seen tapes of waiting subjects, and individuals deemed "deceptive" exhibited behavior ranging from simple nervousness to sabotage of the polygraph itself.

He motioned toward the examination chair. "Mr. Sabini, have a seat."

Sabini sat down.

Ken produced a clipboard that held the sheet of neatly typed questions. "I understand there was some trouble at your company . . ."

Myth's heels clattered on the wooden planks of the Gower pier. Ken checked his watch. Ten on the nose. He leaned against a railing at the far end, looking out at the shimmering mirrors of sunlight on Lake Lanier's choppy waters. The wind was hot, each breeze hitting him like a blast from a blow dryer. He didn't turn as Myth sidled up next to him.

"He's ready," Ken said.

"What?"

"Sabini. He's ready. He's as good a liar as he'll ever be."

"But is he good enough?"

"You mean is he as good a liar as he is a thief? He is now. You should see him. *I* almost believe him."

Ken still didn't look at her. God, he was tired. The late nights had taken their toll. He gazed out at the water with hollow eyes.

"What's wrong?"

He managed a bitter smile. "He took the money. You know damned well he did."

"I don't know any such thing. And besides, you *wanted* to do this."

"I know, I know. It was just so easy. It should be harder for a man to let himself off the hook. But it was easy. So easy." He looked at her. "I see people doing it all the time. Not just on the other side of my polygraph, but everywhere. And it keeps getting easier."

"Ken, you're exhausted. Why don't you try to get some sleep?"

"Yeah. Maybe I'll do that."

"Besides, Sabini's not off the hook yet."

CHAPTER 6

The last thing Ken told Sabini was that it was crucial he get a good night's sleep before taking the D.A.'s polygraph test.

Sabini did not sleep at all.

He spent half the night tossing and turning, practicing his breathing and replaying Ken's test in his head. He spent the other half pacing in his motel room. He considered calling Denise, his wife, to see if she was home. It was something he did occasionally. If she answered, he would quickly hang up; if she didn't answer, he would feel miserable for a day or so. Probably not a good idea to try it tonight, he decided.

He knew Ken and Myth had taken care of everything on their end. The D.A. had sent an approved list of examiners, from which Myth and Ken had made their selection. Ken immediately crossed one name off when he recognized the man as an instructor at his polygraph school. Heavy into the intuitive stuff, Ken thought. A no-no. They needed someone who placed greater importance on the graphs.

They finally settled on Gregory Harmon, a middle-aged examiner who received his polygraph training in the military. Myth insisted the D.A. place a five-year moratorium on Harmon's services to its offices, so the examiner would have no reason to curry favor with the prosecutors.

The groundwork had been laid. Sabini knew it was now all up to him.

Gant wasn't in a good mood as he drove into the Gas 'n Snack station on Cheshire Bridge Road. He had just come from talking to Carlos Valez's widow, who sobbed throughout the entire conversation. She had been under sedation the entire day before, and only that morning had she been able to speak to him. He was troubled not by his empathy for her—but, rather, by his entire *lack* of empathy. He heard time and time again from the police shrink on the subject: It was a normal defense mechanism, and was not in any way a symptom of the officer's dehumanization. Gant wasn't so sure.

The crying woman had quickly identified the "brown-toothed man" who assisted Carlos Valez in the attack on Ken Parker. He was Kevin Farrell, and he often washed car windshields at this station.

Gant pulled to a stop and got out of the car. A tall, thin young man with a scraggly beard appeared from around the corner.

"Wash your windows?" he asked. One of his upper front teeth was dark brown.

Gant shrugged. "Sure."

He watched the man spray his windshield and wipe it clean with newspaper. The window squeaked.

Gant held his badge in front of the man's face. "I'm Thomas Gant. Atlanta P.D."

The man stopped rubbing. "I didn't ask for any money."

"That's not what I'm here about. I have no problem with you making a few bucks. You're Kevin Farrell, right?"

Kevin nodded as he lifted the wipers and sprayed underneath.

"I want to talk to you about your friend Carlos."

"Okay."

"You know he's dead, don't you?"

Kevin moved to the passenger window. "Yeah. I know."

"Someone killed him."

"I heard."

"Any idea who might've done it?"

"No."

Kevin wiped his nose with his sleeve. He stepped around and squirted the rear window.

Gant followed him. "I hear you and Carlos beat up on a guy last week."

"That's a lie!"

"Don't be stupid. There are witnesses. If you wanna go into a lineup, we'll see how far you can hide behind that tooth."

A tall man holding a beer appeared from around the corner. "Kevin, you don't have to talk to that guy."

Gant studied the second man. He wore faded jeans and a ripped muscle shirt, and his face was set in a scowl. "Are you his lawyer?" Gant said.

"I'm his friend. Kevin's not exactly a rocket scientist, so I'm looking out for him."

"It's okay, Jesus," Kevin said. He pronounced the name the same way Anglos pronounced the name of the Holy Savior. Good old Jesus.

Gant flipped back a few pages in his notebook. "Are you Jesus Millicent?" Gant pronounced the name *Hey-Zeus*.

"Don't say it like that. It's Jesus."

Gant snorted. "Okay, Jesus, you just saved me a trip. I want to talk to you too. We heard Carlos Valez holed up with you after he beat up his father. Two officers showed up at your place and you wouldn't let them in for a search."

"I let them in."

"Only after they came back with a warrant. I guess that bought Carlos enough time to get out, huh?"

"What do you want?" Jesus said.

"Stick around. If you have anything to add to the discussion, just chime in."

"What if I don't?"

"Then we can discuss the fact that I can take you in for loitering and for consuming alcoholic beverages on the premises. Pretty minor except when we consider that you're still on parole. Isn't that right?"

Jesus glared at Gant.

"Do you think I killed Carlos?" Kevin asked.

Gant shrugged. "Is there any reason I *should* think that?"

"No. He was my friend."

"What happened last week?"

"I didn't do anything to that lie detector guy. I just *held* him. I—I didn't know Carlos was gonna hurt him that bad!"

"Okay, tell me about it."

Kevin told his story to Gant, from Carlos's anger at losing his job to the blow-by-blow on Ken Parker's beating.

"I know Carlos had a violent temper," Gant said. "Did he have any enemies? People who may have wanted him dead for any reason?"

Jesus stepped forward. "If Carlos did to me what he did to that polygraph guy, *I* would have been his enemy."

Gant looked at Kevin.

"I don't know who would have done that," Kevin said.

Gant gave Kevin and Jesus his card with instructions to call in case they thought of anything else. He looked back at his car. The windows hadn't been so clean in weeks. He checked his wallet; all he had was a five-dollar bill. He gave it to Kevin.

"Good morning, Mr. Sabini. I'm Greg Harmon. How are you today?"

Sabini shook the examiner's hand, relieved that his own palm was dry, not sweaty. So far, so good.

"Fine, thank you," he confidently replied.

Sabini glanced around the office. As Ken had told him, there were large, impressive-looking diplomas on the wall. This office was clean, almost antiseptic, a marked contrast with Ken's shabby, run-down work space. Sabini noticed a full-length mirror on the wall facing the examination chair. A one-way observation window, no doubt.

The examiner motioned toward the chair. "Please have a seat."

The seat.

Sabini stopped short when he saw it. Oh, no. It was the chair Ken warned him about, the Reid seat. He didn't dare try the pucker. Sabini said nothing as he sat and tried to get comfortable.

The examiner picked up a clipboard and sat across from him. "Okay, Mr. Sabini. Apparently, there was a great deal of money missing from your company. Can you tell me what the problem was there?"

Sabini nodded pleasantly. He knew the examiner was fully aware of all the circumstances surrounding the case—otherwise, how could he have made up the list of questions on that clipboard? Ken had drilled him on this part. As Sabini explained in his own words, the examiner would be watching and listening closely, trying to pick up on any verbal or nonverbal cues that might incriminate the interviewee. Eye contact, enunciation, and body language were crucial.

"It started when one of the company's owners was getting divorced." Sabini relaxed and spoke matter-of-factly. "His wife, or his wife's lawyers, demanded an audit of the firm's holdings. It was done, and we were something like twelve million short."

He shook his head as if he couldn't believe it himself.

"We tracked it down and found that the funds were electronically transferred to four different banks in Switzerland, where they had already been withdrawn. By who, we don't know. Some people obviously think I did it, since I know more about this area than just about anyone in the company. But I *didn't* do it," he emphasized calmly. "There's really nothing that links me to this. It's just circumstantial."

The examiner nodded. "All right. I'm going to briefly go through some questions with you. If you're not sure about any of them, or you want me to explain, please let me know."

Sabini listened as the examiner went down the list. By the third question he knew it was the Standard Format Control Question Test. Good.

The examiner was a dry, humorless man whose every look, every glance, seemed accusatory. He spoke with a slight southern accent, yet his words were clipped and precise. He wore a tie and a short-sleeved dress shirt of a style that even Sabini no longer wore.

After the examiner finished previewing the questions, he attached the sensors to Sabini. This polygraph was sleeker and shinier than Ken's, with a frosty silver finish on its sides. Sabini noticed the examiner pressing a foot pedal, which he assumed would activate the Reid seat.

The examiner stood. "I'll be back in a moment."

The man disappeared through a doorway next to the mirror. He closed the door behind him.

Sabini almost smiled, knowing he was being watched from the other side of that glass. He and Ken had practiced this part too. Sabini leaned back in the chair and casually glanced around the office. His eyes finally settled on the wall as he did his best to look bored.

In a few minutes the examiner returned. He sat down, turned on the polygraph, and studied the graph readings. He leaned forward and forcefully clapped his hands together in front of Sabini's face. The needles jumped in response.

"That was to see if you're reactive enough for the instrument's settings. This should be fine."

The examiner positioned his clipboard in front of the polygraph. "Mr. Sabini, were you born in St. Louis, Missouri?"

"Yes."

Sabini concentrated on his breathing. If he could just get a good breathing pattern going, the rest would follow.

"Have you been completely truthful and forthcoming to your company with regard to this case we have discussed?"

"Yes."

"Do you understand that I will inquire only about issues we have already discussed?"

Verbatim from Ken's test.

"Yes."

"Have you ever lied to a superior at work?"

"No."

The first relevant question was next.

There was a pain in his stomach.

His heart pounded faster and faster.

This hadn't happened before. . . .

"Did you, over the course of several months, transfer funds belonging to Vikkers Industries into accounts you opened for your personal benefit?"

Ambiguous question. Many accounts he opened on behalf of his company benefited him personally with regard to ease of use, relationships, and so on. He almost told the examiner so during the pre-exam.

Maybe he *should* have said something.

Stop it, he told himself. He was second-guessing, over-analyzing the situation.

He wanted to look at the polygraph. Was his exploding heart giving him away? All that practice, all that training, it was all falling apart. . . .

"No," he answered.

"Have you ever taken anything from your place of business that did not belong to you?"

"No."

His collar was throbbing, taking the pulse from his neck. He struggled to keep his cool. But the more he struggled, the worse his readings would be. He couldn't win. . . .

"Did you arrange for the withdrawal of your company funds after they were transferred into banks in Zurich, Switzerland?"

There was dampness under his arms. Perspiration.

Oh, God, not now.

Surely the examiner could tell, if not from his polygraph, then from the ever-growing sweat stains.

Sabini tried to relax, pretending he was back at Ken's office, looking at that spot of chipped paint on the wall.

"No."

"Is your birthday March third?"

"Yes."

"Have you ever knowingly violated the rules, regulations, or policies of your company?"

Sabini wanted to swallow.

He didn't dare. The machine would pick it up and brand him forever. One swallow, one movement of his throat muscles, one twitch, could mean the difference between prison and freedom. It could cost him years of his life.

"No."

One more question to go. One more. This wasn't the same as practicing with Ken.

"Do you have specific knowledge of other person or persons who executed the embezzlement of funds from Vikkers Industries?"

"No."

The examiner made another mark on the graph paper.

Sabini stared at the wall, trying to hold it together until the machine was shut down.

The examiner switched off the polygraph, and Sabini felt as if his power had suddenly been cut too. He was drained. As the sensors were removed, he looked at the examiner. The man's face revealed nothing.

"Thank you for coming in, Mr. Sabini. I'll analyze the results and forward them as soon as possible."

It was a long way to Myth's, Ken thought as he crossed Peachtree Street and caught a glimpse of the Fox theater. Traffic was heavy on Ponce De Leon Avenue. Why on this of all nights did it have to be so slow? he wondered. He knew Myth must have Sabini's results, and it was killing him to wait.

He could have called her, of course. But it seemed better for him to be with her when he got the news. Years before, when his father had taken a turn for the worse, his mother called him frantically, begging him to come home immediately. The doctors said his father had only hours to live. Ken took the first flight out of Alaska, and upon his arrival at the Atlanta airport, called Bobby to find out where he should go—the hospital or their house.

"Our house," Bobby told him.

The words went through Ken like a knife. His father was probably dead. But he didn't ask, choosing instead to get the news in person. He hoped Myth would give him better news.

The traffic thinned out closer to Myth's house, and as he turned down the street, he noticed that her house was dark. The porch light wasn't on, and it appeared no one was home. Ken parked and climbed the winding stairs. He was halfway up, when the door swung open.

Myth appeared and sauntered down the stairs to meet him. She came to rest on the step above his.

"Well?" he asked.

She smiled. "It worked."

"He passed?"

"Yes!"

Ken sucked in a huge lungful of air, as if he were a pearl diver breaking through the surface. He laughed and grabbed her around the waist. "*Yes!* We did it!"

She laughed too. She leaned forward and kissed him. It started as a sweet, playful kiss, but suddenly went deeper.

He rubbed his hands over her body, pulling her dress taut at the seams.

"Let's go inside," she whispered.

She made a halfhearted attempt to turn around, but he pulled her down to a half-sitting, half-lying position on the stairs. Cloaked in darkness, they could barely be seen by each other, much less by any passersby on the street.

"Not here," she weakly protested.

Ken's breath moistened her neck, and a long shudder went through her. She pulled him close. "What the hell," she whispered.

He ran wet kisses over her face, behind her ears, and down her neck. Her body relaxed beneath his as he unzipped her dress.

Myth reached for another hors d'oeuvre from the half-dozen platters surrounding her and Ken on her living room floor. They were both naked, wrapped in blankets. "You're supposed to do it in *elevators,* not stairways."

"You don't have an elevator. I had to improvise." He surveyed the feast laid out before them. "Aren't you supposed to celebrate with champagne?"

"I don't like champagne. Have another stuffed meatball. Or a turkey roll."

"I'm still working on the boiled shrimp. Your mother tell you the way to a man's heart is through his stomach?"

"No. Through *here.*"

Under the covers, she grabbed his sensitive lower extremity.

"Okay, okay! Take it easy, it's gonna break off!"

She laughed and let go.

He pulled the blankets tightly around her and dragged her close. "If that's what your mother told you, she's a wise woman."

"Wait till you hear what my father told me."

"I don't even want to know." He tenderly brushed the hair from her face.

"Sabini will pay you tomorrow, in cash," she said. "What are you going to do with it all?"

"What do people say when they win the lottery? That it's not going to change them? Screw that. It's gonna change me."

She laughed.

He leaned against a coffee table. "I can relax a little. My brother's sick, and I've been giving him all the cash I can. It's like a black hole. There's never enough. I can't even think about looking for a new line of work while he's in such bad shape. But with this money, I can take care of him. He can stop worrying. I think that's one of the reasons he can't get better. The stress is just tearing him apart."

"It's been hard on you too."

"Nothing like it's been for him. But this money will help me make a new start for myself. How many people get that chance?"

She smiled warmly at him. "Not many."

"Things are going to be different. Better." He shook his head. "You know, when I said Bill stole Margot away from me, it didn't really happen that way."

He paused to put his thoughts into words. "I think . . . I think I pushed her away. It's not that I didn't think I deserved her. It wasn't that. I guess I just wasn't being very good to myself, and I wasn't going to let anybody else be good to me either. Bill just happened to be there when she needed someone. *I* sure wasn't there for her."

He was surprised at the words tumbling from his mouth. Surprised because he was sharing them with someone, and because they were notions he was forming only at that very moment.

Myth moved closer. "Have you ever wanted her back?"

"I used to. Not anymore. That's all in the past. I'm more interested in the future. I have a birthday coming. It'll be the first one in a while that I'll be able to enjoy. A long while."

She smiled. "I'll enjoy it with you."

He was about to kiss her, when the phone rang.

Myth answered it. "Hello? Yes? Christ, Rogers, what makes you think you can—"

She fell silent, and a tense, anxious look crossed her face. She glanced at Ken.

"I'll be right there," she said.

• • •

Less than half an hour later, Myth walked down a grimy side street in the downtown area, five blocks from the Underground shopping and entertainment complex. As safe and well patrolled as the Underground center was, the surrounding area deteriorated rapidly, with each outlying block more seedy than the previous one. This was not a place for anyone—man or woman—to be walking alone in the middle of the night. She knew she shouldn't have parked so far away, but Ken had insisted on riding with her, and she couldn't risk his being seen waiting in her car.

She rounded a corner and saw, two blocks in the distance, the bright work lights and squad cars that indicated a crime scene. She took a deep breath and pushed onward.

It was always so easy to distance herself from the unpleasantness of the criminal world when she practiced law in luxurious offices and impersonal courtrooms. They were a far cry from the grit and depressing reality of criminal life on the streets. She liked the distance, the detachment. It was the only way she could defend her clients.

She wanted to be anyplace but there.

She stepped closer to the yellow police tape, behind which were the silhouetted figures of several men. Blue flashers from the squad cars bathed the area in a bizarre strobe-light effect, giving those on the outskirts of the scene the appearance of jerky movement, as if in an old silent movie. A familiar form walked toward her.

"Can I show a girl a good time, or what?"

It was Rogers. The assistant D.A. smiled and pulled the tape up.

Myth leaned under and joined him on the other side. "What happened here?"

"Cop thought he was a bum sleeping in the doorway. Poked him with a nightstick a couple of times, but he wouldn't wake up."

She followed him toward the nucleus of all the activity, where the wattage and attention were most concentrated.

He smirked. "I hope you got a big retainer up front."

She tried to prepare herself for the sight, but her breath still left her when she saw it.

Burton Sabini's corpse.

He was lying in the doorway of an abandoned youth hostel. His eyes were open, and he almost seemed . . . *alive,* she thought. He was wearing the same expression he wore in countless meetings with her, sitting quietly in his ever-polite, always-patient manner. But now his chest was covered by a large, sopping stain of blood.

"Multiple stab wounds," Rogers said.

A forensic specialist, leaning over the body, shook her head. "Just one. It was enough."

Myth couldn't take her eyes off Sabini. "Does anybody know what happened?"

Rogers glanced back at the uniformed cops huddled in front of their cars. "Looks like a robbery. His wallet's missing. They identified him from a tag on his keys."

A plainclothes police detective walked past. "Rogers, go home. We're working."

Rogers didn't budge. He was still looking back at the police line, where the first of the scanner geeks had arrived. A young woman's long lens was aimed in Myth's direction.

Rogers nudged Myth and pointed to the scanner geek. "The kid's taken a liking to you. If you're not careful, you might find your photo blown up to poster size in college dorms all over the city. Hmm . . . I wonder if she'd sell one to *me*?"

Myth wasn't in the mood to humor Rogers. She turned from the body.

Rogers put what was supposed to be a comforting hand on her shoulder. "I think the D.A. might be willing to drop the charges now." He shrugged. "Just a hunch."

Hound Dog adjusted the zoom lens on her camera and snapped four quick pictures. Myth Daniels was here. How strange that mere days after being haunted by that face, she should see it in the flesh, Hound Dog thought. And in these grim circumstances, no less. Only after seeing Myth Daniels did Hound Dog realize that the corpse was the man pictured with her in the newspaper.

Hound Dog lowered her camera. Had she seen Myth Daniels at another crime scene? She didn't think so. But if not, then where?

Ken waited impatiently in the car, parked in the shadows of a dark side street. Myth was finally returning after what seemed like hours. He checked his watch. She had been gone only twenty-five minutes. She opened the door and slid behind the wheel.

"Say it's not true," he said.

She just looked at him. It was true.

He sat there, stunned, as she started the car and pulled onto the street.

After a couple of minutes of silence, Myth spoke quietly. "This afternoon he was talking about taking his son to Orlando."

"I can't believe it." Ken shook his head. It was only yesterday that he last saw Sabini. One final pep talk. With the training complete, they wouldn't have had any reason to see each other again. Ken was surprised when Sabini actually hugged him before leaving the office. The last day of school.

And now the man was dead.

"Ken, I'm afraid you're not getting the rest of your money."

He was silent for a long while. "I pretty much figured."

"And I'm afraid we'll have to stop seeing each other. At least for a while. This is a *murder* investigation. Every tiny piece of Sabini's life is going under the microscope. And that includes me. If they link me to you, then they might figure out the rest of our arrangement."

He nodded. "How was Sabini—?"

"Stabbed."

"That's how Carlos Valez was murdered."

"Coincidence."

Ken suddenly felt suffocated by the whole situation. He cracked open his car window. He was still dazed when Myth pulled alongside his parked car.

"I'm sorry about your money," she said. "And I'm sorry about us, Ken."

He still hadn't absorbed any of it. It did not seem real to him; it was almost like waking up from a great dream, only to discover none of it really happened.

She kissed him. "I'll get in touch when I think it's safe."

He nodded and climbed out of her car. Though he was aware she was watching him, he didn't look back as he slid into his MG, started it up, and drove away.

He went home and immediately collapsed. He tossed and turned as the harsh sunlight attacked him through the window blinds of his bedroom. He slept only intermittently, between haunting fever-dream flashes he could never quite remember upon waking.

Late in the afternoon he pulled himself up and stared at the dust-streaked window for a long while. He knew what he had to do.

He had to find that money.

CHAPTER 7

Gant's wife squeezed his hand as the recital began. Diane's students were performing their spring concert, and it was now entirely beyond her control. Gant didn't mind these functions as much as some of the other teachers' spouses. It was rare he was able to see his wife in her element, and he enjoyed the respect she commanded from the students, parents, and even fellow instructors.

Since Sprayberry was a performing arts high school, the recitals delivered more than the typical choir-on-risers snooze-fest. This was a multimedia extravaganza, with elaborate costumes, computer graphics on video monitors, and even smoke and lasers. The kids were in the midst of a rendition of the B-52's "Love Shack," when Gant felt the vibration in his hip pocket. His pager. He tapped his pocket and shrugged apologetically at his wife. She knew what it meant.

He tried to be inconspicuous as he squirmed down the aisle and made his way to the back of the theater. He found a pay phone in the lobby.

"Gant here."

"Hi, Gant. It's Hoover. Sorry to bug you."

Hoover was a detective who worked the evening watch at the station. Gant didn't have much history with him, though their paths did cross on a murder investigation a few years before. The case, which resulted in the discovery of an international counterfeit credit card ring, made the national papers and news weeklies. Unfortunately, the FBI took the lion's share of the credit, and Gant and Hoover, who actually broke the case, barely rated a mention.

"What's up?" Gant asked.

"I'm on a homicide, this Burton Sabini thing."

"The embezzler?"

"Right. There may be a connection between this and your Valez case. The captain tipped me off to it. Can you come down here?"

"Now?"

"It might be a good idea. I'm sorry, Gant, but if you—"

"No, no, it's all right."

Gant didn't like to work nights. He thought of the TV cops who seemed to do nothing but work on their cases morning, noon, and night until they had their man. "Horseshit!" he usually yelled at the screen whenever a detective was still on the job for what seemed to be his eighteenth hour in a single day. But occasionally it happened. Occasionally.

"I'll be right down."

Ken threw open his office door and flew to the desk, looking for the phone bill he had tossed there the day before. Sabini had made several phone calls in their nights together, and if any of the numbers were outside the immediate access area, they would be listed on the statement.

Ken found the BellSouth bill and scanned it. There, listed several times, was a number called during the hours of Sabini's training. Each call was never longer than a minute in duration.

Who had Sabini called between midnight and three A.M.?

"Of course I'm here. I *live* here," Bill said as he walked with Ken down the main office corridor of the Tillinger Savings and Trust.

That Bill was still toiling in his office at eight P.M. had been a safe bet. These days, Ken had an easier time catching Bill at work than at home.

"I need to sneak a peek at the phone directories," Ken said. "The ones where you can look them up by number."

"By number, street address, whatever. We have national listings on CD-ROM, but we also get the Georgia listings in books from the phone company. They cost a fortune, but they're more current."

"Sounds good to me."

"What do you need them for?"

"Deadbeat client. I'm just looking to get paid." Ken was glad he didn't have to lie. All he wanted was the five to ten percent finder's fee that companies usually offered in return for finding missing monies.

"We have them for very much the same reason." Bill spoke in hushed tones, although the place was deserted. "By the way, Margot told me you asked about a loan a couple of weeks ago."

The battery-acid taste was coming back. "I got everything squared away."

"Good. But you could have asked *me,* you know."

"It doesn't matter."

"Of course, the answer would have been the same. We just don't have anything to spare." Bill frowned. "I'm disappointed you didn't feel comfortable talking to me about it. I know you and Margot have all this history, but, Jesus, you and I have known each other twenty years."

Bill didn't get it, Ken thought.

It wasn't a subject they ever talked about, but since Ken had lost Margot, there was a barrier, an invisible wall between him and Bill. They still talked, played football, and ate an occasional meal together, but things were never quite the same. He felt bad about it only when Bill tried to pretend things *were* the same.

It had been a humid July night—was it really six years

before?—when Ken first suspected his wife was sleeping with his oldest friend. They were with a large group to watch the Independence Day fireworks at Lenox Square. There was something about Margot's and Bill's body language that night. . . . Not that they were suddenly too intimate with each other, but just the opposite. They were noticeably awkward and strained. Bill and Margot had always openly joked and engaged in mildly flirtatious behavior, but suddenly that all stopped.

They seemed to be making a conscious effort *not* to hold eye contact for too long. Their verbal exchanges were clipped and stilted. And Bill's manner toward Ken was not unlike a toady sucking up to the boss—ingratiating, overanxious, just a little *too* nice. Since Ken was not in a position to give him a raise or promotion, he suspected Bill was angling for something else.

Forgiveness.

Later the same night, when Ken pulled Margot close to him, there was a certain hesitancy, a resistance. He waited a couple of weeks before confronting her with his suspicions. She listened to him, nodded, and admitted everything. He almost wished she had tried to deny it so he could work up more anger. But she looked so pitiful and emotionally overwrought, he felt angry only at himself.

That was probably why he had been able to remain friends with Margot and Bill. There were some tough times—the first time he saw them hold hands, the first time they kissed in front of him. But he survived. They all survived.

And now, years later, Bill still wanted things to be the way they used to be.

Ken finally replied. "You don't owe me anything, you know."

"Owe you? Why would I owe you?"

Ken didn't look at his friend. They walked in silence until Bill realized what he was talking about.

"That's not what I'm thinking, Kenny. But maybe that's why you won't let me help *you*."

"That's not it. I just—I just got something else going right now. Something that might pan out."

"What?"

"I'll let you know when it happens."

Bill led Ken to the library, which was actually a converted office lined with tall metal shelves. Bill yanked three thick, soft-covered volumes from a shelf and tossed them onto a table.

"I'll be in my office. Come get me when you're done, okay?"

"You got it."

Bill left the room and Ken quickly thumbed through the books, looking for the number Sabini had called. Within a minute he discovered that the calls had been placed to Sabini's home telephone number. To his wife or kid, Ken supposed. But in the middle of the night?

"Just so you know, I'm not going by 'Sabini' anymore. I'm using my maiden name, 'Randolph.'"

Ken sat across from Sabini's widow in the kitchen of her Brookhaven home. It was a pleasant one-story house, decorated with flowered wallpaper and pastel color schemes. The midafternoon sun sliced through open curtains.

Ken slid his briefcase to one side on the table. He had been admitted after he told her he was from Vikkers Industries' insurance company, tying up loose ends in the embezzling case. Denise Randolph had only rolled her eyes in response, opening the door wider for Ken to enter. She had obviously been through this countless times.

Denise appeared to be in her mid-forties. She was a plain woman, but she carried herself with a vitality that made her more attractive than at first glance. She didn't appear to be grieving too much over her husband's death.

"You've changed your name from 'Sabini'?" he asked.

"Yes. My husband's name has been bandied about quite a bit in the last few months. I don't want it anymore, and I don't want my son to have it either."

Ken felt sorry for Sabini. The man's only stab at immortality was slipping away.

"Okay, thanks for telling me," Ken said. He jotted the name 'Randolph' in his notebook. "Honestly, do you think your husband took that money?"

Denise smiled and shook her head. "When this first came out, I would have said there was no way on earth he could have done something like that. No way. It just wasn't him."

"You weren't living together when all this came out, were you?"

"No, we weren't. He had moved out a few weeks before."

"Did that make you suspicious?"

"No. I asked him to move out. It had been a long time coming, believe me." She looked toward the head of the table.

Sabini's place, Ken figured. Even with all the friends and family he had lost over the years, it still amazed him that a person could simply cease to exist. A lifetime of love, knowledge, and experiences erased in an instant.

Poor Sabini.

He deserved better than he got.

Denise looked away. "The only thing he cared about was Jeremy, our son."

"I'm sure he cared about you."

"If he did, he forgot how to show it."

"We know he called you several times in the last couple of weeks of his life. Can you tell me why?"

"He called a couple of times for Jeremy. He never called me."

"Are you sure?"

"Yes."

"We know he made several calls to you between midnight and three A.M."

"Oh, Lord," she said with a long sigh. "Someone was

calling and hanging up. I thought it might be him, but I didn't know."

Calling and hanging up. That explained the short duration of the calls. Sabini had just wanted to hear her voice.

For the first time, Denise was showing genuine sadness for her husband's passing. She cleared her throat.

"Did he have an office here at home?" Ken said, trying to move to a less emotional subject.

She nodded. "I'll show it to you."

She led him to a converted bedroom that was completely bare except for an empty desk and a set of empty shelves.

"Police took the rest," she said. "They stripped the place clean."

Stripped was right, Ken thought. There was no trace of the man who had worked here.

"Did he have a computer?" he asked.

"Sure. One here and one at work. He hated them though."

"Why?"

"His work computer crashed a few times, and once he almost lost weeks of work. I guess some people aren't cut out for the information age."

"You said *at first* you thought he couldn't have taken the money. But what about later?"

Denise looked away and slipped her hands into the pockets of her brown corduroy slacks. "I have to admit that the thought of him doing that was . . . *nice*. It was so out of character. Dangerous. Risky. Do you know what I mean?"

Ken nodded.

"This thing has turned my life upside down. The police came in here and took away half the house. The newspapers, TV, and people like you haven't given us a moment's peace. But it almost would be worth it if he *did* take the money. I liked the thought of that."

"You liked the thought of the money?"

"The money doesn't matter. What matters is that for

once in his life, Burton Sabini may have actually put himself on the line for something."

Ken walked toward Bobby's front door. He had come directly from Denise Randolph's house, and she had given him only one thing remotely resembling a lead. It may have been nothing, but he was interested in the fact that Sabini had so much computer trouble. If someone outside the company had access to his data, maybe the security breach was there. He decided to follow up on it the next morning.

Bobby's wife opened the door before he could knock. "Guess what?" She spoke quietly as she ushered him inside. "The cash fairy floated by and put five thousand dollars in the mail slot last week."

"I wish he'd visit me."

"I think he did."

Ken looked toward the closed bedroom door. "Is Bobby sleeping?"

"Yes. I'd rather not wake him right now. He doesn't get much sleep. Please sit down."

Ken walked to the dinette table and took a seat. He watched Tina as she strode to the freezer and pulled out a small paper bag. She brought it back to the table and sat across from him.

"What's that?" he asked.

She reached into the bag and produced the roll of bills that had come from Sabini. "Where did you get this?" she asked.

"Business has been good."

"I see." Her accent grew stronger, as it often did when she was upset. "This is over one hundred lie detector tests. You once told me that you usually get only two or three examinations a day."

"It's not just the quantity. It's the quality. Some clients pay more than others."

"I haven't told Bobby about this."

"Why not?"

"I don't think he would like it. He doesn't like taking your money."

"That's why I usually give it to you."

"I don't like taking it either. But I know we don't have any choice. I've been keeping a record of all the money you've given us, and one day we will pay you back."

"That's not necessary."

She looked at the frosty roll of bills. "This would upset him. He would wonder how you got it. Just as I wonder."

"I told you—"

"I don't believe you," she said sharply.

Ken nodded. He had rarely seen Tina angry. She was usually so patient, so understanding.

"Tell me this," she said. "Is there any reason we should be ashamed to use this money?"

Ken thought for a moment. "No. No one was hurt, physically or financially. Take it. You need it."

"Yes, we do. If we didn't, I would throw it back in your face."

"Yes, I believe you would."

Outside Bobby and Tina's house, a man sat in a white Acura Legend sedan. Waiting. Watching.

Ken finally walked outside, climbed into his MG, and drove away. After the MG turned the corner, the Acura followed.

The driver had done his homework. On the seat next to him was a thin stack of photocopied map pages, each with highlighted routes to Ken's usual haunts. To his office. To his apartment. To the jogging trail. To Elwood's Pub. In the unlikely event that the man lost his trail, he could use the maps to guess where Ken was heading.

Now, he supposed, Ken was heading home.

But maybe not. Maybe tonight was the night that Ken Parker would make all this shit worthwhile.

The MG swerved into a side street. The man gunned the engine on his Acura and sped past. Had Parker noticed he was being followed?

The man turned at the next street and cut his lights. After a minute, Ken's MG flew past on the main road. The man sighed. He'd have to be more careful. Ken had probably spotted him. Probably thought he was being followed by a cop.

The man chuckled. Ken Parker should be so lucky.

CHAPTER 8

Hound Dog lowered her plastic tongs and moved the print paper around in the developing bath. She checked her watch. Not much longer.

She was tucked away in a corner of the mobile home she shared with Mark, her boyfriend. The makeshift darkroom was fashioned from black tarps draped over a workbench, and she huddled inside, working in the illumination of a red fifteen-watt bulb. The trailer was hot on this sunny morning. The heat was stifling under the tarps.

She could hear Mark working out with his weights, and his every rep rattled the entire mobile home and sent ripples through the photo tray chemicals. She squinted to get a better look at the print materializing before her. It was from a crime scene a few nights before. There was nothing remarkable about it except for Myth Daniels's presence.

The woman's distinct features came into view as Hound Dog stared at the print. She lifted it up, shook it, and slid out from under the darkroom's canvas walls.

Mark ended his set and wiped his forehead with a towel. "What'd you get?"

"Aah, I couldn't get a good shot of the body."

"Too bad."

He was being sarcastic. He claimed to support her unusual avocation, but she knew he would never understand it. Then again, she wasn't sure she understood it herself.

She showed him the photo, and his brows lifted. "Man . . ." He gave a low whistle. "Who is *that*?"

"You're starting to drool."

The woman was beautiful, she had to admit. And Mark was not easily impressed. He worked with dozens of gorgeous women at the city's most popular nude dancing bar, the Gold Club. Mark was a bouncer.

Hound Dog marveled at how incredible Myth Daniels looked in less-than-ideal conditions. The grainy black-and-white photo looked like a perfume ad from a fashion magazine. Hound Dog frowned. "Does she look familiar to you?"

"Should she?"

"I don't know. I saw her in the newspaper last week, and I thought I'd seen her somewhere before."

"And you didn't point her out to me?"

"I'm serious. I know I've seen that face."

"Hmm. Is she a cop?"

"No. She was the dead guy's lawyer. Her name's Myth Daniels. Maybe I've seen her in someone's book. I think I'll make a low-contrast print of this and fax it out to the network."

The "network" consisted of scores of scanner geeks all over the country who regularly sent one another their favorite shots via fax machines. Some even scanned their images into computer files, so hundreds could then be transmitted almost instantaneously. Hound Dog was saddled with a regular manual-feed fax machine, which limited her to one transmission every two minutes.

Mark made a face. "I guess this means you're gonna tie up the phone all night."

"I told you I'd pay for another line."

"Nah. You can't afford it. I'll make my calls now, before you start."

He kissed her and gestured toward the photo. "You're more beautiful than she could ever be."

Hound Dog smiled. "You lie very well, Mark."

•   •   •

Ken threw the yellow pages down on his living room coffee table and thumbed through it. Although he was not up on the latest in information-age technology, he knew there were a few data-recovery services in the city that specialized in retrieving information lost on malfunctioning computer systems. If Sabini had indeed "almost lost weeks of work," perhaps one of these services had restored Sabini's files.

If so, perhaps *they* had access to the information they'd need to rip off Sabini's company.

It was a long shot, but what did he have to lose?

He'd had a restless night, brought on by the nagging feeling that he had been followed the evening before. He thought he had twice spotted the white Acura.

Stop being paranoid, he told himself. Those cars are a dime a dozen.

He found the "Computer Repairs and Service" heading. Only six companies were listed. Ken dialed the first and listened to the receptionist's chirpy greeting.

"Infotron. We're here to help!"

"I hope so," Ken said. "I have a laptop that died on me. There's some stuff on it I need to have. A buddy of mine was there a while back and he raves about you guys."

"Good!"

"The thing is, I can't remember the guy's name who helped my friend. Do you have any way of telling me?"

"Sure. What's your friend's name?"

"Burton Sabini."

Ken heard the clicking of a keyboard as the receptionist looked up the name. "I'm sorry, sir. We have no record of a customer by that name."

Ken hung up and tried the next listing. And the one after that. And the one after that.

On the fourth listing, the cooperative receptionist suddenly turned chilly when Ken mentioned Sabini's name. "I'm sorry, sir," she said. "Our clients' names are strictly confidential."

Bingo.

"He *told* me he went there," Ken said. "I'm not asking you to give me his name. I just want the guy who helped him."

"I can't confirm anything you're saying."

"Fine," Ken said with an exasperated sigh. "I'm coming in with my laptop." He chose his words carefully. "Can I make an appointment with the technician you think I'll be most comfortable with?"

The receptionist got it. "I have a feeling you'll be very happy with Dennis Keogler."

Ken made an appointment for the next morning.

"It's around here somewhere," Margot said as she shone her flashlight into the darkest corner of her basement.

Ken squinted to see past the furniture and boxes stacked against a concrete wall. He yanked the light fixture chain above him, but the bulb remained dark.

"That light hasn't worked for years," Margot said. "Here. Help me move this."

Ken lifted a box off a white wicker laundry basket, which he remembered from his married days. The basket, along with several of the other items here, came from the town house he and Margot had lived in on South Cobb Drive. Funny how a tacky piece from Pier One could take him back. Before he could get too nostalgic, Margot flipped open the lid and directed her flashlight inside.

"Ah-ha!" She reached in and pulled out her old laptop, yanking the power adapter up by its white cord.

Ken took the computer and blew away a layer of dust.

"I don't know what good it'll do you," she said. "It's a 286. A relic. It can't even run Windows."

"That's okay. How much do you want for it?"

"Oh, please. You're doing us a favor by carting it away. I was going to give it to the Salvation Army."

"Thanks." He tucked the laptop under his arm. "Is Bill at work?"

"Naturally. I'd almost rather he was having an affair. At least then he wouldn't be so stressed all the time."

"No, but *you* would be."

"Maybe." Margot sighed. "Bill and I have been out of sync lately. I sometimes wonder if we're going to make it."

It took Ken a moment to register what she was saying. "What happened?"

"Nothing happened. Nothing I can point to anyway. Sometimes I think we've outgrown each other, except . . ." She sighed. "I can't see that we've actually done any growing."

"Maybe *that's* your problem."

"I don't know what our problem is. We don't connect the way we used to. I want to work on it, but I don't even know where to start. It scares me, Ken." He could hear a nasal pinch in her voice as she became more upset. "It makes me wonder if I'll *ever* be able to do this right."

"How long have you felt this way?"

"A few weeks, a few months, I don't know. At first I tried to tell myself it was just a phase we were going through. But it just isn't the same. Sometimes it feels like we're just roommates who have sex."

"And how is the sex?"

"Great."

"Just checking."

"When I'm with him— It's so strange. I've tried to put my finger on it. For a while it felt as if I were with another person. But that wasn't true, not really. I feel as if *I'm* someone else when I'm with him. Does that make any sense?"

He nodded.

"I don't like feeling that way," she said. "It's not his fault. It's mine. I just don't know what I'm going to do about it."

"Have you told Bill any of this?"

"It's not clear enough in my own mind yet."

"It sounds like it's very clear to you."

She shook her head in frustration. "Is there something

wrong with me, Ken? Am I just incapable of sustaining a long-term relationship?"

"You're asking *me*?"

"I don't know. Maybe I'm just running away from my problems."

"No."

"Then maybe you don't know me well enough."

"I know you better than anyone."

She looked up at him as he drew her into his arms. "You do, don't you?"

He nodded.

The hug began as a purely platonic gesture, but he began to feel something else. He thought she was feeling it too, as their bodies pressed together in the dark basement.

She looked at the knickknacks from her and Ken's life together. "We did have some fun times, didn't we?"

"We still do."

"You know what I mean."

"Yeah, we had some fun times."

They went upstairs, and Margot walked Ken to the door. He waved good-bye as he headed down the driveway to his car.

Damn, he thought. Was the whole world going down the tubes?

It bothered him to see Margot so out of sorts. She was the one person he knew who seemed to have her act together; when she was off kilter, the whole world seemed slightly askew. He knew it was unfair to deny Margot the right to her own neuroses, but it still tore him up.

He leaned against his car. For the first time in a long while, he found himself wrestling with his feelings for her. His friendship with Margot was a source of pride. It had not been easy to get to this point, making that leap from husband to friend. "*I* couldn't handle that" was a popular refrain among friends and acquaintances. But he *could* handle it. Or at least he thought he could.

Today she needed him, and that stirred something.

There was a tingling, a charge, between them. The old chemistry.

Ken glanced back to make sure Margot had gone back into the house.

He threw the laptop onto the ground and stomped on it with his heel, cracking the computer's hard plastic casing. He picked it up and tossed it into his car before jumping behind the wheel.

"Man, did you drop it off a building?"

Dennis Keogler sat at his cluttered workbench, holding the shattered laptop computer at eye level. A piece of the broken casing fell to the floor.

Ken shook his head. "Airline baggage handlers. You should see what my suitcase looks like."

"Did the airline make good with you?"

"I think so. Depends on how much you charge me."

Keogler smiled. The guy couldn't have been much older than twenty, gangly but okay-looking. The data recovery specialist worked in the back room of the small downtown shop, where three other technicians toiled over their workbenches. Fluorescent lights buzzed overhead, and thunderous rap music boomed from a portable stereo.

"It won't be cheap," Keogler said. "But I'll see what I can do."

"If it's anything like the job you did for Burton Sabini, I'll be happy."

"You knew Burton Sabini?"

"Yeah."

"I read about what happened to him. Too bad. He was a nice guy."

"Yeah, he was. He said you did a great job for him."

Keogler shrugged.

"Tell me something," Ken said. "In what form will you give me the data you recover from this computer?"

"Any way you want. I can put it on a new hard drive, floppies, backup cartridges, you name it."

It was time to see what Keogler was made of. Ken leaned close and spoke quietly. "And how will you give me the information that was on Burton Sabini's computer?"

Keogler stared at Ken. "What do you mean?"

"I mean, you made a copy of his stuff, didn't you?"

"Why would I do that?"

"*You* tell *me*."

"I don't know what you're talking about."

Ken studied the techie. Keogler swallowed hard. His eyes darted away. He began to breathe through his mouth.

Gotcha!

"Knock it off," Ken said. "You're going to pull the files from this computer, and I'm going to pay through the nose for it. Then you're going to give me the files you pulled from Sabini's computer, and I'm going to pay you much, much more. Right?"

Keogler didn't look at Ken. He stared down at his workbench. "Let's go outside," the kid mumbled.

Ken followed him to a small back patio next to the Dumpster. Keogler paced back and forth.

"Relax," Ken said.

"I can't. Too much diet Mountain Dew. What do you want Sabini's stuff for?"

"A competitive edge."

"Against who?"

"What do you care?"

"Listen, there's no memo that says 'By the way, I hid the twelve million under Centennial Olympic Park.'"

"I didn't expect there would be."

Keogler stopped pacing. "Was he really a friend of yours?"

"Yeah, I knew him."

"I can put everything of his on a couple of ZIP cartridges. How much are they worth to you?"

"A thousand."

"Give me a break. We're talking industrial espionage. Companies pay upward of fifty grand for this kind of stuff."

"How would you know?"

Keogler just smiled.

"Sabini's stuff isn't worth that kind of money," Ken said. "It's months old. What else are you going to do with it?"

"Five thousand."

"Three."

"Deal."

After making arrangements to meet Keogler the next night, Ken left the shop.

The trail was heating up.

"You look like hell. You should get a car with air-conditioning."

The receptionist leaned forward in her chair as she finished folding a paper airplane. She sent the plane sailing into Ken's chest.

"Nice to see you too," he replied as he unfolded it. "What's this?"

"A cancellation. Your two o'clock won't be showing up. He got scared and quit his job. Guess some people really believe in your stuff."

"Imagine that."

The receptionist smirked. "You have a guest waiting outside your office."

"A guest? Who?"

"A cop."

Ken went still. "A cop? What does he want?"

"If he'd told me, I wouldn't be sitting here right now. I'd be out spreading it all over the building."

Ken quickly walked toward his office, trying to smooth out the wrinkles in his shirt. It was like being called into the boss's office. He rounded the corner, only to see Lieutenant Thomas Gant seated on a bench.

"Hello, Mr. Parker." Gant rose to his feet, his face crinkling with a smile. "I need to talk to you. Is this a good time?"

Ken shook the lieutenant's hand. "As good a time as any. Come in."

He unlocked the door and flipped on the lights as he and Gant stepped inside. One of the fluorescent bulbs flickered with annoying vigor.

"Catch any liars lately?" Gant asked as he stepped around the polygraph stand.

"A few. And you?"

Gant shrugged. "Don't know yet."

"Maybe I can help."

"Maybe. Tell me how you knew Burton Sabini."

Ken froze for an instant, just enough to send a clear signal of recognition to Gant. Ken cursed his own reflexes. The cop had blindsided him.

Damage control. "I know the name."

"You know more than that, don't you?"

Ken's mind was racing. How much did Gant know? And how much should he admit? Too much could land him and Myth in all kinds of hot water, but too little might just get him a murder rap.

Time to roll the dice.

"I think he called me a few weeks back. He was thinking about taking a polygraph test for some kind of court case. He had a million questions. He wanted to know how reliable these things are, that kind of stuff."

"That's all?"

"Yeah. That's it."

Gant pulled a grainy photocopy from his pocket. "We found your office number and address written in the message pad of Sabini's Day-Timer. He wrote it there sometime in the last couple weeks of his life."

"He's dead?"

"Murdered. Very much in the same way as your buddy Carlos Valez."

As Gant unfolded the copy, Ken suddenly became aware of the pile of newspaper clippings and papers relating to Sabini. It was the file Myth gave him, and it was sitting on the desk behind Gant, in full view. The lieutenant hadn't seen it. Yet.

Gant showed him the office number and address written on Sabini's message pad. "You never actually met with him?"

"No."

Gant folded the photocopy. Ken tried to hide his anxiety as the detective turned toward the desk, toward all those clippings, and—

—right past them as his attention went back to the polygraph.

The lieutenant seemed fascinated by the device. As he did on his first visit, he picked up the sensors and examined them.

Ken suddenly felt his nervousness give way to a rush of anger. Dammit, this shouldn't be happening. A murder investigation wasn't part of the bargain.

Gant cocked an eyebrow at him. "How much training did you have on this thing?"

"Six-week course."

"Six weeks? You're deciding the fate of entire careers based on six weeks of night school?"

"It's a living."

Gant shook his head. "I don't need one of these machines, Mr. Parker. When you've been at this job as long as I have, you pretty much know when you're being lied to."

"Is that right?"

Gant was staring intently at him. He nodded. "Sometimes I *pretend* to believe them so they can trip themselves up later, but I almost always know."

Another moment passed.

Gant turned toward the door. "You know how to reach me. If you think of anything else, get in touch."

"Sure."

Gant smiled and let himself out. Ken let out the long breath he didn't realize he had been holding.

A spring thunderstorm drenched Ken as he sprinted from his car to the awning of his apartment complex. It was almost ten P.M., and his head hadn't stopped throbbing since

Gant's visit. When was the last time he had been able to relax? He couldn't remember.

His head only felt worse as he walked past the spot where Carlos Valez may have been murdered.

Murdered the same way as Burton Sabini.

Coincidence? Gant sure as hell didn't think so.

Ken inserted his apartment key into the hole, but the door creaked open before he could turn the lock. Startled, he stepped back, his wet hair dripping onto the concrete walkway. He peered cautiously into the dark apartment.

He knew he had locked the door.

Several moments passed. He took one step inside and stopped, trying to get accustomed to the darkness. His eyes darted in every direction, but shadows still cloaked the apartment.

He listened, but all he could hear was the driving, hammering rain.

He made his way to a lamp. He turned it on, and—

"Hello, Ken."

He whirled around, almost knocking the lamp over in the process. His visitor entered from the bedroom, strolling casually into the light.

It was Myth.

"Did I scare you?" She walked over to the still-open front door and closed it tight.

"I wasn't expecting company."

"I let myself in. Hope you don't mind."

He shrugged.

"You really should do something about this lock. I slid my ATM card down the door frame and opened it in about two seconds. But I'm afraid I scratched off my magnetic stripe."

"What are you doing here?"

She stepped closer. "I missed you."

"I thought we couldn't see each other."

"You want me to go?"

"I didn't say that. But what about the police? And all that stuff about Sabini's life going under the microscope?"

"The police talked to me about him. I don't think it's that big a deal. I think this will be worth the risk. Don't you?"

She stepped closer and unfastened the top two buttons of his shirt. She lightly kissed his chest. "Is everything okay?"

He nodded.

She slid her hand inside the shirt and stroked his stomach. "If you don't want this, I can leave."

"I want this."

"Okay, then."

They lay there on his futon, massaged by the sound of the drizzling rain.

She pulled herself up on her elbows and gently blew on his chest.

"I guess you *did* miss me," he said.

"Yeah. I didn't think I would."

"Oh. Thanks."

"No, it's just—I don't get attached to people very easily."

"I can believe that." He rolled over on his side. "What have you been doing with yourself?"

"I've been flooded with calls since Sabini died. There are a couple of interesting cases I may take on. I need to look into them a little more."

"Good."

"What about you? Anything going on?"

"The police visited me again."

She sat up with a start. "Why?"

"They found Sabini's Day-Timer with my name and number in it. I told the detective that Sabini called and asked a few questions, nothing more. But it looks damned suspicious with me being connected to two men who were murdered the same way."

Myth bunched the covers in her hands. "I can't believe it. You did the right thing, though."

"I lied to a cop who's conducting a murder investigation. I wouldn't call that 'the right thing.' Maybe we should admit what we did with the polygraph."

"That's not a good idea. Just stay the course, and everything will be fine."

"That police detective didn't believe me."

"Sure he did. You've seen enough liars to know how it's done."

Ken sighed. "I never thought I was one of them."

"If I had known you were getting this kind of scrutiny, I never would have come here. Is there anything else I should know? Anything at all?"

Like what? he wondered. Like how he was looking for Sabini's stolen money?

"No," he said.

"I shouldn't be here." She settled back slightly.

"What's wrong with wanting someone?"

Myth didn't answer.

"I think it's because then you'd be more vulnerable."

She nodded. "I guess that's part of it."

"Who in your life ever made you think the world's that terrible, that scary?"

"You should talk."

"I'm not gonna pretend that I'm some kind of Pollyanna. But at least I'm not so afraid of the world that I don't know how to live."

"I'll tell you how I've lived. When I was thirteen years old I lived with a stepfather who one day realized he couldn't provide for his family. So he came home, took his hunting rifle off the rack, and put a bullet into my mother."

He might have thought she was joking, so casual was her tone. But as he looked into her eyes, he could see pain and raw emotion there.

She continued, her voice still steady and strong. "His name was Tim. After he lost his job, he killed my mother, then shot me. I played dead. I just lay there on the kitchen floor and watched him turn the gun on himself."

"Christ."

She was facing in his direction, though her eyes were not focused on him or anything else in the room. She spoke dreamily, as if from another time. "He didn't kill himself right away. He sat there with the gun at his head for a long time. Must have been hours. He kept trying, and I kept waiting. Finally he did it. For a while, I didn't think he was going to have the balls. But you know, if he hadn't been able to shoot himself, I would've grabbed the gun and done it for him. I really would've." She paused. "Tim was a real go-getter. He was a ruthless man in a lot of ways. Nothing I did was ever good enough for him, but there was a time when his approval meant everything to me."

"I'm sorry."

"Don't say you're sorry. Just don't try to tell me what living is all about. I know what it's about."

She rolled over, away from him.

He tried to think of something to say, but nothing seemed right. After a story like that, it was no use even trying. He leaned back on the futon and put his arm around her. Her body stiffened at his touch.

It was going to be a long night.

CHAPTER 9

en walked toward the main entrance of Club Renaissance, a Piedmont Road dance club that had changed hands, and names, several times in the past ten years. It was the location Dennis Keogler had chosen to hand over the contents of Sabini's data files.

With the sudden attention from the police, Ken debated the wisdom of continuing to track Sabini's loot. It was riskier than ever to associate himself further with the case. He'd have to be careful. As long as he remained on the periphery, things would be reasonably safe. But the deeper he delved into Sabini's life, the greater the chance of getting caught in Gant's sticky web.

Ken knew his quest would come to a crashing halt if he confessed to Sabini's polygraph training. That fact, more than anything, was keeping him quiet. Myth probably thought he was doing it for her, but he knew better.

She had risen at five-thirty that morning, dressed silently, and kissed him before leaving his apartment. He had no idea when he would see her again.

Ken paid the dance club's stiff cover charge and walked inside to find the place practically empty. But it was early yet. Eight-thirty P.M. The club was creepy with its throbbing music, pulsing lights, and no dancers.

Keogler was seated at a booth, drinking Bud from the bottle. He waved Ken over.

"I picked this place so we'd be lost in the crowd. Some genius I am, huh?"

Ken sat across from him. "Do you have the cartridges?"

"Do you have the money?"

"No."

"What do you mean, no?"

Ken produced a microcassette recorder, held it against Keogler's ear, and pushed play.

The kid's eyes widened as he heard an incriminating snatch from his and Ken's conversation from the day before. They were making the deal for Sabini's data files.

"You son of a bitch," Keogler said.

Ken pulled the recorder away and returned it to his pocket. "Play nice. This could get you into a lot of trouble."

"It doesn't prove anything. No money changed hands. And you can't prove I really have the data."

"If I were a cop, you'd be in cuffs now and I'd be checking out that rectangular bulge in your breast pocket. How much a year do you make selling off this stuff? Two, three hundred thousand? More?"

"What do you want?"

"The way I figure it, you didn't use this information to rip off Sabini's company. I doubt you'd still be at your job. And I don't think you're connected enough to pull it off."

"Then why are you hassling me?"

"Who else have you sold this information to?"

"No one."

Ken studied Keogler, examining him for the slightest hint that he might be fibbing. Almost everyone had subtle, almost imperceptible cues they exhibited when cornered into a lie. It was different for each person, but the day before, Ken had been able to read Keogler only minutes into their first conversation. Maybe he'd get lucky again.

Keogler began breathing through his mouth.

Gotcha!

"Who else?" Ken repeated, pounding the table with his fists.

"Who are you?"

"I'm not a cop and I'm not a fed. That's all you need to know. But I can play this tape for your boss, and I can slip it to the local papers and television stations. Can you see the headlines? 'Computer Technician Steals Secrets from Atlanta's Biggest Corporations'?"

"Aw, man ..." Keogler nervously ran his hands over the tabletop, as if fingerpainting an imaginary piece of abstract art.

"I don't give a damn if you want to keep ripping off your customers. That's your business. And theirs. But I do want to know who else you sold this data to."

Keogler looked up. "That's all you want?"

"That's all I want."

"You won't tell anybody I told you, will you?"

"That would be bad manners."

"My customers are kind of touchy about this stuff. If it gets around that I'm not discreet, I'm in trouble."

"Your secret's safe with me."

Keogler bit his lip. "Sabini worked for a metal-works company. I looked up its competitors and made some phone calls. A VP at Crown Metals bought the stuff from me."

"What did he want with it?"

"What do they *ever* want with it? Sabini was a financial officer. Crown could see what Sabini's company had bid on contracts, what the financial arrangements were, and so forth. Then they could swoop in and make better deals. That's what I figured anyway."

"What was the guy's name?"

"Don Browne. With an 'e' at the end."

Ken jotted the name down on a cardboard coaster.

Keogler grinned. "You can look through this data all you want, but there's nothing here that could have helped anyone steal that money. No access codes, no electronic funds transfer numbers. If that's what you're looking for, you're out of luck."

"We'll see about that."

"Carlos Valez was an animal. He got what he deserved."

Liz Benton walked toward the spacious center court of the Packard Hills Shopping Center, inspecting the kiosks and pushcarts before the mall opened for the day. Gant kept pace with her.

"Ms. Benton, is there anyone here who may have wished him harm?"

"Besides me?"

"I'm serious."

"So am I. He scared the hell out of me. I didn't know if he was going to come back and kill me, or just slice a few fingers off."

"You should have called the police."

"I did. They wouldn't even send an officer out. He didn't make an explicit threat. Apparently, ransacking my office and advancing on me with a wound-up phone cord wasn't enough to justify your department's time."

"I'm sorry."

"To answer your question, no, I don't know of anyone who had any reason to kill him. I didn't know him well, but I never heard of any problems."

"What made you suspect him of stealing the video equipment?"

"It was a combination VCR/TV unit used for training tapes, and at the time it was stolen, only half a dozen employees had access to it."

"Including Carlos Valez."

"Right. So we sent them all in for polygraph tests. I have to tell you, I don't have a lot of faith in polygraphs. Anyone who watches *60 Minutes* will tell you those things are unreliable. But our developer swears by them, and I have to follow company policy."

"Tell me, how did you come to choose the polygraph company you did?"

"Luck of the draw. We had been using an older gentleman downtown, but the last few times I talked to him, I got the distinct impression he had been drinking. So I decided to try someone else."

"Ken Parker."

"Yes. I just stabbed a finger in the phone book. I figured one of those guys is as good as the other."

Gant watched as the woman kicked an unsightly power cord underneath one of the pushcarts, out of sight. Convinced that the cart was now presentable, Liz continued her inspection.

"Were you satisfied with the job Ken Parker did for you?"

"Well, he returned my calls, did the exam, and promptly sent over his report. In that sense, yes, I was satisfied."

Gant sensed hesitancy in her voice. "But . . . ?"

Liz stopped and turned toward Gant. For the first time, she seemed to be giving him her full attention. "Something interesting has happened. Something I should tell you about."

What do you say to a thief?

Ken shoved a quarter into the pay phone and punched Don Browne's office number. He still wasn't sure what he was going to say.

Hey, how 'bout those stolen data files?

A secretary answered, and Ken identified himself only as a friend of Burton Sabini's. She put him on hold, and Browne picked up almost immediately.

"Don Browne."

"Hello, Mr. Browne."

"Who is this?"

"I want to talk to you about some computer data you purchased. They belonged to Burton Sabini."

"What?"

"Let me guess. You don't know what I'm talking about."

"No." Browne practically choked out the word.

"Don't bullshit me. Let's get together and talk about it."

"Not until I know who this is."

"We'll talk about that later too."

"Are you trying to blackmail me?"

"All I want is information."

Browne paused. "Like what?"

"We'll talk about that when we meet. I'd like to see you today."

"Today?"

"Yes."

Another pause. "I'll meet you tonight," he said. "Call back here at seven-thirty. I'll tell you where I'll meet you."

"Seven-thirty." Before Ken finished speaking, Browne hung up the phone.

The fax machine hummed and shuddered as the halftone transmission slowly uncurled into the tray. Hound Dog held the end as she cut the thermal paper loose with a pair of scissors. It was a photograph from a fellow scanner geek in Colorado, sent in response to her query a few nights before. A handwritten note came with it. Hound Dog held the photo up as Mark looked over her shoulder.

"What is it?" he asked.

"It's her. The same woman. I knew I'd seen that face before. She's younger here, but it's definitely the same one."

The photo was a crime shot of Myth Daniels being led away by police from what looked like a condominium complex. She appeared to be in her early twenties. Hound Dog almost shuddered. She now remembered the photo, and what had struck her about it.

The woman's cold, unforgiving face. There was no pity, no regret, despite the fact that she had just killed someone.

Hound Dog picked up the accompanying note. It read simply, "Call me."

"Who sent it?" Mark asked.

"A guy named Gary Conway. He lives in Colorado. I met him at a photography convention about a year and a half ago. I guess that's where I saw this photo of her."

She omitted the fact that the scanner geek had made several overt passes during the course of the convention, all rebuffed.

Mark returned to the kitchen table, where he was doing his homework. He was almost half finished with a bachelor's degree in accounting, accumulating credits through correspondence courses. By the time he would have to attend actual classes, he hoped to have enough money saved so he could quit his job as a bouncer.

Still holding the fax, Hound Dog picked up the phone and dialed Conway's number.

He answered on the first ring. "Hi, Hound Dog."

"How did you know it was me?"

"I just sent you the fax. I figured you'd want the scoop on it."

"And you knew nobody else would be calling? Get a life, Conway." Hound Dog looked at the picture again. "Well, that's definitely her. What *is* the scoop?"

"This was a while back, maybe twelve or thirteen years ago. In Denver. That woman had just shot a man in cold blood. Killed him."

"I remember that."

"Yeah. She had tried to charge the guy with rape a few weeks before, but it didn't stick. The next thing everyone knew, he was dead on her doorstep. She said he'd broken the door and was coming in with a knife."

"So she blew him away."

"You got it."

"You get any shots of the stiff?"

"Nah. It was all taped off by the time I got there. This made some headlines, though. There was some question whether or not it was really self-defense."

"What do you mean?"

"It could have been a setup. She knew the guy, she could have asked him to come over. You know what she looks like, *I* would have gone over."

"Was she ever charged?"

"No. Just a lot of speculation. What's the story with your Madeleine Walton shot?"

"Who?"

"Madeleine Walton. Isn't that who we're talking about?"

Hound Dog flipped through her pocket notebook. "The name *I* got was Myth Daniels."

"Check it again."

Hound Dog crinkled her nose as she looked at Conway's photo next to her own. It was unmistakably the same person. She wrote the name "Madeleine Walton" in her pad with a large question mark beside it.

"I'll look into this. Anything else?"

"Yeah. When are you gonna dump that big, dumb brute of a boyfriend of yours and give me a chance?" He paused, then added, "I'm not on a speakerphone, am I?"

"Lucky for you, no. Thanks, Conway. I'll be in touch."

She hung up and stared at the two pictures for a moment longer. Mark stood, approached her from behind, and massaged her shoulders.

"What's wrong?" he asked.

"I don't know," she said, still staring at the photos. "But it's time I found out."

Ken walked down a long ramp in the building that housed Crown Metals, Don Browne's company. It was seven-twenty P.M., and his telephone appointment with Browne was only ten minutes away. It was an appointment Ken was going to miss.

He decided to drop in on Browne instead. There was no way to tell how deeply involved Browne was, and it didn't seem like a smart move to let him call the shots and arrange their meeting. Surprise was the best strategy.

Ken made his way past the empty attendant booths until he found himself in the building's subterranean parking garage. Cool. Dark. Not particularly inviting. He could have walked through the front door, but he wanted to avoid the guard desk in the lobby. He preferred to arrive unannounced. Ken's footsteps echoed in the nearly empty parking level.

He found the elevators and rode up to the eighth floor, where most of Crown's corporate offices were located. The reception area was empty. Good. No one to intercept him. Ken scanned the directory and found Browne's office number. Suite 8023.

He walked down the hallway as if he had a legitimate reason to be there. It was a stellar performance, but there was no audience to appreciate it. Surely there were a few workaholics still toiling in their cubicles. But with each turn of a corner, Ken could see only vacant corridors. He followed the numbers toward Browne's office.

The lights turned off.

Ken stopped. He wasn't in total darkness; traces of sunlight were still coming through windows in a few of the open offices. He squinted to see his watch. Seven-thirty sharp. The hallway lights were probably on a timer.

Ken saw a ribbon of fluorescent light spilling from a doorway. Browne's office. Ken stopped to listen.

There was a continuous rapid-fire clicking coming from behind the door. It was a familiar sound, but Ken couldn't quite place it. He crept closer to the door and peeked through the crack.

All he could see were bookshelves.

He placed his fingertips on the door and shoved. It swung inward, revealing more bookshelves, a window, a desk . . .

And a man slumped over the desk.

No way in hell.

Ken froze. This couldn't be happening.

The man's face was lying on his computer keyboard,

causing line after line of letters to scroll down the monitor screen. It was making the clicking sound.

Ken still hesitated. Then he heard a sound. Voices in the hallway. Coming his way, naturally.

Ken stepped inside and pressed himself against the wall. The voices came closer, as did the sound of casters rolling across the carpeted corridor. A vacuum cleaner. Cleaning people.

The voices faded as the workers turned the corner.

Ken stepped away from the wall. What now? Maybe the man wasn't dead. Maybe he'd had a heart attack and was just unconscious. He should check.

He walked over—and saw a tiny bullet hole in the man's forehead, with only the tiniest trace of blood. Jesus.

Should he report the murder? No. He was already linked with two murders. How would this look?

As he was pondering what to do next, he noticed the lock on a file drawer in the desk. He had come here for information, and the stubborn part of him refused to leave without it. He reached for the drawer. It didn't open.

He had a good idea where to find the key. He pushed back Browne's chair and thought for a moment. Did he really want to do this?

No. Yes. Maybe.

Hell no, he didn't want to do this.

But the stubborn part took over again. He jammed his hand into the corpse's right pants pocket. Wet. Browne had pissed in his pants at the moment of death.

Ken fished for the keys, finally hooking them with his middle finger. He pulled them out and unlocked the desk drawer. It was jammed with files. He thumbed through the tabs until he found one labeled v.i.

Vikkers Industries?

He reached inside. No paper. Shit. But as he pulled out the folder, a thin, rectangular piece of metal slid out. He picked it up. It appeared to be an aluminum sample cast with a dark purple hue. A series of numbers and letters were etched on one side. He pocketed the sample and put the folder back into the drawer. There didn't appear to be any other relevant files.

Ken held up the keys. Was it absolutely necessary to put them back where he found them? Yeah, probably so. He once against stuck his hand into Browne's damp pocket and deposited the keys.

He looked at the computer. It could be holding more information, but there wasn't time to guess at the password. It was time to get out.

He leaned into the doorway, checked both directions, and walked down the corridor. He reached the elevator bank and punched the button. It didn't stay lit. He tried it again. Again, the light didn't stay on.

Damn. It must have switched over to key access only, probably at the same time the lights went off.

Ken followed the glowing green exit signs to the stairwell. He ran down to the sixth floor, where he found the covered walkway that crossed Spring Street to another office building. He crossed the bridge, took the other building's elevator, and emerged on the street below.

As Ken walked to his car, he cast a glance up at Browne's lighted office. First Carlos Valez, then Sabini, now this guy. Three people he had recently come into contact with. No way was it a coincidence.

What had he stumbled into?

Christ. If he didn't wind up in jail, he might just end up as corpse number four.

"I have some news for you."

Early the next morning, Ken was walking across his office parking lot, when he heard Gant's voice.

Lieutenant Gant.

Again.

Ken felt the metal strip in his pocket. Shit. If Gant

somehow found out that he had been in Don Browne's office, the hunk of metal might be evidence enough to bury him. It had been a sleepless night, and the morning obviously wasn't going to be any better. He was still shaken from the experience of finding Browne's body.

Did it show? Could Gant see that he was half out of his mind? "What do you have?" Ken asked.

"I'm afraid you botched a test."

"What test?"

"The test you gave Carlos Valez. He *didn't* steal the VCR."

Ice water surged through Ken's veins. "How do you know?"

"The mall manager told me. Someone tipped her off, and they found the unit at another guy's house. Did you test someone by the name of Robert Finlayson?"

This wasn't happening. Christ almighty.

"Yes," Ken answered in a low rasp.

"That was the guy."

Ken nodded. One of his worst fears had finally come true. He had been proven wrong. Shit.

"I guess it happens," Gant said. "You can't be right all the time."

How about half the time?

Was he right even that much?

Carlos had said he lost his job, his home, and his family because of that damned machine. No, not because of the machine. Because of the examiner.

"Thanks for making my day," Ken said. "Is that what you came to tell me?"

"That and the fact that this gave Carlos Valez even more reason to have been angry at you. If you want to admit anything, your position would be stronger than ever. He was obviously furious with you."

"There's nothing to admit!"

Gant said nothing.

"Do you want to arrest me? Huh? Jesus. Okay, so I

screwed up his exam. I have to live with that. I didn't kill him though. What more do I have to say?"

"Nothing," Gant said. "You don't have to say another word."

Ken half expected handcuffs to be snapped around his wrists, but instead Gant turned on his heel and walked away.

Ken entered his building, sailing past the smirking receptionist on the way to his office. Did she know what a fraud he was?

Probably.

Ken flew into his office, slammed the door behind him, and kicked the polygraph stand. The machine crashed to the ground. A knob flew off and spun furiously on the floor.

That felt good.

Ken settled into his desk chair and looked at the mess. Why had Gant come? The fact that the exam was botched didn't have any real bearing on the case; it didn't suggest that he was responsible for Carlos's death. No, Gant wanted to throw him off balance, hoping to upset him and get a confession out of him. That was it.

The man was just doing his job.

The way he had been doing *his* job when he screwed over Carlos Valez.

Ken rubbed his face with his hands. What the hell was happening? Don Browne's murder was reported on the morning TV news, but there was no apparent motive, no suspects, no anything.

Was he fooling himself by thinking he could find that money?

Maybe.

But the money, Ken realized, wasn't all he was after. With the police breathing down his neck for a pair of murders he didn't commit, he was driven to discover what was happening around him. He suspected that the twelve-million-dollar booty was in the eye of this storm, and if he could find it, a lot of other answers would follow. Answers he just might need to stay out of jail.

But the quest was getting more risky by the moment.

"What the hell are you doing?"

Myth pushed her way into Ken's apartment. It was two thirty-five A.M., and Ken, in his grogginess, had answered his door without checking the peephole first.

"I'm trying to sleep," Ken replied. "You're not helping."

She glared at him. "I was talking to Sabini's widow, and she said an insurance investigator was there to see her. I checked around, and none of the agencies would admit to it. Then she described the car he was driving. *Your* car."

"Yeah, so what?"

"Looking for Sabini's money will only attract attention from the police."

"We also agreed not to see each other. That didn't stop you from coming over to my place the other night."

"I admitted that was a mistake."

"Fine. You make your mistakes, I'll make mine."

"This involves both of us, Ken. If you blunder into that police investigation, you risk exposing everything we've done."

"I'll be careful."

She sat on the sofa. "It's a waste of time. Tell me, are you any closer to finding the money?"

Ken wiped the sleep out of his eyes. "Maybe," he said.

"What do you mean?"

"I know that some information from Sabini's laptop was copied and sold by a data recovery guy."

This got her attention. "When?"

"A few weeks before they found the money missing. It was sold to an executive at a competing company, who happened to have been murdered last night."

Myth stared at Ken for a moment. "Are you talking about the man at Crown Metals?"

"One and the same."

"How did you find this out?"

"I asked around."

"Do the police know all this?"

"I don't think so."

She sat still, thinking in silence. "I wonder if Vikkers Industries knows."

"Sabini's company? How would they know?"

She hesitated before speaking. "Did you know Vikkers Industries is under investigation?"

"For what?"

"They recently completed a very lucrative merger with Lyceum Metals. The Securities and Exchange Commission is investigating charges of misconduct on the company's part."

"What kind of misconduct?"

"I'm not sure. The investigation is still in the preliminary stages. The SEC doesn't like to publicize these things because it can have an adverse effect on the company's stock."

"What does this have to do with anything?"

"Maybe nothing. But if someone is murdered just a few weeks after obtaining Vikkers' privileged information . . ."

"You think Vikkers may be involved."

"Was the murdered executive the only one who had access to this data?"

"As far as I know. Why?"

"I've heard this strictly off the record, but several executives around town are reputed to have received Vikkers' sensitive financial data in the weeks prior to the merger. It actually discouraged other companies from trying to ace Vikkers out of the merger with Lyceum Metals."

"Why?"

"It didn't paint a pretty picture of Lyceum. Vikkers completed the merger with no other bidders in the running. The top Vikkers guys made out like bandits."

"Maybe Don Browne spread the information around before he got killed."

"Possible. But why would he help his rivals? I'm sure he paid dearly for that data, and he'd want the advantage of having it to himself."

"Maybe someone killed him for it."

"Maybe. But the other firms have supposedly had that data for weeks. We're only assuming, of course, it *was* Sabini's data."

"If they all had Sabini's data," Ken said, thinking it through, "then there *is* an explanation."

Ken shoved Keogler against a telephone pole behind the data recovery service. The kid was petrified.

"Who else?" Ken demanded, leaning into Keogler's face.

"What—what do you mean?"

"Don Browne wasn't the only guy you sold this information to, was he?"

"Yes, I swear!"

"Bullshit. This information is all over the place. I want to know who else you slipped the data to."

Keogler squinted in the midmorning sun. He was sweating despite the mild temperature. "I can't do that."

"Sure you can. And while you're at it, tell me who else knew Don Browne had the information."

"No one else knew. I wouldn't tell anybody that."

"Except me, huh? Right. You're forgetting I still have the tape of our conversation. And a copy of the data that you gave me."

"Come on, give me a break, will you?"

Ken shoved a pen and paper into Keogler's chest. "Start writing."

Keogler took the pen and paper, fumbling with them as he glanced meekly at Ken. He turned, and using the phone pole as a backing, began writing. "I didn't tell anyone besides you that Browne had the data. I didn't tell any of these guys that I'd sold it to anyone else. It wouldn't be good for business."

"Why did you originally give me Browne's name and no one else's?"

Keogler clicked his tongue. "He was a deadbeat. He wouldn't pay the balance of what he owed me. He tried to say the information was bogus. Can you believe that? So it didn't exactly break my heart to give you his name." Keogler shook his head as he continued writing. "Man, that data must be hotter than I thought."

"Have you looked it over?"

"Of course. But there are no access numbers in there. Like I told you, no one could have used it to rip off the company. I checked." Keogler handed Ken the pen and paper.

Ken glanced over the list. There were four names and companies.

"You know," Ken said, "maybe you should take another look at that data."

"Why?"

"Because there's more there than just sales figures and marketing strategies. You're naïve, stupid, or both if you think Don Browne's death didn't have a thing to do with those data files."

"Well, it occurred to me that *you* might have killed him." Ken glared at Keogler. "Why would you think that?"

"Well, he died less than twenty-four hours after I gave you his name. Seems like a pretty big coincidence."

"I didn't have anything to do with it."

"Maybe, maybe not. But if you rat me out to the cops, you can bet I'll tell them about this."

The kid had a point. "If you're straight with me, I won't have any reason to rat you out."

"I hope not, for both of our sakes."

"Will you take another look at those files?"

"What am I looking for?"

"I don't know. But Vikkers is under investigation. Maybe there's something in there that will tell us why."

"Are you sure you're not a fed?"

Before Ken could answer, he looked up and saw a familiar sight.

The white Acura sedan.

Again.

It was at the end of the alley, crossing at the next block. In the past few days, even when it wasn't tailing him, it always seemed to be there.

Near his apartment.

In parking lots.

Wherever he went.

The car slowed, then continued across until it was out of sight.

"I'm no fed," Ken said. "I'm just looking to collect on a debt."

Hound Dog clutched the Lexis/Nexis card as she walked through the front doors of the Georgia State University Law Library. It had taken her a good fifteen minutes to sweet-talk her friend out of the access card, and it had cost her dearly. She had to promise to spend her Friday night at a party with the guy, who was a second-year law student.

The Lexis/Nexis system was a computer database that offered full-text retrieval of literally thousands of newspapers, magazines, and legal documents. Articles could be accessed by a name, subject matter, or even the appearance of a phrase. For example, it would be a simple matter to call up every article in the past ten years that contained the words "gravy-sucking pig," an entry Hound Dog had, in fact, once tried. She discovered thirty-four articles.

The Lexis/Nexis system could be found in law firms all over the world, but usage charges ran into the hundreds of dollars an hour. Many universities, however, were given access for bargain-basement prices. It made good business sense to hook law students in to depending on the system for which they—or their firms—would later pay dearly in the real world.

She slid her friend's access card into the computer terminal and waited for the prompt. She typed the command "NAME MADELEINE WALTON." In a few seconds, the screen informed her there were seventy-seven articles that contained that name. She knew some of these were probably other people with the same moniker. She typed "CITE" for a full listing of the articles. Immediately the list came up. Most of the stories came from Denver sources, and their headlines made it clear they were about the murder Conway told her about. She selected a few to save in her print file, then noted the last appearance of the name in the system.

Over twelve years before.

Since then Madeleine Walton didn't exist as far as the database was concerned.

Hound Dog typed "NEW SEARCH," then "NAME MYTH DANIELS." One hundred and ninety-four entries. She studied them, and was not surprised to see they began only after Madeleine Walton's entries stopped. Most of the articles revolved around court cases, up to and including the Burton Sabini matter.

She selected several of them to save in a print file. She typed the "PRINT" command, and in less than five minutes she picked up all her articles at the circulation desk, neatly collated and stapled.

She thumbed through the stories as she made her way back to her motorcycle. She had never encountered anything like this in her years as a scanner geek. Murderers posing for her, cops flirting with her, and victims screaming at her, maybe, but this case was something new.

Hers was often a lonely life. Most people thought she was a nutcase, and she didn't socialize much with the other scanner geeks. Many of them *were* nutcases.

But she couldn't imagine ever leading a different life. Not when the night beckoned. Not when there was a world of wonder, excitement, and intrigue waiting for her.

Not when she was now literally clutching a mystery in her very own hands.

CHAPTER 10

G ant pressed the surgical mask hard over his nose and mouth in an attempt to block stray particles of aluminum dust from his respiratory system. He was visiting a Vikkers plant, where company president Herbert Decker was spending the day.

The plant was located in nearby Kennesaw, an Atlanta suburb best known as the site of a bloody Civil War battle fought as General Sherman's forces advanced. The town's recent notoriety stemmed from the fact that it was the one municipality in the country that passed a law *requiring* each home to have a gun. This was done in the name of deterring crime, but it actually just provided the national press with "aren't-those-rednecks-funny" news stories.

Gant strained to see through the dirty goggles given to him by an assistant foreman. Huge aluminum presses roared as he walked toward a glass booth at the factory's far end. He climbed a short flight of stairs and entered the booth.

"Lieutenant Gant?" A short man with a booming voice stepped toward him.

Gant closed the door and pulled off the mask. "Yes. Herbert Decker?"

"That's me." Decker shook Gant's hand, squeezing hard. The man's firmer-than-firm handshake, loud voice, and expansive gestures struck Gant as indicators that

Decker was trying hard to compensate for his small size.

"Have a seat," Decker said. "I'm sorry I have to meet you here, but I like to spend time in the field every month. It keeps my finger on the pulse."

"No problem. I take it you know why I'm here."

"My secretary said it was about Burton Sabini. But I've already spoken to another detective."

"He's still on the case. But his plate is pretty full right now, so I'm picking up some of the slack."

"I'll help you if I can, but I really don't have any more to say."

"Have you ever heard of a man by the name of Carlos Valez?"

"Can't say I have."

Gant believed him. Damn. It was a stab in the dark; he was hoping to make some kind of connection. "How about Ken Parker?"

Decker shook his head. "Are they suspects?"

"I'm sorry, I can't discuss that. How did the people in your company feel about Burton Sabini?"

"I don't think we felt much of anything. He did his job well, he was a nice guy, but that's about it."

"What about after the embezzlement?"

"Well, the senior management team and I were understandably upset. But among the rest of the employees, I think the feeling was 'attaboy!'" Decker shrugged. "It wasn't their money."

Gant nodded. "That's often the case with big-company embezzlement cases." He checked his notebook. "Speaking of money, you and the senior management team made quite a bit of it last year. It must have run into tens of millions."

"You're talking about the merger."

Gant nodded. "Did Burton Sabini share in that windfall?"

Decker took on a defensive posture. "No, he didn't. He didn't have a stake in the company."

"Why not? I understand other executives who had been here less time profited very well."

"It wasn't in his deal. Some people had shares, some didn't. Compensation is dealt with on a case-by-case basis. And I should tell you our profits are only on paper. None of us can cash in our shares yet."

"It's only a few more months though, isn't it?"

Decker didn't reply.

"Sabini watched everyone else here get rich after the merger, but he got nothing."

"He got paid a good salary!" Decker roared.

A screamer. Every employee's worst nightmare. "I'm just trying to understand what motivated him to embezzle from your company," Gant said.

"He was a fucking thief!"

"Please calm down."

Decker tossed his paperweight against a cork bulletin board, knocking down a few pieces of paper. "You people haven't done a damn thing to get that money back. I don't give a fuck who killed him. Where's the money he took from us?"

Gant remained calm. "Maybe someone killed Sabini out of revenge."

"For what? Stealing from us?"

"*You're* obviously angry about it."

Decker shook his head. "We didn't want him dead. He was our only chance of getting that money back. No one *here* killed him. Trust our greed, Lieutenant."

"I find that amazingly easy to do."

The white Acura was in Ken's parking lot.

Once again.

Ken had just finished repairing his polygraph, when he stepped outside to see the car parked in the shadows of an oak tree.

Ken turned toward the glass doors of his building and

looked at the Acura's reflection. A man was in the passenger seat, and he appeared to be watching him.

Ken pushed open the door and ducked into the hallway. He jogged down the corridor and cut through to a stairwell at the rear of the building. As he ran down the stairs, his mind raced. Who would be following him? Not a cop. The car was too nice. For tailing suspects, police generally liked older, plainer cars. Less conspicuous.

It probably wasn't a creditor either. He was paid up on all of his delinquent accounts, and collection agents didn't waste their time spying once they found their man.

Ken still had not formulated a plan when he stepped out to the alley alongside his building. Keeping an eye on the Acura, he sprinted around to the other side of the parking lot. He ducked behind a pickup truck and peered through the cab windows. The man still sat in the Acura's passenger seat, watching the office building.

The guy knew what he was doing, Ken thought. Sitting in the passenger seat was an old surveillance trick. It gave the appearance that the observer was waiting for a driver.

Ken crouched low and slid between parked cars in the lot, slowly creeping up on the Acura. He stopped a few feet away, behind the driver-side door. The man was heavy, balding, maybe fifty years old. No one Ken had ever seen before. Shit-kicking country music blared from the car stereo.

Ken rubbed his hands on his jeans. He didn't have many options. He could walk away and ignore the guy. Or he could call the police, but without the threat of physical danger the case wouldn't warrant much attention. Or he could confront the man. But how? He was sure the guy would deny following him if questioned point-blank.

Better to shake him up.

Ken straightened to peer through the driver-side window. The keys were in the ignition; it was hard to miss the bright orange rabbit's foot dangling from the steering column.

He threw open the door and slid behind the wheel. The man jumped with a start, gasping as he spilled soda all over himself.

"My name's Parker," Ken announced as he pulled the car door shut. "But I guess you already know that, don't you?"

He started up the car, put it into gear, and peeled out of the lot. The tires squealed as he roared onto Roswell Road, barely missing a car in the adjacent lane. His passenger, speechless, held his armrest in a white-knuckled grip.

Ken glanced over. "I know you've been following me."

"I don't know what you're talking about!"

"The hell you don't. Well, here I am. You got something to say to me, say it."

The man stared out the windshield in horror. "Jeez, just . . . slow down, all right?"

"Oh, I'm just getting started. Wait until we get out of this traffic."

"Come on, man!"

"I know you're not a cop."

"I can still bust your balls, you know that? This is kidnapping, grand theft auto, reckless endangerment—"

"Sorry."

Ken sped through a busy intersection, jerking the wheel to avoid a truck.

The man raised his arms. "Watch it—*shit*!"

"I figure this is the only way we can talk. You can't hurt me. You do, and we both die. So if you got a gun—"

"Who do you think I am?"

"Good place to start. Who are you?"

"Uh, can't we just pull over and talk about this?"

"I'll think about it. I'd think a lot better if you started talking now though. Who are you?"

The man nervously pulled at his seat belt, fumbling to fasten it around him. "Okay. All right. My name's

Michaelson. Ted Michaelson. I was following you. Okay? I admit it."

"Big of you. Why?"

"Twelve million dollars."

Ken gave him a sharp look.

"Isn't that reason enough?" Michaelson glanced ahead. "There's a hot dog stand in the parking lot up there. I'll buy you a dog and we'll talk. Okay?"

Ken swerved into the parking lot. "You're not going to run, are you?"

Michaelson laughed as he pinched six inches of fat on his midsection. "What do *you* think?"

"Sabini's company hired me," Michaelson said after taking a massive bite of his bratwurst. "They wanted me to look in on things, see if I could get a fix on what he did with their money."

Ken sat on the hood of Michaelson's car, a chili-cheese dog in hand. "So you're a private investigator?"

Michaelson nodded. "Freelance, but I do a lot of contract work for Vikkers. Mostly paperwork, background checks, a little surveillance. Small stuff."

"I guess I fall under the 'small stuff.' "

"Not at all. I was tailing Sabini the last couple of weeks of his life. I *know*."

"You know what?"

"About you, about Myth Daniels, about everything. Sabini spent some serious time in your office. Rehearsing for the big event, I'd say."

Ken's first instinct was to terminate the conversation immediately. A Vikkers investigator was the last person he should be speaking to. But he thought of something.

"You didn't report this back to the company," Ken said. "They would've been screaming bloody murder if you had."

"Kept it to myself."

"I wonder why you'd do a thing like that."

"Vikkers offered me five percent of any money I locate. That's a lot . . ."

"But not enough?"

"It occurred to me you and the lawyer might be in on it. It occurred to me *I* might get in on it."

"In on what? The money?" Ken laughed. "You sorry son of a bitch. You know, they say you can't take it with you. But for all intents and purposes, Sabini *did* take it with him. We don't know where it is."

"I'd like three million dollars."

"Wouldn't we all?"

"With what I know, I can make things uncomfortable for you and your lawyer friend."

"You're blackmailing us? Sabini died *owing* me money."

Michaelson studied him. Ken shook his head in disbelief as he finished his hot dog.

Michaelson nodded. "Okay, maybe you're not in on it. That'd make sense too. Why would she need you when she could keep it all to herself?"

"What are you saying?"

"I got a theory. A theory maybe Sabini was killed by someone he knew. Someone like . . ."

"Who?"

"Somebody who already got what she wanted from him. Someone smart. Someone beautiful. Someone who knows how to make a man stop thinking with his head."

"Myth was with me that night."

"At eight-twenty P.M.?"

Ken didn't reply.

Michaelson nodded. "I was following him, remember? I was about a block away when he got it. I kept waiting for him to come out the other end of that alley, but he never did."

"You didn't see who did it?"

Michaelson shook his head. "No, but I got ideas. She wasn't with you then, was she?"

Ken tried not to let Michaelson see how the conversation was affecting him. His stomach was churning and his throat was closing. He felt a layer of sweat on his forehead.

Michaelson talked louder and more quickly. "What do you know about her, really? That she's great in the sheets? Yeah. I know about you and her. But what do *you* know?"

"You're wrong. She didn't do it."

"I can afford to be wrong. You can't. If she *did* kill Sabini and get the money, you're in an awkward position. You helped her perjure a client. You got something on her. To her, you're a loose end. Know what you do to loose ends? You clip 'em off."

"I believe her a hell of a lot more than I believe you."

Michaelson grinned at Ken. He finished his bratwurst, crumpled up the wrapper, and tossed it into the trash can. He stepped around and opened his car door.

"I'm sure Sabini believed her too." Michaelson motioned toward the passenger-side door. "Want a lift?"

That night, Ken spotted Myth near the illuminated fountains at Centennial Olympic Park. They had chosen this meeting place since locals never ventured there after office hours, and, as expected, only a few tourists were present. Ken glanced around, realizing that he had not gone there since the Olympics. How different it was without the pavilions, without the vendors, without the people. It seemed lonely without the crush of visitors that had once so defined the character of the place.

Ken stepped over the plaza's personalized bricks, remembering that Bill had bought one for him. He never got around to looking it up, though he knew it was somewhere on the side facing Martin Luther King Drive. He'd have to find it someday. Given Bill's sense of humor, the brick was probably an insult for everyone to see.

Ken gestured toward the fountain as he approached Myth. "If you need to cool off, it's okay to jump in."

"You mean I won't get arrested?"

"It's not that kind of fountain. And if they saw *you* with your clothes wet, you'd probably get the key to the city."

"I'll pass, thank you."

"Your decision."

"What have you found out? Anything?"

Ken paused. He thought about telling her of his conversation with the Vikkers private eye, but decided to keep it to himself. At least for a while.

"I know that a number of people got their hands on Sabini's computer files. I have a list of names, and they check out. They're also alive and well, unlike our friend Don Browne. If he was killed because he had those files, the others were spared for some reason."

"Maybe he wasn't as discreet as the others."

"Maybe. But from what I've been told, there's nothing in those files worth killing for."

"We'll know that only when we know who killed him."

Ken stared at her. Was *she* a killer? Could she really have snuffed Sabini with a blade to the heart?

Ken tried to picture her doing it.

The image came to him easily.

Jesus.

"What about on your end?" he asked. "What have you found out about Vikkers?"

"Not much, I'm afraid. The SEC investigation has everyone clammed up tight. No one likes talking about it."

"I'm sure you could persuade them." An edge crept into Ken's voice, despite his best efforts to suppress it.

Myth hesitated. The fountains stopped, then began their cycle again. "I made a man's acquaintance . . ."

"I'll bet you did."

She eyed him curiously. "Is there a problem?"

The back of his neck felt hot. "You made a man's acquaintance to get what you wanted from him. Just like you made my acquaintance."

"We can stop this right now. I thought this was what you wanted."

"What did he say?"

"He's a high-level executive at another company. He saw the stolen data. The thing is, it turned out to be *wrong*. The figures were incorrect."

"What does that mean?"

"It means that they had extensive financial reports, but the information had almost no basis in reality."

"Then what use was it?"

"No use. Not to any of the people who purchased it. The phony data may have hurt them more than it helped."

Ken turned to avoid the lens of a tourist's camera.

Hurt more than helped.

"Maybe that was the point."

"It was this way when we got in this morning."

Ken was staring at Keogler's workbench, now barren where there had once been tools, a boom box, and tacked-up Victoria's Secret catalogue pages.

Ken turned to the receptionist and one of Keogler's co-workers. "He didn't call in?"

The receptionist shook her head. "No. He was supposed to be here at nine. But when we got in, his workbench was cleared out. I've been trying to call him all morning, but there's no answer at his apartment."

"Where does he live?"

The receptionist hesitated. "I really can't tell you that."

"He has my computer. Give me his address before I start screaming to the Better Business Bureau."

The receptionist looked toward a technician, who replied with a "what-the-hell" shrug.

Ken followed her back to her desk, where she consulted a small card file. She jotted down the address on a Post-it note and handed it to him.

"If you find Dennis," she said, "tell the jerk I never thought his Somalia jokes were the least bit funny."

. . .

Ken pulled to a stop in the parking lot of Keogler's complex, finding a space near the tennis courts. Nice place. How many illicit data sales a month did it take to live here?

It was a security building, but Ken was able to catch a door as it closed behind two bikini-clad women who were stepping out to the pool. He bypassed the elevator and climbed the four stories to Keogler's apartment.

The door was wide open.

Ken poked his head inside, but the place was empty. Not a stick of furniture, not a single hanging print.

Not a living soul.

"Hello?" Ken said.

No answer.

He took a quick tour of the apartment. Empty. And clean. Aside from the occasional nail hole in the wall, it was as if no one had ever lived here.

He ran downstairs to the building manager's office. The manager was an overweight woman with long, painted nails and green eye shadow.

She held up a set of keys. "These were dropped in the mail slot sometime in the last hour or so. No notice, no note, no nothing!"

"You didn't actually see him?"

"No, he didn't even stop in to say good-bye. Chickenshit little bastard skipped out on his lease. I'll tell you one thing, he ain't getting his deposit back!"

"So you had no idea he was leaving?"

"Do I *sound* like I had any idea?"

"Did he leave a forwarding address?"

"Nope!"

Ken walked back to his car. Why had Keogler suddenly bolted from his job and apartment, leaving without a trace?

If, indeed, Keogler *had* bolted. Was it possible that someone had snatched him and taken all his stuff?

Get real, Ken thought. Too many conspiracy movies had warped his brain.

As he drove out of the parking lot, he caught sight of a red Camaro with a U-Haul trailer hitched behind it. It was coming from behind the building. Ken squinted to look at the driver.

It was Keogler.

Ken cut his wheel hard to the left, blocking the Camaro's way out of the lot.

"You asshole!" Keogler shouted out his window. He braked to a stop, his face tensing as he recognized Ken.

Ken jumped out of his car and ran to Keogler's side window. "Where are you going?"

"Vacation. Get the hell out of my way."

"Unh-unh. What's going on?"

"I gotta get out of here *now*."

"Why?"

"Man, I don't have time for this shit."

"Make time."

Keogler slumped in his seat. "If I find that all this is your fault, I'm gonna kill you."

"All *what* is my fault?"

Keogler rubbed his face in his hands. "I haven't slept, and I have one hell of a long drive ahead of me. Please. Just get out of my way."

"Not until you tell me what's going on."

Keogler anxiously looked around. "Shit. Get in. I'll give you the *Reader's Digest* version."

Ken climbed into the passenger seat and slammed the door behind him. "Talk to me. What's going on here?"

Keogler gazed out the windshield. "I did what you told me. I took another look at those data files."

"And?"

"I found a pocket program. A program that hides in a file, between lines of programming code. It's hard as hell to find, but I ran across some red flags that started me digging deeper."

"What's in this program?"

"It caused Sabini's computer to malfunction."

"Like a virus?"

"Much more elaborate. It had to have been put there by someone who was very familiar with the programs already in place. He was using custom programs, so that doesn't leave many possibilities."

"Someone at his company."

"You got it. The amazing thing is, at the same time, this program replaced Sabini's data files with new data."

"Fake data . . ." Ken said.

"Yeah, that's what it looks like. His company referred him to me. They wanted the computer to malfunction, they wanted it brought to me, and I think they wanted me to pass the data along." Keogler shook his head. "I thought I was covering myself, man. I didn't know anyone was on to me."

"*I* found you out pretty easily."

Keogler looked as if he were going to cry. "I screwed up. That's why I gotta skip town now. If the company knows, then the feds could be on my ass. I got greedy. Stupid and greedy."

Ken couldn't argue with that. Vikkers had used Keogler to disseminate bogus information to its competitors. The kid walked right into it.

"So if you don't mind, I have to get the hell out of Dodge," Keogler said, leaning over Ken and opening his door for him.

Ken swung his legs out of the car and stood up. "Maybe there's another way. Running's not the answer."

"Neither is jail. Move your car, please."

Ken moved his car. Keogler's Camaro, with the U-Haul trailer attached, sped out of the lot, barely slowing for the speed bumps.

Gant thought the receptionist in Ken Parker's building was a nice enough kid, but her tight-lipped smirk unnerved him. It was the amused look a high school girl might have if a guy's fly was open, or if he had a "kick me" sign taped to his back.

"I answer the phone for him only if he's out of the office," the young woman stated flatly. "Sometimes I'll give directions to his clients if they can't find their way to him. That's it."

"Do you keep a phone log?"

The receptionist shook her head and lifted up a pink message pad. "It all goes here. I tear the sheets out and give them to the tenant. When are you going to tell me what he's done?"

"When I know he's done something. Have you noticed anything different about him in the past couple of weeks? Anything strange, out of the ordinary?"

"Strange, always. Out of the ordinary, no. Except that he's been really down in the dumps lately."

"Really?"

"Yeah. No wonder though. As far as I can tell, his business has been worse off than ever."

Gant made a mental note of this. It didn't quite jibe with his findings that Parker had recently spent several thousand dollars repaying delinquent loans.

The lieutenant produced photographs of Burton Sabini and Carlos Valez. He showed them to the receptionist. "Recognize either of these guys?"

She immediately dismissed the photo of Sabini, but stared at the Valez picture.

She pointed to it. "Maybe this guy. He might have come in here once."

"Just once?"

"That's all. Ken doesn't have regular customers. It's not that kind of business." She took the photograph and held it closer. "This guy's dead, isn't he? I saw this same shot on the news."

Gant nodded.

The receptionist grimaced. "This is one terrible picture. It's bad enough someone croaked him, but then he has to have this awful picture on TV. That reminds me . . ." She opened her desk drawer and pulled out a miniature television with a five-inch screen. "I'd appreciate getting this over with as soon as possible," she said. "*General Hospital* starts in two minutes."

"I can't compete with *G.H.*" Gant tossed a business card onto her desk. "Call me if you think of anything else."

He made his way out to the parking lot, thinking about what the receptionist had said. Parker's business was apparently worse than ever. Where had his money come from?

As the late afternoon sun dipped low in the sky, he glanced at the neighboring buildings. One in particular caught his eye. Its side entrance faced the west side of Ken's building, and over the door was a security camera.

Gant stepped closer. He couldn't make out the camera's angle through the smoked glass bubble, but it appeared to be pointed in the general direction of Ken's building. He knew these devices were, as often as not, actually "dummy cameras" that did not function, but served only to deter thieves and vandals.

However, if this was a real video camera . . .

He walked inside, waved his badge around, and within minutes found himself talking to a six-dollar-an-hour security officer who was employed to sit at a console and watch the bank of monitors.

"Show me the east entrance," Gant ordered.

The security officer punched a button, and Gant squinted at the black-and-white screen. A good portion of Ken's office building and side parking lot were in plain sight.

He turned to the security officer. "Do you record these?"

"Yeah. Eight hours to a tape, twenty-four hours a day. We keep them thirty days, then tape over 'em."

"Good. Don't erase any more. Gather the tapes from this particular camera. I'll be back with a court order."

"What do you have for me?" Decker leaned forward in his large leather desk chair, anxiously staring at Michaelson.

"Well, I'm keeping my eyes on Sabini's widow. She just got a passport. She may be making plans to bolt the country."

"The authorities have looked at her a thousand times. Don't you think you're barking up the wrong tree there?"

"Maybe, maybe not. The authorities didn't even dig deep enough to find out that she has family in Europe."

"You're kidding."

"Nope. They could have helped with the bank withdrawals there. I'm sifting through the bullshit right now, but I might have something for you pretty soon."

Michaelson shifted in his small chair. Decker was buying all of it. Just like always.

"I think I'm close to finding the person who has the money," Michaelson said.

Decker nodded. "Keep me posted," he said. "The board of directors has been all over our asses. They want new systems in place, but they have no idea what *kind* of systems. In the meantime, we have a business to run. It's a goddamn mess."

"As soon as I find out anything, you'll know about it."

Decker spoke quietly. "What about Matt Lansing?"

"He's been approached four times by the feds. Steven Lars was there three of those times. He's an FBI agent who specializes in antitrust cases."

"Did you believe Lansing when he said the wire didn't work?"

Michaelson shrugged. "Those things can be temperamental. If you go into a cluster of buildings, the signal can get buried, just like with your cellular phone. I'd say there's a fifty-fifty chance he's being straight with us."

"I don't like those odds."

"I'll try to adjust them in our favor."

"How do you propose to do that?"

"Don't worry," Michaelson said. "I have an idea I'm working on. I'll get back to you on it."

"Sooner rather than later?"

"You got it. Listen, I might be able to do a better job if I knew what you're afraid of. What did you guys do?"

"It's best that you remain on a strictly need-to-know basis."

"And at what point will I need to know?"

"The point at which all hell breaks loose." Decker stared glassy-eyed out the window. "Which may come sooner than any of us would like."

"Are you out of your goddamned mind?"

Hound Dog tried not to look irritated at Mark's latest outburst. He didn't understand. He said he did, but it was more and more obvious he never could.

He glared at the Lexis/Nexis printouts and Department of Motor Vehicle request forms. "This is sick!"

"It's a hobby!"

"Riding around on your motorcycle all night, taking pictures of car accidents and murder victims, *that's* a hobby. Barely. But this is going over the edge."

"Look at this!"

"I don't want to look. It's none of our business."

"This is all stuff I got at the library. I'm not doing anything wrong. I'm just trying to figure this out. Madeleine Walton and Myth Daniels are the same person. But why the different names?"

"Who cares?"

"*I* do. She's one of the best attorneys in the city, and she's hiding from another life. Aren't you at least a little curious?"

"I'll wait for it to turn up on *Hard Copy,* all right?"

"What's your problem? Why are you being such a wad about this?"

He turned from the articles and photos littering her workbench. It was another hot day in their trailer, and it was only getting hotter. He pulled a curtain and turned the tiny crank to open a roll-slat window.

He turned back. "I'm worried about you."

"Worried? Because you think I'm nuts?"

"No. Because I think you might get yourself hurt. You don't know what it's like for me, sweetheart. I come home from the club at three or four in the morning, and most nights you aren't even home."

"You knew that's what it would be like."

"Yeah. But I see from your pictures the places you go, some of the neighborhoods you're in at all hours of the night. Honey, those are places I wouldn't go in my *car*."

"I always carry the cellular phone you gave me. And I'm perfectly able—"

"And don't tell me you can take care of yourself."

"Well, I can."

"Taking care of yourself has nothing to do with it. Things just happen to people. Especially people who take the chances that you do."

"Should I move out? Is that it?"

"No," he said quietly. "That's the last thing I want."

"Why is this suddenly such an issue with you? You didn't used to give me a hard time."

"Well, maybe . . ." He hesitated. "Maybe I *care* more now. All right?"

She felt some of her anger drain away.

He continued. "The longer we're together, the more I can see a *future* together."

Surprised, she stared silently at him. They had never discussed their relationship in terms other than the here and now, and Mark generally was not one to express his feelings so openly.

"I don't want to lose you, honey," he said simply.

"You won't."

She snuggled close and kissed him. She didn't want to lose him either.

She had met him a year and a half before. There was a car accident outside his club, and he was one of the rubberneckers. When she arrived, he had just gotten off work. His starched white shirt was unbuttoned at the collar, and his bow tie was undone and hanging at his lapels. He stood watching, his hands in his pockets, the tux jacket draped casually over his left forearm. The wind lightly tousled his thick, wavy hair.

He was beautiful.

She took some obligatory shots of the accident scene, but she couldn't resist turning her camera on this incredible figure of a man. He approached her, and they went to breakfast together. Since that night, she never even considered dating anyone else.

She had said "I love you" to other guys before, but only with Mark did she realize what the words really meant. She was lucky, so lucky, to have him.

Mark looked down at the information and photos she had collected. "You shouldn't dig into this woman's private life. Maybe she had a good reason for changing her name."

"Like what?"

"I don't know. But I think you'd be better off if you left it alone."

"You know I'm not going to do that."

"Maybe Myth Daniels has a long-lost twin."

"No. Madeleine Walton's Lexis entries end just before Myth Daniels's begin. It's the same person, but an entirely new life."

"Okay, it's the same person. Now what?"

She plopped down onto her red beanbag chair. "Now I think it's time I went to the source."

At home that afternoon, Ken thought about what he had learned from Myth and Dennis Keogler. If Vikkers had purposefully spread fake data around, had Sabini been in on it too? Maybe not. The "pocket program" had done all the work. If Sabini had been party to it, he would have been able to adjust the figures himself. Would Myth have any idea where to go from there? Even if she did, he wasn't sure if he could trust her.

That private eye had made sense. Damn him.

Ken went to his bedroom window, peered through the

blinds, and there, on the street below, was Michaelson's Acura. The P.I. was in the passenger seat.

"Son of a bitch," Ken said under his breath.

Ninety seconds later he jerked open the door of Michaelson's car and plopped down in the seat next to him. Ken sat there listening to the whiny country-western song on the radio.

"Good afternoon," Michaelson said.

Ken looked over at him. "Is it my day to be watched?"

"Yeah. Myth Daniels is tied up at the courthouse all day. Not much going on there." Michaelson lifted up a red thermos. "Want some lemonade?"

"What makes you think you can get your hands on that money?"

"Because I know Sabini didn't work alone. It's not that he wasn't smart, but he didn't have the *kind* of smarts he'd need to pull this off by himself."

"Who would've?"

"The twelve-million-dollar question. But if there's still someone out there, he or she might still screw up."

"*Or she*. You still think Myth had something to do with it."

"I'm keeping an open mind. So are you, I guess."

"What do you mean?"

"You're here talking to me, aren't you? I'll bet you're not so eager to share your bed with her now. You'd have to lie awake, thinking that she was gonna murder you in your sleep. Am I right?"

"You talk too much, Michaelson."

The P.I. chuckled. "She wouldn't kill you in your own place anyway. Too risky. Someone might see her coming or going. A woman like that, people remember. It'd have to be somewhere out of the way, like where Sabini got it."

"This is all bullshit. If I'm going to believe you, I need more than these stabs in the dark. What makes you think she might be in on this?"

"Did you know she was sleeping with Sabini?"

The words sliced right through Ken. It was getting harder to pretend he wasn't bothered by the investigator's insinuations.

"How do you know?"

"I was following him. He stayed at her place a few nights. *All night* a few nights. And you should have seen 'em when they thought they were alone. They were all over each other. It sure looked funny. Can you imagine the two of them going at it? The goddess gyrating on that little dweeb?"

"Fuck you."

"Ooooh. I guess you *can* imagine it. But that's what leads me to imagine a lot of other things. I don't think she was attracted to his magnetic personality or his smoldering good looks. Do you?"

Ken didn't answer. He was trying to remember the times he saw the two of them together, and he could not think of one instance in which they appeared to be anything other than business acquaintances.

Michaelson snickered. "You're getting a lot of unwelcome attention from the cops right now. And Myth Daniels doesn't have a care in the world, not really. Except if you crack, then it's all over for her. If I were you, I'd watch my back."

"If you were me, you'd know I have nothing to worry about."

"If you say so. But *I* know you helped Burton Sabini out with the polygraph. Doesn't that worry you?"

"No, because I know you're doing a number on the company that's paying you to find their money."

"If push came to shove, I'd just say I was playing all the angles on their behalf. I'd tell 'em I was *pretending* to blackmail you to determine if you had the dough or not. They'd buy it."

"You wouldn't take that chance."

"You wanna try me?"

Ken sighed. "What the hell do you want? I already told you I don't have the money."

"Let's just say you owe me a favor. I'll collect on it in the near future."

Ken sat for a moment longer, listening to another twangy song on the radio. He leaned forward and switched the station to hard-driving rock and roll.

"Hey, hey, hey!" Michaelson objected.

Ken opened the car door, climbed out, and turned back. "I hate country music."

He slammed the door and walked away.

CHAPTER 11

It was half past eight on a clear, balmy evening when Ken pulled the starter on Bill's boat. The engine sputtered to life, coughing fuel through the sun-cracked hoses. A quiet sunset cruise was exactly what he needed just then. Away from all thoughts of Burton Sabini, Myth Daniels, Ted Michaelson, and the mess he had gotten himself into.

If Myth had been sleeping with Sabini, the guy probably would have told her anything she wanted to know. Anything. So she may actually have the stolen money. That would explain her initial resistance to looking for it. She had participated in Ken's investigation only after it was clear he was pressing forward without her. Maybe she just wanted to keep tabs on him, to make sure he didn't catch on.

But could he trust Michaelson? It was obvious the P.I. still suspected that he and Myth had worked together to stash the money away. Michaelson was keeping him under observation, and the warning was probably intended to arouse his suspicions and shake out information. Ken just wished to hell he had some information to give.

He backed the *Vivianne* away from the slip. He'd wait until he was farther out to crank up the stereo. There were probably people sleeping in some of the other boats, and they wouldn't appreciate Van Halen blasting them awake.

Ken steered away from shore for fifteen minutes. He

finally eased back on the throttle, and the engine dropped to a gentle purr. He looked up. Stars. How long had it been since he had noticed the stars?

Too long.

If only his brother were with him. Bobby had loved tagging along on these excursions, relaxing as the *Vivianne* gently rode the waves. Bobby would be here again, Ken thought. Someday.

A warm breeze caressed Ken's face as he turned starboard into the wind. He took a deep breath. There was a scent of pine in the air, drifting from a dense forest on the darkened shore.

He cut the engine. Blissful silence. Playful waves lapped against the *Vivianne*'s hull. For the first time in weeks, Ken felt himself relax. He grabbed a beer from the cooler and popped the top. The solutions to his problems weren't any closer, but they didn't have to be. As long as he could forget for a while.

He heard something.

The faint roar of another boat.

Ken looked fore, aft, port, and starboard. Nothing. But as the roar intensified, he thought it was somewhere off his port side.

He switched on the running lights to make his presence known. The roar was getting closer, but Ken still couldn't see another boat.

A couple of kids out for some makeout action, probably. City kids had their cars, farm kids had their haylofts, and lakeshore kids had their boats. Ken had been a lakeshore kid.

The roar grew closer still. Where were the boat's lights?

He switched on the mounted spotlight and turned it toward the sound.

Still nothing. The roar became louder.

Suddenly a gray hull broke the spotlight's beam fifty yards away. It was a much larger boat, maybe a thirty-footer. It slowed to a stop and idled in the glare of the *Vivianne*'s halogen spotlight. No lights emanated from the mystery vessel.

Ken looked incredulously at the boat. It was like sitting in an empty movie theater and watching a stranger walk in and take the seat right next to you.

As he considered averting the spotlight beam, the other craft revved its engines. What the hell? Was someone looking for a race?

The other boat lurched forward and hurtled toward his port side.

Holy shit.

Ken gripped the wheel and braced himself. The impact knocked him to the deck. He scraped a leg across sharp rigging as he went down. The larger boat's engines rang in his ears. Deafening. Angry. Violent.

The *Vivianne* spun away from the other vessel, rocking in its powerful wake. Ken clutched his right knee. It was damp.

Blood.

He pulled himself to his feet. His right leg couldn't support him. He eased down behind the wheel.

The other boat was circling back.

Ken punched the starter. Nothing.

Again. Still nothing.

Come on, you son of a bitch . . .

The big boat rammed his stern, jolting Ken as the *Vivianne*'s fiberglass hull cracked. Water seeped onto the deck.

Ken struggled with the starter.

Come on, come on, come on . . .

The engine finally roared to life. It was far weaker than the monster that was after him.

Ken glanced up. The bigger boat was coming back for another run.

Why?

He throttled the engine. Gotta outrace it. His life depended on it.

He looked back at the vessel. Could he beat it back to shore?

Not a chance. It was gaining fast.

His leg was killing him.

More water sloshed on the deck.

The boat rammed his stern again. And again. And again. Each collision shook his boat with ferocious intensity. The craft moved alongside his own.

Ken squinted to see who was at the wheel.

He saw no one. There were no lights on deck. The vessel loomed large, a shadow against the night sky.

It struck the bow. A starboard window shattered, and glass sprayed across his face. Some of it stuck like day-old stubble. He opened his eyes and gunned his engine harder.

Bam!

Another hit on the bow.

Ken veered away. He glanced around, frantically trying to get his bearings.

Bam!

He gripped the wheel hard. It was sticky with blood. He smelled the oily stench of his craft's engine overheating.

How much more could the boat take?

How much more could *he* take?

Water sloshed around his ankles.

The pump. Gotta find the pump.

He threw open the storage locker and fished out the water pump. He had never used it before. How did this thing work?

Bam!

Hell of a time to learn.

Ken plugged it in, threw the hose over the railing, and prayed the pump would do its thing.

It did. At least for the moment.

Ken jumped behind the wheel. He spun it hard to port, leaving the larger boat behind. He had more maneuverability, which was his only advantage.

Unless he found a way to exploit that advantage, he'd be dead meat.

Up ahead, Ken recognized what locals called "Klang's

Thicket," a dense patch of trees, vegetation, and overgrown weeds. It was big enough that the larger boat could still follow him, but that was the plan.

If only he could make it there.

The boat struck his stern again. Engines roared and water churned. Ken couldn't feel his right knee.

The pump was working overtime, but cool water continued to wash across the deck.

He gripped the wheel harder. He had to be careful. If he was off by only a few feet, he would bury himself in the trees and probably stall. He'd be a sitting duck.

But he needed speed so the larger boat couldn't easily follow.

One . . . two . . . three!

Ken yanked the wheel hard starboard and flew into the thicket. The larger boat whizzed past.

Perfect. He probably had thirty seconds before it could circle back and come after him. He aimed his spotlight forward and plunged past the water pines. This was his old makeout territory. Was the other boat's pilot as familiar with it?

Ken swerved into a clump of weeds and cut the lights and engine. He waited, listening as the other boat roared through the thicket, snapping low-hanging branches as it barreled through.

Surely it wouldn't be going so fast if the wheelman knew what was ahead.

Ken held his breath as the boat sped past.

It was still going!

After another few seconds he heard the sweet sound of the larger boat's hull being ripped apart by the rocks of Klang's Thicket.

His first impulse was to confront the murderous bastard, but he could barely stand, much less fight.

Whoever it was would be there for a while.

Ken punched the starter. Nothing.

He tried it again. It started. He backed out of the weeds

and left the thicket. There was less water in the boat than before.

As Ken sped for land, he felt his leg again. Cold and numb. It was a mess.

He beached the boat on the sandy shore. If he docked the vessel, it would probably sink before the hull could be repaired.

He hopped back to his MG on one leg, casting a nervous glance back to see if he was being followed. Not as far as he could tell.

Ken started up his car and drove. His leg hurt. His head ached.

He saw a Waffle House. As expected, there was a blue-and-white Forsyth County police car in the parking lot.

Ken pulled in and honked his horn. He waved at the cop through the glass window. The cop waved back and resumed his conversation with the counter girl. Ken honked again. This time the cop scowled, left the counter, and walked toward him.

"What's your problem?"

Ken gestured down to his leg. "Take a look."

The cop approached cautiously, as if Ken might have an assault weapon in his lap.

He recoiled at the bloody mess Ken's leg had become. "Jesus Christ."

Ken gritted his teeth. God, it hurt. "Nail the bastard who did this to me. I'll tell you where he is."

The officer reached for his walkie-talkie. "We gotta get you to the hospital, pal."

"But the guy who did this—"

"We'll take care of that later."

Ken gave his statement in the waiting area at the Kensington Hospital emergency room. He felt better after his leg was X-rayed, cleaned, and bandaged. The knee didn't look so bad.

It took an hour and a half before the doctor could see him. While he waited, the police officer returned.

"Here's the story," the cop told him. "We sent a patrol unit out and found the boat. It's right where you said it was. There's no one inside, and we're conducting a search of the area."

Ken assumed the cop was invoking a general "we," since he obviously hadn't left the cozy confines of the hospital. "Do you know whose boat it was?"

"Yeah, it was stolen this evening from a dock on the lake. The owner didn't even know it was gone. They're dusting for prints."

"Whoever it was tried to kill me."

"Is there anyone who would have reason to do that?"

Ken found himself shaking his head. "No."

"Look, it's my guess some kids stole the boat and went joyriding. It happens all the time. You were just in the wrong place at the wrong time."

Joyriding. Right.

The doctor put twenty stitches in his leg and informed him that there did not appear to be any permanent damage. He suggested a crutch, but after Ken hobbled around the room a few times, the idea was rejected.

He paid the emergency room tab with his credit card, deciding not to look at the total until the next morning. He wasn't in the mood to deal with it.

He limped back to his car and drove home, all the while wrestling with the inevitable question: Was Myth behind the attack?

Maybe Michaelson was right.

Ken cast a nervous glance in his rearview mirror. All clear. For now.

Since he was limited in what he could tell the police, he was entirely on his own.

So what else was new?

Another of Gant's least favorite clichés of police TV shows was that of the department's seemingly inexhaustible resources. Apparently, money and manpower were always in plentiful supply, and officers could have as much time as it took to crack every case.

This simply was not true.

He knew it was certainly different in small towns, but on a big-city police force there came a time when it was wiser to cut one's losses. If, after a few days, there were no strong suspects in a homicide investigation, the detective had to present a strong argument for continuing full-time on the case. There were other, solvable murders that required more immediate attention.

He knew the cutoff time was coming on the Carlos Valez investigation. The autopsy report hadn't turned up anything useful, and the only suspect, Ken Parker, had no priors and no evidence against him. It also did not help matters that Valez was a lower-class Latino with a criminal record. That, coupled with the fact that he died in a poor area, didn't bode well for the case. Gant ruefully noted that if Valez had been a white physician murdered in fashionable Buckhead, the investigation would continue indefinitely. At least until well after the local media coverage stopped. For an unemployed janitor, alas, the incident merited a story the day of the murder, but nothing more.

The Burton Sabini killing was another matter. Sabini had been a public figure due to the high-profile embezzling case that had caught the attention of the local business community. And it did not go unnoticed that another recent murder victim, Don Browne, had worked in the same industry as Sabini. What were the odds of two Atlanta metalworks executives being murdered within a week of each other? Gant had spoken with Serena Misner, the investigating officer on the Browne case, but so far there was no other apparent link between the two men.

In Sabini's case, the lack of a strong suspect was crippling the investigation. His murder looked more and more like a random mugging turned deadly. Sabini had been drinking at the Blues Junction bar at the Atlanta Underground entertainment center, apparently celebrating his passing the D.A.'s polygraph test. He left alone, and the next time anyone saw him, he was dead in an alley four blocks away.

It was possible he staggered into the wrong place at the wrong time. That was certainly the way it looked. But here, as in the Carlos Valez case, there was a connection to Ken Parker. Maybe Sabini *did* have Parker's name, number, and address so he could telephone him and ask a few questions. Gant wasn't sure. But he knew the only likely solution to cracking the mysteries rested with Parker. Otherwise, the cases would soon just stall, residing in the "unsolved" files, likely to forever remain that way.

Gant strode into the audiovisual lab at nine A.M. sharp, greeting the two officers on duty. A/V patrol was a popular slot for cops sidelined with injuries. Carlton and Wittkower were manning the consoles, and both had crutches next to their chairs. Carlton had been shot during a drug bust, and Wittkower had slipped on a cupcake wrapper in the squad room. Ironically, it looked as if Carlton would be the one to recover more fully.

"What's going on, guys?" Gant asked as he peered over their shoulders.

"Not much," Carlton groused. "I'm just logging in the Michael Moss show."

Gant looked at the monitor, and sure enough, there was Officer Moss in his uniform, giving a sobriety test to a suspected drunk driver. The video camera was mounted inside the police car, recording the officer's each and every move.

"Look at the way Moss keeps playing with his hair," Carlton pointed out. "And he always tries to keep the right side of his face to the camera. He thinks that's his good side."

Gant laughed as he kept watching. He caught a brief glimpse of Moss's left profile. "I'll be damned. His right side *is* better."

Carlton smiled as he noted the time on a log sheet. "He thinks he's gonna be on TV. Maybe *Cops*."

Gant turned toward Wittkower. "What do you got for me?"

"Nothing yet. You know that expression, Doing nothing but watching the grass grow? I've just been watching the grass grow. Literally."

Wittkower motioned toward the monitor above him. There, in black and white, was the side of Ken Parker's office building, with the tape being played at several times faster than normal speed. Wittkower turned the dial to slow it as he saw someone. He pushed a button, and the picture zoomed in on a man entering the building. Wittkower compared it to photos of Ken and Sabini taped onto his console. Satisfied it wasn't either of them, he continued scanning.

"How much do you have done?"

"About twelve and a half days. I haven't even seen Parker yet. He obviously doesn't use this entrance. Do you really think we'll find anything?"

"We might. Keep watching, Wittkower."

Ken walked with a slight limp as he tried to make out the worn house numbers along St. Charles Avenue. It was a pleasant street in the trendy Virginia-Highlands section of the city, but Ken couldn't enjoy the scenery.

Someone had tried to kill him.

Who was behind the wheel of that boat?

Was it the same person who killed Sabini? Don Browne? Carlos Valez?

Ken glanced around. That person could be any of the people he saw walking on this sunny street. Just waiting for another chance at him.

Ken had never visited this address before. It belonged to one Stan Warner, a self-described "information broker." Ken had met him the year before, when the man's then-employer, Greenfield Electronics, suspected Warner of stealing computer time from a mainframe at the firm's New York headquarters. When he came in for a polygraph test, he offered Ken his own unique services to coax a passing grade. His lucrative side business involved the selling of personal information, ranging from credit histories to driving records to unlisted phone numbers.

Ken failed Warner, who was immediately fired from his job. But Ken was intrigued by his "information brokering" service, so he kept the address.

This was a stupid move, Ken thought as he walked toward the duplex. Warner would probably K.O. him before he could get two words out. Oh, well. What was one more bruise?

Ken rang the doorbell. After a few moments, a shirtless, wild-haired young man swung open the door. He eyed Ken suspiciously.

"Stan Warner?" Ken asked.

"Yeah."

"I'm Ken Parker. I'm a polygraph examiner, and you failed a lie detector test I gave last year."

Warner looked closer and burst into a broad smile. "I'll be damned! Come on in!" he said with a thick southern accent.

He flung the door open wide and stepped back into his home. Ken hesitated. He hadn't expected a warm greeting.

Warner called back as he stepped into another room. "Don't worry. I got only one dog, and she doesn't bite."

Ken followed to a messy living room area, with newspapers, magazines, and tractor-feed computer paper everywhere. The only illumination came from the sunlight peeking from around the roll-down shades. Warner cleared away some papers from his couch, making just enough room for Ken to sit.

"What brings you here?" Warner asked as he plopped down on a stool.

Ken was still taken aback at Warner's gregarious manner. "Do you remember who I am?"

"Sure. You flunked me. Made me lose my job."

"I thought you might be mad about it."

"Nah. You caught me. I was guilty as hell. I'm just glad they didn't have me arrested." He gave Ken a curious look. "You didn't come here to apologize, did you?"

"No, I—"

"Because you don't have anything to feel bad about. Losing that job was the best thing that ever happened to me. I never would have had the guts to leave on my own. I work only for myself now. I love it. But what am I talking about? You know how it is. It's great, isn't it?"

"Yeah. Great. That's kind of why I came to see you. You're still in the information business, aren't you?"

"Of course!"

Ken instinctively distrusted people who were this peppy. Either they were on drugs, or they were masking deep-rooted anxieties that could result only in their going berserk at a playground with an AK-47.

"I need information on someone. As much information as you can find."

"Do you have a social security or driver's license number?"

"No. Sorry."

"Don't be. You're the one who'll be paying extra for it."

"How much are we talking about here?"

Warner presented Ken with a rate card listing his entire range of services. Ken smiled at some of the items: UNLISTED PHONE NUMBER $50.00, UNLISTED HOME ADDRESS $40.00, COMPLETE POLICE RECORD $275.00, MEDICAL HISTORY $225.00.

"How do you decide on the prices?"

"Depends on how hard it is for me to get the information, how risky, or how much *I* have to pay. I have sources, and they don't come cheap. I think I have the lowest prices in the city though. If you can find any lower, I'll beat 'em."

After some haggling, Ken finally settled on a "general background" package that Warner assured was becoming increasingly popular among older, wealthier women who wanted to check out their young suitors. Warner showed him a few samples, reminding Ken of his own file at Myth's house.

"Okay," Warner said. "All I need now is the name."

"Two names. The first is Burton Charles Sabini."

Warner scribbled it down. "Fine. What's the other?"

Ken paused a moment before answering. "Daniels," he finally replied. "Her name is Myth Daniels."

"What is it?" Margot asked as she fingered the blue-purple metal bar Ken had found in the late Don Browne's office.

"I was hoping you could find out for me." Ken leaned against the deck railing outside Elwood's Pub. Bill and their other friends were watching a Braves game inside.

"Why?"

"It might be important. You guys run tests all the time. No one would notice if you had this analyzed, would they?"

"*I* would notice," she said. "And before I send this to the lab in my company's pouch, I'd like to know why I'm doing it."

Ken looked away. Of course she'd like to know. How could he explain that he was keeping her in the dark for her own good? Just because he was up to his ass in muck didn't mean he had to drag her down with him.

He could always make up a lie.

No. Not with her. She deserved better.

"I can't talk about it right now, Margot. It would help me if you would do this, but if you don't feel comfortable with it, that's fine too. You have to know that I'm not telling you about this for a reason, and that when I can discuss it, I'll answer any question you want. But right now I just need you to trust me."

Margot was silent as the Braves fans went wild inside. She squeezed the metal bar in her right hand.

"Will you do it?" he asked.

She finally nodded. "I'll send it out to the lab first thing in the morning. I give them a lot of business. I'm sure they won't mind doing it for me gratis."

"Thank you, Margot."

"You're welcome. When you feel like talking, just remember I'm here. Sometimes I think you forget that."

"I never forget."

Ken returned home to hear the phone ringing. He answered it. "Hello?"

"It's time." Michaelson's voice.

"It's pretty arrogant to expect people to recognize your voice after only a couple of conversations."

"I'm just giving you credit. Since you're a trained observer and all."

"Uh-huh. So what is it time for?"

"It's time for the favor you owe me. What are you doing early tomorrow morning?"

CHAPTER 12

Ken had never tested a more nervous subject.

Matt Lansing was trembling as Michaelson escorted him through the door of Ken's office. Lansing licked his lips every few seconds, and his eyes darted furtively around the room. Although it was normally Ken's job to keep his interviewees on edge, this young man was already terrified.

Michaelson's "favor." Shake the guy up, bully him, and see what he has to say. You know all the tricks, right?

Of course he knew all the tricks. It was all part of his job. He didn't want to do it, but he believed Michaelson when he said he could make things uncomfortable for him. The last thing he needed was a loudmouth P.I. rocking the boat.

He extended his hand to Lansing. "It's really not that bad."

Lansing managed a weak smile. "Then *you* take the exam for me."

"If I could, I would. Have a seat."

Lansing sat down next to the polygraph, looking at it as if it were a bomb that could go off at any moment. He took short, quick breaths.

"Don't hyperventilate," Ken said. "It's hard to get a good reading if you're unconscious."

Lansing smiled, but his breathing didn't improve.

Ken turned to Michaelson and motioned toward the door. "Wait outside. You can come back when the test is over."

"You're the boss," Michaelson said. He left the office and pulled the door shut behind him.

Ken looked back and saw that Lansing's condition was improving. Michaelson's presence obviously rattled him.

"Okay," Ken said. "Let's talk about why you're here."

"My company doesn't trust me."

"That's not necessarily true. Businesses have all kinds of reasons for testing employees. There are parent companies, investors, and board members who often require these tests. They just want to examine all the options."

"Right," Lansing said caustically.

"That said, you were sent here for a reason. Can you tell me why your company wouldn't trust you?"

"Some investigators have approached me about possible securities violations on Vikkers Industries' part. I haven't told them anything, but they keep coming back."

"That's all?"

"That's all."

Ken fixed Lansing with a doubtful stare. The man looked away, then back. He squirmed.

Keep the heat on . . .

"Okay," Ken said as he picked up his clipboard. "Let's see what we have here."

He went over the questions with Lansing, who was eager to respond. Ken told him to save his answers for the exam. As Ken pulled the polygraph cords across Lansing's chest, he made a point of feeling the wireless microphone Michaelson had told him about.

"What's that?" Ken asked.

"Uh, it's a microphone."

"You're recording this?"

"No. Vikkers has been making me wear it ever since this stuff started."

"You wear it all day?"

"And at night. I never know when I'm going to be approached."

Ken smiled. "What about when you're with your girlfriend?"

"I don't have one at the moment. But if I did, I don't think I'd treat that investigator to a show."

"I don't blame you. You should take the wire off. The polygraph is a very sensitive instrument. The radio waves from that mike could throw off the readings."

"Okay. But please tell that to Michaelson when he asks why I'm not wearing it."

"Sure."

Ken knew, of course, that Michaelson was listening to their every word on a Walkman outside. Another mike had been planted on the desk, and Ken was quite sure the radio waves would have no effect on the test readings.

He did the card trick for Lansing, who was appropriately impressed by the polygraph's "accuracy." With that out of the way, it was time to begin the test.

"Are you presently an employee of Vikkers Industries?"

"Yes."

"Will you be completely truthful to me regarding the subjects you've agreed to discuss?"

"Yes."

"Do you understand I will inquire only about the issues we have discussed?"

"Yes."

"Have you ever stolen anything from an employer of yours?"

"No."

"Have you divulged your company's confidential information with investigators from any sector of the law enforcement community?"

"No."

Lansing's response was reasonably stable, but Ken frowned

at the graph as he made a mark with his felt-tipped pen. He
had to lay the groundwork here.

"Have you ever lied to keep from getting into trouble at
work?"

"No."

"Have you discussed confidential details of your company's merger with Lyceum Metals with members of the
law enforcement community?"

"No."

Mention of the merger sent Lansing's blood pressure
through the roof.

"Is your name Matt Lansing?"

"Yes."

"Have you ever violated any laws in the preparation of
business or personal tax documents?"

"No."

"Have you accepted an offer of leniency or immunity
from prosecution in exchange for providing law enforcement agencies with confidential information about your
company?"

"No."

Lansing was getting comfortable. His last response was
milder than those for the earlier irrelevant questions.

"Let's do it again," Ken said.

He ran the test once more, and again Lansing's blood
pressure soared upon mention of the merger.

Why was the merger freaking this guy out?

Ken tore off the graphs and took them to his desk. He
studied them intently, making meaningless marks with his
pen. He moved back toward his interviewee.

"Let's talk about the men who came to see you. I'm sure
they asked you a lot of questions, and it's only natural that
you would answer a few, if only to get them to leave you
alone. Am I right?"

Lansing shrugged.

"I know you told these guys more than you're letting on,

and if I were in your shoes, I might have too. Those government types are pretty scary."

"I told you the truth," Lansing said.

"If you ask ten people for the truth, you'll get ten different answers. It's all a matter of perspective. I'm sure you didn't *want* to talk to those guys. Anything you said, I'm sure you said under incredible duress. They probably threatened you with everything under the sun. I know you wouldn't have talked to them otherwise, and I'm sure your company knows it too. So although on one level you feel you didn't do anything wrong, deep down you're disturbed about something. It's all over these graphs. Unless you can talk to me about it, I'm afraid it's going to look much worse than it really is."

"Maybe your polygraph needs an adjustment."

"The equipment is fine. Remember the playing card test?" Ken smiled. "I'm afraid you're an open book. That's not a bad thing though. It shows you're an honest man at heart."

"Even though you're calling me a liar," Lansing said.

"That word doesn't fit you. You're between a rock and a hard place, and you're not sure of the best way out."

Lansing looked down at the floor.

Stand your ground, Ken thought. Don't fall for this shit. Can't you see what I'm doing here?

"Are you sure there isn't something more you want to talk to me about?" Ken asked. "It would look good for you if we can clean up these readings."

Lansing rubbed his temples. "This whole thing has been a nightmare."

"You can stop it. Explain what I'm seeing on these graphs."

Don't fall for it, Lansing. The graphs don't say squat.

"Do you have anything to drink around here?"

"Sorry."

Lansing clasped his hands together until his knuckles turned white. "I keep telling myself that it's just a job. Nothing more, nothing less."

"Just give me the truth."

"I think I'm gonna be sick."

"These readings are too strong to ignore. Are you working with the feds? Is that it?"

"No!"

"That's not what your boss is going to think after he's read my report."

"It's not true."

"Then tell me what *is* true."

Lansing cleared his throat. "It's not that bad."

"Then *tell me*. It's for your own good."

Lansing's lips quivered. He *wanted* to talk.

"Tell me!"

Lansing sighed. "The FBI wants me to gather information about Vikkers. They have a list of people in the company they want me to approach."

"Approach for what?"

"Information. The FBI wants to know all about the inner workings of Vikkers Industries."

"Why?"

Lansing ignored the question. "I didn't talk to any of those people. The feds can say whatever they want, but I'm not going to spy for them."

"Did you report this to your bosses?"

"No."

"Why not?"

"I don't know. Could this be why my readings are the way they are?"

"It could be part of it, but I have to tell you something, Lansing. You're still holding back a hell of a lot. You know it, I know it, and my machine knows it. And when I make out my report, your company will know it."

Ken looked at the pulse needle. The man's heart was about to explode.

"Come on," Ken pressed. "Talk to me."

"The FBI threatened me with prison. They said my career will be ruined and my life won't be worth a damn."

"Does this have anything to do with Burton Sabini?"

"In a way. Sabini was disgusted with the company. That's why he did what he did."

"Why was he disgusted?"

"Because he was a decent man."

"We're talking in circles here. Out with it. What's going on?"

Lansing eyed Ken for a moment. "This is really outside the scope of the exam. I don't think I should be discussing this with you."

"Your company hired me to find out the truth. They trust me. Let's get everything out in the open, okay? No secrets."

The door flew open and Michaelson hurried into the room. He was holding a Walkman and the headphones were down around his neck. "The test is over," he said.

"The hell it is," Ken replied.

Michaelson tore the blood pressure cuff from Lansing's arm. "Come on, we're getting out of here."

"I'm not finished," Ken said.

"Yes, you are. I know what I need to know."

"You were listening?" Lansing asked.

"You bet. Did you put the feds in touch with any other Vikkers employees?"

"No."

"I want those names. Every last person the FBI wanted you to approach, got it?"

Lansing glanced nervously at Ken. "Uh, sure."

"I was still talking to him," Ken said.

"I'll finish up my own way," Michaelson replied.

Ken spoke to Lansing. "Tell me about the merger!"

"Not a word!" Michaelson barked.

"Just thinking about the merger scares the hell out of you, doesn't it, Lansing?"

Michaelson fumbled with the perspiration sensor and chest cords, freeing Lansing from the polygraph. "Come on," he said as he pulled Lansing to his feet.

"Tell me about it!" Ken shouted.

But Lansing was silent as Michaelson pulled him out of the office and down the empty corridor.

Ken stepped to the doorway. Dammit. Lansing was *so close* to saying more. Why was Michaelson suddenly so skittish? If information was what he wanted, why did he shut down the session?

One subject sent Lansing's blood pressure soaring and compelled Michaelson to yank him out of the room.

The merger.

It all kept coming back to the merger.

"This takes time, Kenbo. The stuff comes from a lot of different sources. You gotta be patient." Stan Warner rifled through a stack of papers.

"That's something I've never been good at." Ken stood next to Warner. He had known it was probably too early for results, but the Q&A with Matt Lansing whetted his curiosity. After Michaelson pulled the plug, Ken had driven to Warner's to see if the information broker had uncovered anything of use.

Warner handed Ken two legal-sized photocopies. "This is it so far. It's their DMV reports."

"What good is that?" Ken took them.

"You'd be amazed. It's the gateway to a lot of other information. It has the birth date, social security number, sometimes place of birth. Anybody with four-fifty can get it on anybody else. *If* you want to wait four to six weeks. It so happens I got a buddy down there who can get 'em for me right away."

"Good for you."

"Good for you too. Because he tipped me off to something the DMV would never tell you."

"What's that?"

"Someone else has shown an interest in Myth Daniels in the past week."

"What kind of interest?"

Warner handed him a small sheet of scratch paper. "This chick requested a file on Daniels just a few days ago. My friend gave her name and address to me. It's all yours. No charge."

Ken looked at the name Warner gave him: Jessica Barrett.

"Anyone you know?" Warner asked.

Ken shook his head.

"Me neither." Warner sat on the floor and crossed his legs.

Ken stepped across the dirty room, still staring at the name. "Why would she want this?"

"Myth Daniels is an attorney, right? Maybe it's someone who's thinking about hiring her. Or maybe someone who's going up against her. You never know. The people who hire me want information for all kinds of reasons. Which reminds me, you never told me why you want background on these people."

"That's right, I didn't."

"That's cool. I'm into the discretion thing. As long as you know I could probably find out if I really wanted to."

"I don't doubt it."

Ken pocketed the paper and headed for the door. "When you get anything else, let me know."

"Just another half block, Bobby."

Ken gripped his brother's arm. It was the first time Bobby had been outside in months, and he was struggling to finish the walk back to his home.

"I just—have to catch my breath," Bobby said.

"It's okay. No rush."

"This was a terrible idea. This is your revenge, isn't it?"

"Revenge for what?"

"For me and my buddies yanking down your sweat pants in front of Cathy Morrison."

"That was in high school. Besides, Cathy worshiped me after that."

Bobby started to laugh, but a weak cough overtook him. "We should have brought the wheelchair," he grumbled.

"Nah. You'll be fine." Ken glanced around to see if he was being watched. All clear, as best as he could tell.

"What's wrong?" Bobby asked.

Ken looked back at him. Bobby had enough to worry about. "Nothing. Tell me how things are with you and Tina."

"She's amazing. She's been calling and writing every politician she can. And she's still working two jobs."

"Incredible."

"Our love life is for shit though. Sick and tired. I'm too sick, she's too tired."

"That'll change."

Bobby resumed his slow, measured steps back toward the house. Ken kept a tight grip on his arm.

"When I get better, I'm never going to take anything for granted again. Walking, talking, breathing . . ."

"Yeah, you will. Until the next time you get sick."

Bobby walked in silence for a moment. He turned to Ken. "Thanks."

"For what?"

"I know you're the only reason we're still in our house."

"That's what families are for."

"I get really scared, Kenny. I get these panic attacks in the middle of the night. Sometimes it seems like there's no way out, and there's no way things can get better. Do you ever feel like that?"

"Yeah. But there's always a way out. It may not be the way you want to take, but it's there if you look hard enough."

Bobby winced as they walked a few more steps. "The Gulf War Veterans Group wants me to go to Washington. They want me to testify at some congressional hearing. I guess they want to trot out all their sick and crippled."

"Are you going?"

"Yeah. But you know how much I hate talking in front of people."

It was true, Ken thought. Bobby had always been the shy one.

"It'll be a good thing for you," Ken said.

"Yeah. Tina thinks so too. They'll pay my way and everything."

"That's great."

"It'll be great if I can walk more than a block without puking my guts out."

"Just a few more yards, Bobby."

Myth wanted to go home. She had spent the entire day at a deposition, and the last thing she wanted to do was return to her office. But her assistant, Zachary, had left early for a dental appointment and she had to pick up her messages, mail, and faxes.

It was a quarter after five before she made it back to her desk. Zachary had mercifully weeded out the unnecessary or uninteresting mail, leaving her with a contract and a few briefs. She scanned the phone log. No one she especially needed to call back that night. Just the usual, boring . . .

Except one.

It leapt out at her. A name she had hoped never to see again.

Madeleine Walton.

Someone identifying herself with that name had called at three-ten P.M. There was no phone number; Zachary had checked the "Will Call Back" box on the log.

Myth reached for the caller I.D. unit sitting on her desk. It automatically recorded the phone numbers of all incoming calls, with a maximum memory of forty-eight calls. It worked only for phone numbers within the area, so if the call came from out of state, she was out of luck.

She repeatedly pushed the button, scrolling through phone numbers on the LCD screen and comparing them with those on the log. She scrolled back to when the Madeleine Walton call came in. She flipped to the one previous, then to the one after. This had to be it. As she jotted the phone number, she noted that the prefix was for De Kalb County. She was tempted to dial the number immediately, but that wouldn't be smart.

She would have to be smart about this.

CHAPTER 13

E very workday for years Gant had purchased a cinnamon roll from the street vendor around the corner from headquarters. But that was before his doctor told him that his cholesterol level was too high. Gant's wife pleaded with him to adopt a low-fat diet, but it was not necessary; both of his parents had died early deaths from heart disease, and he had no desire to continue that particular family tradition.

So it was a whole wheat bagel he was eating as he walked into the squad room. He was surprised to see a visitor at his desk. It was Alicia Valez, Carlos's widow. Gant had spoken to her shortly after the murder, but had not seen her since.

"Mrs. Valez, how are you?"

"Not so good," she replied without a trace of emotion in her voice. "It's been hard."

He sat behind the desk and angled his chair in her direction. He nodded as if in understanding, though he could not imagine how it would feel to lose Diane.

"We're doing everything we can to find the person who did it."

"I think I know who did it," she said.

She did not look at him. She stared into the distance, mouth tight and frozen.

"There was a man . . . He hated Carlos. He told Carlos he would kill him."

"Who?"

She moistened her lips. "His name is Ken Parker."

"He threatened your husband?"

"Yes. Carlos took a lie detector test from this man. Ken Parker told Carlos that if he paid him five hundred dollars, he would tell Carlos's boss he passed the test. If Carlos didn't pay, he would fail."

"That's extortion."

"My husband didn't pay, so he failed. He lost his job. He went to see Parker to talk about it. They had a fight. My husband had a temper."

"So I gathered. Why didn't your husband go to the police?"

"He told Parker he was going to. That's when Parker said he would kill him."

"Your husband told you this?"

Alicia nodded. "After he and his father fought, I guess he was afraid to go to the police."

"Ms. Valez, if I remember correctly, your husband struck you too."

"Carlos was angry and confused. He was scared."

"I read the report. In your statement, you didn't mention anything about this. Nothing about Ken Parker except to say that your husband had taken a polygraph test. Am I correct?"

She did not reply.

"Am I correct?"

"I don't remember. I was upset."

"And when you and I spoke, after your husband was killed, you didn't mention it then either. Why not?"

"My husband ... my Carlos— He was dead. I wasn't thinking."

"It's been a couple of weeks. It took you all this time to start thinking again?"

Tears streamed down her face.

He hated to ride her, but there wasn't any alternative. Her story was so riddled with holes that he had to confront her before she could think of convenient lies to plug them.

"You told me to see you if I thought of anything else."

"I appreciate that you're here, Ms. Valez. I just need to know you're absolutely certain about this."

"I wouldn't have come if I wasn't sure."

"Tell me something. If your husband thought Ken Parker might kill him, why was he at Parker's apartment building?"

"I don't know," she whispered.

"Who else have you spoken to about this?"

"I don't remember." She huddled in her chair as if he were attacking her.

"Think about it. I have time. Would you like a cup of coffee?"

She shook her head.

He stood, walked across the room, and poured himself a cup of decaf. He kept an eye on Alicia as he stirred in the no-fat creamer. Her story didn't hold water, but it was the closest thing he had to a real break so far. After he thought she had had enough time to consider the question, he returned to his desk and sat down.

"Okay. Who have you discussed this with?"

"No one. Carlos talked to me about it, but I didn't tell anyone else."

"Not even your father-in-law? You're still living at his house, aren't you?"

"I'm still living there, but no, I haven't talked to him about it."

"So you're telling me that you told *no one* about the extortion attempt and death threat before now?"

"Yes."

"Weren't you worried about your husband?"

"Carlos said it would be okay. I believed him."

He looked at her doubtfully. "Ms. Valez, your husband was found dead at the apartment complex of a man he had fought with only days before. That's a fact. A reasonable person might suspect that man of killing him. *You* might suspect it. And, knowing that no arrests have been made, you might be tempted to come forward with a lie to help the case along."

"It's not a lie!"

"You have to be completely truthful with me. Otherwise, you could be in a lot of trouble. Obstruction of justice, perjury—"

"I'm telling the truth!"

He nodded as he pulled a report form from his desk. "Okay, Ms. Valez. Let's go through it again."

As Ken drove into his complex's parking lot, he saw a car in his space. A police cruiser. Shit.

He pulled into a visitor space and hurried up the stairs to his apartment. The door was wide open. Voices came from inside. He entered to see a pair of uniformed officers going through his kitchen drawers. Gant stepped from the hallway.

"Hello, Mr. Parker."

"What's going on?"

Gant presented a document with an official-looking seal on it. "Search warrant. For your car too. Is it downstairs?"

Ken waved toward the open door. "Help yourself."

His mind raced. What could they find in here? Anything that could connect him to Myth or Sabini?

Or Don Browne? That's all he would need.

The officers emptied the contents of his kitchen drawers onto the floor.

"You guys don't clean up after yourselves, do you?"

Gant shook his head. "Sorry."

"That's okay. It'll force me to get off my ass and finally straighten up around here. What are you looking for? Maybe I can help."

"Murder weapon."

"Can't help."

Ken opened the sliding glass door and stepped onto his balcony.

Gant joined him. "Carlos Valez's widow says you threatened her husband's life."

"It was the other way around. *He* came after *me,* remember?"

"She also says her husband failed your polygraph test because he wouldn't pay you off."

"Bullshit. I don't take bribes."

"Been offered many?"

"A few."

"It seems like a way for an Answer Man to make a lot of extra money."

"I wouldn't be living *here* if I did."

Gant looked at the gray, cloudy sky. It was about to rain. "Her statement is going to take this thing to an entirely new level. If there's anything you want to tell me, you'd better do it now."

"I've told you everything already."

"Okay. Just so you know."

"Does her statement give you the right to trash my place?"

"I could have gotten a search warrant at any time. But her statement made it mandatory."

"She's lying."

"Perhaps." Gant went inside.

The search was over in less than an hour, owing more to the sparseness of Ken's apartment than to any particular efficiency of the officers on duty. They, of course, left empty-handed, but only after photographing each and every knife in the silverware drawer. None was even close to the size and character of the blade suspected in both Sabini's and Valez's murders.

The officers gave Ken a card with a number to call in case he discovered anything broken as a result of the search. The cops could not promise the department would reimburse him, but at least the complaint would be logged. Ken immediately threw the card away.

An entirely new level, Gant had said. Whatever that meant. Police surveillance? Phone taps, maybe? Ken wasn't sure. But he knew it was more dangerous than ever to contact Myth.

He felt his pocket for the name and address Warner had given him. Jessica Barrett. She didn't live far away.

Maybe he'd take a drive tonight.

Heading east past Peachtree City, Ken ventured into a section of De Kalb County he had never explored. The neighborhoods deteriorated, then slightly improved as the afternoon sun softened into twilight. What would he do once he found the address? He wasn't sure.

He checked the rearview frequently to make sure he wasn't being followed. Between Michaelson, the police, and whoever tried to dunk him into the lake the other night, he imagined himself leading a veritable parade down the two-lane highway. But he was alone.

To his surprise, the address was on the main thoroughfare of a mobile home community. As he proceeded slowly down the main drag, he noticed the trailer park was a cut above most, with orderly, well-kept lots and tree-lined streets. Still, it did not appear to be the neighborhood of anyone who could afford to hire Myth. He slowed as he approached the address. He stopped. There was a motorcycle parked out front and a light in one of the windows.

As he sat idling, trying to decide what to do, a petite young woman appeared from behind the trailer carrying a laundry basket. She was walking toward the trailer's front door.

Jessica Barrett?

He jumped out of his car and jogged over to the woman. "Jessica Barrett?" he asked.

"Yeah," she replied cautiously, shifting the basket between them.

"What's your interest in Myth Daniels?"

"Who?"

"Myth Daniels."

"Never heard of her." She stepped up to the door, but Ken leaned against it, preventing her from pulling it open.

"I think you have. You requested her data sheet from the Department of Motor Vehicles, didn't you?"

She hit him with a jab to the stomach. While he was off balance, she knocked his hand off the door. He fell forward, cracking his chin against the side of the mobile home.

"Christ!" he yelled.

She jumped inside the mobile home, closing and locking the door behind her.

He kicked a plastic patio chair. He whirled toward a window, where he could see her shadow against the curtain. "I just want to talk, okay?"

No answer.

"Jessica?"

"Did she send you?"

"Who?"

"Myth Daniels."

"No. As far as I know, she doesn't even know about you."

"Then why are you here?"

"Good question," he murmured, more to himself than to her. He stroked his sore chin. He hadn't expected a new set of bruises. "Look, I just want to know what you've found out."

"What's it to you?"

"Is there any other way we can talk about this? It's starting to get dark out here."

The porch light came on.

"Thanks," he said dryly. "I found out about you because I'm doing the same thing. I'm trying to find out what I can about Myth Daniels."

"Why?"

He'd already said more than he probably should have. But if he expected her to be forthcoming, he'd have to pony up some info of his own. Even if he had to make it up.

"Because I'm thinking about hiring her for a big case," he said. "And I'm not sure I can trust her. I've heard rumors."

"What kind of rumors?"

"Unh-unh. You next. And I'm *not* going to talk to you through this window all night."

She was silent for a moment. Then he saw her silhouetted form pick up a cordless phone and dial a number.

He heard her say, "Change your greeting, Marcie, it's getting old. It's me, Hound Dog. I'm about to talk to a guy on my front porch. He drives an MG with the license plate HVK11A."

Ken was impressed. He knew she could not see his license plate at the moment, so she must have glimpsed it before going inside.

She rattled off his physical description and concluded with "If anything happens to me, make sure this guy gets nailed to the wall. Bye."

She hung up the phone, opened the door, and stepped outside. What looked like a thin pile of eight-by-ten photographs and proof sheets were in her hand.

He smiled at her. "Very good. C.Y.A."

"C.Y.A.?"

"Covering Your Ass."

"Scary world out there. What's a girl to do?"

"You're doing it."

"We'll stay outside." She gestured across the street, where a few elderly neighbors were sitting on lawn chairs. "I like their company."

"Fine."

She sat on a patio chair, and Ken righted the chair he had kicked. He sat next to her.

"Do you have a strong stomach?" she asked.

"Yeah."

She handed him the photographs. He thumbed through them, stopping when he realized what he was seeing.

Sabini's murder scene.

There, in grainy black and white, was Sabini's corpse. Ken flipped through the rest of the pictures, pausing at a shot of Myth.

"Where did you get these?"

"Took 'em myself."

"You work for a newspaper?"

"No. I do it for fun."

"Something tells me you're not being sarcastic."

"Something tells you right."

"Okay, so you were there. Why the big investigation? Why Myth Daniels?"

She gave him a suspicious look. "I still don't know if I should be talking to you about this. You could be working for her."

"What if I were?"

"Are you?"

"No. I told you that—"

"Yeah, you told me. I'm just not sure I believe you."

"Worst-case scenario. What could happen if you trust me and I *am* lying to you?"

She thought for a moment. "Well, I wouldn't be telling you anything I'm not prepared to tell her. As a matter of fact, I tried to call her today."

"Then tell me."

She handed Ken the fax of Myth at the Denver crime scene. "Meet Madeleine Walton."

His eyes never left the photo as she related to him the entire story of her investigation. He barely even glanced at the Lexis/Nexis newspaper printouts she handed to him.

After she finished her story, Ken looked away. Lies. Myth had lied to him. Would they ever stop?

"Hey, I'm sorry," she said.

"For what?"

"This isn't just about business, is it?"

He did not reply.

"She's very beautiful," she said, taking back the photos and fax. "But tell me something, what made *you* investigate her?"

"There's a lot about her I don't know."

"Obviously."

"Is this all you got?"

"Yeah. I tried to call her. She wasn't in all day. The last time I called I left a message. I told her secretary my name was Madeleine Walton. I figured that would get her attention."

"I bet it did."

He stood up and walked toward his car. "I gotta go."

"Hey . . ." She rose and took a few steps toward him. "Let me know how it comes out."

"I will. Thanks, Jessica."

"Call me Hound Dog."

Matt Lansing drummed his fingers on the conference table.

Michaelson had deposited him there twenty minutes before, promising—or threatening—a meeting with Herbert Decker. Lansing hated his confrontations with Decker, which almost always ended with the company president screaming at him about something. How would he react this time?

Lansing had withheld information from the company's investigator, and he knew that Decker would not be pleased. It went against everything Vikkers preached to its employees. Commitment. Teamwork. A unified front. The Sabini embezzlement had dealt a blow to the corporation, and this was only packing salt into the wound.

Lansing hadn't asked for any of it. The FBI agent, Lars, had approached him three times, on each occasion affecting a loose, casual demeanor even when he was threatening poverty, prison, and public scorn. The guy acted almost as if he *didn't* want Lansing to cooperate, so he could take him down with the rest of the company.

Vikkers Industries hadn't exactly been supportive either. Although Decker and the investigator maintained that the wireless mike was there only to study the FBI's line of inquiry, Lansing suspected it was also to make sure *he* didn't reveal anything. He patted his chest to make sure the wire was still in place. It had become a habit, like feeling if he still had his wallet.

Damn Herbert Decker.

Lansing stifled a gasp as Decker walked into the room. Don't be a wuss, he told himself. Decker couldn't read minds, even if it sometimes seemed like it.

"Relax, Lansing. Stress kills, don't you know that?"

Then why hadn't this job killed him years ago? Lansing rolled his shoulders, trying to loosen up.

Decker sat on the other side of the conference table. "Ted Michaelson said you and he had an interesting conversation."

"Yes. Do you want me to recap it for you?"

"Not necessary. He told me what I needed to know. Did you give him the complete list of executives the FBI wants you to put them in touch with?"

"Yes."

"What took you so long to tell us about this? The FBI may have gotten to these people by now."

Lansing cleared his throat. He wasn't supposed to mention the polygraph exam to Decker. That was probably to protect the company from liability since his taking the test violated the terms of the Employee Polygraph Protection Act. Michaelson told Lansing to pretend he had decided to come clean on his own, which would make him look better anyway. "I was confused," Lansing said. "The feds have a way of screwing with your mind, I gotta tell you."

Decker's face turned red. "You fucking moron. Would you accept that excuse from one of your subordinates?"

Probably, Lansing wanted to say. Instead, he replied, "Of

course not. That's why I'm talking to you now. Don't I get some points for that?"

Decker patted his pathetic comb-over as he suddenly became calm. The change in mood frightened Lansing even more than the angry outburst. That, at least, had been predictable.

"Don't worry," Decker said. "You'll get *exactly* what you deserve."

CHAPTER 14

Mark was right, Hound Dog thought. Her inquiry into Myth Daniels's life suddenly seemed childish. It was all a big game to her. But after meeting her visitor, she felt ashamed. He obviously had a reason for needing to know, and his pain was real. The truth mattered to him in a way it never could to her.

She took solace in thinking she may have helped him with her information, but it wasn't enough. She felt rotten.

Maybe she'd skip the scanner surfing tonight.

Or maybe not. She wasn't going to feel better hanging out in the trailer, that was for sure. After flip-flopping on the issue a few times, she finally attached her multiband scanner to the belt of her black jeans, pulled on her helmet and denim jacket, and set out on her motorcycle at ten-thirty P.M.

There wasn't a lot of activity on the streets—a few non-fatal accidents and a drug buy gone bad that ended in the shooting death of a seventeen-year-old boy. Hound Dog was squeezing off pictures of the boy's family when his bereaved mother, a hugely overweight woman in her late thirties, started screaming and had to be restrained from attacking her. Hound Dog backed off. At the urging of the police on the scene, she hopped on her motorcycle and left.

She didn't get a shot of the body, but that was no great

loss. She had seen plenty of dead bodies. Her first had been a teenage girl who was the victim of a serial rapist. Hound Dog had brought her camera but couldn't bring herself to use it. She stood on a bluff overlooking the crime scene, just sobbing. It was the last time she had cried at a crime scene. She still refused to photograph dead rape victims whose bodies were exposed; it would be like perpetuating the rape, becoming an accessory after the fact.

Cruising east on Ponce De Leon Avenue, she spotted the blinking neon FRESH DOUGHNUTS sign at Krispy Kreme, meaning a batch had just come out of the oven. She rolled to a stop near the shop's plate glass windows. The harsh fluorescent lights were so intense, she had to squint to see inside. At the counter were the usual four A.M. customers: prostitutes, bartenders, a homeless guy. But no cops. Good, she thought. Officers on the graveyard shift made a habit of harassing scanner geeks, and they knew her. She had to be especially careful of traffic violations, since the police relished each and every opportunity to ticket her.

She dismounted, went inside, and bought a doughnut and a cup of coffee. She kept her scanner on as she sat at the counter. Her right earphone dug uncomfortably into her ear, and after checking it, she discovered the foam had almost worn through. She put it back on, mostly to discourage conversation from the guys staring at her a few seats away.

A 10-71 crackled over the scanner. A shooting.

"Murphy sixteen, Murphy sixteen. Code 10-71. Unidentified white male wounded, paramedics en route. Perpetrator at large. 15614 Corsair, repeating, 15614 Corsair. Please respond."

Hound Dog felt as if she were yanked outside her body, looking at herself from above.

Mother of God.

She grabbed her helmet and bolted for the door.

It was her home address.

•   •   •

Hound Dog pushed her motorcycle harder than she had ever pushed it before, tearing through deserted streets, through red lights, through a construction site. She had to get home.

To Mark.

No further details came through on the scanner; police had not reached the scene yet. She gritted her teeth and roared through an intersection.

Mark had to be okay. He just had to.

She raced into the trailer park, catching sight of two sets of police flashers in front of her home. She threw the bike down and ran for the open front door, pushing past the half-dozen neighbors standing outside. An officer tried to block her.

She yelled at him. "Goddammit, I live here! Where's Mark?"

Before the officer could answer, she slipped past him. Mark was lying on the floor.

He wasn't moving.

His white shirt was soaked with blood.

Hound Dog dropped to her knees and screamed.

Another officer tried to lift her up, but she shook free and scrambled toward Mark's motionless body. She grabbed his hands.

Ice cold.

Not him, not Mark. Jesus Christ almighty, not Mark.

Come on, honey. Please . . . don't die, don't leave.

She sobbed, bunching the bloodstained shirt in her hands.

A beefy officer knelt beside her. "Ma'am, an ambulance is on the way. We're gonna help him, but you have to step back. Okay?"

Her face was so twisted in anguish, she could barely see through the narrow slits between her eyelids. "Please, you've got to let me—"

She couldn't make herself choke out the words. She finally let the officer pull her away as she heard the approaching sirens of a paramedic unit.

• • •

In the hours that followed, Hound Dog remembered only that she talked to a great many people about the same things over and over. Doctors, nurses, paramedics, police officers . . . No one was listening. She kept telling them they had to save Mark, but they were ignoring her.

He went into surgery at five thirty-five A.M. While she waited, police officers took her statement. A picture of the event began to take shape: Someone had broken into the trailer and was surprised by Mark coming home from work at four-fifteen A.M. They scuffled, and during the fight Mark was shot once in the stomach with a handgun. The assailant escaped to an unseen car just outside the trailer park.

Most of this information was gleaned from an insomniac neighbor who heard the gunshot and squealing tires. The neighbor investigated, found Mark, and phoned the police.

Thank God, Hound Dog thought. Otherwise, Mark might not have been found until daybreak. Then it would have been too late.

It might still be too late, she thought.

"No news is good news," one of the nurses quipped, and Hound Dog supposed she was right. But as the morning wore on, she looked toward every person in a scrub suit for some sign, any sign.

None looked back.

Ken was eating lunch at the corner deli when the television blared news of the shooting. He almost missed the story entirely, registering it only when he glanced up and saw the mobile home he had visited the evening before. There it was: the two plastic lawn chairs, the plant boxes, the awning . . .

He rushed from the deli and jumped into his car. His first fear was that something had happened to Jessica Barrett, but the gunshot victim was actually a twenty-three-year-old male in critical condition at St. Vincent's Hospital. Apparently it was a botched burglary attempt.

Apparently.

Ken arrived at St. Vincent's, parked his car, and followed a confusing series of colored stripes on the hospital floor until he arrived at Intensive Care. He found Hound Dog alone in the waiting area. She looked like she should be in a hospital bed herself, he thought.

"I heard what happened, Jessica."

"I told you to call me Hound Dog," she said dully. "What the hell are you doing here?"

"I thought this might somehow be related."

"Related to what?"

"To what we were talking about last night."

"It's not my fault."

"I didn't say it was. I'm just thinking—"

"Goddammit, it was a burglar! That's all. There've been four other trailers broken into during the last month."

"Okay, fine," he said, trying to soothe her. "What was stolen?"

"Nothing. Mark surprised whoever it was before they could take anything."

Ken sat next to her. She had started crying. Now her head bobbed wearily and finally came to rest on his shoulder.

"Do you have any family?" he asked.

"They live in Illinois, and I can't call them."

"Why not?"

"Because I'm supposed to be in North Carolina. My parents think I'm an English lit major at Duke University."

He stayed until she had pulled herself together and convinced him she was okay. So different from the tough number he had met the night before, Ken thought. Poor kid.

He drove downtown as he considered the unpleasant possibilities. If *he* found out about Hound Dog's investigation of Myth, anyone could. The scanner geek had not been exactly secretive about her actions, and her carelessness just may have gotten her boyfriend shot.

It was time to confront Myth.

Ken arrived at the closest of the courthouse parking lots, and after some driving around, he found her car. He parked, waited, and watched. Within half an hour Myth stepped into the lot and headed for her car. Ken jumped out and approached her.

"Hi," she said nervously. "What's wrong?"

"You tell me."

He filled her in on Gant's searching his apartment, which Myth quickly dismissed as an act of desperation. She was also unconcerned about the statement by Valez's widow.

"Hearsay," she assured him. "Most of it is inadmissible. Anything else?"

"Yeah. How come I've never been introduced to Madeleine Walton?"

He wasn't sure what kind of reaction he had expected, but there was no gasp, no jerking of the head, not even an arched eyebrow. She looked no more disturbed than she would if he had asked for the time.

"Because Madeleine Walton doesn't exist anymore."

"What the hell does that mean?"

"Exactly what it sounds like. How do you know about this?"

"I have my sources."

"I need to know."

"There are some things *I* need to know. Like who you really are. What you're hiding from. I'm not going to let you dick me around."

"Is that what you think I'm doing?"

"I think it's a distinct possibility. Start talking."

"Ken, not here. We can meet someplace else. Maybe in a couple of days—"

"Bullshit! Tell me right here, right now. Or I go to the police and spill everything."

"You won't do that."

"The shit's starting to come down on me hard, and I'm

not going to stand here without an umbrella. Tell me what I need to know right now, then we'll talk about what I will or will not do."

She cast a nervous glance around. "I've been honest with you, Ken. I told you I'm not happy about the person I used to be. I—I killed a man. In self-defense. There was a scandal. . . . Some people thought it was premeditated."

"But you were never charged."

"You know about this too?"

"Yes."

"Some reporters started dredging up my parents' death, speculating that maybe I killed them too. Can you believe that? I knew if ever I was going to make something of my life, I had to be someone else. So I left Madeleine Walton behind and became Myth Daniels."

"Myth," he said. "Appropriate name you chose for yourself."

"None of the top law firms would have hired a woman with my past. That's one of the reasons I struck out on my own. I was constantly afraid I'd be discovered."

"And now you have been."

"How did you find this out?"

"I think I've had about enough. I want off this ride."

"Before you make up your mind ... we should give some more attention to that idea you had."

"What idea was that?"

"Looking for the money."

Myth raked her hair back, flipping it over her shoulder. "Enough time has gone by that I think it's all right. I have some ideas."

Now she had some ideas. When he started to back away, she began to come closer. "Let's hear them," he said.

"I need time to come up with a plan. Can we meet in a few days?"

Part of him wanted to tell her to go to hell. But only part of him.

He nodded. "When?"

"I'll call and let you know. We'll have to be careful though. You're still getting a lot of attention from the police."

"Bumping off customers *can't* be good for business."

The receptionist turned off her television as Ken walked in. She was the only one in the building who dared mention it to him, though he knew it was on everybody's lips.

"Neither is a receptionist who watches TV on the job."

"If you had more clients coming through, I wouldn't have to. It gets boring around here. Except when the cops come and interrogate me."

"They can interrogate all they want. It doesn't mean I did it."

"Don't say that. I *like* thinking that you did it. And so does everyone else."

"Why?"

"It gives you a little style. It shows you have more initiative than we gave you credit for. And it also gives us something to talk about. Something besides the copier that still doesn't work."

"I'm glad I can oblige."

"Watch out for Downey though. He's looking for a reason to kick you out."

"So what else is new? Anyway, I'm paid up through next month."

"This isn't about money. He thinks you're degrading the character of the building."

"Is that why he leases offices to a phone sex service on the first floor?"

"We call it a *telemarketing* firm. Besides, Downey's their biggest customer."

Ken smiled and walked back to his office. There was a message on the machine from Margot. She rarely called him during work hours, so it might be important.

He dialed her work number and she answered. "Margot Aronson."

"Shrug off the suit mode. It's me."

She laughed. "Easier said than done. Where did you get this hunk of metal you wanted analyzed?"

He sat up straight. "You got the results back?"

"It's an aluminum-based alloy that no one's ever seen before. How did you get it?"

By rooting through the urine-soaked pockets of a dead guy, Ken thought. He didn't answer her question. "So what's so special about it?"

"Well, no one thinks it's a piece from an alien spacecraft, if that's what you mean. But it's a unique formulation, light yet strong, and it's not commercially available."

"What about those numbers and letters etched on the side?"

"They're probably production codes to tell which batch this sample came from. One of the guys at the lab thinks Lyceum Metals uses those particular codes."

Lyceum Metals. The company Vikkers was merging with. Ken jotted down the name on a scratch pad. Interesting, but still nothing to indicate why Don Browne was murdered.

"I don't suppose you would care to tell me what this is all about?" she said.

Before he could reply, a thunderous crash sounded behind him.

He spun around.

White-hot flames leapt into the air, singeing his eyebrows. He couldn't breathe. It was as if all the air in the room had been sucked out, replaced by thick black smoke.

It was a firebomb.

He stood and pushed his chair into the wall of fire.

Ducking low, he raised his arms, shielding his face. He bobbed and weaved, dancing with the flames as he stumbled for the door.

Something hit hard against his thigh.

The polygraph stand.

He gripped its handles and pushed onward, the stand's casters sliding across the burning oil-and-gasoline mix.

He rammed the door. It didn't budge.

He tried once more. The hollow-core entranceway cracked.

He charged at it again. And again.

The blaze tore through the office, swirling over the desk, the bulletin board, all around him. . . .

Throwing all his weight behind the stand, he rammed the door repeatedly until with a glorious *crack,* he finally broke through. He hit the floor of the corridor.

Oxygen-hungry flames lunged after him.

He jumped to his feet, twisting and turning in the billowing smoke. He screamed in agony.

The back of his shirt was on fire.

He felt himself being shoved down the hallway, pushed to the floor.

Another roar. Snowflakes falling all around him.

Snowflakes?

Standing over him was a wiry man with a fire extinguisher. The accountant from down the hall.

The man ran toward the flames, trying to contain them in the office. Another man appeared from around the corner, armed with a second extinguisher.

"Get back!" he yelled at Ken. "Get the hell away!"

The men fought the flames, advancing, then retreating as the fire gathered strength.

The fire alarm rang. Shrill, earsplitting.

Tenants emerged from their offices, curious, then panic-stricken. They ran for the stairwells.

Ken pulled himself to his feet, choking on smoke and ash. His back hurt like hell.

He stumbled toward the nearest set of stairs. The others pushed and shoved past him. He didn't remember this many steps. . . .

He still couldn't catch his breath. His eyes stung. He gripped the handrail and followed it down, down, down. . . .

The first floor. Finally.

He staggered to the parking lot, coughing as flakes of soot floated onto the cars around him. He turned to watch the fire.

Already it had spread to the next office, and was in danger of taking out the one after that.

He peeled off his shirt. The wind licked against his burned skin. He slowly sat down, angling his body against the breeze. He was light-headed and nauseated.

He was going into shock.

He fought it by taking slow, deep breaths. The queasiness passed. He looked up, and by the expressions on his neighbors' faces, his back was not a pretty sight.

"I forgot to wear my sunscreen," he muttered.

The fire crew arrived within minutes, and they extinguished the flames with only three offices lost to the blaze. Five, however, were temporarily unusable due to water damage.

Ken allowed the paramedics to salve and bandage his burns, which were diagnosed as first and second degree. While he argued with them about the necessity of having to go to the hospital, the arson investigator arrived.

Ken gave him the full account. The man wrote down the details and promised to call later. He seemed more interested in the characteristics of the fire than in the identity of the arsonist, Ken thought.

He then called Margot back from a pay phone in the parking lot, apologizing for the abrupt end to their call. He didn't mention the fire. She had worried about him enough.

He went to his car, opened the trunk, and found a grass-stained T-shirt rolled up next to the spare tire. He slid it over his head and walked back to his office building. The air was still thick with a sharp, smoky odor that tickled the back of his nose. The smell would probably hang for weeks.

The building's front doors were propped open, and as he walked inside, the first thing he saw was his polygraph. Somebody had moved it downstairs. He ran his hands over the vinyl cover, brushing pools of water onto the floor. He fingered a few places where the vinyl had melted, effectively welding the cover to the polygraph's metal surface.

He ripped the cover off with one fierce yank. The machine seemed okay.

The damned thing was indestructible.

"You burned down my building, you bastard."

Ken looked up to see Downey. The manager wasn't joking.

"Impossible," Ken replied. "This place is a hundred percent asbestos."

"Very funny. I'll start laughing when you're out of here on your ass. Maybe even in jail."

"You're in for a long wait. By the way, I need a new office. I understand mine's being remodeled."

"Sorry. Got no place to put you."

"Then we'll go to court. I'll sue you."

"Sue me? For what?"

"For the suffering I just endured in this deathtrap of a building. I'll trot out all the building code violations."

Ken was immediately relocated to a slightly smaller office on the short end of the L-shaped building. Downey opened the door, threw the keys at him, and stomped away. Ken rolled his polygraph into the empty room. He tried the light switch. Sickly blue-white fluorescent lights flickered and buzzed.

He glanced around. It was a dingy, depressing office with green paint chipping from the walls. Just like the old one. He snuffed the lights and left.

He drove to the nearest record store, where he found a copy of *Creative Loafing,* Atlanta's alternative weekly newspaper. He walked back to his car, flipping to the classified section. As he sat behind the wheel, the burns on his back itched, and he could feel a stinging sensation as the topical medication wore off. He shifted in his seat because of both his itch and the discomfort at what he was contemplating.

The classifieds were open to the "firearms" heading.

He had never owned a gun before, but he had taken a marksmanship class to satisfy a phys ed requirement during his short college career. And now, with two attempts on his life in the space of a week, it seemed like a good idea to carry some protection. Buying secondhand meant he wouldn't have to ride out the mandatory waiting period. Five days, was it?

He circled two possibilities, walked to a pay phone, and dialed. No answer.

He tried the other number, and it was answered by a friendly-sounding guy in nearby Smyrna. They agreed to meet that afternoon.

Hound Dog didn't want to leave the hospital. It had been hours since the operation, and she wanted to be there when, not if, Mark regained consciousness.

But the police had urged her to go home and report anything that was missing. It might help them find the shooter.

She made a lightning-quick trip to the trailer, politely brushing off her well-meaning neighbors who wanted details of the morning's excitement. She glanced around the ransacked mobile home. Papers and photographs were strewn about, and every drawer had been pulled out, emptied, and cast aside. Her stomach turned when she saw the stain on the linoleum floor. Mark's blood.

It was so frustrating. When there was something to be done, some action to be taken, she was always ripe for the challenge. But when all she could do was sit and hope, she was completely out of her element. A victim-in-waiting.

Mark should *be* here, making love to her or maybe just doing his homework. She found one of his shirts on the floor, a big Georgia Bulldogs sweatshirt. She pulled off her shirt and slipped on Mark's. It felt good. It smelled like him.

She found his gym bag and packed a change of clothes, remembering to take his address book. She had to call his friends and family.

She looked around the trailer again. She couldn't see that anything had been stolen, but it was obvious the burglar was looking for something.

For what?

She didn't want to believe it had anything to do with Myth Daniels. If that were the case, what had happened to Mark was her fault. She couldn't live with that.

But why hadn't anything been stolen? The intruder had obviously taken a lot of time to search the place. Time that could have been spent carting off the television, stereo system, and the silver candlesticks that had belonged to Mark's mother. Anything of value was untouched.

Only the papers and photographs were disturbed.

What if Ken was right?

She went to her darkroom bench, pulled up the tarp, and looked underneath. There, sitting where she had put them the night before, were the photographs she took of Sabini's murder scene, plus the faxed Madeleine Walton picture.

She picked up the photos, put them into the gym bag, and left the trailer.

CHAPTER 15

Ken took careful aim with his Smith & Wesson N-Frame
.44 special. He squeezed the trigger, and the gun kicked
back as the roar echoed off a hillside.

He was at a rural dump site, where locals deposited
old refrigerators, water heaters, and other junk. Forty
feet in front of him was a row of beer cans set up on an over-
turned refrigerator for target practice. His first shot was a
miss.

It was an overcast day, and a sprinkling rain began as he
lined up his next shot. Staring through the sight, he shut
one eye, even though that would have meant points off in
marksmanship class. Any gunslinger worth his salt keeps
both eyes open. Maybe later.

He squeezed off the shot, blowing away the second can.

He quickly aimed for the next one, squeezed, and it, too,
was shredded.

He readjusted his grip on the handgun. It had a heavier
kick than others he had used. The man he bought it from
was a little guy, slight of build, whose main achievement in
life was having gone to high school with Julia Roberts. He
sold the gun for two hundred and twenty-five dollars. Ken
had no idea if it was a good deal or not.

He aimed for the next target, pulled the trigger, and
nicked the can, causing it to spin wildly on the refrigerator.

He tried firing after a few quick draws. Not only did he

miss the cans, but had there been a barn in front of him, he doubted he would have hit its side.

"The Sundance Kid I ain't," he said out loud, his voice ringing eerily in the deserted field.

He discarded the empty shell casings and reloaded.

As he continued his target practice, he was struck by an odd sensation. He thought holding and firing the gun would give him a feeling of power, of control. But he felt just the opposite. Relying on this gun made him feel weak, and therefore strangely vulnerable. Maybe this was why he had never owned one before.

After thirty minutes, he felt reasonably secure in his marksmanship abilities. So he could hit a few tin cans. But could he hit a moving, breathing target?

It was dusk as Ken climbed the stairs to his apartment. With the cardboard box containing the gun tucked under his left arm, all he could think about was getting to bed. His right leg still hurt, and his back was stinging. It had been a rough few days.

He unlocked the door, stepped inside, and stopped.

He heard something.

A whisper. Some shuffling.

He turned to see several figures huddled in the darkness, silhouetted against his living room window.

They were moving toward him.

Ken knelt low and tore into the box, struggling to pull out his new revolver. He clawed at the Styrofoam packing material, breaking and crumbling it as the pieces wedged under his fingernails. The figures moved closer. He gripped the gun and waved it in front of him.

"Stand back! Move and I'll splatter your goddamned brains. You hear me? I got a gun!"

The gun's shiny barrel caught what little light there was in the room.

The figures were still advancing, and he took aim at the one closest to him. He gripped the gun harder, and . . .

The lights came on.

"Holy shit . . ."

The room was decorated with balloons and streamers.

The first person he saw was Margot. She was coming from his kitchen with a candle-laden cake.

As he looked around, he saw almost everyone he knew. Twenty-five friends wearing party hats and holding noisemakers. His flag football buddies, their spouses, and friends from Elwood's.

"Happy birthday to you . . ." the guests started to sing, but their voices trailed off as they saw Ken kneeling with the gun.

Dead silence.

Some of the guests started to laugh. Just a chuckle at first, but it built until almost everyone was roaring.

Colby, whom Ken had squarely in his sights, stepped forward. "How did you know?" he whined. "Aw, crap. Bill leaked it, didn't he?"

Ken shrugged as he looked at Bill. "You never could keep a secret, Fred."

Bill went along. "I sure tried, Barney." Bill looked around at the group and cut loose with a near-perfect imitation of Ken. *"I'll splatter your goddamned brains!"*

The gang roared again.

As Ken stood up, he glanced at Margot. She wasn't laughing.

In the next two hours, more guests arrived and the party went into high gear. The refrigerator was soon overflowing with beer and wine, and eardrum-shattering music threatened to raise the neighbors' ire. Ken, drinking both beer and Jägermeister, proceeded to get wasted. It was the only way he could get through the evening; he wasn't in the mood for a party, particularly not one in his honor.

Margot was avoiding him, even shunning eye contact from across the room.

Bill finally approached him in a reasonably secluded corner of the apartment. "That was a grand entrance."

Ken smiled. He hadn't been this drunk in a long time.

"You didn't know about the party," Bill whispered. "Not from me or anyone. What the hell's going on?"

"I didn't know *who* was in here. I just wanted to defend myself."

"Since when do you carry a gun?"

"Since today. A birthday present to myself."

"Why?"

Ken didn't respond. He finished his drink and surveyed the party. "This is cruel. You know how much I hate birthdays."

"Talk to me. Before you get totally hammered."

"Too late."

"Are you dealing drugs? Something like that?"

"Hell, no."

"Then what? Why are you so jumpy? Are you still upset about what happened with the boat the other night?"

Ken looked at Margot through the crowd. "Your wife's avoiding me. She knows something's up."

"Nah. She thought you were joking around with the gun, like everyone else."

"She didn't believe that."

"Sure she did. If she didn't, she'd be here talking to you like I am."

Ken shook his head. "She doesn't want to talk to me because she doesn't want to hear me lie. You know, Bill, that's why I lost her."

"You lied to her?"

"No. I lied to myself. All the time. It's a bad habit."

He leaned back against the counter, struggling to maintain his balance. He managed a crooked grin.

"A habit I need to break . . . if I want to stay alive."

Squirt.

Ken woke up on the sofa with a nasty hangover. And was that water squirting in his face?

Squirt.

Ouch.

His whole body ached. His head throbbed.

The morning sun blinded him even though his shades were drawn.

Squirt.

He looked up to see Hound Dog standing over him, aiming a water-filled Windex bottle at his face.

"Are you awake?" she said.

"No."

Squirt.

"Stop. Please."

"Are you awake?" she repeated.

"Yes."

"Good answer."

Ken sat up. He glanced around the apartment. It was amazingly clean, considering that a party had been there only hours before. Margot probably led the cleanup crew.

He turned to Hound Dog. "How the hell did you get in here?"

"I knocked, and you said, 'Come in!' The door was unlocked."

"Oh. I guess I wasn't quite awake yet." He rubbed his cheeks. "I had a birthday party here last night, and things got out of control."

"Belated happy birthday."

"Thanks. How's your boyfriend?"

"Hanging on. No more, no less. No one can tell me if he's going to make it. They have my cellular number if he wakes up . . . or anything."

"Try not to dwell on the 'or anything.'"

"I won't. That's why I'm here. I want to find who did this to him."

Ken looked at her. She was dead serious. She carried herself with such strength and confidence, yet she had a face that was so youthful and delicate.

"What makes you think I can help you find who shot him?" Ken rubbed his temples. Dull, throbbing pain.

"I've had some time to think about it. Maybe you were right. Maybe it *did* have something to do with Myth Daniels. You know her and I don't, and you must have some reason for suspecting her."

"I just offered her up as a possibility. You were digging around in something she'd rather keep hidden."

"There's more to it than that, isn't there?"

Ken didn't answer.

She shoved his legs aside and sat on the sofa. "I want to know everything, Ken. I let you slide by on that half-assed story about hiring her for a case. We both know that was a lie. I think I deserve to know the truth. Don't you?"

He was silent for a moment. Since this whole mess began, he hadn't discussed it with anyone but Myth. Not with Margot. Not with Bill. Not with Bobby. Now this young woman wanted some answers.

She was entitled, he thought. She had suffered for it.

He told her everything. About Myth, about Burton Sabini, about the money.

Hound Dog listened intently, nodding occasionally.

"Do you think Myth Daniels is behind your firebombing and boat attack?"

"I don't know. I'm watching my back though."

She sighed. "Mark told me not to do this. I wish I had listened to him."

"You can't think that way. No matter what, it's not your fault."

"I've been in scary situations before. I've seen some pretty wild things. But it was always *my* neck on the line, no one else's. It didn't even occur to me that I might cause someone else to be hurt, least of all Mark."

She sat down on the couch as tears welled in her eyes. She was reverting to that scared kid in the hospital waiting room.

Ken quickly changed the subject. "Why do you do it?"

"You mean the scanner surfing?"

"Yeah."

"I don't know. Why do some people jog seventy miles a week? Why are some people addicted to the Net?"

"Is it something you *have* to do?"

"Like an obsession? I don't think so. It started when I was in high school. I used to listen to a police scanner my grandfather gave me. When I moved away from home, I started going to the places I'd hear about. Then I started taking pictures, and it kind of grew from there."

"Unusual hobby."

"It gives my life ... *texture*. I grew up in the northern suburbs of Chicago. My family always had a lot of money, and they used it to shelter me from everything that didn't belong in their charmed little world. I never even saw a cemetery until I was in high school."

"You're lucky."

"Yeah, maybe. But I was a boring, insipid little girl turning into a boring, insipid young adult. There are enough of those around already."

" 'Boring' is not a word I'd use to describe you." He added, " 'Insipid' neither."

"Thanks for tacking that on. I'm grateful for what my parents gave me. I love them, but I need to go my own way right now."

"You're certainly doing that. Just how do you make your parents believe that you're a college student in North Carolina?"

She smiled. "What a tangled web we weave ... When I decided to leave, I couldn't bring myself to tell them. They would have freaked. I was there on scholarship, so money isn't an issue. I lived in a house off-campus, and my old roommates take my parents' calls, phone me with the messages, and forward any mail from them. And my family has never expressed any desire to visit me at school. It's been amazingly easy to pull off."

"If you say so."

Hound Dog thought for a moment. "It seems to me you're already doing a good job of checking Myth Daniels's paper history. What if I take it a step further? Talk to some people, maybe follow her a bit, see who she's talking to?"

"I can't let you do that."

"You're not *letting* me do anything. It's my decision. If she's the reason Mark is in that hospital room, I want to know. I'll share whatever I find with you, and you can do the same with me. We'll be partners."

Ken felt uneasy, but a part of him liked having someone to work with. He suddenly felt less alone, less isolated. "You could go to the police," he said.

"And tell them what? I'll wait until I have proof."

She stood and bounded toward his kitchen.

"What are you doing?"

She opened his refrigerator. "I know a great hangover cure. Got any relish?"

Breaking and entering.

That's exactly what he was going to do, Ken realized. He was parked across the street from Don Browne's house, which had been for sale even before the man's death. A call to the Realtor had told him that the house was unoccupied, and a quick glance through a window told him that the house was still fully furnished. And now he was going to break in like a common thief.

Ken spent a few moments trying to talk himself out of it. What did he expect to find? Surely the police had already investigated.

But the police didn't know about Sabini's stolen data files. Maybe there was something in that house that would tell him why Don Browne was killed, while the other executives with Sabini's data were spared.

It was worth the risk.

Ken walked toward Browne's house with the Super Soaker squirt rifle he had just purchased at Target. He glanced around as he approached the garage doors. No one was watching.

He inserted the Super Soaker barrel into the garage door

opener's key receptacle. As he squeezed the trigger, water blasted into the key mechanism and conducted a charge between contact switches. The motor kicked on and the door rose to a fully opened position.

Wow. Ken looked at the squirt rifle with newfound respect. He had seen the trick on the evening news, but he wasn't sure it would actually work. How many burglars had learned the trick the same way?

He threw down the Super Soaker and walked through the garage. He tried the door into the house. Unlocked, just as he had hoped. Real estate agents hadn't bothered to secure it, probably assuming the locked garage doors would be enough. Ken pushed a wall switch and brought the garage door back down.

He stepped inside the house. The air was still and musty. The kitchen was first on his tour, and he proceeded to check out the dining room, living room, and two of the bedrooms. He moved quietly, as if the slightest sound might alert the neighbors. Even the carpet rustling beneath his feet unsettled him.

Finally he found a home office, or what could be better described as *half* an office. The other half was a mini-museum of data processing equipment, dating from the dawn of the personal computer. Ken recognized a mid-seventies Altair and an early-eighties Apple II, but Browne's most recent system seemed to be an IBM. Ken turned on the computer and waited for it to boot up. Would Browne have opened Sabini's data files on his home computer? There was a chance, Ken thought. It would probably be safer than loading them onto his system at work.

Ken pointed and clicked his way to the directory. There were 1700 files in the system, and he didn't know the name of the one he wanted. He scrolled through the list, looking for any names that would ring a bell. There was no appearance of Sabini, Vikkers, or other likely possibilities.

But there was a file named POCKET.PGM.

Pocket program? That was the phrase Keogler had used.

Ken clicked on it. Hundreds of lines of programming code appeared, annotated by yellow boxes of text. The code itself was indecipherable, but the annotations were fairly clear. They were Browne's step-by-step analysis of the programming code, and several conclusions. As Ken read, he saw a few key words: VIKKERS PRO-FORMA. IMPLANTED DATA. ERRONEOUS INFORMATION.

Browne had known about the pocket program.

He knew the figures were wrong.

But there was more. It wasn't just financial figures that were faked, but test results. According to Browne's notations, lab reports were also inserted by the pocket program. The reports suggested that Lyceum Metals' highly anticipated new alloy formulation, RC-7, would become brittle in subzero temperatures.

It was one of the many items Browne had labeled "ERRONEOUS?" with a yellow text box.

Maybe Browne was trying to take the question mark away from the notation.

Maybe the metal sample in his file drawer was RC-7.

Maybe that's what got him killed.

CHAPTER 16

Hound Dog sat in an oak-paneled phone booth on the hospital's first floor, waiting for Dorothy Weiss to answer the phone. Weiss was the mother of the young man Myth Daniels had shot in Denver. Hound Dog knew she should have called from home, where she could have recorded the conversation on her answering machine. But after an uneventful day of tracking Myth Daniels, she decided to call on her way to visit Mark.

"Hello?" a frail voice answered.

"Dorothy Weiss?"

"Yes?"

"My name is Susan Flesher. You don't know me, but I was a friend of your son's. We went to high school together. I've been in Chicago for the past few years, and I ran into someone who told me Charles had been . . ." Hound Dog's voice trailed off.

"Killed," the woman finished for her.

"Yes. I'm sorry, Ms. Weiss. I know it's been a long time and you may not feel like talking about it, but I'm curious to know what happened."

"Who did you say you were?"

"Susan Flesher. Charles may have mentioned me."

"No, I can't say he did."

"Oh. That's all right. I probably didn't mean that much to him." Hound Dog instantly despised the self-pitying wimp she was portraying for this woman's benefit. But if it made her talk, it would be worth it.

"What do you want to know, dear?"

"Who killed him?"

"A woman he had been seeing."

"I heard that."

"Her name was Madeleine Walton."

"But she shot him in self-defense, right?"

"No. In retribution."

"Retribution for what?"

"For raping her."

Hound Dog was surprised at the frank admission. "You don't think she made that up?"

The woman sighed. "I should think that, shouldn't I? He was my son. But I believe the best way to honor the dead is to learn from their lives. I knew Charles. He'd been in trouble before. There were other women, other incidents. This was just the only one that made it to the district attorney's office."

"What happened?"

"I don't know all the particulars."

"I know this isn't easy to talk about, Ms. Weiss."

"Sometimes talking is easier than *not* talking." The woman cleared her throat. "The district attorney threw the case out. Acquaintance rape is difficult to prove. I wished they had tried a little harder."

"You wanted your son to go to jail?"

"There at least he could have gotten some help. Maybe he would have learned his lesson. As it was, the only lesson he learned was at the end of a thirty-eight-caliber revolver."

"Where did it happen?"

"At the woman's condominium complex. She claimed he was coming to attack her again. But I know that's a lie. It was cold-blooded murder."

"What makes you think that?"

"I'm sure he didn't want to attack her again. That wasn't Charles's style. He called her just a few minutes before, probably to gloat about the charges being dropped, though *she* claimed it was to threaten her. I think she purred into the phone, whipped him into a frenzy, and invited him over. Then she murdered him."

"The police didn't agree with you."

"No, and neither did the district attorney's office. I think they were more interested in dating her than prosecuting her."

"Even though she had just killed a man?"

"Maybe *because* she had just killed a man. There are some sick bastards in this world."

Hound Dog finished by thanking the woman and promising to visit her son's grave the next time she was in Denver. She hung up the phone and walked to the elevator. The conversation hadn't convinced her that Myth Daniels was evil incarnate. As Hound Dog punched the button for Mark's floor, she wondered what *she* would do if some guy raped her and got away with it.

Kill him?

No. Mark would do it for her.

But barring that, she wouldn't let it go unpunished. Maybe Myth Daniels was on the right side of this one.

The elevator doors opened, and Hound Dog walked down the hallway. As she stepped into the ICU, she saw a crowd of orderlies at Mark's bed.

Oh, no, she thought. Something's happened.

Hound Dog ran through the room and elbowed past the hulking attendants. "Mark . . ." she cried.

She yanked the curtain aside. But he was fine. Or at least his condition was unchanged. Hound Dog looked up to see what had attracted so much attention.

Three beautiful strippers from his club were leaving flowers, balloons, and signed cards. The room was aglow with white teeth, big hair, dark tans, long legs, giant breasts, and skimpy, form-fitting clothes.

The strippers greeted her with polite "hellos," minus the phony southern accents they put on for the out-of-town

conventioneers. One by one, the women said their good-
byes to the comatose Mark, accompanied by a peck on his
cheek or forehead.

"Bye-bye, big guy."

"See you soon, honey!"

"You better get better!"

The women filed past, whispering good wishes to Hound
Dog as they left the room. The orderlies disbanded, leaving
Hound Dog and Mark alone.

Hound Dog's friends often asked her if it drove her
crazy that Mark worked with so many beautiful naked
women.

"No," she always replied with a smile, "because he's seen
me naked."

She pulled up a chair and sat down. The strippers didn't
really worry her, because she trusted Mark completely. He
always made her feel special. With every look, every em-
brace, and every smile, he let her know that she was terrific,
that he was proud and lucky to have her on his arm.

She wanted him back.

She rested her head on his legs and fell asleep.

Hound Dog woke up at eleven-thirty, her back stiff from
the awkward sleeping position. The nights at Mark's bed-
side were wearing her down. She looked at her jacket and
scanner lying on the chair next to her. It hadn't occurred to
her to scanner-surf since Mark had been shot, but tonight
she had the restless feeling she got when she was away from
the streets for a while.

How twisted was that? No wonder Mark worried about
her.

She picked up the scanner and fingered its smooth surface. Just the touch of it made her feel better. She could slip
on the headphones and listen for a while, but it wouldn't be
enough. It was never enough.

She grabbed her jacket and camera bag. She knew if
there was any change in Mark's condition, the staff would

call her on the cellular. She kissed him on the forehead and left the hospital. Just for a few hours, she promised herself.

She felt herself relax before she even hit I-85. She turned up the scanner to hear it over her motorcycle's roar. Was she addicted to this routine? Did she need it like a narcotic?

Now wasn't the time to wrestle with that one. Just go with it.

Shortly before midnight she found herself in front of a coin-operated amusements company in College Park, where a ring of thieves had tried to cart off several pinball machines and jukeboxes.

She snapped a few shots of the handcuffed perps lined up in front of their moving truck. Four squad cars were surrounding the vehicle, and the pinball machines were spread between the truck and building. A few cops had plugged in a game called Fireball to an exterior power outlet, and they were taking turns playing. Their fun abruptly ceased when they noticed Hound Dog taking their pictures. A plump cop turned toward her and grabbed his genitalia, and she captured this gesture on film too. The cop wasn't pleased.

"Still making friends, I see."

Hound Dog smiled as Laszlo, a fellow scanner geek, approached her. He wore Italian loafers, khakis, and a green Polo shirt, and his camera hung from his neck on a Nikon strap.

"Laszlo, you look like a tourist on vacation."

He attached a flash unit to his camera. "When you come right down to it, aren't we all tourists? Sightseers on that grand vacation called life?"

"You can be the sightseer. I'd rather *live* life."

"By squinting into that viewfinder every night?"

"No. By leading a happy, productive life, free from unfortunate wardrobe choices and dead battery packs."

Laszlo looked down to see that his flash unit ready light wasn't on. "Aw, man. Just my luck. I don't suppose you can loan me one."

"Sorry."

"Well, that cuts *my* night short." He looked at the row of pinball machines in the street. "This would make a great shot. See if you can line 'em up to look like tombstones. With the light of the flashers behind—"

"Already done. You're not the only one around here with a sense of ironic imagery." Hound Dog took a few more pictures, then moved closer to the scene.

"No security system," Laszlo noted. "All that merchandise and nothing to protect it. Pretty dumb, huh?"

Hound Dog remembered her parents' using their household security system to keep tabs on her comings and goings. They would get activity reports faxed to them once a week, and they would know if she came home late or left after the system had been activated. She hated that thing.

Something occurred to her. "Wait a minute," she said.

"What?"

Her mind raced. Was it possible?

"What is it?" Laszlo asked.

Hound Dog ran back to her motorcycle.

Early the next morning, Gant stood in Ken Parker's office parking lot, staring in amazement at the burned-out shell of the polygraph examiner's office. He turned to Joe Downey, the building's crusty old manager.

"You have no idea who may have done this?"

"No idea," he said. "But I'm sure it's that bastard's fault."

"Which bastard?"

"Mr. Lie Detector. Ken Parker."

"You think he threw the bomb?"

"No, but he probably had it coming. Maybe he pissed someone off. He doesn't show a lot of respect for people, you know."

"People like you?"

"People like me, people like anybody!"

Gant looked toward the side of the building. "If someone

had walked up there and thrown it through his window, the fastest way down would be that west stairway, right?"

"I suppose."

"Thanks," he said to Downey. Gant walked toward the building next door.

Ken looked through his blinds, watching Gant as he disappeared around the side parking lot. What was Gant doing? Looking for new and different ways to pin a murder on him, no doubt. Ken had assumed Gant was asking Downey for the location of the new office, but the cop was now headed in the opposite direction.

Ken picked up the notes he had transcribed from Don Browne's computer the day before. Better get these out of sight. He opened the side panel cover of his polygraph, which contained the paper roll. He folded the notes, put them inside, and replaced the cover.

The pieces were finally falling into place. Don Browne had figured out that Vikkers was disseminating phony information, and he had secured a sample of Lyceum Metals' RC-7 formulation to determine if the test results were bogus. Perhaps in the process of investigating the data Browne had called attention to himself and was murdered for his trouble.

There was one person who might talk about this, Ken thought. Matt Lansing. Ever since Michaelson had ushered Lansing out of the polygraph test so quickly, Ken wondered what more the man might have told him. Something about the merger had sent his readings sky-high. If Lansing had really wanted to talk about it, maybe it was time to give him another chance.

Ken left his building, checking to make sure Gant wasn't watching him. The detective was nowhere in sight. Where had he gone? Ken walked to a pay phone and thumbed through the directory for Vikkers Industries' main switchboard. He dialed it and waited for the receptionist to answer.

"Vikkers Industries."

"Matt Lansing, please."

"I'm sorry, Mr. Lansing doesn't work at this office anymore."

Ken hesitated before continuing. "Where may I find him?"

"Let me transfer you to Jason Danvers. He's handling his accounts."

Before Ken could say another word, he found himself on hold. In a few seconds, another voice came on the line.

"Jason Danvers."

"I'm looking for Matt Lansing."

"He's not here, I'm afraid. Is there something I can help you with?"

"Uh, no. Actually, it's personal. Do you know where I can find him?"

Danvers laughed. "No one can find him."

Ken tensed. "What do you mean?"

"He's scouting for new markets. I believe he's in Indonesia right now. If you'd like to leave your name and number, I can pass it along next time he checks in. It may be a while though."

"When do you expect him back?"

"Probably not for a year."

"A year?"

"Yup. He's living on the road. Are you sure there's nothing I can do for you?"

Ken hung up the phone. Vikkers was covering all their bases. They had made sure Lansing wouldn't talk to anyone.

Dammit.

Maybe his "partner" had done better.

Ken paced across the living room of Hound Dog's trailer. "Don Browne knew Sabini's figures were fake."

Hound Dog spoke from behind the canvas walls of her darkroom. "So you think that's why he was killed?"

"As far as I can tell, it's the only thing that separates him from the other people who had the data. Vikkers wanted people to think that Lyceum Metals' new aluminum formulation was a bust."

"So no one else would be interested in partnering with the company."

"Right. So Vikkers implanted fake test results. This merger was worth hundreds of millions to them. They weren't about to let anyone stop them."

Hound Dog emerged from the darkroom and pinned four wet prints to a small clothesline stretched before a rotary fan. The fan was stained by the dried blood of a friend who had tried to duplicate a David Letterman "Stupid Human Tricks" segment. The dumbass had attempted to stop the fan blades with his tongue. Hound Dog swore he still spoke with a lisp.

"Surely you don't think Myth Daniels killed Don Browne," she said.

"I don't know. I don't know if she's the one who tried to kill me. I don't know if she's the one who broke in here that night either."

"Funny you should say that," Hound Dog said. "Because I have a way we might be able to find out."

"How?"

She pointed to her drying photos. "Look."

It took Ken a moment, but he soon realized he was seeing Myth's front yard. Two of the photos showed a security service sign next to the mailbox. Ken read the company name aloud: "APEX ALERT."

"It's an alarm company. If she left her house, they would know it."

"As long as she had activated her system."

Hound Dog nodded, smiling at him.

"I see what you're getting at," Ken said. "You want to see if she was home the night your boyfriend was shot."

"Or the night that boat rammed you."

Ken thought about it. "Good idea, but the alarm company won't turn that information over to just anybody."

"They would turn it over to the police."

"With a court order, maybe."

"Without a court order. Those armed response security firms are mostly ex-cops anyway. They're all one big happy family."

"So how does that help us?"

Hound Dog was already flipping through the yellow pages for Apex Alert's number. She found it, grabbed her cordless phone, and dialed.

"What are you doing?" Ken asked.

"Shhh." She listened, then spoke in a casual tone. "Good afternoon, Linda, this is Tamara Brooking calling from the Atlanta P.D. How are you doing?"

Ken rolled his eyes.

Hound Dog gave him a shove as she walked across the room with her phone. "Good. Listen, I'm looking into a burglary complaint. The victim thinks it may have been a member of her own family, so she doesn't want any paper on this until she knows for sure. I'm keeping it out of the system, but I'd appreciate it if I can get a copy of her activity records for a couple of dates."

Hound Dog picked up a pen and notepad and tossed it to Ken. He scribbled the day and time of the boat attack and flashed it to her.

She nodded and spoke into the phone. "The address is 2525 Sandy Plains Road. I need records for June third and June fifth, all day for both." Hound Dog turned to Ken. "She has me on hold."

"You're nuts."

"I hear that every day of my life."

"I don't doubt it."

"This will work!"

"*That* I doubt."

Hound Dog spoke into the phone again. "Yes? Okay. But can't you read me the entries now? I see. I was just hoping to save myself a trip. I understand."

Ken gave her an "I told you so" look.

Hound Dog wrinkled her nose at him as she continued

speaking into the phone. "Okay, but I won't be able to make it by until this evening. Can you leave it with some-one? Okay. Great. That's Sergeant Tamara Brooking. B-r-o-o-k-i-n-g. Thank you, Linda." Hound Dog hung up the phone.

"Well?"

"The records will be at the guard desk in their lobby. The guard will hand them over when Police Sergeant Tamara Brooking comes in and shows her badge."

"How is that going to happen?"

"It's not. There is no Tamara Brooking."

"Exactly."

"Well, at least we know where the records will be." Hound Dog put the phone back in its cradle. "We'll just have to go steal them."

"*We?*"

Gant huddled with Sergeant Andrew Stanton, watching the video monitor carefully. It had taken most of the day to get a court order freeing up the building surveillance tape from the other morning. If, as Gant suspected, the fire-bomber had made an escape around the back of Ken Parker's building, the camera may have picked it up.

Gant stared at the digital time stamp in the lower right-hand corner of the picture. "We're getting close. It happened at about nine-forty A.M."

Stanton turned the jog shuttle dial, running the video at two times normal speed. He slowed the picture, freeze-framing it when a figure stepped into view. It was a person wearing jeans and a hooded sweatshirt, and carrying a small paper bag.

"There," said Gant. "Can you zoom in?"

"I can do it, but it's pretty blurry. These security camera lenses aren't the fastest in the world. Let me see if I can find a frame that's sharper."

Stanton shuttled back and forth on the tape, but none of the images were noticeably more defined than the other. He zoomed in on the face, but the result was a diffused black and white mess.

Gant sighed. "Let's go forward a minute or so. Let's see if our friend comes back."

They watched, and after a few moments the figure returned. The bomber turned to look back for an instant, then continued across the frame.

"Look, no bag," Gant said intently. "That was the firebomb. A Molotov cocktail."

"We may be in luck," Stanton said as he ran the picture back. "I might be able to get a good still shot here."

Stanton froze the picture. He zoomed in on the bomber, and the result was a grainy yet identifiable picture.

Gant burst into a broad smile.

"Anybody you know?" Stanton asked.

"Yeah."

CHAPTER 17

enjamin Dietz liked graveyard duty. The other guards in
his building preferred days, but he relished the peace
and quiet of the eleven-to-seven shift. His post at the
guard desk was particularly serene, given that there
were seldom visitors to hassle him. The only overnight
activity in the twelve-story building was from Apex Alert
on the second floor, which employed only a small night staff
to monitor their alarm systems.

Yes, this was his favorite job ever. Much better than the
armored car company where he'd worked for seventeen
years. Better than the Coweta County sheriff's deputy job.

His only real responsibility tonight was giving a manila
envelope to some lady cop. If she even showed. The guard
on the previous shift had passed it along, and it rested on
the counter in front of him with the name SGT. T. BROOKING
printed on its front.

He'd been on duty twenty-five minutes, when he heard a
scream.

He looked right and left. Where had it come from? Inside or outside?

He stood up as a young woman ran in front of the building's glass entrance. She fell to the sidewalk. Behind her, a
man pounced and pinned her down.

Dietz ran around the guard desk and unsnapped his holster. The woman's assailant, wearing a stocking cap, looked

Dietz in the eye. The woman threw a vicious punch to the attacker's face and threw him off. The man, still eyeing Dietz, jumped to his feet and ran down the street.

The guard pushed open the glass door and kneeled beside the woman.

"Ohhh. God, it hurts . . ." She was clutching her stomach.

"Take it easy, honey. What did he do to you?"

The woman looked up. She was about the same age as his daughter, a junior at the University of Georgia. "He just came after me. He hit me in the stomach with a pipe or something, then he chased me."

"I'll call an ambulance."

"No." She pulled herself up. "It's not that bad. If I could just—have a drink of water."

"Sure, honey. I'll get it for you."

"Don't leave!" she said, her gaze darting down the street. "I'll come inside with you."

He helped her to her feet. They walked through the entrance and he pulled out his stool behind the guard desk. "Sit down."

"Thanks."

The woman sat as Dietz picked up a paper cup and walked across the lobby to a water fountain. He filled the cup and came back with it.

She sipped the water. "Thanks."

"Just relax, honey. I'm going to call the police."

"Don't bother. The guy's gone."

"You should still file a report."

"Why? What do you think they'll do about it?"

Dietz picked up his phone. "Don't be silly. They'll be here in five minutes."

Her hand came down on the hook. "Please. I just want to go home and go to bed."

"You're just upset."

"You got that right." She pulled her hand away and stood up. "Thanks for your help, but I just want to forget about this."

"Are you sure?"

"Very sure. Good night, Officer. Or whatever you are."

Dietz watched her leave. He put the phone back on the cradle. Crazy kid.

He looked down at the counter. Where did that manila envelope go?

"Who taught you to punch like that?" Ken gingerly touched his cheek. He drove down International Boulevard as Hound Dog pulled the envelope from under her shirt.

She tore into it. "I got carried away. Spirit of the moment."

"That *hurt*."

"No pain, no gain."

"Uh-huh. So what exactly did we gain?"

Hound Dog angled the printouts into the streetlights' glare. "Let's see. Her alarm activity is here in military time. On the day of your boat attack, she deactivated the alarm at twenty hundred and eleven hours."

"Eight-eleven P.M. When she got home from work."

"Right. Then activated it again at twenty-three hundred and fifty-eight hours. Eleven fifty-eight P.M. Probably when she went to sleep."

"So she was home."

"That's what it looks like."

"What about the time your boyfriend was shot?"

Hound Dog flipped to the next report. She studied it and let the pages fall to her lap. "Home. She was home."

Ken didn't know whether to feel discouraged or relieved. "She didn't do it. Either time."

"It doesn't mean she wasn't behind it. It just means she didn't do it herself, that's all."

Twenty minutes later they pulled up to Hound Dog's trailer. "Are you heading over to the hospital?" he asked.

"A little later. I'll call right now to see if there's any change. Maybe I'll ride around for a while, to unwind."

"Scanner-surfing?"

"Yeah." She climbed out of the car. "Good night, Ken."

"Good night."

Ken watched as she shuffled across the patio and walked up the three short steps to her trailer's front door.

As much as she tried to hide it, her boyfriend's condition was hitting her hard, Ken thought. After seeing that she was safely inside, he drove back to his apartment.

The phone was ringing when he entered. He ran across the room and picked up the receiver. "Hello?"

"Where have you been?" It was Myth.

He was still clutching her security system activity reports. He tossed them onto his coffee table. "Out and about," he said.

"I'm ready to discuss my ideas for finding Sabini's money."

"Okay. Discuss."

"Not over the phone. Let's meet tomorrow night. The pier again? Ten P.M."

"Why there? Why so late?"

"You're a suspect. We can't be seen together, or it's all off. It has to be this way."

"If you say so."

"It'll be good to see you, Ken. I've missed you."

"Yeah."

There was hesitation, as if she wanted him to say more, but finally she just said, "Good night."

"Good night." He hung up the phone.

What was he going to do?

He couldn't meet her. Could he?

Ken paced the small living room, remembering Michaelson's warnings. Myth would have to kill him "somewhere out of the way," the private eye had said.

The pier certainly qualified.

With all that had happened, he'd have to be an idiot to trust her. But he still wasn't entirely convinced of her guilt.

Ken looked at the alarm activity reports again. If Myth wasn't behind the attacks on him and Hound Dog's boyfriend, who was?

•   •   •

There was a full moon that night, for which Gant was grateful. There were no streetlights on the block.

Gant, Lieutenant Jim Ringland, and two uniformed officers approached the two-story duplex nestled in a neighborhood of brick row houses. Gant had known Ringland for years, and was happy when the detective offered to help with the pickup. Gant had not worked with him since transferring to day shift six years before.

"Fireworks?" Ringland asked.

"I'm not expecting any. If our firebomber shows a gun, he goes away for a long time."

"If you're right about this, he's going away for a long time anyway. It might not matter to him."

"I'm not going to argue with that."

Gant drew his revolver and checked the chamber. Ringland and the other officers also produced their weapons. Gant motioned for Ringland and one of the uniforms to cover the rear of the house as he and the other approached the front door.

Gant took a good look at the cop accompanying him. He was a kid fresh out of the academy, and his ruddy cheeks were offset by a square jaw and bright blue eyes. Gant remembered how he felt in his own days as a uniformed cop. On these pickups, where the shields called the shots, he had always felt like the anonymous expendable crewmen on *Star Trek* who got killed whenever they beamed down to a planet with the principals.

Gant read the officer's nameplate. "Okay, Gordon, let's make an arrest."

They walked quietly up a set of stairs to the front door. Gant rapped on it hard. He waited, looking toward the adjacent window. One of the horizontal blinds pulled up slightly.

"Open up. Police!"

Retreating footsteps pounded inside. In the same instant, Gordon broke the door open in one ferocious kick. The two officers rushed into the house, guns drawn, as they barreled through the living room and down a narrow hallway.

Shattering glass echoed in the back bedroom. They hurtled through the doorway to see a broken window frame with pieces of glass still falling and breaking on the floor. Gant holstered his gun and leapt through the second-story window, grabbing hold of a tree branch outside.

He yelled back to Gordon, "Get Ringland's ass out here!"

Gant half fell, half climbed down the tree, all the while trying to keep an eye on his suspect. For a moment he thought he lost him, but he spotted the man as he reached the ground. Gant dropped the last few feet and literally hit the ground running.

Middle age and a little extra weight had not slowed him much, and what he lacked in speed he more than made up for in endurance. He was well known for his ability to wear down a fleeing suspect; the detective just kept going. When the suspect glanced back to see if he was still being chased, Gant always felt encouraged. When the suspect looked a second time, he knew the collar was his.

They had run three blocks when Gant heard the squealing tires that told him Gordon or one of the other officers was in the car and joining the pursuit. The suspect looked over his shoulder, cueing the lieutenant to put on an extra burst of speed.

The car roared behind them, and Gant watched as the man cut across a yard toward a tall wooden fence. His suspect jumped for the gate and scaled it. Sliding across the dew-soaked grass, Gant sprinted for the gate and yanked on it. He swung the gate forcefully against the brick side of the house, hammering the man's face against it. The suspect collapsed in a heap at his feet, moaning as blood spurted from his nose.

Gant pinned the man's shoulders and cuffed him. He turned him faceup. It was Jesus Millicent, Carlos Valez's smart-ass friend.

"This is your lucky day, Jesus. If one of those hothead rookies had caught you, they'd be having a nightstick party on your skull."

Jesus squirmed and shouted, "Man, I didn't do nothing!"

"You mean you didn't do *anything*."

"What are you, a fucking teacher?"

"No, but my wife is. I don't appreciate your lack of respect for the profession."

Gant turned him over. Ringland and the other uniformed officer ran up, guns drawn. Ringland grimaced at Jesus's bloody face. "What'd you do to him, Gant?"

"I opened the gate. He happened to be on it."

Ringland gave Gant a knowing look. "That's the way it looks to me."

"Really," Gant insisted. "He was trying to climb over, I swung it open and he hit the wall."

"Of course," Ringland said with a conspiratorial smile.

Gant decided to let him think what he wanted.

"Let me get this straight, Jesus. You didn't firebomb this building. But you just happen to have canisters of gasoline and oil, and a ripped-up rag, in the backseat of your car."

Jesus looked at Gant and Ringland on the other side of the table in the small interrogation room. Two pieces of brown washroom paper towel protruded from his nose, sticking out at odd angles.

"Man, my nose is starting to bleed again."

Ringland tore off another piece of the brown paper towel. "Here. Put this between your upper lip and gum."

"I want a lawyer, and I want a doctor."

Gant smiled. "We told you. A public defender is on the way. You don't have to talk to us. But you've already resisted arrest, and that's a violation of your parole. We can put you away. Even if we don't get anything else, you're in lockup for two more years."

"Aw, shit . . ."

"You get a lawyer in here, he'll tell you to clam up, and

you're gonna piss us off. And even if we can't get this other stuff to stick, we'll get you for big-time parole violation, and we'll make sure you serve it out."

"I didn't do it!"

Gant nodded. The grueling process of interrogating suspects was one of his least favorite parts of police work. Other officers loathed the tedium of stakeouts, but there at least the cop could listen to music or sit with his thoughts. Gant had no fondness for the psychological back-and-forth of getting a suspect to spill his guts.

He glanced at the video monitor. It was almost time to play the tape. Almost. It was good to let Jesus lie a little more before playing this trump card; the typical suspect's fear at having been caught in a lie was good for getting them to 'fess up to other, possibly related crimes. They did this in hope of "making good" with the cops to whom they had just fibbed.

Gant looked at Ringland. "He says he didn't do it."

"That's what he says," Ringland replied.

"I told you *ten* times! I'm not saying another word until my lawyer gets here."

"Fine." Gant stood and motioned toward the monitor. "While you wait, we'll let you watch a video."

The next morning Ken had been in his office only ten minutes when he heard a sharp knock at his door. He opened it to see Lieutenant Gant.

"Good morning," Gant said. "Can we talk?"

Ken gestured wide for Gant to enter. What now?

Gant stepped inside and looked around the new office. "I have some good news for you. We got your bomber."

Ken froze. "The bomber? Who was it?"

"It was a buddy of Carlos Valez's. His name is Jesus Millicent. He thinks you whacked his friend."

"He told you this?"

"We picked him up last night. He got real talkative after we showed him tape from a security camera on the building behind yours. It's aimed at your rear entrance. Revenge, pure and simple. He also admitted to stealing the boat that tried to sink you at the lake last week."

What a relief. The attacks were totally unrelated to Myth and Sabini. But before he could get too euphoric, he thought about what Gant had said.

A security camera aimed at the rear of his building.

Ken tried to remember if he, Sabini, or Myth had ever wandered within its range. He wasn't sure. Shit.

"You're lucky to be alive. He really had it in for you," Gant said.

"Now all I have to worry about is you."

"Only if you're guilty."

"I'm not. But that didn't keep me from almost getting killed. Twice."

"Mistakes happen."

"Thanks for the comforting words."

Gant studied the polygraph. "This doesn't look any worse for wear. At least you still have your livelihood." He chuckled. "The first time I saw one of these gadgets, I swore it was going to electrocute me if I lied. It was one of the most terrifying experiences of my life."

"Maybe that's why you tested so poorly."

"That's not supposed to make any difference, is it?"

"A lot of examiners will tell you it doesn't. I think it does."

"That's refreshing to hear. I've always wondered how I'd test now."

"You'll never know unless you try it."

"Is that an invitation?"

Ken paused. "Actually, no. I don't know what it would prove."

"You're probably right. It would be more interesting if I hooked *you* up to this machine."

"Me?"

"Yes. I already know what it's like to take a test, but I have no idea what goes into *giving* one."

Ken looked at the examination seat and forced a smile.

He had never taken a polygraph test in his life. He had tried on the sensors when designing Sabini's training exercises, but that was the extent of it. "Examiners make the worst possible subjects," Ken said.

"Why is that?"

Because we know how to beat the damn things, Ken wanted to say. Instead, he just shrugged.

"Let's try it," Gant said. "It'll be a learning experience for me *and* you."

"You're serious?"

"Of course."

Ken let out a long breath. "I don't think so."

"Why not? I don't see any customers here."

Ken thought about it. Gant wasn't an examiner, and even if he was, this machine couldn't get the better of him.

"You're not afraid of anything, are you?" Gant asked.

Ken rolled up his left shirtsleeve and sat in the examination seat. "Put that blood pressure wrap around my arm."

Gant threw the wrap over Ken's left bicep and fastened it with the Velcro ends. He squeezed the bulb until Ken motioned for him to stop.

"That's good enough," Ken said. "We don't want to cut off *all* the circulation, unless it's one of the really tough cases and you need to torture a confession out of the subject."

Gant smiled and followed Ken's directions for fastening the respiration sensors around the torso and the perspiration sensor to the finger.

"What now?" Gant asked.

"Turn on the power. It's on the front lower right-hand corner."

Gant flipped the switch and watched as the chart paper began rolling across the trembling needles.

Ken pointed to the desk. "Somewhere over there you'll find a standard test I use for employee theft cases. Just fill in the blanks."

Gant picked up the test and read from the sheet. "Is your name Kenneth Parker?"

"Yes."

Gant looked at the graph paper as Ken pointed to the sensor needles and told him what each one represented. Gant nodded before reading the next question. "Are you employed by Polygraph Associates?"

"Yes."

"By the way," Gant said, looking away from the page, "did you ever really have any associates?"

Ken shrugged. "No, it just sounded good."

"I see. Okay, is there any information pertaining to the Burton Sabini case that you have withheld from me?"

Ken glared at Gant. "I don't think that's on the page."

"No, but it didn't seem right to ask if you embezzled from yourself." Gant looked at the needles. "Looks like I got a rise out of you with that one."

"No," Ken said. "The answer to your question is no."

Gant nodded. "Have you ever lied to keep from getting into trouble at work?"

"No," Ken said. Jesus, why did he ever agree to this? He thought he was building up goodwill with the lieutenant, but this was turning into an interrogation.

"Did you murder Burton Sabini?"

What the hell was he doing?

Gant smiled and checked the needles.

"No," Ken replied.

"Interesting," Gant said as he examined the readings.

Ken tore off the blood pressure wrap. "I think that will do it for our little demonstration."

"I'm sorry. I thought it would give me a truer picture of what this test is all about."

"I hope it was informative."

"Oh, it was," Gant said as he walked to the door. "It's amazing. I practically accused you of murder, and your blood pressure didn't budge." He smiled. "Maybe you can explain that to me sometime."

Gant left the office.

Ken yanked off the perspiration sensor and pushed the door closed. Shit.

Shake it off, he told himself. Gant was just trying to get under his skin. And the man had come with good news.

At least he knew Myth wasn't behind the attempts on his life. There was no reason not to meet her. He could now face her at the pier with a little more trust.

CHAPTER 18

While in daytime the Gower pier possessed a friendly, almost quaint atmosphere, its character was transformed completely at night. As the fog rolled in, swirling over and around the choppy waters of Lake Lanier, the pier's wooden planks grew wet and slippery, and they reflected back only moonlight from the night sky; there was no other source of illumination. Nearby pine trees cast eerie, threatening shadows onto the pier's entrance, like gargoyles lording over a Gothic manor. Wind whistled through the understructure, creating a chorus of low howls and frantic, desperate shrieks.

It was five minutes to ten as Ken walked from the dirt road next to the entrance. His eyes were quick in adjusting to the moonlight. He stepped onto the wet planks. They creaked and groaned with each step.

At the end of the pier, Myth was leaning against the railing. She was looking out at points of light miles away, dotting a hillside on the lake's north shore.

She spoke without turning to face him.

> "Trust not before you try,
> For under cloak of great
>   goodwill
> Does feigned friendship lie . . ."

He stepped closer. "What?"

"I'm sorry, Ken. I'm sorry I got you mixed up in this."

"I'm sorry too. But we can still make it worth my while."

"You don't understand."

She turned and leveled a silver snub-nosed revolver at his chest.

"This isn't easy for me," she said.

He stared uncomprehendingly at her. His first reaction was not of fear, but of overwhelming anger. *Why hadn't he learned?*

He had trusted her. And now it was going to cost him everything. Never before did he actually think he was about to die. Not when the boat tried to sink him, not when his office was firebombed. But now he knew it was all over.

"Why?" he finally asked.

He expected her to respond by pulling the trigger, but she answered, "Because you're dangerous."

"*I'm* dangerous?"

She nodded. "As long as you're alive, as long as you can talk, I can't be completely safe."

"How do you figure that? You know I'll keep my mouth shut."

"Maybe, maybe not. If the screws start to tighten, I can't predict what you'll do. And, Ken, the screws are tightening."

"Whose fault is that?"

Still she did not fire. She was stalling; maybe she really didn't want to do this, he thought. He turned slightly and slid his hand toward his jacket pocket.

Slowly, a bit at a time . . .

"You already have Sabini's money, don't you?"

Myth did not reply.

He slid his hand a little closer, in what he hoped was an imperceptible movement . . .

"Then you have what you want. You don't have to do this."

"There's no other way. I've tossed it around, looked at it from every angle. This is the only way it gels."

His fingers stretched for his pocket. Just a little more . . .

"There's another way. Make me a partner."

"A partner?"

"Give me a cut of the money. Just what Sabini owed me. You'd be buying my silence. That would make me an accessory after the fact, wouldn't it? I wouldn't be in any position to give you away."

She shook her head. "The frame's already been built, Ken."

"What frame?"

"The frame that pictures you as Sabini's murderer."

The nails of his right hand clutched at the fabric of his jacket, pulling the pocket closer.

She continued. "And for that frame to work, it has to look like you disappeared with the money."

"I can't believe it."

"The evidence has already been planted. It solves both of my problems. Someone to take the murder rap and to distract the authorities from finding the money."

"It won't work."

"Why not?"

"Because I'm not gonna die tonight."

He drew his gun.

Her eyes widened in horror. "No. It's not what you think!"

"Then, what is it?"

Before she could say another word, a gunshot rang out, exploding in the night air.

Her blouse ruffled slightly. A dark stain spread from her chest. She stumbled backward.

But Ken had not fired.

Another shot echoed across the pier, and she twisted violently. She fell to the wet planks, trembling, choking, and gritting her teeth.

Then she lay still, her agony dissipating in one long, last sigh.

There were pounding, running footsteps on the pier behind him.

He whirled around.

It was Michaelson. The P.I. was holding a gun. "Christ, kid. Are you all right?"

Ken was too stunned to speak. Michaelson leaned down to examine Myth, feeling her neck for a pulse.

"I'm sorry." Michaelson shook his head with regret. "I knew she was up to something, but I couldn't tell you. I didn't know if you were in on it or not. So I followed you."

"You killed her. . . ."

"It was her or you. Don't think I didn't consider letting her finish you off. She still might have led me to the cash." Michaelson looked up. "By the way, *you're welcome*."

"Goddamn."

"You got that right."

Ken couldn't summon any gratitude; he was still too angry. Angry with Michaelson for being right about her.

"Do you have a phone in your car?" Ken asked. "I'll call the police."

The P.I. shook his head. "Wrong. They get into it, we lose all that money she died for."

"Are you out of your mind?"

"You're not thinking, Parker." Michaelson's smile showed more gums than teeth.

"You killed her. Are we just supposed to ignore that?"

"She was going to kill you. Before you go bringing the police into it, don't you think you'd better undo what she's done? She's framed you for murder, remember?"

"How?"

"I'll tell you. After you take care of the body."

"Go to hell."

Michaelson picked up Myth's small handbag and rifled through it. "You don't have much choice. If you go to the police, I'll deny everything. Remember, I'm still Vikkers' official investigator on this case. And believe me, this lady did a good job of setting you up for Burton Sabini's murder."

Michaelson threw the purse aside. "Do we have a deal?"

Ken cursed at the night sky. From beyond the grave, Myth was *still* screwing him over. Except that she didn't have a grave. He was being asked to provide that too.

"We can turn this around," Michaelson said. "We can find the money, make it look like *she* skipped town with it. But to do that, we can't just leave her here. I have to do a job for another client in less than an hour. That means *you* take care of the body."

"What about the frame-up?"

"I'll take care of it. But I gotta know I can count on you."

Ken looked at Myth's body. She was still beautiful, as if she were sleeping.

The next few minutes were almost surreal to Ken, as if someone had inhabited his body and was directing it to do things beyond his control. He found himself helping Michaelson roll Myth's body into a blanket and found himself being struck by the sight of her thick, lustrous hair spilling out of the end as they carried the blanket to his MG.

He was only vaguely aware of Michaelson's sick jokes as they crammed the body into the small trunk.

His vision almost blurred as Michaelson fished around in his own trunk and came up with a rusty hoe. Ken settled behind the wheel of his car, and the P.I. handed the gardening tool to him.

"What you wanna do," Michaelson instructed, "is head up Highway 92 until you think you're in East Bumblefuck, then you go *another* twenty minutes. You dig, you bury her deep. Got it? She's gotta vanish."

Ken kept the top down as he drove, hoping the wind would slap him back into reality. It didn't work. Her betrayal, her death, and now this had all happened so fast. He was too angry to grieve, and yet he felt he had lost a part of himself on the pier that night. Or maybe he was still losing it.

He drove as Michaelson had instructed, until he found himself on an isolated gravel road miles from anywhere. He finally came to a stop near a densely overgrown field.

He didn't want to do this.

He cut the engine, climbed out of the car, and paced back and forth. The gravel crunched beneath his feet. He stopped, lit up a cigarette, and inhaled.

Who would have guessed that he'd end up here? Miles from anywhere, a woman's body in his trunk, and a murder investigation still hanging over him.

He rubbed his sweaty hands on the legs of his jeans. Time to get on with it. He took a deep breath, inserted the trunk key, and turned. He hesitated before lifting the lid.

He took another breath, threw up the trunk lid, and . . .

Myth was staring at him.

He took a step back.

Then, slowly, she sat up.

"Don't panic," she said.

He drew his gun, wondering if he had finally gone insane.

"You're panicking."

He waved the gun in front of him. "What the hell is going on?"

"I'm sorry to have put you through this."

"What exactly have I just been through?"

Myth climbed out of the trunk, rolling her cramped shoulders. "Didn't you hear me? I've been yelling for the last half hour."

He shook his head as Myth unbuttoned her blouse. She reached inside, and he raised his revolver. She slowly, carefully, produced two tape-lined plastic packets.

She held them up. "Explosive blood packs."

"What in the holy hell—?"

She motioned toward Ken's gun. "You don't need that."

"Maybe I do, maybe I don't."

"Let me explain."

"Please."

She stared at his gun, but there was no way he was going to put it away. "Michaelson and I have been working together. He's a dangerous man. He shot somebody the other night, almost killed him. And it was my fault."

"Are we talking about Mark Bailey?"

She gave him a surprised look. "How did you—?"

"Never mind. Keep talking."

"I got a call from that number. Someone identified herself as Madeleine Walton. I asked Michaelson to check it out. I didn't know he was going to break in and search the place. I didn't want anybody to get hurt."

"Christ. Then what is tonight all about?"

"It's supposed to be about me killing you out here, in the middle of nowhere. That's what Michaelson thinks."

"You could have done that back at the pier."

"We could have, but do you know where most murderers mess up?"

"Excuse my ignorance."

"Disposing of the body. It's easy to kill someone, but the real risk comes afterward. The old French crime bosses knew that. When they wanted to rub out one of their men, they'd give him the task of disposing of a body. So this person would take all the precautions and make sure he wouldn't be seen. Once he got to wherever he was going, the supposed 'body' would rise up with a garrote and kill him. It was perfect. The victim himself picked his final resting place before a murder had even been committed."

Ken was fascinated in spite of himself. "You and Michaelson—"

"We embellished it a little. If we had killed you at the pier, there would always be a chance we'd be discovered disposing of your remains. This way you take the risk before there really is a murder."

"So you're supposed to—"

He stiffened warily as she reached into the trunk. She pulled out her gun by the barrel and tossed it to the ground near his feet.

"I was supposed to kill you out here. Preferably after you had already dug my grave." She leaned back against the car. "I could never do anything like that, Ken. Not to you or anyone . . . There's nothing more horrible than seeing a life taken away. You never forget it."

"You didn't kill Sabini?"

"No."

"I'm having serious trouble absorbing this."

"You gave me a scare tonight. We hadn't counted on you having your own gun. I was afraid you'd shoot me before Michaelson could *pretend* to shoot me." She shook her head. "The whole plan just got out of hand."

" 'The whole plan'? Look, I want you to tell me everything. About you, about Sabini, about Michaelson. What the hell is going on?"

"Let's go. I'll tell you everything you want to know."

They climbed into Ken's car and drove back down the dusty rural roads with the ragtop up. Wisps of fog snaked in front of them, enveloping the car as the engine's roar attacked the quiet surroundings.

"Michaelson first approached me when I was researching Sabini's case," Myth said. "I like to know *everything* about the people I work with. Information was something he had plenty of. After a while, we started having discussions."

"What kind of discussions?"

"He and I were sure Sabini took the money. So while Michaelson worked on tracing the funds, I worked on Sabini."

"Did you sleep with him?"

She didn't answer. They drove in silence.

"Shit," he muttered.

"I didn't sleep with him. Some men are more turned on

if you keep just out of reach. Sabini was that type, even if he didn't know it."

"So what happened?"

"I got Sabini to tell me how he got the money back here from Europe. He bought some rare letters. One of them was even signed by Napoleon. He smuggled them back with some business memos. I told Michaelson."

"So Michaelson killed Sabini and took the letters."

"That's what I thought. But he said he didn't touch Sabini. Michaelson did find the letters, but it turns out they were worth only a fraction of the twelve million." Her lips curled into an ironic smile. "Sabini lied to me."

"I taught him well."

"Michaelson was furious. He suspected me, you, everyone. He knew all about you because I had him do the file you saw on your background. He knew I wanted you to train Sabini, and after you agreed to do it, he continued his surveillance to make sure you weren't telling anyone about it."

"*You* wanted him to spy on me?"

"Only at first. I called him off, but after Sabini died, he was watching both of us pretty close. He thought we had the money. After you confronted him, he started working on the next step in his plan."

"My murder?"

She nodded. "I know he did what he could to make you suspicious of me . . . in case you and I were holding out on him."

"He told me you were screwing Sabini and that maybe you killed him."

"Did you believe him?"

"I didn't know what to believe."

"I can't say that I blame you. But, Ken, you have—"

"Why the hell didn't you tell me all this before tonight? Why did you make me go through it all?"

"It was better this way."

"Better for who?"

She was quiet for a moment. She leaned over and whispered, "I have a plan."

Michaelson stood next to his car, nervously drumming his fingers on the roof. He was parked behind Myth's home, adjacent to a pool house that bordered the property line. Myth was twenty-five minutes late, and he was having second thoughts about her convoluted scheme to eliminate Ken Parker. It was possible Parker changed his mind and went to the police, in which case the coroner would be surprised to find a very live corpse in the car trunk. Unlikely, Michaelson thought, with the threat of a frame-up coupled with the lure of Sabini's fortune. He was pretty sure Parker would do as he was told.

There was the chance Parker could have overpowered Myth at the burial site. Also not likely, since she would have the element of surprise on her side. She should have been able to squeeze off six shots before the guy knew what hit him.

Michaelson checked his watch again. Anytime, baby . . .

As long as she didn't screw this up, everything would fall into place. Within forty-eight hours he was certain a sizable chunk of the cash would be his, with no Ken Parker to mess things up for him. He couldn't let Parker live and squeal to Vikkers. And he sure as hell wasn't going to split his take with the guy.

And then there was the kid who came back to his trailer unexpectedly the other night. Who *came home* at four in the morning? Nudie bar bouncers, Michaelson noted ruefully after reading about his victim in the next day's paper. Mark Bailey was still in a coma, and with any luck would never recover. He would have to monitor Bailey's progress, because he was pretty sure the kid could identify him.

A flash of headlights speared down the alley. As the car drew closer, he recognized Ken's MG. The top was up, and

Myth was driving. She pulled to a stop behind the pool house and climbed out.

"How many?" Michaelson asked.

"How many *what*?"

"How many shots did it take to kill him?"

"Shut up, Michaelson."

She unlocked her back gate and strode to the pool house. He snickered as he followed her.

Once inside the well-lit structure, he could see her dirt-stained clothes, skin, and hair. She stepped into a changing room and slid on an old denim shirt and a pair of sweat pants.

"He didn't open the trunk until he had already finished digging," she said.

"Well, it saved you the trouble of doing it."

"It took him forever. Then it took me a while to cover him up."

"Good work."

She emerged from the changing room. "This had better be worth it. You'd better be as close as you say you are."

"Tough talk, lady. I guess I should watch myself around you." He smiled. "Or else I'll end up like our friend."

"Don't be cute. What do you know?"

Michaelson approached a small wet bar and poured himself a shot of vodka. "I gotta admit I suspected you of partnering with Sabini on the embezzlement. The guy had almost no friends. I didn't know who he could have worked with. But you, you're sharp, crafty . . ."

"I never met Sabini before the investigation began. And if I *had* been involved, I never would have represented him."

"I believe that. So then I thought Sabini told you what he did with the funds, and you were holding out on me."

"You don't think that anymore?"

"No. Because now I have a pretty good idea who *does* know."

"Who?"

"The same person who helped him rip off all that money."

"Who is . . . ?"

Michaelson shook his head and chuckled. "Unh-unh. That's my secret for now."

"We're in this together, Michaelson. I killed a man for you."

"For me? I don't believe you were thinking about me."

"I know why you really wanted him dead. Your bosses at Vikkers wanted him that way, didn't they?"

"I work for myself."

"Get real. They found out Ken was poking around in their misinformation campaign, didn't they?"

"Let's just say the company is very sensitive about that particular subject."

"Does that mean you also killed that man at Crown Metals who was poking into their business? Don Browne?"

"No comment."

"None necessary. That's some company you work for. They *used* Sabini. They didn't even tell him they had implanted that program, did they?"

"They didn't have to."

"Just like they didn't have to share the profits of that merger with him either. I hope they realize that's why he stole the money from them. He felt betrayed. He thought he had it coming to him."

"Life isn't fair."

"I'm pretty sure his partner didn't work for Vikkers. I want to know who it is. Now."

Michaelson, in one quick movement, whirled and slapped one hand over her neck. He slammed her against the paneled wall.

"You think I'm fucking stupid?" he whispered. "If I tell you, I'd be mighty expendable, wouldn't I? Just like Burton Sabini. Like Ken Parker."

"You're a stupid, scared little man."

"Do you have any idea what I could do to you right now?"

"How about what *I* could do to *you*?"

Michaelson heard the sharp, distinct click of a revolver

being cocked. He looked down to see Myth's gun pointed at his genitals.

"Do what you need to do," she said.

He let go and backed off.

She pointed the gun away. "Don't do that again."

Michaelson smiled. He laughed out loud.

He was still laughing as he left the pool house and climbed behind the wheel of Ken's MG.

CHAPTER 19

Good news is something I don't get enough of," Gant said as he strode into the A/V lab in response to a message from Officer David Wittkower.

"You're getting it this morning," Wittkower replied, twisting a jog/shuttle wheel on the video console. "Check this out."

The monitor showed two men standing outside the rear entrance of Ken Parker's office building. They were talking and smoking cigarettes. Wittkower activated the zoom function and zeroed in on the men. Ken Parker and Burton Sabini.

Gant nodded. Only minutes before, he had received a telephone report that showed several one-minute calls from Ken Parker's office to Sabini's residence.

"Clear as day!" Wittkower exclaimed. "Here they are together just a few nights before Sabini's death. Twelve-fourteen A.M. You can't ask for much better than this. We got him cold."

"Parker said they had never met."

"When a murder suspect says that about the victim, then turns up on *Candid Camera* with him, that's what's known as a break in the case."

"Thanks for the lesson."

Ken took a deep breath, inhaling the warm, sweetly scented air around Myth's remote cabin. Located forty-five minutes north of the city, it was often used to house her high-profile clients to keep them from media scrutiny. He didn't like being stranded without his car, but Myth and Michaelson had already arranged to leave the MG at his apartment building. They wanted to delay notice of his disappearance for as long as possible.

Ken paced the length of the large wooden porch, wishing Myth would get back. The more he thought of her plan, the less he liked it, and he liked being manipulated even less. He knew she hadn't told him of the "French crime boss" scheme in advance for fear that he might not go along with it. After he had participated, albeit unwittingly, it was a much simpler matter to convince him to let Michaelson's search come to its promised conclusion.

What the hell was he doing? And why?

He wasn't doing this for her. It was for Bobby, wasn't it? That's what he kept trying to tell himself. He had gone this far, and he might as well ride it out a little farther. But where would he draw the line?

The line. He had crossed it the moment he agreed to test Sabini on the polygraph. So he had simply drawn another one, he thought ruefully. And another one. And another one after that.

Just as his interviewees did.

Ken wandered inside the cabin, which was in reality a house. It was a rustic two-story structure with dark cedar beams and a freestanding fireplace that centered the large living room. As peaceful as the setting was, the silence unnerved him. He found an old magazine, which he read from cover to cover before hearing the sound of a car coming down the isolated country road.

He cautiously approached the window and peered outside, trying to see through the trees. It was Myth's car. He met her at the door.

"What's the story?" he said.

She kissed him. "We're in a holding pattern for another day or so. Michaelson thinks he knows where the money is."

"Where?"

"He won't tell me."

"So, in the meantime, I don't have a life."

"Ken, it's almost over. I promise. Michaelson needs to believe I'm with him on this."

"So what's he going to believe when he finds the money?"

"That you're our partner, whether he likes it or not. What's he going to do?"

"Kill us both."

"It won't happen."

"This is a dangerous game we're playing. We know what the guy is capable of."

"I can handle it."

"Famous last words."

"Not mine."

"Be honest with me."

"About what?"

"What if I hadn't gone along with this? What if I told you there was going to be no treasure hunt, and all I wanted to do was go to the police?"

"That didn't happen, did it?"

"What if?"

She was silent for a long while. She finally replied, "We would have gone to the police, of course."

Decker left his car with the valet and walked into Iverson's, a restaurant known for its high prices, rude waiters, and excellent food. The place was closed for a private party hosted by the Friends of the Atlanta Ballet, and although Decker had never been to a performance, his company was a generous supporter.

Decker surveyed the main dining room, where the Georgia elite were mixing and mingling, trying to look like they gave a shit about the performing arts. Decker didn't see whom he was looking for.

Decker noticed clouds of cigar smoke billowing from a smaller party room. Ah-ha. Where he should have looked in the first place.

Decker entered the smoking area. He glanced around until he met eyes with the man he was there to see.

Governor Walter Holden.

Holden cocked his head to the right, then continued his conversation with a local sports team owner.

Decker knew what it meant. He stepped through a pair of French doors to the balcony overlooking Butler Street. He waited two minutes before Holden joined him.

"How are things?" Holden asked. He took a puff from his cigar.

"Not good. In the vernacular of your friend in there, I need you to run some more interference."

"What's happened?"

"The feds. They're swarming all over us. I have a list of fifteen employees they want to spy on us. Who knows how many they've gotten to?"

"It's messy."

"That's why I need you to do something."

"Like what?"

"Call off the dogs. Cash in a few favors."

"I've *already* cashed in a few favors. If I do any more, it may look suspicious. Already I've gone far beyond the realm of merely helping a constituent."

"Most constituents aren't giving you a twenty-million-dollar nest egg to retire on. Your future's at stake, Governor."

"I held up my end of the bargain. The merger was approved."

"Yes, but we can't cash out for another six months. Before then, if the SEC digs deep enough, we can get wiped out."

Holden shook his head. "You never should have pursued the Sabini matter the way you did. If ever there was a time you didn't need the spotlight on your company . . ."

"What was I supposed to do? Let him walk with twelve million of my money?"

"You could have cut him a deal."

"I tried that."

"You didn't try hard enough."

"We've been through this before. It's in the past."

"Except we're still paying for it!" Holden spoke in a sharp whisper, almost spitting on Decker's face. "I don't know what you're doing to keep things on track, and I have a feeling I don't *want* to know."

"Come on, Walter. Are you still trying to tell me you didn't have Sabini taken out of the picture? You know, so the spotlight's glare on us wouldn't be so intense?"

"Don't be stupid. In case you haven't noticed, people are looking at your company harder than ever. His death is the worst thing that could have happened."

"If you say so," Decker said.

"I've done all that I'm going to do. I still expect the balance of my payment in five months and twenty-six days."

Decker looked at the street below. "I have a joke for you, Walter. What did the death row inmate say to the governor?"

Holden just glared at him.

Decker smiled. "I beg your pardon."

"Don't count on it."

"I'm going to the cafeteria. Would you like me to bring you back anything?"

Hound Dog shook her head in response to the nurse's question. "No, thanks. I might head down there myself after a while."

"Okay."

Hound Dog sat up in her chair as the nurse left the room. Mark was still in Intensive Care, and he was making progress, becoming semiconscious several times that afternoon and evening. Hound Dog even thought he recognized her for a few brief moments. A spiderweb of electronic equipment was wired to her boyfriend, humming, beeping, and clicking, making sleep for her more impossible than it was already.

She looked at her watch. Ten forty-five P.M. On most nights, she would be heading out at about this time. And Mark would be throwing out obnoxious drunks who couldn't keep their hands off the strippers.

But tonight she was just sitting, watching, waiting. And Mark just looked weak. Tired.

She suddenly felt restless and claustrophobic. Gotta get out of here, she told herself. Just for a few minutes. She wouldn't ride the streets tonight though. If Mark woke up, she needed to be nearby. She kissed him on the cheek and left the room.

The hospital cafeteria boasted the usual fare: hours-old food in heat wells, complemented by stale breads and pastries. There were only a few people around. Interns talked at a table in the corner. An elderly woman cried as she ate a bowl of soup. A large maintenance man read the paper and snacked on a bag of Fritos.

The Frito muncher left as Hound Dog bought a pack of crackers. She took a seat near the exit.

Michaelson climbed the hospital's rear stairwell, pausing when he reached the fourth floor. The maintenance uniform was a lousy fit. The jumpsuit's crotch rode up uncomfortably. If he raised his arms, he was sure he would castrate himself.

He had spotted Mark Bailey's girlfriend in the cafeteria, which gave him a window of opportunity to visit the kid's room. Bailey was making progress, and Michaelson knew this might be his only chance to silence him before the police could get a description.

He had done a lot of work in hospitals, generally to sneak a peek at confidential patient records, so he knew that the maintenance worker garb was a good disguise. Doctors and nurses held laborers in low esteem and didn't usually look at their faces. That was fine with him, but for good measure he had slicked his hair back and donned a thick mustache.

He carefully opened the stairwell door and peered down the corridor.

Intensive Care.

This would make things more difficult. There were fewer rooms on this floor, and no patient was more than a couple of steps from a nurses' station. Also, each patient's vital signs were being constantly monitored, and any downturn would set off an alert. He would have to move fast once the job was done.

He walked down the hallway, at first tentatively, then confidently, as an orderly passed him by. He walked past the nurses' station. No one noticed. He grabbed a mop sitting in a pail, then followed the numbers until he found himself at Mark Bailey's room. The door was cracked open, and he could see that three of the four beds were occupied. The kid was in the bed near the right wall.

Perfect.

Michaelson went to the next room, where all four beds were taken. He spoke in broken English to the nurse on duty. "Clean bathroom, me?"

She gave him a puzzled look.

"Room 924?" he said.

"Yes."

"Clean bathroom, me," he said, walking to the bathroom with his mop. He cast a glance back to see if she was picking up her phone. She wasn't. She didn't suspect a thing.

He pulled the door closed and tried the door on the opposite side. Locked. Behind the door was another bathroom for Mark Bailey's room, and beyond that was the kid's bed. Michaelson had done his homework.

He picked the lock in less than twenty seconds. He crept through the other bathroom and stepped into Bailey's room. His curtain was drawn, blocking the bed from the nurse on duty. The girlfriend had probably drawn it.

Michaelson crept toward the bed. Mark Bailey was lying flat on his back, eyes closed, still unconscious.

Michaelson reached into the pocket of his coveralls and pulled out a large-sized plastic Ziploc freezer bag, one with the green "freshness stripe." In his experience, pillows were not much use in suffocation, unless they were the heavier one hundred percent down pillows. Porous foam material allowed the victim to suck air through, allowed him to breathe even with the pillow jammed against his face.

He looped a drawstring around the freezer bag's opening. Careful not to upset the equipment sensors, he pulled Mark's head forward. He lowered the bag over it and pulled sharply on the string. Within seconds the bag crumpled in on itself and pressed flat against the kid's nose and mouth.

Michaelson expected some resistance, some twitching perhaps, but there was none.

Just another few seconds . . .

He glanced at the equipment monitors. No alarms yet. He made a mental note never to stay at this hospital.

Mark's head turned slightly and his chest quivered, but that was his only protest as life eked slowly from his body. Michaelson gripped the top of the bag, preparing to yank it off and make a run for it.

The curtain behind him pulled open.

Oh, shit.

He spun around.

It was the girlfriend.

"Get the hell away from him!" she screamed, rushing toward the bed.

Michaelson immediately adopted a stooped posture and an indeterminate foreign accent. "Help him!" he exclaimed as he pulled off the bag. "I just found him!"

"Oh, God, Mark!" Hound Dog cradled his head as Michaelson pushed past her.

"I'll get some help!" he shouted. He bolted through the bathroom but slowed his pace as he grabbed the mop and calmly walked past the nurse in the other room.

•   •   •

Hound Dog pinched Mark's nostrils, took a deep breath, and placed her mouth on his.

She exhaled.

His chest expanded beneath her shaking hand.

What now?

She hadn't done this since high school, when she entertained the class by Frenching the plastic training dummy. If only she'd been paying better attention . . .

Two nurses burst into the area. Hound Dog backed away as they descended on Mark's bed.

"Help him! Please. Someone just tried to suffocate him!"

"What?" one of the nurses asked in disbelief.

"He had a plastic bag over his head. Goddammit, do something!"

One nurse checked the instruments while the other refastened his oxygen mask.

Hound Dog thought she could see his chest moving. Or was it just wishful thinking?

No, she realized with relief. He was breathing.

"The janitor found him," she said. "When I got here—"

"What janitor?"

"The one who—"

Hound Dog stopped as she realized it was the Frito-eating guy who left the cafeteria just as she entered.

She ran from the room. The elevator? No. He wouldn't have wanted to wait.

She ducked into the stairwell.

She listened.

There were running footsteps far, far below her.

It had to be him.

The elevator chimed open behind her, and she ran for it. The doors started to close before she could get there, but she wedged them open with her elbow and shoulder.

She pressed "L" and the "doors closed" buttons. She hopped impatiently as the elevator descended five floors to the lobby.

Or was he headed for the parking garage? No, not if he were looking for a quick getaway. Probably parked on the street. Maybe, just maybe, there would be a security guard at the hospital's front entrance. Someone who would help her get the son of a bitch.

She flew out of the elevator and pushed open the hospital's front doors. No security guard.

But there was the rotund man, still in his coveralls, running down the block.

She bolted after him.

He was heading toward a car. Dammit! Can't let him reach it. He wasn't getting away with this.

The man was slow, and although he had a lead, she was gaining. Almost there . . .

The man turned.

Hound Dog jumped and hit him with a ferocious tackle. She pounded his cheek against the asphalt sidewalk.

"You fucker!" she screamed.

He threw her off. Before she could regain her balance, he elbowed her on the side of her head. Twice. Then he hit her again, this time on the back of the neck.

A white flash. The sidewalk rushed toward her.

In what seemed like an instant, she was aware of the car starting on the street beside her.

Had she been knocked unconscious?

Still unable to move, she tried to focus on a streetlight as the car roared away.

She pulled herself to her feet. She was nauseated and woozy. A creeping darkness fogged her vision.

She stood motionless, fighting to remain conscious.

The wooziness passed.

She kicked clumps of grass growing between cracks in the sidewalk.

Goddammit!

She should have kept her distance. She could have caught the guy's license plate number and let the police pick him up. Now she might never know who he was or why he wanted to hurt Mark.

Mark . . .

She sprinted back to the hospital.

Margot knocked on the door to Ken's apartment. It was a quarter to nine in the morning, and she wasn't getting an answer.

"Ken?" she called out.

She knocked again. Still no reply. She reached into her purse, pulled out a set of keys, and unlocked the door. She let herself in.

She looked around, and as she was about to close the door behind her, a strong hand gripped it. She gasped and turned to see a worn silver badge and an Atlanta P.D. photo ID card. It identified the bearer as Lieutenant Thomas Gant.

"Can I help you, ma'am?"

"Why would I need your help?"

Gant didn't reply. Instead he asked for her name and relationship to Ken.

She answered, then said, "What are you doing here?" She got a sick feeling in her stomach. "Is Ken okay?"

"I thought maybe you could tell me."

"I don't know. That's why I'm here. I haven't heard from him, and he hasn't returned any of my calls. I was worried. What the hell is going on? Where's Ken?"

"We don't know. Why do you have his door keys?"

"He gave me a set. In case he ever lost his."

"How long have you had them?"

"A few months."

"How long has it been since you've seen Ken Parker?"

"We had a birthday party for him last Tuesday. What's all this about?"

Gant closed the door behind him. "If you knew where he was, would you tell me?"

She looked at him incredulously. "You think that I—"

"Did he send you here? Did you come here to pick up a few things for him? Some clothes, maybe?"

"No. I told you why I came."

"Yeah. Yeah, you did. Ms. Aronson, we've sworn out a warrant for his arrest. He's wanted in connection with a murder. We've uncovered some evidence very damaging to him, and we need to talk to him about it. The longer he stays out of sight, the worse it will be for him."

She couldn't have heard him correctly. "A murder?"

Gant nodded.

"What evidence do you have?"

"I'm sorry, I can't discuss that."

She slowly shook her head. "I really don't know where he is."

"If you say so."

"You actually think Ken killed someone?"

"He's a suspect."

"There's no way. I *know* him. He's just incapable of that."

"I hope you're right."

"The hell you do."

"Think what you want."

"I don't need your permission to do that."

She walked out of the apartment.

Michaelson pulled to a stop in the Carter Library parking lot. He had never been inside this learning center dedicated to the thirty-ninth president of the United States. He didn't know anyone who had. Tourists, maybe. And kids. Lots of kids.

Children poured from school buses into the white orientation building. Good, Michaelson thought. He had chosen the spot well. He wanted a lot of people around.

After all, he had an appointment with a killer.

He had made the call that morning. "We have a mutual acquaintance. Burton Sabini. I know who you are and what you've done," he had said. "We'll meet to discuss it at ten A.M. in the courtyard at the Carter Library."

He heard only stunned silence from the other end of the phone. Bull's-eye. He had found Sabini's partner.

It was now a good forty-five minutes before the designated meeting time, but he wanted to hide and watch for a while. He wanted to make sure Sabini's partner came alone. Normally Michaelson would have recruited a "cover" to stake the situation out and watch his back, but he didn't want to risk bringing anyone else into it. He was already into Myth Daniels for a piece of the dough, and he didn't want to split it any further.

He parked on the other side of the school buses. Here he could watch the courtyard benches without being easily seen himself.

A white van pulled up to the main entrance, and a group of senior citizens emerged. They shuffled to the sidewalk, clutching their blue and white tour tickets.

Michaelson hit the armrest control, lowering his window a few inches. He settled back in his seat. His legs were still sore from his sprint from the hospital the night before. If only Mark Bailey's girlfriend hadn't returned so soon.

Shit. Just one more thing to worry about.

The money would make it all worthwhile, he thought. All those years eating shit, doing the spying and dirty work for executives who thought they were too good for him. Until they needed him for something. Then they came crawling.

Screw 'em.

He climbed out of his car and looked around. Maybe he'd come back to the museum someday to see what all the fuss was about. Nah, probably not. He was never a big fan of Carter's.

He walked to the courtyard and ambled around the benches. How much should he ask for? Two million? Three million?

Three million.

He would negotiate from there.

Satisfied that the courtyard would be a safe and visible

meeting place, he walked back around the school buses and climbed into his car.

Something wasn't right.

It smelled . . . different.

He heard something behind him in the backseat. He looked in the rearview mirror.

He wasn't alone.

"You got some major heat on you, Kenbo. You're not gonna stiff me, are you?"

Ken paced across the living room of Myth's cabin, cradling the cordless phone against his shoulder. He had called Stan Warner to see if the information broker had uncovered anything. "Take it easy. What are you talking about?"

"There's a warrant out for your arrest."

Ken could almost feel his throat closing. It had finally happened. "How do you know?"

"I got sources, all right? What I wanna know is, are you going to pay me for Sabini's info packet? I'm sitting here, looking at it, and it's a thing of beauty. But I'm afraid you're not going to have much use for it in jail."

"I'll be in touch," Ken choked out.

He hung up the phone.

It had to end. Enough was enough.

He heard the sound of a car outside. Myth wasn't supposed to be back until that evening.

The police?

He stepped onto the porch. It was Myth. Her Mercedes rolled to a stop in front of the cabin.

As she climbed out of her car, he could see she was upset. She must have heard.

"You know about my arrest warrant?" he said.

She looked puzzled. "No," she whispered. She sat on the edge of the wooden porch swing.

The news didn't even faze her. "Then, what is it?" he asked.

Her face was ashen. "Michaelson and I made arrangements to meet today."

"I know. What did he say?"

"He didn't show."

"Jesus. You think he skipped out on you? That's it, isn't it? He got the money, and he skipped out!"

"No . . . Ken, no."

She looked as if she were going to be sick. He joined her on the swing.

She sounded hollow. "Michaelson's dead."

Ken let the bombshell lie there for a moment, without poking or probing it, which would normally have been his first impulse. He was too stunned to react.

She looked away in the direction of the wooded area near the cabin. "They found him in his car at the Carter Library. Someone killed him. Stabbed him."

"Stabbed like Sabini. Like Carlos Valez."

Myth didn't respond.

Ken looked down. "I've had a lot of time to think out here, and I don't like what this has done to me."

"*What's* done to you?"

"The money. What it's done to all of us. Or maybe you were like this before, I don't know. But people are dying for this goddamned money. It's not worth it. You make a good living, why are you in this?"

"Please, Ken."

"You like it, don't you? Does it make you feel powerful, manipulating men this way? Does it?"

"No. Ken . . . I love you."

"I don't like myself very much right now. Along the way I've found out some things about myself I really hate. This thing has gotten out of hand."

"I'm sorry, Ken."

"Give me your keys."

"What?"

Ken snatched the keys from her limp fingers. "I'm not staying here one more minute. Let's go."

"Where?"

He grabbed her arm, pulled her to her feet, and walked with her toward her Mercedes.

"I'm taking you home. I can't go back to my apartment, so I'm borrowing your car. Any objections?"

"Some."

"Deal with them."

Ken pulled into Myth's driveway, slowing as he neared the house. He jerked to a stop and stared at her. How could a woman this beautiful repulse him so much?

"Tell me something," he said. "Why did Sabini ask for me personally? How did he know me?"

"I don't know. Maybe you did some work for his company?"

"No. Never."

"Who knows? He could have heard about you anywhere."

Not likely, Ken thought. "I'll get in touch with you later."

"Shouldn't we go to the police?"

"Not yet. First I need to check on some things myself. When I decide to go to the police, you'll hear from me."

"You despise me, don't you?"

Right on target, he thought. As usual. "I can't trust you," he said sharply.

She spoke in a desperate tone he hadn't heard from her before. "What can I do? What can I say?"

"Nothing. That's just it." He looked down. "I've been thinking about Carlos Valez. Maybe someone killed him to *protect* me. It was important I stayed alive to finish Sabini's training, wasn't it?"

"Ken, you can't believe that *I*—"

"I don't know. But I do know you were supposed to see Michaelson, and now he's dead. What am I supposed to think?"

"I don't know," she replied weakly.

He leaned forward and opened her door. "Good-bye, Myth."

She was trying to effect a stoic, hardened expression, but the tears on her cheeks betrayed her. She climbed out of the car and ran up her front steps.

He wanted to think that she actually gave a damn, but he couldn't. He slammed the Mercedes into reverse and backed out of the driveway.

She had played him for a fool, and the fact that he had seen it coming didn't make it any easier. He had been willing to sell his self-respect for the first serious offer that came along. He could never forgive himself for that. He could never forgive her.

He pulled onto the street and raced down the block.

Why had Sabini chosen him? There had to be some link, some connection. Maybe the cops could find it, but they might be happy to nail him to the wall for Sabini's death and let it go at that. Going to the police would only be a last resort.

But he knew that *not* going in was risky too. If the cops picked him up before he could turn himself in, he'd look guiltier than hell. That meant his apartment, his office, his friends, and his usual haunts were off-limits.

But there was one place he could still go.

CHAPTER 20

Carlos Valez's widow was screaming and sobbing in Interrogation Room #2 as Gant and a female officer sat on the other side of the table. Gant looked to his colleague, half expecting her to comfort Alicia. The female officer was merely acting as a witness, per departmental procedure when interrogating females. She obviously did not feel it was her place to calm Gant's witness, as much as he could have used the help.

"Please stop, Mrs. Valez."

"They are going to take my baby away!"

"Nobody said anything about that."

Alicia was doubled over, holding her stomach and rocking. Gant had seen it many times: the "breaking" of witnesses, when all their nervous energy was finally expunged in a massive crying fit. He had just gotten Alicia to admit she had lied about her husband's statements concerning Ken Parker.

"He said Carlos's killer would go free if I didn't say those things."

"Who? Who told you to say them?"

She leaned forward and pleaded with the female officer. "My baby . . . Don't take my baby away."

The female officer did not react.

"Mrs. Valez, everything will be all right if you're honest with me."

She tried to compose herself, but she was hindered by a sudden case of hiccups. Gant poured her a glass of water, and she gulped it down.

"Jesus told me to say those things."

"When you say Jesus, you don't mean God."

"No."

"Jesus Millicent?"

"He said Ken Parker killed Carlos, and he was going to get away with it. Jesus said the only way for my husband's murderer to be punished was for me to say that he threatened Carlos."

Gant nodded. It was exactly what he had suspected. He had doubted her statement from the very beginning, and the subsequent capture of Jesus led him to believe that the man may also have orchestrated this particularly insidious attack against Parker. It was the one thing Jesus wouldn't admit, probably because he didn't want to get Alicia into trouble.

"So what exactly did your husband say about Ken Parker?"

She shook her head as more tears rolled down her cheeks. "Nothing. He never mentioned his name to me."

"Never?"

"No, never. What is going to happen to me?"

As satisfied as Gant felt with having pulled the truth from her, it didn't help him piece together Parker's involvement in the case. Just that morning he had sworn out a warrant for Parker's arrest, but it was entirely possible the suspect had already skipped town. Unless, of course, Parker was responsible for the P.I.'s murder at the Carter Library. Just minutes before, Gant received word that the investigator had been working on the Vikkers Industries embezzling case.

It came back to that case again.

"Follow the money" was standard procedure in cases such as this. Find the money, and the rest of the pieces fall into place. Or so the reasoning goes. Gant suspected it was sound advice in this particular instance, but none of the agencies had been able to come up with anything. Not the Atlanta P.D., not the FBI, not the D.A.'s office.

He had to find Ken Parker.

Gant's thoughts were interrupted as Alicia started sobbing again. "I'll have to give the money back to Jesus," she said.

"What money?"

"He gave me five thousand dollars the day I talked to you."

"Five thousand? Where did he get that kind of money?"

"I don't know. But he said there might be more if I did what he wanted."

Gant turned to the other officer for a reaction. This time the woman looked interested.

"*Five thousand dollars?*" she said.

Gant glared at Jesus through the eggshell-white bars of the jail a few floors above his office. Jesus was copping major attitude.

"Got nothin' to say to you, man."

"Where'd the money come from? The sick and the elderly don't ordinarily have that much cash on hand, and they're the only ones you'd have the guts to rob. I've seen your record."

"Maybe I've moved up in the world."

"Why was it worth five thousand dollars to you for Mrs. Valez to incriminate Ken Parker?"

Jesus yanked down his pants and sat on the steel toilet in the corner of his cell. He smiled at Gant. "Enjoying the show?"

"Charming. Where did the money come from?"

"What do you care?"

"I care if someone else had reason to kill or otherwise harm Ken Parker."

"You got your man. Leave it at that."

"Sorry."

"Well, then, you'd better be prepared to deal."

"I am."

"Will the D.A. back that up?"

"If I ask him, but I have to know you're not bullshitting me. Why do you want to deal now? You could have talked the night we arrested you."

"I thought I might be getting some high-priced legal help, or maybe some money to make it worth my while. Neither has been coming, so I figure I'm on my own."

"Spill it."

Jesus leaned back against the toilet. "Talk to the D.A. I'll need something in writing."

"What do you have for me?"

"This is good. Don't worry, it'll be worth it."

Hound Dog motioned for Ken to enter her trailer. "Where have you been?"

"Dead," he said, closing the door and locking it. "Sorry I've been out of touch."

"I haven't really noticed. I've been busy with Mark. Someone tried to kill him the other night."

Ken felt sick. "Is he okay?"

"Yeah, but if I had come in a minute later, he wouldn't be. I can't tell you how scared I was."

Ken listened as she filled him in on the events of the other night. "Was it a big guy, heavyset, with a ruddy face?" he asked.

"Yes," she said in surprise. "Who is it?"

"He's dead. You don't have to worry about him anymore."

Rather than taking comfort in his words, she seemed suspicious. "How do you know?"

Ken took a deep breath. He had to tell her. Where should he start?

He told Hound Dog about Michaelson's plans to kill him and the frame-up for Sabini's murder.

Hound Dog looked down. "I'm glad he's dead," she said. "It's horrible to say, isn't it? But that's how I feel."

"I can't say I blame you. If I had known he'd come after your boyfriend, I would've warned you. I'm sorry."

She nodded. "What now?"

"I need to find out how Sabini knew me. Why he chose me for his test."

"Luck?"

"Maybe. But if he really had a partner in this scheme, it's possible his partner suggested me. Maybe someone I've worked with before, someone who hired me. If I can find that link—"

"You might find the murderer," she finished for him.

"Right."

"How are you going to find that link?"

Ken walked across the small living room and turned toward her. "I have a pretty good idea."

"He's lying! I've never even heard of this man before." Herbert Decker filled the small interrogation room with his booming voice.

"Jesus Millicent gave us a complete statement," Gant said. "You hired him to kill Ken Parker. When his first attempts failed, you had him convince Carlos Valez's widow to incriminate Parker in her husband's death."

"That's ridiculous. I don't know any of these names."

"Are you sure you don't want your attorney present?"

Decker sputtered, "I don't need a lawyer. I didn't do anything! Why would I want to kill this guy?"

"That was my question. And Jesus couldn't help me answer that one, because you never told him. You never even told him who you were, which was a smart move, but he saw you on television the other night. You were hamming it up at a fund-raiser."

"That's a crime?"

"No. But let me introduce you to someone who has an idea why you would want Ken Parker dead." Gant turned to the wiry, dark-suited man at his left. "This is Special Agent Lars from the Federal Bureau of Investigation."

Lars stepped forward, taking command of the room. Gant noticed how these FBI types liked to do that. "Mr.

Decker, we know that in addition to other Securities violations, your company disseminated false information about Lyceum Metals in order to facilitate your merger with that company."

"Lies."

"We arrested the computer specialist who sold the information to your competitors. He was in Tennessee headed to who knows where. He told us all about your pocket program, and also that Ken Parker was on your trail. We suspect you found out too. We found some photos and surveillance records in the office of your late investigator, Ted Michaelson, that prove he was watching Parker. Maybe Parker was getting too close to the truth, so you wanted him out of the way. He happened to be a murder suspect, and you chose Jesus Millicent because, as a friend of Carlos Valez's, he would have a built-in motive for wanting Ken Parker dead."

"Just as you wanted Don Browne dead," Gant added. "We think he knew about the pocket program too."

Decker burst out laughing. "Utterly fantastic. You can't prove a bit of it!"

"You went after Parker with a two-pronged attack," Gant said, leaning into Decker. "After Jesus failed in his attempts to murder him, Carlos Valez's widow made up those lies. You hoped he would be arrested, which would have effectively put the brakes on his investigation."

"You still can't prove any of this."

Lars ticked the points off on his fingers. "We have Jesus Millicent, we have your pocket program, and we know your only in-house programmer who could have designed it. He'll talk to us. And as we speak, we're zeroing in on Matt Lansing, even though you sent him on an around-the-world tour to keep him away from us."

"This is crazy."

"Is it?" Lars said. "We have a secretary at Lyceum Metals who says that her boss called you to say that Don Browne may have obtained a sample of their RC-7 metal formulation. This was just a day before he was killed."

Decker chuckled, but Gant could see a hard swallow in his throat. "I think I'd better talk to my lawyer."

Gant smiled and opened the door, motioning for Lars to join him in the hallway. They left the room and locked the door behind them.

"I want to work on him awhile longer," Lars said. "But it looks good. I think we got him."

Gant nodded. "This solves your problem, but not mine. I have three murders and twelve million dollars still unaccounted for."

"Kenbo, I hit pay dirt on this Sabini guy. You're sure getting your money's worth."

Ken and Hound Dog sat on stools in Stan Warner's cluttered living room, thumbing through the contents of a bulging file folder. There was a veritable biography of Burton Sabini, complete with press releases, photos, and report copies. It was far more than he had ever expected.

"Where did you get all this stuff?" Hound Dog asked.

"Well, I shouldn't say . . ."

"Okay."

"What the hell. I'm kind of proud of it. I think I've outdone myself this time. I got a lot from the morgue at *The Atlanta Constitution*. They keep clip files on people there, and I got a contact who helps maintain it. She pulled the whole file and gave it to me."

Ken shook his head, squinting as the early afternoon sun beamed through a dirty window. "This is incredible."

"Thanks. I do what I can."

Ken stood and pulled out his wallet. "Two hundred bucks, right?"

"Yeah. Cash only."

Ken counted out ten twenty-dollar bills and handed them over.

Warner turned to Hound Dog. "If there's ever anything I can do for you, just let me know. Maybe a background check? There are some creepy guys out there, and a pretty girl like you might like to know who she's getting involved with."

"Thanks," Hound Dog said, "but I already have a guy."

"How well do you know him?"

"Well enough."

"If you say so." Warner turned back to Ken. "Listen, it's only a matter of time before you're arrested for this Sabini guy's murder."

Hound Dog gave Ken a surprised look. He hadn't told her about the arrest warrant.

"I know," Ken said. "That's why I want this stuff. I don't have long to try to figure out what's going on."

"Be careful with this file. Don't tell anybody where you got it. I gave you a bargain. Don't repay me by bringing the cops down on my operation."

"It's a deal."

It had been a good ten years since Ken had visited Jerry's Billiards, a hole-in-the-wall pool hall downtown. There was a laughable "restaurant" section where customers could enjoy their drinks and microwaved sandwiches in tall booths in the back. Ken noticed that the place was even more run-down than he remembered, with beer stains coloring the pool tables' worn felt tops. But the booths were still there. Good. That's all he needed. A little privacy.

He and Hound Dog slid into a booth. "Nice place," she said sarcastically. "But where else would I expect a fugitive from justice to take me?"

"I'm sorry. If you'd rather not risk being with me, I understand."

"Don't sweat it." She ran her fingers over the razor-marked tabletop. "Is this from cutting lines of coke?"

"That's what it looks like."

"You sure know how to show a girl a good time."

He spilled the file's contents on the table. "Here goes nothing."

"I'm afraid I won't be much help. Only you will know if

there's a link between you and Sabini here." She began sorting the file's contents. "But I'll try to get this stuff into some kind of order."

Ken sifted through the packet one piece at a time. It reminded him of the file Myth had given him, but this was much more comprehensive, including several photos and press releases sent out over the years by Sabini's various employers.

Twenty minutes passed, and they had barely made a dent in the file. Maybe he was wasting his time, Ken thought. There wasn't anything here.

Faded pictures of people he didn't know.

Companies he'd never heard of.

A lifetime of dreams and accomplishments reduced to a single file folder.

Poor Sabini, Ken thought as he looked at a photo of the man's smiling face. The guy really got in over his head.

Ken leaned back and picked up a black-and-white photo of a groundbreaking ceremony, obviously part of a company press kit. There was a row of business-attired employees, one of whom was Sabini, standing in the middle of an open field.

Ken was about to toss it aside, when something caught his eye.

Or, rather, some*one*.

He moved the picture closer to his face and squinted at it. There, next to Sabini, was a face he knew. A smiling face, seven or eight years younger than the one he still saw several times each week, but quite recognizable nonetheless.

"What is it?" Hound Dog asked.

"God," Ken whispered. He gripped the photo and stared at the face, wishing it would miraculously change into another.

This couldn't be happening.

It was the one person he didn't believe—*couldn't believe*—he'd see in these photos.

"Who is it?" Hound Dog asked.

Still holding the picture, Ken stood up. "I'm sorry. I have to go."

"You're *leaving* me?"

He could barely think straight. "Take MARTA, okay?" He fished around in his pockets and came up with a twenty. "No, take a cab. I'm sorry."

"Don't cut me out of the loop!"

He ran from the pool hall.

CHAPTER 21

Ken drove down Piedmont Road, dropping a few cassettes on the seat beside him to keep the photo from blowing away. It was just past six P.M., and the happy-hour nightspots were in full swing. Cars lined up for spaces in the jammed parking lots. Decks overflowed with buzzed customers.

Ken ran his hands through his hair a few times, breathing automobile exhaust fumes noxiously combined with a citrus odor from one of the restaurants. He glanced back down at the photo. The face was still there, only inches from Burton Sabini's.

Margot.

His ex-wife, best friend, and closest confidante.

He felt like hell.

Had the indicators been there the whole time and he just didn't pick up on them? Margot's sudden restlessness, her detachment from Bill . . .

Ken drove for the better part of an hour, finally finding himself in Margot and Bill's neighborhood.

He had to talk to her.

He slowed to a stop in front of his friends' house. Bill, hunched over the engine of his old Vette in the open garage, glanced up. He ambled down the driveway.

"Ken Parker lives!" he yelled out. "Where'd you get the wheels?"

Ken remained sitting, staring at the photograph as Bill stepped alongside the Mercedes. "Where's Margot?"

"Where she always is at this time."

Ken checked his watch. "The jogging trail."

It had been a couple of weeks since he had run with her. The evenings they spent running and talking were some of his favorite times. Even when everything else was turning to shit, he always had the jogging trail with Margot.

"What's wrong, buddy?"

No more secrets. Ken cut the engine. "I'll tell you what's wrong."

He told Bill the whole story, from his very first encounter with Myth at Elwood's.

"I figured that Sabini's partner killed him because he didn't want to risk being exposed at Sabini's trial. Michaelson, the private detective, told Myth he knew who the partner was. He planned to approach him and blow the whistle unless he got a chunk of the money. So Michaelson was killed too."

"Jesus."

"I suspected that Myth killed Michaelson," Ken said. "She was working with him, and he might have told her who Sabini's partner was, even though she said he didn't."

"You don't trust her?"

"I wasn't sure. But listen to this. Sabini wanted *me specifically* to help him get ready for the polygraph test. But he had no way of knowing me unless maybe his partner did. So it occurred to me this person might be someone he and I both knew."

Bill looked at him questioningly.

Ken took a deep breath, grabbed the photo from the seat next to him, and climbed out of the car. He handed the picture to Bill.

Bill looked at it incredulously. "Margot?"

Ken nodded.

"Where did you get this?"

"I have a source."

"You're out of your mind."

"I don't like it either. But it's the only way it makes sense. Margot and Sabini worked at Allied Industries at the same time."

"So what? That was over five years ago. I never heard her talk about this guy."

"You think it's just a coincidence?"

"It can't *be* anything else." Bill glared at him. "Christ, you're pathetic. You never could forgive her, could you?"

"Bill, that isn't—"

"Don't take it out on her. You wanna get mad at somebody, get mad at me!"

"Do you think I *want* her to be involved in this?"

"I can't believe this! Whenever you needed help, I always did whatever I could to—"

"Bullshit. I *never* asked for your help!"

"You needed it!"

"No! You needed to *think* I needed your help. And you needed for the whole world to think I did too. It's always been that way. You needed that to feel good about yourself. Never mind how you made *me* feel."

"Fuck you."

Ken grabbed the photo and jumped into the Mercedes.

"Where are you going?" Bill shouted. "Wait!"

Ken roared away without casting another glance in his direction.

He should be running with her, Ken thought. Laughing, joking, forgetting his troubles. He shifted on the hood of the Mercedes. The car was parked on the street, facing the jogging trail. Margot would be coming any minute now.

Ken lit a cigarette. Why did it have to be her?

The last tinges of sunlight were disappearing when he caught sight of Margot coming over the hill. She drew closer, obviously surprised to see him. She stopped and pulled off her Walkman headset. "The police are looking for you."

He didn't say anything. He took another long drag on the cigarette.

"What's going on, Ken?"

He searched for the right words. "You know, there haven't been a lot of people I could count on in this world. Not really. Nobody who tells the truth to himself or anybody else. Nobody except you."

She frowned. "What's this about?"

"Even when you left me for Bill, it was because I practically pushed you out. You were always honest with me."

She gave him a bewildered look.

Maybe she *was* bewildered, he thought. Maybe she didn't know any of this. God, he couldn't stop hoping.

"Why'd you do it, Margot?"

"What are you talking about?"

"You know exactly what I'm talking about. You and Burton Sabini."

"Burton Sabini?"

"Christ, Margot. *Don't fucking lie to me!*"

"What is this all about?"

"Look, I want to hear your side of it."

"Side of what?"

She was looking at him as if he were crazy. He studied her. He probably knew her better than he knew anyone, and she seemed genuinely perplexed.

He forged ahead. "I didn't come here for you to lie to me. I want you to explain. Tell me *why*."

"There's nothing to explain! I barely knew Burton Sabini. We worked at the same place for a while. He just got me the job there."

Doubt was starting to creep in. Margot wasn't this good a liar. . . .

She continued. "Bill arranged it with him, and I was there until—"

"*Bill* knew him?"

"They were in the reserves together. I needed a job, and

Bill talked him into giving me a good word. Dammit, Ken, are you going to tell me what this is all about?"

She was telling the truth. She did not have the slightest idea what was going on.

Bill.

He hadn't mentioned knowing Sabini. And now Bill knew *everything* there was to know about this case. Including the fact that Myth might know the identity of Sabini's partner.

"Holy shit," Ken whispered.

Myth ran her hand under the showerhead, feeling the water and letting it spray against the beveled glass door.

She hoped the hot shower would help her relax, but that would probably take a tranquilizer.

It was happening again. And she couldn't stop it.

Gossip had already begun to circulate about her conduct in the Burton Sabini case, and more was certainly to follow in the days to come. Even if formal charges were not filed against her, such talk could have a devastating impact on her career.

Career? That was only part of it. Ken was gone, and she was alone again. But that's how she functioned best, wasn't it? No one to answer to, no one to tell her what to do . . .

She scowled at her reflection in the mirror. She knew she'd lose her looks someday, and she'd be as ugly as she felt inside.

Good, she thought. She couldn't wait.

She peeled off her robe and stepped into the shower, letting the water massage her face and neck. She could not hear the phone ringing a few feet from the bathroom door.

"If you're there, pick up!" Ken yelled into the pay phone. *"Pick up!"*

No one did.

He spoke urgently. "Sabini's partner is Bill Aronson! If you get in, lock up and don't open your door for anyone but me. I'm on my way over."

He hammered the hook and dialed another number.

"Hello?"

"Hound Dog, it's me."

"I'm not talking to you."

"I'm sorry, but I need you to do something."

"Tough."

"Please. You're closer than I am. Go to Myth Daniels's house. If she's there, get her out. If she's not, don't let her go in."

"What's wrong?"

"She's not our killer, but she could be in danger. Be careful. If you get there and there's a sign of anything wrong, get the hell away. I'm heading there right now."

"I just grabbed my keys and helmet. I'm on my way."

Ken slammed down the receiver and bolted for his car.

Bill wasn't ready to give up his life.

He walked up Myth Daniels's long driveway and approached the winding stairs.

Maybe he should've hopped the first plane out of the country. Maybe he should've skipped town as soon as he had the money. But no. He didn't have the guts to start over.

The whole time he and Sabini had planned their heist, it seemed so simple. Get the money, split it, and live happily ever after.

But how? He could never tell Margot. He'd have to leave her. He couldn't stay in the United States either. Not if he wanted to actually spend the money.

He felt cheated. There had been the hard work: the research, the clandestine meetings with Sabini, coordinating the connections through his bank. All to make sure the transactions couldn't be traced back to him. He thought Sabini's ass was covered too. If only that special audit had come a few months later.

But Sabini was indicted and the bastard got scared. He wanted to give back the money and call it a day. Which would have meant giving up Bill too. They had argued for months, until Sabini finally told him he was going to plea out despite having passed the D.A.'s polygraph test.

Bill couldn't let that happen.

That night near the Underground, Sabini didn't even fight back. Maybe he was drunk, or maybe he really wanted his sad, miserable life to be over.

Bill knew he would eventually come up with a plan. As soon as he was through stomping out these annoying fires, he could concentrate on his future.

The humid wind howled through the trees. It was getting dark.

He stepped quietly toward the front door and tried it. Locked. He rang the doorbell.

He waited a full minute, but there was no answer.

He slipped on a pair of work gloves and punched a stained glass window next to the door frame, shattering it. He pulled apart two of the heavy wire borders and reached through to unlock the door.

As he stepped over the threshold, he saw an alarm panel. No flashing lights, no alert. Myth Daniels had not yet activated her alarm for the evening. Bill cautiously stepped into the foyer, looking and listening for any sign of her. He heard a shower on the floor above.

He turned and climbed the oak stairway.

Upstairs, Myth turned off the water and stepped out of the shower. God, she was tired. She shrugged on her robe, pulling the terry cloth against her body. She opened the bathroom door.

Bed. She needed to forget everything until—

A blade snapped to her throat. An arm hooked around her waist.

She gasped.

"Are you going to scream?"

She could barely hear him. Her attention was riveted on the blade at her throat.

"Are you going to scream?" he repeated.

"No," she whispered.

"Good. Then show me where you keep your files."

She still did not move.

He shook her violently. "Your *files*!"

She carefully led him down the hallway, aware that any sudden movement could drive the razor-sharp blade into her larynx.

Her breathing was slow and measured even as her heart pounded furiously. She felt hyperaware of her surroundings.

The sound of the man's breathing.

The stench from his oil-stained T-shirt.

The coolness of the tiled floor on her bare wet feet.

They passed an etched mirror on the wall. She stole a glance at it, recognizing the man immediately. She'd seen him the first night she had met Ken, at Elwood's.

He caught Myth's glance but did not react.

He didn't care that she could recognize him, she realized. Because he was going to kill her.

Traffic was piling up on the I-75/85 downtown connector, and it appeared to Ken that all the southbound lanes were jammed up ahead. Probably a Braves game, he thought. Shit.

He took the shoulder and raced over mini–speed bumps to the next exit. He would have to try his luck on surface roads. The Mercedes slightly resisted the steep climb up the exit ramp, but gained power as it neared the traffic light at the top.

He braked to a screaming halt behind an old pickup truck. Two teenagers sitting in the flatbed stared at him as he waited for the light to change.

Please let her be away from home, he thought. If he was right about Bill, Myth could be in danger. And it would be nobody's fault but his own.

"Open it."

Bill stepped back as Myth turned the key in her tall

rosewood lateral file. The top drawer pulled open just below her eye level.

"You know who I am, don't you?" he asked.

She nodded.

"Then I'm sure you know what files I want. Everything you have on Sabini."

She started pulling out folders. "*You* were his partner."

Bill smiled. "So were you, in a way. I need all your records for this case."

"Most of them are in my office."

"All in good time. Nothing can be left behind . . . except for these."

Still keeping a watchful eye on her, Bill reached into his jeans pocket and pulled out two rolled-up certificates, now quite crumpled, each with a gold seal.

"Treasury notes?"

"From Denmark. The cops will do some checking and find that a large number of these notes were purchased right after the money was stolen. They'll find these notes that you accidentally left behind."

That *she* left behind? Myth tried not to look as terrified as she was.

"You should appreciate this," he said. "I'm just using your own plan. Yours and Michaelson's. Kenny told me all about it. This way it'll look like *you're* the one who left town with the loot. Not Ken. Same scheme, different victim." He smiled. "You're a beautiful woman. I can see why Sabini was so nuts about you. He was in love with you, did you know that?"

She didn't reply.

"You *did* know," he said with a chuckle. "I saw him only a few times in those last couple of months, but whenever I did, you're all he talked about. He never even told you, did he?"

Still she did not reply.

"Did he?"

"No."

"That's because he was weak. Scared. He had big dreams, but he didn't have what it took to follow through. This whole scheme was his idea. *He* approached *me*. But he tried to chicken out half a dozen times. Right up until the end."

"You killed him," she said without looking up. "Just like you're going to kill me."

He said nothing.

Hound Dog skidded to a stop in Myth Daniels's driveway. She dismounted and looked at the house. There were no lights on. She crept up the front stairs, inching her way to the door.

It was ajar.

The glass panel next to it was broken.

She was too late.

Hound Dog whipped out her cellular phone to punch 911. But before she could punch the second "1," a hand reached out and pulled her into the house.

The phone hit the floor.

The door slammed shut behind her.

A man with a knife pulled her close. "You must be Hound Dog. Ken just told me about you . . . and your motorcycle."

She tried to ignore the knife at her stomach. "And you would be . . ."

He grabbed the back of her neck and guided her toward the stairway. With the knife rising to her chest, he steered her up the stairs and down the upstairs hallway.

She tried not to cry out when she saw Myth Daniels bound and gagged on the office floor. Hound Dog couldn't tell if the woman was alive or dead.

"Why are you here?" he whispered.

Hound Dog took stock of her surroundings. There had to be a way out. If she died tonight, it wasn't going to be without a fight.

"Did you hear me?" the man said, pressing the knife into her. A drop of blood appeared on her sweatshirt.

"Yes," Hound Dog said. "Don't kill me. Please."

"We've already established that you're going to die. The only question is, How painful does it have to be? The choice is yours."

Hound Dog nodded, and then, in one lightning-fast motion, she pulled sharply on the file drawer and rammed him on the chin.

He stumbled back.

His blade lunged at her.

She ducked, but wasn't fast enough. It swiped the side of her neck.

The slash felt cold. Wet.

He fell to the floor.

She stumbled, but regained her footing as she hurtled through the doorway. She could hear him pulling himself up behind her.

Not much time, think fast . . .

She jumped through a doorway and yanked the door closed behind her. It was a large closet, but she could see light underneath another door at the far end. She moved through the closet, pushing and burrowing through the clothes and boxes. Keep pushing, a little farther . . .

She reached the other door, and turned the knob.

Locked.

Dammit!

She fought desperately with the knob.

She froze.

He was coming down the hallway. His footsteps stopped in front of the closet.

Did he know she was in there?

She didn't breathe.

Why didn't he move on?

He was listening.

Waiting for her to do something stupid.

The seconds ticked by. She had to take a breath. Surely he would hear her.

He moved away. She heard his footsteps echoing in the hallway.

Tap. Tap. Tap. Tap.

They receded, then became muffled as he entered the other room.

The bastard had a plan, she thought. She was pretty sure the only way down to the first floor was the staircase at the far end of the hall. He was starting at that end so he could work his way back.

He was sealing her in.

Escape was out of the question. She had to get to a phone.

Maybe there was one in the room on the other side of the closet door.

If only it wasn't locked . . .

Her neck still felt cold. Numb. She yanked a sweater down and dabbed it against her wound.

She crept back toward the hallway and listened.

The man was still in the bedroom.

She peered out, then silently moved toward the next room. Her eyes were trained at the end of the hallway, where he could appear at any moment.

As she approached the door, she noticed it was slightly ajar.

Would it creak? Better not take the chance. She sucked in a deep breath and shimmied through, brushing only slightly against the door.

Please, please, please let there be a phone.

In the dim light she saw one on the end table. She lifted the receiver.

Before she could dial, she heard that tapping sound on the hallway tile.

His footsteps.

She dropped the handset and scrambled for the door, pressing herself against the wall behind it.

She waited.

Tap. Tap. Tap.

The footsteps stopped.

The door slowly creaked open. It swung closer and closer, stopping only inches from her face.

She imagined he was looking around the room. The phone was off the hook, dangling from the end table.

"We can work out a deal, young lady."

She didn't breathe.

He took a step inside.

This was it, she thought. Her last chance . . .

She threw herself against the heavy wooden door. It swung at the man, striking his back and shoulders with bone-crunching force.

He doubled over and staggered a few steps.

Hound Dog jumped from the other side and grabbed his wrist with both hands. With more speed than strength she shoved his fist—and the knife—into his stomach.

He dropped to his knees. A crimson stain grew on his shirt.

She jumped over him and started running toward the staircase. Out of the corner of her eye she saw a shadow coming after her. Before she could react, he slid across the hallway and grabbed her ankles.

She screamed.

She tumbled down the first flight of stairs, her arms and legs banging and bruising as she tried to slow herself. She caught brief glimpses of the man sprawled above her, waiting to pounce again.

She finally collapsed on the landing. Her right leg throbbed. Was it broken? God, no . . .

The man jammed his knife into a wooden step and pulled himself down. He pulled the blade free and jammed it into the next one.

He was working his way down to her, one step at a time. . . .

Ken's stomach lurched at the sight of Bill's car parked at the curb.

He was too late.

He sped into the driveway, barely clearing the brick mailbox, then braking to avoid hitting Hound Dog's motorcycle. He leapt from the car and ran up the front stairs two at a time.

A woman screamed.

He looked to the bay window at his right.

They were on the landing. Hound Dog's back was to him, and Bill was standing over her.

Ken threw his legs over the railing, calculating the distance. Seven, maybe eight feet across.

A moment of doubt. Don't think, he told himself. No time.

He kicked away from his perch, keeping his head low as he crashed through the bay window.

His first sensations were purely of sound.

The smashing of glass.

The low-pitched breaking and splintering of wood.

He felt his skin sliced in a dozen places at once—his head, shoulders, arms, legs . . .

His eyes closed, he collided with Bill. They fell against the stairs.

The knife spun crazily out of Bill's hand.

Stunned, Ken was vaguely aware of Hound Dog jumping for it, but Bill was faster. Bill grabbed the knife and held it against Hound Dog's throat.

"Don't move. I'm finishing it, Kenny!"

"No, you're not."

Ken stood and pulled out his gun. Warm wind whistled through the shattered windowpanes, but he couldn't have felt more chilled.

"You don't get it, do you?" Bill pulled Hound Dog closer to him on the landing. "She's not important. We're set, buddy. The money . . . it's ours!"

Ken aimed the gun down at Bill. "It's over."

"It doesn't have to be."

"Yes, it does. Put the knife down."

Bill kept the knife where it was. "Kenny . . ."

"When did life get so cheap to you?"

"I didn't want it to be like this."

"Then how did it happen?"

"I had to do it, Kenny. I didn't want to go to jail. Sabini was gonna fold. And that investigator was gonna turn me in if I didn't cut him a piece!"

"Then why didn't you pay him off?"

Bill didn't answer. He leaned over, grimacing in pain from his still-bleeding puncture wound. He kept the knife at Hound Dog's throat.

Ken took a step closer to him. "Drop it."

"I was looking out for you, man. That's why I sent Sabini to you in the first place! I knew you needed the money."

"Don't pull this bullshit with me. You were out for yourself."

"Kenny, that Valez guy was gonna kill you. If I hadn't—"

"Murdered him?"

"He would have killed you."

"You wanted me around to finish Sabini's training. That's all."

"No. Look, we can carve up the money. Just me and you. Margot doesn't even know about it!"

"I said it was over!"

"No. It's not. Listen to me. Sabini gave me the codes I needed to monitor Vikkers' secret transactions. Channels they use to bribe foreign politicians to get contracts, that kind of stuff. Get this: They've been funneling money to the governor. *Our* governor!"

"I don't care."

"I have the printouts to prove it. Don't you see? He can grease the wheels for us."

"Drop the fucking knife!"

"I'm trying to *help* you!"

Ken shook his head. Bill actually believed his own bullshit. Just like everyone else in the world.

Blood started beading on Hound Dog's throat.

Ken squeezed the trigger. The gunshot echoed through the house.

Bill spun around, wheezing and gasping for air as his chest was ripped apart. He tumbled down the stairs.

"Liar," Ken said.

Ken paced in the driveway of Margot and Bill's house, looking at the surreal scene playing before him. Swarms of police officers scurried about, some with dogs, others with high-powered flashlights. Several arc lamps lit up the garage and yard, casting the house in a harsh white glare. It was a quarter past four in the morning.

Ken felt sick.

Bill.

The guy he had known since he was thirteen years old.

They had taken their first sip of beer together.

Their first cigarette.

On the night Ken lost his virginity, Bill was the first person he told.

And tonight he had ended his friend's life in a fraction of a second.

Hound Dog stepped toward Ken. She, like he, was now accessorized in gauze bandages.

"They don't need all this," Ken said. "I told them where it was."

"How are you so sure?"

"I'm sure."

She followed him to the garage, where police mechanics were conducting a search of Bill's vintage Corvette. As they watched, an officer rolled out from under the car with a plastic-wrapped bundle.

"Lieutenant!" the officer shouted.

Gant stepped forward and took the bundle into his plastic-gloved hands. He peeled back the wrapper to reveal a hefty stack of treasury certificates and accounting forms.

Gant joined Ken and Hound Dog in the driveway. He motioned back to the car. "You were right."

Ken nodded. He hadn't had any doubts.

Margot appeared in the doorway. Ken had been the one to tell her about Bill, and she had reacted with shocked disbelief. When he left her side, he still wasn't sure the death had really registered.

She now looked at Ken silently, with eyes that communicated more sadness, more disillusionment, than he had ever known. If only he could take that pain away.

She turned and went back inside the house.

She was gone forever, Ken thought. Like Bill.

"We have a lot to sort out," Gant said. "I just talked to the hospital. Myth Daniels will be okay. I need statements from all of you."

Ken nodded.

Gant held up the accounting forms. "Electronic fund transfers," he read aloud.

"Someone should look at those," Ken said. "They may show that the governor of Georgia has been earning some extra cash from Vikkers Industries. At least that's what Bill said."

Gant shook his head as he put the forms and treasury notes into an evidence bag. "I'll make sure the FBI is present for your statement. They'll want to hear this." He pointed to the garage. "How'd you know where to look?"

Ken looked down at the Corvette. "Bill always said this car wasn't for driving. He said it was for dreaming."

EPILOGUE

In the days and weeks that followed, Ken couldn't shake the image of his friend twisting and twirling backward, his chest blown open, eyes rolled upward, mouth pulled into a horrible grimace.

It was the worst thing he had ever seen.

Or done.

When the police lab called to tell him he could have his gun back, he thanked them and said he would pick it up the following day. He never did.

The investigation continued, and though he was called upon to clarify aspects of the case several times, he was never formally charged. Neither was Myth, though the state bar took a close look at her actions. She was helped by the fact that the National Polygraph Association refused to admit that it was possible to beat polygraph exams.

That did not, however, prevent the trade group from suspending Ken's license for ninety days.

No sooner had that missive come down, when he was contacted by the Emory University psychology department. They wanted him to assist in a new study relating to polygraph effectiveness. Apparently, media coverage of his case prompted the study, and Ken suddenly found himself making more money than he had ever made as an examiner.

The Vikkers president, Herbert Decker, was headed for trial for Securities violations and conspiracy to commit murder. Although the man was suspected of ordering Don Browne's killing, he was not charged, due to the fact that his presumed hatchet man, the late Ted Michaelson, was incapable of turning evidence against him.

The accounting forms did incriminate Governor Holden, helping to cement the government's case against Vikkers Industries. Holden claimed to be unaware of the numbered account the company had credited, but the FBI, following the same trail Bill had discovered, traced it back to the governor. Decker refused to confirm their findings. As the government's probe continued, Holden announced he would not run for another term so he could launch his own investigation and clear his name. In the meantime, he quietly began to solicit financial support for a U.S. Senate campaign.

Ken missed Margot. He had not seen her since Bill's funeral, a day he wished he could forget. He felt more alone than ever, unable to share his grief and frustration with anyone.

Margot told him she wanted some time to herself. He understood, but he still jogged every Monday, Wednesday, and Friday, hoping to see her one day at her usual start-up point on the trail. He began to realize he'd been right about losing her that night.

One Saturday afternoon he finally made himself look for the brick that Bill had bought for him in Centennial Olympic Park. It took some searching, but eventually he found it. It wasn't the good-natured insult Ken was expecting. Instead, it read KEN PARKER—BESTEST BUD.

He wished it had been an insult.

He visited Hound Dog and her boyfriend, and happily, Mark was on his way to a full recovery. Hound Dog was back on the streets every night, scanner on, waiting for crime scene info.

One bright spot in Ken's life was seeing his brother testify before the congressional committee in Washington. Ken surprised Bobby by driving all night to be at the hearing. Bobby spoke eloquently, with passion and conviction, moving other witnesses to tears. Ken had never been prouder of his younger brother. Although no money had yet been appropriated, the fact that it was a congressional election year could work in Bobby's favor.

Ken spent a lot of time driving, trying to reconcile himself to the changes in his life. Bill was gone, Margot was out of the picture, and Myth . . .

He made no attempt to contact her, though she had tried to call him several times. It didn't feel right. She had shown him a part of himself he hated, a part of himself he would always associate with her. The liar. The master of self-deception. If there was any good in this, he thought, it was that he had finally confronted who he really was. And maybe, just maybe, he had beaten back his darker side.

He was finally evicted from his office building, not for late rent payments, but because Downey had determined he was a "disruptive presence" in the building. Ken knew he could have fought it, but there was no use. He still had several weeks to go on his license suspension, and the rent was only a drain on his funds.

"Keep or throw away?" Hound Dog held up a stack of polygraph industry newsletters.

"Throw away."

It was Ken's last day in the office, and Hound Dog was helping him pack up. He folded in the flaps of a large cardboard box. "I think I'm actually going to miss this place," he said.

"It's been a big part of your life."

"It's ugly, dilapidated, and probably unsafe, but it was comfortable. I almost feel like I'm abandoning a crippled, one-eyed dog nobody wants. I'll even miss the receptionist."

"*I* won't," Hound Dog said. "She gives me the creeps."

A knock sounded on the open door. They looked over to see a young man with a baseball cap. "Ken Parker?"

"Yeah."

"I have a delivery for you, sir."

The kid handed him an envelope. Ken signed for it, and while he tried to decide whether to tip him, the messenger disappeared.

"You should have tipped him," Hound Dog said.

"Yeah, yeah, yeah." Ken opened the envelope and pulled out several papers. On top was a note handwritten on Myth's letterhead.

> Dear Ken,
>
> I'm not writing to apologize, though I am sorrier than you will ever know for what has happened.
>
> Enclosed is a promissory note from Vikkers Industries' insurance company for the return of the stolen funds. I want you to have it all, Ken. I hope it gives you an opportunity for the "new start" you've been looking for.
>
> Myth

He looked at the papers underneath. After wading through the legalese, his eyes zeroed in on the numbers.

Five hundred and sixteen thousand dollars.

The finder's fee. It was all his.

Five hundred and sixteen thousand dollars. It was a fortune, but still a pittance compared to all he had lost.

He handed the papers to Hound Dog. She read the letter and found the dollar amount. "That's great, Ken."

"I want you to have half."

"No."

"You earned it."

She shook her head. "I'm getting a trust fund in a few years that makes this look like spare change. If, of course, my folks don't cut me off."

"See? You may need it."

Hound Dog thought for a moment. "Maybe you can give

a little to Mark, so he doesn't have to work at the strip club anymore."

"Sure."

"We'll discuss it over dinner. You're still coming, aren't you? Mark's making one of his specialties."

"Wouldn't miss it."

Hound Dog tied a plastic trash bag and hoisted it over her shoulder. "I'll meet you downstairs, okay?"

"Okay. Thanks."

"Cheer up. If you're real good, maybe later I'll tell you why everybody calls me Hound Dog."

He smiled. "It's a deal."

She gave him a squeeze on the arm and left the office.

He looked around. Everything was neatly boxed and ready to go.

Go where?

To his apartment? He had enough junk there already, he thought. And that's what all this stuff was. Junk. Artifacts of a life he'd just as soon forget.

He reached into his pocket, pulled out his trick deck of cards, and tossed it into the waste can. He turned off the lights and took one last look around.

There, silhouetted in the room, was his beat-up old polygraph. With its sensors removed, it looked like a quadruple amputee, helpless on its metal stand.

How fitting, he thought.

He walked out of the office, slowly pulling the door closed behind him. It groaned and creaked, finally swinging shut with a click. Ken took a deep breath, taking in the building's familiar musty smell one last time.

He never looked back as he walked down the stairs and stepped into the pale orange light of dusk.

ACKNOWLEDGMENTS

This book would not have been possible without the support of so many people who helped nourish the story throughout its long and unusual genesis:

Patricia Karlan, Don Roos, Courtenay Valenti, and Bruce Moccia, who lent such vital encouragement when the book was in its earliest stages.

My literary agent, Andrea Cirillo, who first urged me to try my hand at novel writing, and my motion picture agent, Joel Gotler, whose belief in this story continues to inspire me.

My editors extraordinaire, Beth de Guzman and Nita Taublib, whose skill and gentle guidance gave me a terrific introduction to the publishing world.

My lovely wife, Lisa, the most honest person I've ever known.

And last, but certainly not least, I owe a debt of gratitude to the polygraph examiners I visited—and their complete inability to determine that I was lying to them.

ABOUT THE AUTHOR

ROY JOHANSEN'S first screenplay, *Murder 101,* was produced for cable TV and won an Edgar Award as well as a Focus Award, which is sponsored by Steven Spielberg, Francis Ford Coppola, George Lucas, and Martin Scorsese. He has written projects for Disney, MGM, United Artists, Universal, and Warner Bros. He lives in southern California with his wife, Lisa.

Look for Roy Johansen's next novel

BEYOND BELIEF

available in hardcover April 2001

Here's a sneak peek.

Maybe tonight was the night he'd learn to believe in magic.

Not damned likely, Joe Bailey thought.

Over the years, he'd received too many calls that promised something extraordinary but never actually delivered. Why would tonight be any different? He unbuttoned his overcoat as he climbed the polished granite front stairs of a mansion on Habersham Drive. He checked his watch: 1:40.

The call had come only fifteen minutes earlier from Lieutenant Vince Powell, who headed the evening watch at the station. There had been a homicide.

"I'm in bunco," Joe told him. "You're sure I'm the guy you want?"

"I know who you are," Powell said. "You bust up all the phony séances, psychics, and witch-doctor scams."

"Among other things, yeah."

"Well, we got something right up your alley. It's scaring the shit out of the officers on the scene. You wanna take a look?"

No, he didn't want to take a look, but he was here anyway. He strode through the open door. It was a cold February night in Atlanta. Mid-thirties, he guessed. He could still see his breath in the air as he walked through the foyer and looked for the uniformed officer who usually secured a crime scene.

Probably upstairs getting the shit scared out of him.

There were voices echoing down the stairway. Not the matter-of-fact grunts he'd heard at the few murder scenes he'd visited; the words were the same but uttered faster and louder. A totally different energy.

But whatever it was waiting for him up there, he was sure it wasn't magic. He always tried to allow for any possibility, but in his six years on the bunco squad, he had yet to see the genuine article. He'd been a professional magician in his twenties and early thirties, so the smoke-and-mirrors stuff had quickly become his specialty. It was still only a small part of his job, but when the squad needed someone to pull apart spirit scams or sleight-of-hand cons, he was the man.

He'd never been asked to investigate a murder.

"Who the hell told you that you could be a *real* cop?" a voice drawled from the top of the stairs.

Joe looked up to see Carla Fisk, a detective he had once worked with on a beauty-juice investigation. The perp had been selling bottles of tonic that supposedly made its female users flower into beautiful specimens of womanhood. Carla, who cheerfully admitted that her face looked like the "before" picture of almost every beauty ad ever printed, had worn a wire and purchased a few of the bottles. She was no glamour girl, but she was one of the most beautiful people Joe had ever known.

He smiled. "It's past your bedtime, Carla. You're not working nights, are you?"

"Nah, I was down the street at Manuel's Tavern. Everyone wanted a look at this one."

"Why?"

"You'll see. How's that little girl of yours?"

"Furious. She wasn't happy about being woken up and shuttled to the neighbor's place so I could go check out a Buckhead murder scene."

"She'll understand."

"Maybe if I come back with Yo-Yo Ma tickets."

"You gotta talk to your kid about the music she listens to. People are gonna think she has a brain." Carla grinned, flashing yellow teeth. Then she cocked her head down the hall. "You'd better get down there. They're waiting for you."

He walked down the long hallway, feeling a sudden chill. Was it getting colder? No, it was probably just his imagination, fed by the nervous voices at the end of the hall.

What was in that room?

He stepped into the doorway and froze. He thought he was prepared for anything, but he was wrong.

Suspended high on the far wall, a man was impaled by a large spiked sculpture.

The sight was so odd, so out of the realm of belief, that Joe looked away, then back, as if another glance would help it make sense.

It didn't.

He was staring into a large room with tall ceilings, perhaps fifteen feet high. There were grand bookshelves, two towering windows, a seating area, and a grand piano. The corpse was suspended at least eight feet. The chrome sculpture, a skyline of gleaming spikes, was driven downward into the victim's chest, sticking him to the wall like pushpins into a paper doll. A pool of blood had collected on the floor below, along with one of the man's shoes.

"Unbelievable," Joe murmured.

"Is that your professional opinion?"

He turned to see a tall, tanned, fiftyish detective standing next to him. The man didn't offer to shake hands.

"Are you Bailey?"

"Yeah."

"I'm Mark Howe, Homicide. Have you ever seen anything like this?"

"No."

"How did this happen?"

"I have no earthly idea."

Howe clicked his tongue. "That's not the answer I wanted to hear. You've never investigated a homicide, have you?"

Joe shook his head. "No, I'm in bunco."

"Right. The Spirit Basher."

Joe sighed. "The Spirit Basher" was a nickname he'd picked up after several high-profile busts in which he had debunked phony spiritualists and psychics. The local papers championed the headline-ready nickname whenever he ventured into that territory.

"Yeah," Joe said. "Some people call me that."

Howe made a face as if he had just bitten into a lemon. "For the record, I didn't ask for you. It was my boss's idea to call you in."

"I'm glad we got *that* straight."

"No offense, but you spend most of your days breaking up insurance scams, gas station pump fixes, and auto repair con jobs, am I right?"

"And you spend most of your days investigating drug deals gone bad and domestic disputes settled at the end of a firearm. I'd say we're both in foreign territory here."

That shut him up.

Joe glanced around the room. Two fingerprint specialists were dusting every flat surface, and a medical examiner was walking from side to side, staring up at the corpse. A photographer was snapping pictures of the scene.

Joe studied the corpse's face.

It wasn't possible.

"Christ. I know this man," Joe finally said.

"What?"

As if this weren't bizarre enough. "I know him. This is Dr. Robert Nelson."

"That's right," Howe said, surprised.

"He was a professor at Landwyn University. He co-chaired the parapsychology program."

"Friend of yours?"

"He despised me. I do some part-time work for the university. The head of the humanities department doesn't believe in that stuff, and he brings me in to debunk the psychics and spiritualists they study."

Joe couldn't take his gaze from Nelson. The professor had been in his early fifties, and his strong chin and cheek bones were tensed in a horrible grimace. It almost appeared as though Nelson were still feeling the agony of that sculpture rammed through his chest. Blood had run down his blue oxford-cloth shirt to his khaki slacks and dripped from the cuffs. Another bloodstain ran down the wall behind him, obviously from the exit wound.

"Who found him?"

"Girlfriend. Eve Chandler. She's in the next room. She let herself in around eleven and found him. She said there have been some disturbances here the past few nights."

"What do you mean?"

"Objects moving around, furniture shifting, and that piano tipping over. All by themselves."

"Did she see these things happening?"

"That's what she says. She's sure they were caused by the same person who made the statue fly into her boyfriend's chest."

"And who would that be?"

"An eight-year-old boy."

"That little bastard murdered him, I know he did."

Eve Chandler leaned back on Nelson's sofa. She was an attractive woman in her early forties, and she had obviously taken a heavy dose of sedatives. She was slurring her words, and her eyes were thin slits. Tears streamed down her face, and she occasionally wiped them from her neck with the back of her hand.

"Who is this boy?" Joe asked.

"It's a kid Robert was studying. His name is . . . Jesse Randall. He makes objects move with his mind."

"Even five-foot sculptures?" Howe asked skeptically.

"All kinds of things. Robert was very excited about him. He said this boy was like no one he had ever seen."

"Why would the boy want to hurt him?" Joe asked.

She stared at Joe as if he were suddenly speaking a foreign language.

Howe leaned forward. "Miss Chandler, are you on medication?"

She nodded. "Valium. Lots of it. I have a prescription. Wanna see the bottle?"

"That won't be necessary," Joe said. "I know this is hard for you, but we need you to focus. It's important." Eve nodded, but Joe still wasn't sure she understood. He spoke slowly. "Can you tell us why the boy would want to hurt Dr. Nelson?"

"He and Robert had some kind of disagreement. I'm not sure what happened, but he didn't want to see Robert anymore. That's when the shadow storms began."

"What?" Howe asked.

"Shadow storms," Joe said. "Supposed psychic phenomena caused by angry or emotional dreams. While the telekinetic sleeps, objects will move around, flying off shelves and smashing against walls—that kind of thing."

She nodded. "It always started just after nine o'clock, which Robert said was Jesse Randall's bedtime. All hell broke loose after nine o'clock."

"You saw these objects moving around?" Joe asked.

"Mostly we heard them, but a couple of times we saw things flying through the air."

"Can you show me what you actually saw moving?"

"They were both downstairs."

"We'll go down with you."

Howe shook his head. "We have some other things to sort through first."

"Now," Joe said.

"I have a few other questions first," Howe said.

"They'll keep," Joe said. "This is evidence that could be tampered with, stolen, or otherwise compromised." He stood. "Please, Ms. Chandler, will you show us?"

She led them to a sitting room adjacent to the foyer, where she picked up a small decorative musical instrument made up of five bamboo reeds tied together by red twine. She handed it to Joe. "We heard this playing from the next room. Every time we went in to look, the playing stopped. Once, when Robert went to look, it flew out of the room and almost hit him."

Joe inspected the instrument, but there didn't seem to be anything unusual about it. "Did either of you see it rise from the shelf?"

"Hell, we saw it flying toward his *head*."

"That's not quite the same. Did you see it rise from the shelf?"

She thought for a moment. "No. He may have though." She wiped more tears from her face and neck. "Jesus, I can't believe this."

Howe offered her a handkerchief, but she waved it away. "Keep it," she said. "I gotta be pretty close to running dry."

Joe sympathetically pressed her arm. "Can you tell me what else you saw?"

She nodded. "It was in the kitchen. I'll show you."

They followed her into the large, magnificently decorated kitchen, which was centered by a ten-foot marble-topped island. A rack hung above it with dozens of pots and pans.

"Sometimes, during the night, these pans would swing by themselves and start banging together." She shuddered. "They'd make a terrible sound."

Joe pushed some of the pans, and the eerie, hollow clanging sounded like dozens of out-of-tune gongs.

"Imagine hearing that in the middle of the night," Eve said. "We came downstairs, and as we got closer to the kitchen, the pots started to bang together harder and harder. By the time we made it in here, a few of them were even flying off the hooks and hitting the island and the floor. We watched them swinging and clanging into each other for more than a minute, making that horrible sound. Then they just stopped."

"You have no idea what caused it?"

"Robert had an idea."

"The little boy and his shadow storms," Howe said sarcastically.

"Yes." Eve's expression hardened. "Can you arrest him?"

Howe shook his head. "There's the matter of proof. We don't have any evidence that links the murder with Jesse Randall."

"How else could it have happened?"

Howe turned to Joe. "You wanna take that one?"

Joe faced Eve, but he was speaking to Howe as much as he was to her. "Ms. Chandler, in my experience, telekinesis does not exist. Part of what I do in my job is to expose con artists who try to convince others that they have paranormal abilities. I've never seen a psychic claim that couldn't be explained in another, more plausible way."

Her face flushed. "I know who you are and what your feelings are, Mr. Bailey," she said fiercely. "Robert told me how difficult you made his job. I loved that man, and his life's work was based on the fact that this phenomenon *does* exist. If you refuse to believe that, then maybe they should throw you off this case."

Howe put a comforting hand on her arm. "There's no need to get upset. I'm in charge of this investigation. We've just asked Detective Bailey to come here and see if he can help explain what happened." He turned to Joe. "Do you want to take another look at the scene?"

Joe nodded. Howe would obviously have better luck finishing Eve Chandler's interview alone.

He left the house and walked toward his car. It was colder now, and a harsh, biting wind had kicked up. He opened his trunk and pulled out a large black suitcase. Its leather finish was worn and scuffed, and the brass latches and hinges were tarnished. It was his spirit kit, which he used to inspect the scenes of séances and psychic demonstrations. Made up of an odd assortment of sophisticated test equipment and ordinary household items, he generally kept it in his car trunk, where it would be handy for both his police investigations and his debunking work for the university. The last time he left it at the station, some joker had plastered a *Ghostbusters* "no ghosts" insignia on its side, and the sticker had adorned the case ever since.

He carried it back into the study, where the police videographer was filming every inch of the room with a digital camera. The still photographer was now chatting with a few of the officers who came to gawk at the site.

The nervousness among the officers had given way to morbid humor. Joe overheard cracks about Nelson's taste in decorating, and how a nice tapestry might have been a better match for the wall.

They were trying to be funny, but he could hear a slight edge in their voices. Lieutenant Powell had probably been right about his men getting the shit scared out of them.

Joe had just popped open the suitcase's lid, when Howe walked into the room. "Where's Eve Chandler?" Joe asked.

"Passed out downstairs. Between the Valium and you

running her all over the house, she was wiped out. Thanks for neutralizing my witness, Bailey."

"You'll get more out of her tomorrow anyway." Joe pulled a small black box about the size of a hardcover book from the spirit kit. Its high-impact plastic case surrounded a five-inch view screen.

Howe squinted at the instrument. "That looks like a bomb squad gadget."

"It is. It's a McNaughton handheld sonar pulse reader that I grabbed from the bomb squad's scrap heap. It's a little out of date, but it still does the job."

"*What* job?"

Joe attached a battery pack to the unit's top edge. "It tells me if there's anything on the other side of these walls I should know about. It throws out sonar waves that detect any mass behind scanned surfaces. It was made to find explosives, but it also works to detect flying rigs, projectors, or anything else phony spiritualists use." He screwed a telescoping rod onto a bracket on its base and extended the rod out to its full eight-foot length. He flipped the red power switch, and the unit revved to life with a high-pitched whine.

The other cops in the room stopped talking as he slowly swept the reader across the walls and ceiling.

Ping . . . ping . . . ping . . .

Joe took note of a few spots where the sonar reader detected areas of greater mass. He was hoping to find some evidence of a contraption that could have sent the sculpture flying into Nelson, but the readings indicated only support beams.

He glided the reader along the wall where Nelson was impaled. No significant variances.

Damn.

He put down the reader and pulled out a large aerosol can. He turned toward the other cops. "Are you guys finished in here?"

One of them nodded. "Knock yourself out."

Joe sprayed the can high on each wall and over the entire ceiling.

Howe snorted. "If it's the smell you're worried about, that usually isn't a problem until the corpse has been around for a few days."

"It's not room deodorant. It's phosphorous clearcoat."

"What?"

Joe was used to the smart-ass comments and questions. Most cops had only the vaguest notion of what he did, and he always tried to patiently explain the tools of his trade. "It coats everything with phosphors that will show up under an ultraviolet light. If there are any thin wires or mesh up there, this will light them up."

Joe reached back into his kit and produced a high-wattage battery-operated fingerprint lantern. He switched it on. A faint purple light emanated from its rectangular lens plate, and the phosphors that had settled on his sport jacket took on an intense white glow. He aimed the lamp toward the ceiling and slowly walked around the room. Except for a few cobwebs in the corner, nothing showed up under the light.

He turned off the lantern.

Howe's lips twisted. "Well, *that* was impressive."

"It wasn't meant to impress you." Joe's patience was almost at an end. "It was only supposed to narrow the field of possibilities, which it did."

"Uh-huh. So what you're telling me is that you're no closer to figuring out how it was done."

"You're always closer if you can eliminate some of the possibilities."

"Now I'm *sure* you don't know what you're doing. You're actually spouting the bullshit that McCarey and Stevens teach at the academy."

"McCarey and Stevens?" Joe smiled faintly. "They must have been before my time."

"Screw you."

"This isn't their bullshit. It's mine, and it's what made your boss call me at one in the morning when you couldn't even begin to figure out what was going on here."

"I can handle this."

"I'm sure you can, and after tonight, I'm sure you will. I'm just here to scope things out and help where I can."

"Which doesn't appear to be much."

"We'll see."

Howe relaxed slightly. "Hmm. Were McCarey and Stevens really before your time?"

"Yep."

"Damn, that's depressing." Howe turned toward the door. "I'm gonna rouse Ms. Chandler and see if she needs a lift anyplace. I'll check back with you."

"Fine."

Joe pulled out a tape measure and extended it to the base of the sculpture, which was angled up at a forty-five-degree angle. Eleven feet four inches from the floor.

He measured the entire room, noting the height and width of the one door and two windows. The measurements could come in handy later, when comparing various heavy lifting methods typically employed by magicians and psychic scam artists. He could immediately eliminate the Harrison winch due to the rig's large size and lack of portability, and others, like most pulley systems, would not work due to the high center of gravity necessary to drive the sculpture so forcefully into the wall. And he knew of no rig that could explain Nelson's elevated position.

A sharp crack sounded in the room.

Joe spun around.

It was Nelson's other shoe. It had finally slipped off his foot and fell on the floor, spattering blood against the wall.

As Joe walked out the door, no one was making cute comments about Nelson or anything else. It was obvious they just wanted to get the hell out of there.

He headed downstairs, trying to make sense of what he had just seen. Even if he could figure out how it happened, who would kill Nelson in such a bizarre manner? And why?

He stood in the foyer, jotting down a few last impressions of the crime scene, when Howe came through a doorway with Eve.

"Any ideas?" Howe asked.

Joe put his notebook away. "Not yet. I need to do some checking around."

Howe nodded. "I'm going to take Ms. Chandler home. We'll touch base tomorrow."

Howe said it more like an order than a simple statement. Joe let it pass.

Eve walked toward him until her face was only inches away.

"Just what *do* you believe in, Mr. Bailey?"

He stared back, unsure how to respond.